RESISTANCE

Mara Timon is a native New Yorker and self-proclaimed citizen of the world who began a love affair with London about 20 years ago. She started writing short stories as a teenager, and when a programme on the BBC caught her interest, she followed the "what ifs" until a novel began to appear. Mara lives in London and is working on her next book. She loves reading, writing, running, Pilates, red wine, and spending time with friends and family – not necessarily in that order.

Also by Mara Timon
City of Spies

MARA TIMON

RESISTANCE

ZAFFRE

First published in the UK in 2021 by
ZAFFRE
An imprint of Bonnier Books UK
4th Floor, Victoria House, Bloomsbury Square, London WC1B 4DA
Owned by Bonnier Books
Sveavägen 56, Stockholm, Sweden

This is a work of fiction. Names, places, events and
incidents are either the products of the author's
imagination or used fictitiously. Any resemblance to
actual persons, living or dead, or actual
events is purely coincidental.

A CIP catalogue record for this book is
available from the British Library.

ISBN: 978-1-83877-466-0

Also available as an ebook and an audiobook

1 3 5 7 9 10 8 6 4 2

Typeset by IDSUK (Data Connection) Ltd
Printed and bound in Great Britain by Clays Ltd, Elcograf S.p.A.

Zaffre is an imprint of Bonnier Books UK
www.bonnierbooks.co.uk

For Matthew and Alexandra

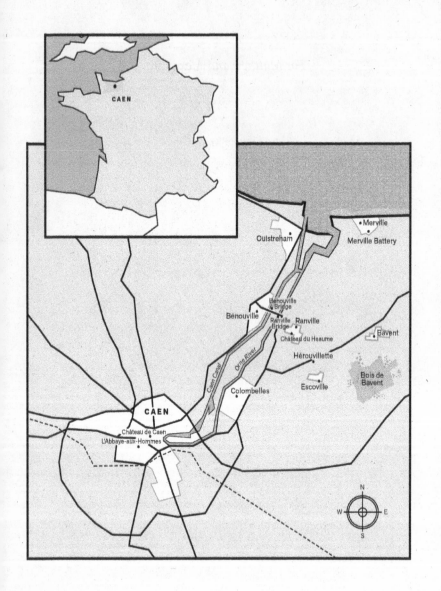

Character List

England

* **Vera Atkins:** Assistant to section head Colonel Maurice Buckmaster, and his de facto second in command, responsible for the recruitment and deployment of British agents in occupied France

* **Barbara Bertram** turned her West Sussex home into a staging house, providing hospitality for operatives coming into/out of France

* **Maurice Buckmaster:** ('Buck') Leader of the French section of Special Operations Executive

~ **Elisabeth de Mornay:** (code name Cécile, aliases include Katrin Hügel and Cecil) An SOE agent

* **Leo Marks:** Cryptographer and SOE's head of agent codes

Eileen: A wireless operator working for Special Operations Executive in London

Virgil: A wireless operator in France, presumed captured by the Germans

Léonie: (alias Lene Deines) An SOE agent, and Cécile's commanding officer

France

Marcel Beaune: One of the heads of a resistance network in Normandy

Jacques Mandeville: One of the heads of a resistance network in Normandy

Alain Sablonnières: One of the heads of a resistance network in Normandy

Pierre, Antoine, Guillaume: Members of a resistance network in Normandy

Dominique: (alias Anna Severin) An SOE agent whom Cécile trained with in 1942

~ **Eduard Graf:** Wehrmacht colonel, formerly Abwehr, now working with Rommel

Felícienne / Silke Kellen: A Hungarian refugee

Jérôme: (alias Olivier Severin) An SOE demolitions specialist whom Cécile trained with in 1942

Thierry de la Hay: (alias Big André) An SOE weapons trainer whom Cécile trained with in 1942

* **Erwin Rommel:** ('the Desert Fox') Field Marshal, Commander-in-Chief of Army Group B and architect of the Atlantic Wall

***Hans Speidel:** German Lieutenant-General and chief of staff to Rommel from April 1944

Pascal: the wireless operator in Beaune's *réseau*, executed before Léonie and Cécile landed

Zeit: Wehrmacht colonel

Rannulf Kühn: – Wehrmacht Lieutenant-Colonel, one of Zeit's clique

Lorenz: an SS major

Eugene Vallentin: an SS captain

Hermann Mönch: a planner in the Todt organisation

* **Lieutenant-Colonel Peter Luard:** commander of the British 13th Parachute Battalion

Other Persons of Note

~ **Edith Renard:** A friend of Elisabeth's, with links to the Resistance in Paris

* **Gerd von Rundstedt:** German general and commander in France

* **Johanna Solf** presided over a group of anti-Nazi German intellectuals

* **Erich Vermehren:** A former Abwehr officer who defected to England in early February 1944

* **Hauptmann (Captain) Karl Heinrich Wolter (deceased):** Commander of the Merville Battery until his death in an RAF strike on 19 May 1944

* **Oberleutnant (Lieutenant) Raimund Steiner:** Succeeded Wolter as commander of the Merville Battery

* **General Carl-Heinrich von Stulpnagel:** A German general later executed in Berlin on 30 August 1944 for his role in the failed 20 July Plot to assassinate Hitler

Chapter One

It wasn't late, but my eyes felt as if they had been rubbed with sandpaper. Eileen, sitting beside me, pulled off her headphones and tossed them onto the table. She stared at them for a few moments before speaking.

'I don't need to translate that message. The raid failed. This . . .' She nudged the paper with the agent's message. 'This will only confirm who was arrested. The girls in Grendon can decode this one. I don't want to hear who was arrested or shot. Who's missing. I don't want to know. I just can't.'

She pressed her shaking hands to her forehead. 'Look, I know we're not supposed to get attached to them, but they're real people, not just sounds from the other end of the line.' She turned away to compose herself, then gave me a watery smile. 'Of course, you know this, you're one of them. And still you spend your free time here, helping us.'

'What better way to find out what sort of mess I'm going to drop into, once I deploy?' It was the easy answer, if not the full one. I adjusted my headset and held up a finger to indicate an incoming transmission. 'Virgil is on time, maybe for the first time in his life.'

With a cigarette clamped between my teeth, I translated the Morse dots and dashes into characters, confirmed receipt of the message and signed off. Stared at it for a few seconds, and muttered: 'Shit.'

Eileen's eyes met mine, visibly bracing herself. 'What's wrong?'

'That wasn't Virgil,' I said.

'What do you mean?'

'It didn't sound like him. Virgil crashes about when he transmits, but this one sounded light. Confident.'

'Shit,' she echoed, closing her eyes. 'Not another one.'

'Let's decrypt it before we make any decisions.'

The new voice came from the doorway, surprising me enough that I reached for the blade I usually wore, strapped to my thigh. My hand fell away when I saw Vera Atkins calmly light a cigarette. Officially the assistant to the head of F Section, Maurice Buckmaster, she was in fact his intelligence officer, responsible for the recruitment and deployment of agents going into France, as well as the running of the female agents.

'Can you decode the message, Cécile?' she asked.

'Yes,' I said, reaching for a piece of squared paper.

If the sender really was Virgil, that small pile of paper wouldn't be enough. His indecipherable transmissions were legendary with the codebreakers in Grendon.

I cracked it on the third try: he acknowledged a shipment of firearms, and requested explosives, timing pencils and money for bribes.

They'd clearly known about the last drop, but the one before had delivered enough explosives to take down Versailles.

'Vera, has Virgil's *réseau* attacked anything within the past week?'

Her blue-grey eyes narrowed. 'No.'

'Damn.' I pushed back from the table, ignoring the bang as the chair hit the wall. 'I need to see Virgil's last few transmissions.'

I brushed past Vera and, with Eileen close behind, sprinted down the hall to the filing room. I snatched the folder from the drawer and leafed through the documents, scanning the top sheets with their neat translations.

I eased onto a chair and started again, this time looking at the handwritten pages.

'What are you looking for?' Vera asked.

'We just sent them explosives. I want to know if he reported them going astray.' No, that wasn't quite right and I shook my head. 'I want to know how long he's been compromised and we've been sending supplies to the Boche.'

I rubbed the bridge of my nose and kept reading. The Norgeby House operators weren't supposed to get attached to field agents, and field agents weren't supposed to get attached to each other. It happened, anyway. The words blurred, but I couldn't stop. There had to be something in there.

'What makes you so certain it wasn't Virgil?' Vera asked. 'Because he asked for more explosives?'

Rotating my stiff shoulders, I answered. 'Sometimes there are variations in a pianist's – an operator's – style, the cadence to how they transmit. Their "fist". But these changes are slight, like their handwriting. You know that.' I waited for her nod. 'If you think of it like music, tonight's message sounded more like *The Magic Flute* than Virgil's usual *Carmina Burana*.'

A small crowd was forming behind Vera at the door. She ignored them, flicking her lighter and watching the orange flame dance and die.

'You trained Virgil, didn't you, Cécile?'

'No,' I answered. 'He was trained here, like the rest of us, but I helped him get settled once he dropped into France.' I closed the file and rubbed the back of my neck. 'He's a skinny little thing. Bald as an egg, with wide eyes and a stutter, but he has a heavy "fist". And he can't spell very well, which is why it takes the girls so long to decrypt his messages.'

And he sang Welsh lullabies to the baby daughter he'd never met while he transmitted.

She smoothed the immaculate lay of her jacket. 'What do you think happened?'

'I don't know, but I'm certain he's been compromised, maybe dead.' I corrected myself. 'He's probably dead. If he were alive, I think they'd have had him code it, and maybe check the message before he transmitted it. That way they'd have a better chance of fooling us, but this was a different person, Vera. And they have his credentials.'

'Not something he would give up easily,' she murmured to herself.

'No. He'd have made them work for those codes.' It was small consolation. 'Give me some time, Vera. Let me see what I can find.'

She hesitated for a moment, and then stepped back into the hallway. She closed the door behind her, leaving me alone with a half-empty packet of cigarettes and the mystery of what had happened to Virgil.

The third pass through Virgil's folder yielded no new insights, and I returned to the filing cabinets.

4

'*Why bother, when you already know what happened?*' my inner voice asked. '*Virgil is lost.*'

I took a deep breath and moved past the French files, towards the area holding the files on the situation in Germany. Flicked through files categorised by agent or operation. I pulled each one out and scanned it for a familiar name, but there was no mention of him, and what I learnt was grim: the arrest of Johanna Solf and more than seventy of her friends in January, after speaking too freely in front of a Nazi informer, had neutralised her circle of anti-Nazi intellectuals in Berlin. Despite some of them being well placed in the German government as well as society, they'd proved too trusting of a stranger.

Other files detailed arrests following the defection of Abwehr officer Erich Vermehren, and the many, many plots to assassinate Hitler.

Sharp steps in the hallway heralded Vera's return. I closed the drawer and sidestepped to the French cabinet as Vera entered the records room. Her steady blue-grey eyes met mine, and she asked: 'Did you find what you were looking for?'

She knows.

I cleared my throat. 'To be honest, no.'

She lit a cigarette. Inhaled deeply, blew the smoke into the hallway, and waved the glowing tip to urge me to explain.

'The previous transmissions were almost certainly Virgil. The challenges were met, and the spelling was typical of him, to the point where the person decoding indicated how many times she tried before she was able to unlock the message.'

It had taken about five seconds to find that out, but Vera didn't need to know that.

'There was simply no indication that Virgil was in any way concerned about being exposed. Or, at least, not more than any of us transmitting in the field,' I added. 'Based on an assumption that he was caught between the last drop and the one before, we're looking at some time over the past three weeks.' I leant against the cabinet, careful to stick to facts that she could corroborate. 'I checked the files from Spiritualist, Inventor, and any of the other *réseaux* that might have interacted with Virgil's. Bit of a bugger, that. Most of the Resistance cells I checked seemed to have stopped existing from the spring of '43 – about the time the Gestapo decided they were interested in me, and I left Paris.'

I crossed my arms over my chest and asked, 'What happened, Vera? Why were so many circuits blown last year? Why are they being blown now?'

'You became a target when you turned down a date with your neighbour, and he took that rejection straight to the Gestapo,' she reminded me. 'Unfortunately, that happens all too frequently. The Germans have become far too good at hunting our people.' Her answer explained one-offs, maybe a lot of them, but not the scale the files had shown. Nonetheless, her calm tone made it clear that she wasn't about to be baited. 'If you're finished here, Buck has a few questions for you.'

She knew I'd look. She knew, and she let me. Why?

Because she knew there was nothing to find here.

But there would be a file on him somewhere, I just had to find it. Find *him*.

'Of course.'

I stubbed out my cigarette, and followed her from Norgeby House's now-empty halls and into the fading daylight, realising just how much time she'd allowed me with the files. We crossed Baker Street, passed the sandbagged entrance of Michael House, and climbed the stairs to Maurice Buckmaster's office.

The lights were off and the blackout curtains open. To the south, barrage balloons hovered above the skyline. The chief of F Section stood by the window, his tall frame held still, hands clasped behind his back. Vera closed the door quickly behind her, her brisk footsteps receding down the hall.

'Hello, Buck.'

'I understand that you think Virgil was compromised?' he asked, forgoing the usual small talk.

'It would appear so, yes.'

For a few long moments, Buck remained intent upon Hyde Park's searchlights, scraping the darkening sky. Then he turned to face me, his intense blue eyes studying my face.

'Is there any chance another operator was transmitting? Someone he was training?'

It was a good question, but I was shaking my head before he finished the sentence.

'He didn't have clearance to train anyone else, and another operator would use their own credentials.'

'So, the Germans.'

As much as I wanted to rail against losing Virgil, the best way to serve him would be to prevent anyone else from being caught in the Nazis' trap.

'We have to assume that, Buck.'

Buck's breath expelled in a soft whoosh. 'Thank you, Cécile.'

'And it won't be just him.' I braced myself to voice the unim-aginable. 'If he's been compromised enough to hand out his codes, he might have been forced to betray others.' They weren't nameless, faceless casualties. They were brave men and women that I knew – had worked alongside. 'What will you do?'

He responded by throwing the question back to me.

'What do you think I should do?'

Tired and tense, I answered without thinking.

'Do to them what the Nazi bastards did to us. Play along for a while. See how far their net was cast, and who else might be compromised. Send them enough false intelligence to set a trap and see how many you can catch in it. But if you're going to send weapons, you might want to send in a fair percentage of ones that have already failed inspection.'

'Yes,' Buck murmured.

'If there's anything you can do to save . . .'

Buck made a sound, not unsympathetic. He knew that any warning we sent would be too late; that the only option was to try to contain the situation. He glanced at his wristwatch, even though it was too dark to see its face.

'It is getting late, Cécile. Go home. Go to whichever officers' club you frequent and fleece anyone foolish enough to play cards with you. Do whatever it is you do, but try to get some rest. You'll need it.'

I had reached the door when his last sentence registered.

'Why would that be?'

Rain began to tap against the window, getting harder with each moment. Buck stepped away from it and closed the curtains.

'You've been training in Milton Hall for the past four months for a reason, Cécile. We need you. We need your skills, and we need your tenacity.'

My heart rate accelerated. 'You mean me? You want me to handle the situation?'

'No, Cécile. After last year, your face would be too well known in Paris. Someone else will handle that.' He raised a hand to stop my protest. 'Don't worry, we'll let you know what we learn of Virgil.' A tired smile raised the corners of Buck's mouth. This was his way of preventing me from trying to find out on my own. 'Consider yourself on leave until noon on Wednesday. Vera will drive you and Léonie to the aerodrome. You'll have your final briefing then.'

'I'm going back?' A fierce joy hit me with an almost physical force. 'I'm finally going back to France?'

Once there, I might be able to learn news of my husband. Buck had to know that, but his expression gave nothing away.

'Enjoy your leave, Cécile, and do endeavour to stay out of mischief.'

He returned his attention to the window and added, 'For once.'

Chapter Two

Barbara Bertram secured the wireless set inside my valise and closed the false bottom.

'It's smaller than the one I took last year,' I observed, peering over her shoulder. 'At least I can take more than a single change of clothes this time.'

'Not much more.' She pushed a pile of neatly stacked clothes towards me. 'Change into those now. You're jumping in shoes, not boots. We'll tape your ankles and get you into the jumpsuit when it's closer to time.'

'Thank you, Barbara.'

'Your necklace and the other items were cleared by Miss Atkins, but your wedding ring is the wrong colour gold.'

She waited patiently, hand held out. I twisted it to the first knuckle and paused. It had been on my finger for less than a year, and although Buck and Vera had indulged me in letting me continue to wear it, it felt wrong taking it off.

'It was purchased in Portugal, not England.'

'Which is not consistent with your cover story. I *am* sorry.' Her sympathetic smile didn't fool me; this was an argument I wouldn't win. 'You know how important details can be.'

She waited patiently until, muttering curses to myself, I pulled it from my finger. Something caught my eye, and I moved to the window. I held the band up to the light, squinting to read the script etched inside. *Forever*, it said. With the date of our wedding.

The date of our wedding, but not our initials, because he knew that if I got caught, wearing a wedding ring with a different set of initials from my cover story would give me away. I closed my eyes against a wave of grief, and turned away so Barbara couldn't see.

'I'll keep it safe until you can collect it,' Barbara said, her expression understanding.

She handed me its replacement and waited for me to slip it on before tucking my ring into a little box. It would go into a larger box, with the rest of my belongings, including a letter I had written to my husband, to be sent on in case I didn't make it back.

Assuming they would be able to find him.

Barbara paused halfway to the door.

'Cécile?'

'Yes?'

Her face softened. 'Take care of yourself, my dear.'

She closed the door and I remained at the window for a few moments, watching Barbara slide into the car that would take her back to Bignor Manor, and wondering how she got into this business.

I slipped out of my dress and into a cream silk blouse and pencil skirt, smoothed the skirt over the sgian dubh strapped to my thigh. The Scottish 'sock knife' was the legacy of a now-deceased friend, and was easier to hide than SOE's standard-issue Fairbairn Sykes blade, although I'd take that as well.

The woman in the looking glass shook her head. My naturally auburn hair had been dyed blonde and set in a style made popular by Veronica Lake. In fact, with the blonde hair, my resemblance to the American actress was uncanny. If Buck and Vera expected me not to be noticed in this guise, they'd be proven sadly wrong.

I straightened the collar of my blouse, and then my shoulders. As prepared as I could be, I made my way to the parlour downstairs, to find out just what Buck had planned.

Léonie perched on the edge of a large leather armchair beside the dormant fireplace, her back ramrod-straight, her attention locked on a map of France pinned to the wall beside the window. I'd been offended when I'd learnt that she would be my commanding officer. I'd been one of the first women to be recruited as an SOE field agent in '42, and spent a year operating in France and Portugal. But while I didn't know Léonie's background, despite her small stature, she'd proved adept over the last couple of months when we trained together in Milton Hall, and as a tactician she was brilliant and ruthless. Moreover, she was willing to listen before making any decision.

I wouldn't say we were friends, but we did respect each other, and as long as she didn't expect me to kowtow to her, we'd get on just fine.

To her right, Vera Atkins, elegant in her blue-and-grey tweed suit, leant against a bookcase, shrouded in a cloud of smoke and mystery. Both women were completely no-nonsense, sharing little of themselves, and while I had heard rumours that Vera could let her hair down when the situation allowed, I held no such suspicions of Léonie.

Vera straightened and moved towards the map.

'Let's begin,' she said. One long finger circled an area a few miles east of Caen. 'You'll drop here.'

12

'The Resistance is active in the area,' Vera continued. 'But as you can imagine, so are the Germans. You'll separate upon landing for your own protection. Cécile, you make contact with the Resistance. They recently lost their wireless operator, so you'll need to support them. It'll give you the opportunity to assess their strengths and weaknesses. And, of course, their potential. We have agents working with them, but they've been there for some time. A fresh pair of eyes will be useful.'

'Anyone I know?'

She continued as if I hadn't spoken. 'Dr Olivier Severin, your contact, is a demolitions expert. We have another man in as their weapons instructor.' Using the burning tip of her cigarette as a pointer, she swept around the area in a wider loop. 'What we know of the area – Field Marshal Erwin Rommel built the "Atlantic Wall" to fortify the ports and coastline. He remains in charge of these, while von Rundstedt controls the forces further inland.' She indicated the various units and designations, where the headquarters and supply depots were. 'We need you to validate this information. Anything new, including information on order of battle or troop movements, we need to know as a matter of priority. Léonie, you will take the lead on this.'

'Understood.'

'The Jedburgh teams you've been training with are set up in what we consider to be an ideal configuration for field agents. Two officers, and one radio operator. It's small and agile. In your case' – she inclined her head towards us – 'all three of you are officers, and the third member of your team is already in situ.'

That didn't sound good. Without training with her, without knowing her, we had no idea of what she was capable of.

Vera held up a hand to still any protests. 'Anna Severin is quite adept, by all accounts.'

'Severin? Connected to Olivier Severin?'

'His wife.'

'She's not one of ours?'

'She is, and has worked with the Resistance in Normandy for almost a year, and elsewhere in France before that. I can assure you, you will have no complaints about her.'

'She hasn't been back at all during that time?' I asked.

'No.' Vera set a large envelope on the table, closing the matter before I could comment on how rare it was for an agent to stay in the field for more than six months. Usually they needed a break. Or they got caught. Whoever she was, this woman must be good.

'What are her skills? And what makes you think she'll work with us?' Léonie asked, but my mind was already whirling.

'Madame Severin can handle a gun as well as almost anyone I've seen.' This was high praise, coming from Vera. 'And she has worked as a courier. She's smart, resourceful and familiar with the area. As for her willingness?' Vera paused. 'She will do what's required.'

As she's seen.

'Wait,' I said, holding up a finger. 'Dr Severin is the demolitions expert?'

Vera inclined her head again. 'Correct.'

There couldn't be many men who were trained as medics, much less doctors, who specialised in demolitions. I knew a man like that once. We met on the first day of training, and parachuted together into Paris a few months later. Once, with a wry grin, he'd explained it to me: by attacking things – bridges

14

and tunnels and factories – he could do his part for the war without forcing him directly to break the Hippocratic Oath.

It was almost too much to hope for, but I asked anyway. 'Is it Jérôme? Is Jérôme Dr Severin?'

Vera's eyes met mine, neither confirming nor denying my theory. It was enough to make me continue.

'And if Jérôme is Dr Severin, then Anna Severin can be none other than Dominique. She's still alive, then?'

Vera's eyes held mine for almost a minute before she nodded.

'Well done, Cécile. Dr Severin is indeed Jérôme, and your friend is now known as Anna Severin. She will be the third woman on your team. I trust you'll find her acceptable?'

'There's no one else I'd rather have,' I said in complete honesty. I turned to Léonie to fill her in. 'We began our SOE training together back in '42. Last year, when we were in Paris, Dom found out the Boche were planning to ambush us, and risked her life to warn us. While most of us survived the day, the Gestapo picked her up afterwards. No fault of hers – she knew she'd be in their crosshairs when she warned us. They arrested her and took her to their headquarters on Avenue Foch.'

Mad with fever from the two bullets I'd taken in the ambush, hidden in Madame Renard's cellar, I was unable to protect Dom, unable to assist in her rescue as the Boche transferred her to Fresnes Prison. It was something that had haunted me until the day I fled Paris, when Madame Renard had given me a postcard Dom had sent from Marseilles, telling me she and Jérôme were safe.

'She was never in Marseilles, was she?'

15

'Of course not.' Vera's tone made it clear that the discussion was over.

'What are her motivations?' Léonie asked.

Vera looked at me. 'Cécile?'

I crossed my hands in my lap, and assumed a beatific expression. 'We were instructed not to speak about our past during training. Ourselves either, for that matter.'

'Quite right,' she said, her flat tone telling me she wasn't fooled. 'What were your impressions then?'

Touché, Vera.

'From their accents, I'd say she – and Jérôme – are both British and well educated. I suspect Jérôme comes from a diplomatic family, and may have spent an extended period of time in France before the war.' Coming from a diplomatic family myself, it was a safe guess, although I hadn't actually met him until that first day of training. 'Dominique speaks both English and French as a native. I would guess that one of her parents was Parisian.'

'And their motives?'

'Damned if I know.'

Vera waited patiently for me to elaborate.

'I really don't know, so this is only my guess. Jérôme is medically trained, but I don't think was in the medical corps. I think something happened to push him into the infantry. As for Dom, I think probably the same. Something happened to make her want to fight back. And Vera wasn't joking, Dom is a sharpshooter.'

'Good to know,' Léonie acknowledged, glancing at Vera to elaborate.

Instead she reached into the large envelope and removed two smaller ones, handing one to Léonie and the other to me. Inside were identity cards, ration cards, the works. The forgers knew what they were doing, but I'd spent enough time in France to know that this set was all wrong: the weight of the paper, the colours, everything. With these papers, I'd be caught in a heartbeat. Why would Buck and Vera bring me back from Portugal, only to sacrifice me in Caen?

Vera, usually so meticulous, remained calm under my glare, her expression unchanged, and if anyone wilted, it was me. Vera was fiercely protective of 'her girls'. She wouldn't sacrifice me, or any of us. Not willingly.

I took a second look at the papers, feeling my eyebrows raise at the eagle, the swastika. The name.

'Katrin Hügel?' I read the name on the papers aloud and stared at Vera. 'You mean, I'm *German*?'

Chapter Three

Thick yellow fog clung to the ground and swirled around the legs of the ground crew as they loaded the cargo. Even with a recent coat of non-reflective black paint, the Halifax looked heavily modified. Its running lights and dorsal turret had been removed and its armaments faired over. The guns had been traded in, maybe for space, maybe speed. Whatever the reason, the result was the same: if we were caught in a dogfight, this dog would die.

The pilot and co-pilot walked around the plane with the engineer, not bothering to look at us as, trussed up in our harnesses like Christmas turkeys, we crossed the tarmac. I paused in front of the bomber, and turned to the trio.

'The last time I flew into France, it was in the belly of a Lancaster. It took some damage crossing the Channel and we had to jump blind. I was lucky to land safely. This time, get me there in one piece, will you?'

The co-pilot patted the side of the plane. 'We'll do our best, ma'am.'

The familiar stench of petrol and kerosene assaulted me as soon as I ducked through the bomber's door. Breathing through my mouth, I shuffled towards the back of the plane, where the cage holding our belongings was secured in front of several other crates.

Léonie settled on the bench across from me. Her jumpsuit was too big for her, rolled a few times at her wrists and ankles. Maybe SOE didn't have something small enough to fit her, or maybe it was intended to be too large to disguise her height in case the Germans found it. The 'chute, enormous on her tiny frame, made her look like a turtle, a comparison I was loath to voice aloud. She would be the last one to complain, but equally, wouldn't find my observation amusing.

The dispatcher, a stocky man a few years shy of forty, winked and hooked us onto the bar.

'I don't always get it right. You'll notice if I haven't.' It was an old joke, and we smiled politely.

A freckled face appeared from the wireless operator's compartment below the cockpit.

'Don't worry, Hobie knows what he's doing, and our pilot is the best in the business. Report says the weather'll clear over the channel. If not, if our Rebecca here can't find her Eureka, we come home.' He opened his mouth to explain.

'Yes, yes. The signal from the ground. I know. I'm familiar with the device.'

He cleared his throat and looked away. 'Good. Get ready, then. We'll be moving shortly.'

He ducked back into his compartment moments before the engine came alive. The Halifax rocked back and forth a few times, the feel almost comforting, then we began to roll forward. The plane picked up speed, bumping over the tarmac. Outside the window, the brick-and-ivy cottage disappeared; inside, I breathed through my mouth and gripped the seat, trying not to fall off.

19

'You'll be fine!' Hobie yelled into my ear.

'I know!'

'Hang on, though – you'll feel the turbulence as we pass the storm. Then we go in high over the Channel, then swoop low after we pass the coastal defences.' He used his left hand to illustrate the words while the right one gripped the bench. 'Then we wait for the green light. You know about the green light, don't you? Nothing, and I mean nothing, happens until we see it. Understand?'

The Halifax's nose rose and the old bomber lifted off, heading for the south coast, and then France.

I closed my eyes, and uttered a silent prayer.

The Halifax banked, jerking me awake. The sun had set but outside, light flashed as something exploded.

'Flak,' Hobie the dispatcher said. 'Pretty typical when we clear the coast. We should be through in another couple of minutes. You two will drop just beyond.'

The stench of cordite assaulted my nose, and I breathed through my mouth. With a loud *ping*, a shard pierced the fuselage, burying itself in the wall. We watched it quiver for a few seconds before the dispatcher joked, 'Missed me by a good coupla feet. Good thing Jerry's a bloody bad shot!' He laughed, but the tremor in his voice gave him away.

Without warning, the plane rolled, dropping altitude and changing direction. I tumbled from the bench, my knees smacking the floor. Léonie leant forward but the dispatcher was faster, grabbing the back of my flight suit.

'Not yet, lass. We're just trying to get around the flak. Wait for the green light, remember?'

I glared. 'Keep it up and you'll go out the door before I will.'

He grinned. 'Good lass.'

Another shard pinged, and I swivelled to sit on the floor. It had embedded itself in the bulkhead where my head had rested only seconds before. I swallowed the bitter taste of bile and cursed.

'Bad shot.' I repeated the dispatcher's words and scrambled back to the bench.

'Be grateful for it.' He yanked me onto the bench. 'We're almost through it.'

Unless they scramble the fighters.

The plane dipped again and an engine stuttered.

Léonie's eyes met mine.

'We haven't passed the defences yet,' she murmured.

'*Searchlight!*' the freckled kid bellowed.

'Brace yourself!'

The dispatcher held my harness as the plane corkscrewed towards the ground. The crates in the rear of the plane strained against their restraints and something crashed.

The plane steadied itself, and I gulped in acrid air until the dispatcher pushed open the heavy door. Cold air whipped through it, making my eyes water. I secured my flight glasses and joined him at the door.

Directly below us was a small town, not far away from two silver ribbons that must have been the river Orne and the canal. At least we were in the right area. Hobie tugged on our static lines, reassuring himself they were still secured to the anchorage, tightened our straps and checked our harnesses.

'Remember – not before the green light.'

21

We gazed out into the night sky. Below, an oblong field passed by, slightly humped, with dark shadows mottling it.

'Rommel's asparagus!' Hobie shouted. 'Jerry plants telephone poles in the fields to prevent gliders and small planes from landing. Doesn't stop your lot, 'course. But be careful. They're dangerous.'

There were no lights down below, and the one on the wall remained red.

We braced ourselves as the plane banked over a field. Each circle increased the chance the wrong person would see us, of the Germans waiting for us below.

'He can't find it!' I yelled at Léonie.

She cocked her head, then pointed to her eye. *Will you go in blind?* she asked.

Two trips to France, and two blind drops. I didn't like the idea, but it was the only sensible option and I gave Léonie the thumbs up.

She disappeared into the slipstream before the dispatcher could grab her.

'Crazy bitch,' he muttered, but didn't move fast enough to restrain me.

I took a deep breath and leapt into the night. My head jerked as I slid past the plane's undercarriage. With a sharp tug, the dark cream silk of my parachute unfurled in front of the full moon as I finally returned to France.

Night played with the shadows. Verdant fields were dark, the trees darker. A gust of air pushed me closer to the line of trees, and towards the pole, maybe fifteen or sixteen feet tall, jutting from the field in front of me. I raised my legs, hoping to clear it. My heels grazed the top, then pushed against it, thrusting me forward. Relief turned to fear as I jerked backwards, my 'chute caught on the top. I bounced against the pole once, twice, then dangled, my feet a yard or so above the ground.

'Damn.'

I extracted the Fairbairn Sykes from a pocket, and sawed at the harness. It suddenly gave way, and I fell, jolting my shoulder against the post and tumbling to the ground. Pain shot up my right leg as I landed. Winded, I lay there for a moment, staring at the sky and catching my breath. My shoulder wasn't dislocated, and my ankle didn't feel broken. It wasn't a picture-perfect landing by any standard, but I was alive, and there was no sergeant major waiting nearby to yell about my form.

A breeze lifted the 'chute, and for a second it billowed before resting back against the pole. It wouldn't be easy to get down, and the canisters would already inform the Germans of the drop. All this would do, would let them know that an agent had dropped as well. And even if I freed it from the pole, they'd probably find it anyway.

'Welcome back to France, Elisabeth,' I muttered to myself, knowing it would be the last time I would hear my real name for a while. The Resistance would know me by my code name, Cécile, and the Boche would hopefully only see Katrin Hügel. I removed the remains of the harness and stepped out of the flight suit. We were supposed to bury it, but there was never time. And, for once, my height was a blessing. When they found the jumpsuit, they'd look for a man.

I quickly unwrapped the bandages that protected my left ankle, stuffing the linen strip into a pocket. The right one would have to remain, to stabilise it and prevent any swelling. I removed my shoulder bag from where it had been secured around my waist and slipped my Walther PPK into my skirt's waistband, underneath the money belt, stuffed with a ridiculous amount of forged francs to pass on to the Resistance. The moon was bright enough, so I moved the torch into my bag with the rest of my kit. I slung the strap diagonally across my chest, and with the PPK now in my hand, hobbled across the field to the middle of the field, where Léonie, already out of her harness, was forcing open the cage that contained our belongings. At least the dispatcher had had the presence of mind to send that after us.

With another rumble, the plane passed overhead, releasing a small trail of canisters containing whatever provisions the *réseau* had requested of London. Our three 'chutes were a risk, but the Nazis wouldn't be able to miss the dozen or so that blossomed on the sky.

Ignoring the canisters settling to the ground around us, Léonie thrust the valise with the wireless Jed Set into my hand.

'Let's go. The Nazis won't be far behind.'

'You know where we are?' I asked, my internal compass telling me that we were a couple of miles from the expected landing zone.

'Roughly. I don't think we're far.'

We slogged through the muddy field, crops tangling around our feet. While it provided some cover now, if the farmer was working with the Boche, he'd report a pair of intruders to them . . . if they didn't find us first.

We heard an approaching vehicle and dropped to the ground. It didn't sound like a motor car, but it wasn't loud enough to be a transport. Maybe a lorry, the sort that farmers used? We waited, our eyes fixed.

The earth was damp, its smell overpowering. The motor didn't slow, didn't stop. When we couldn't hear it anymore, we slowly made our way to the road. Léonie held up her hand, halting me. Clutching her own gun, she inched towards the road.

Seconds turned into minutes. The Nazis would know a plane had made it through the coastal defences, and would have been blind not to notice our parachutes. What had the pilot been thinking, releasing the canisters?

As the minutes drew out, I reached for my valise, ready to take my chances on the road. I hadn't made it more than a yard or two before I heard the furtive rustle of Léonie's return. She gestured, took her valise, and led the way. We separated at the road, with a murmured reminder to meet at the Abbaye aux Hommes, Saint-Étienne's church, on Sunday.

If we lived that long.

Chapter Four

It was a long walk, exacerbated by the heavy valise and protesting ankle. The Germans would already be en route, likely alerted by a 'good citizen' who had seen the parachutes, if they hadn't seen anything themselves. Another vehicle approached and I threw myself, and case, into the shrubbery at the side of the road.

Within seconds, two khaki-painted hunters rumbled into sight. A troop transport carrying half a dozen men and a Radio Detection Vehicle, its rotating aerial seeking a wireless transmission, although with the Resistance's operator captured, who did they think would be transmitting?

A new operator. They knew a new operator was arriving. And they must think I'd be stupid enough to transmit from the landing field.

They passed me, heading to the drop site. The men would fan out as soon as they reached the field with the bloody canisters. I hadn't seen a dog, but that didn't mean there wasn't one with them. They'd find my jumpsuit – and, unless the kerosene-and-petrol stench of the plane masked it, my trail. I needed to move, and quickly.

I crawled out of the bushes, brushed myself off and pulled the valise free from the hedge. The moon, already clouding over, still provided enough light. With no other option, I started plodding along the road, moving as fast as my ankle would allow, hoping for a river, a stream or anything to throw off our scent.

The case became heavier with each mile, but I couldn't risk leaving it. One step after another, until the first house came into view. My ankle pulsed with pain, and my determination had taken me as far as it could. I had to stop. The house looked nice enough – small, with large windows and wisteria that wound up the stone façade. But that could mean anything. The couriers claimed nine out of ten homes would open the door to a Resistance member, but that one in a hundred would summon the police.

Those were odds I was willing to take. Exhausted as I was, I was about to approach the house, one arm raised to knock, when I saw the wooden shed at the corner of the garden, behind the house but not quite hidden from the road.

It was a much better option, and I limped towards it, careful to stay out of the moonlight. I moved as quickly as I could past the house, stooping as I passed a darkened window. Easing the shed door open, I looked inside. It was larger than I expected, with gardening tools neatly hanging, and a set of crates against one wall.

I stowed my case behind a crate and sat down on it. I would have killed for a cigarette, but the smell would carry through the open windows of the house, and there was no point in alerting them to my presence. I glared at the bandaged ankle ballooning on top of my filthy shoes. Sighing, I pulled a clump of mud from my heel. Re-wrapped my ankle with the clean bandage, found my tin of shoe polish and used the old linen strip to coax a shine out of the old and still-damp leather of my shoes.

There was still a couple of hours until daylight. The best option was to stay here for now, and rest my ankle for a bit. I'd leave once the sun was up, and there wouldn't be as many questions about a lone woman hobbling down the road with a valise.

A vehicle was coming, the engine protesting as the driver changed gear into a bend. There was a lot of activity on the roads for such a rural place. I waited for it to pass, but instead of accelerating, the car stopped. Reaching for my gun, I eased towards a crack in the wood to investigate. A dark Citroën Traction was parked in front of the house. There weren't many people who could afford petrol, and if they could afford it, access was a problem. Unless, of course, you were German.

Or a collaborator.

And even so, curfew had come and gone hours ago. Who was this person, that they were free to move about in the middle of the night? Silently, I cursed my decision to stop here.

A petite woman stepped from the passenger side of the car. Shadows and a smart hat obscured her face as she exchanged a few words with the driver and, with a jaunty wave, she walked down the flower-lined path. The Citroën pulled away from the kerb, but it was the woman I watched. Just before she disappeared from my view, her shoulders twitched. She slowed, her gaze slowly raking the area with an expertise uncommon in civilians.

Back straight, she continued to the house, closing the door behind her. She had sensed me. With my wounded ankle, running wasn't an option, but as long as she didn't alert her gendarme friends – as long as it was only her and me – I had a chance.

28

I pushed the crates further against the wall, slid the PPK into the back of my skirt, and with hands free, I waited, confident she would come.

She didn't take long. Now clad in dark trousers, with her hair fastened at the back of her head, she moved through the night like a cat. A cat holding a silver Colt pistol in her hand. She was taking no chances, and neither was I. The gun's report would attract attention, so whatever move I made would need to be silent and decisive. And if I couldn't defend myself against a woman half my height, then SOE had failed and I had no business being here.

The shed door inched open. The Colt should have been too large for her slim arm, but her grip was confident. She eased inside, keeping her back against the wall.

'I know you're in here,' she said. The words were pitched low, and her French was perfect, with the slightest hint of a Parisian accent. 'You might as well show yourself. I won't hurt you.'

For Christ's sake, would anyone believe that line while she held a small cannon in her hand?

She took another next step, and I struck. My left hand grabbed her hand, smashing it, and her gun, against the wall. Jammed my right forearm against her throat, cutting off her air supply.

Her foot smashed my tender ankle and I staggered back, freeing her left arm. Retaining custody of her right, I propelled her, face forward, against the side wall. Tightened my fingers around her wrist until her fingers loosened. Pried the weapon from her grip, but she was already moving. Dropping low, her foot lashing out.

I allowed myself to fall forward, crashing both of us to the ground, and landing atop her. Half in, half out of the shed, I could finally see her face, the familiar features rearranged into something I no longer recognised.

Once she had been almost like a sister to me, and by far the last person I'd expect to be working for the Germans. And yet, here she was. I'd been betrayed before – an acquaintance who'd taken rejection badly. This was a thousand times worse. The single word felt as if it had been torn from my soul.

'Traitor.'

Chapter Five

Bright green eyes widened as I rested the gun's muzzle against her forehead, just hard enough to let her know that I wasn't afraid to shoot her.

'Cécile?' Her voice broke, her breathing fast and shallow. 'Get off me. You, of all people, should know that I'm no traitor.'

'The Dominique I knew wouldn't be collaborating with the Boche.'

'The Dominique you knew worked hard to gain their trust, so that she could pass on information to the Resistance. And she still does that. Now, *get off me!*'

She stopped struggling, her eyes locked on mine.

'Oh, for heaven's sake, Cécile. You were there when I was arrested. You had to know they wouldn't give me an easy time of it. You know I wouldn't work for them – didn't Miss Atkins tell you what I did?'

'She did not.'

'She should have, she certainly knew what I was doing. We told her. And if you can't trust me, at least trust her.'

There weren't many people I trusted, but I knew the commitment Vera Atkins had to the women she was responsible for in the field. And yet, trust was a luxury I couldn't afford, especially when my contact had just got out of a gendarme's car. Even if that contact was Dominique.

I cocked the gun. 'Last I knew, the gendarmes didn't run a taxi service.'

Her Cupid's bow mouth curled into a faint smile. 'They're much better at picking people up,' she conceded. 'But looks can be deceiving. You know that.' She tried to shift out from under me. 'Move, will you, I can't breathe.'

'Pity.'

'Get off me, Cécile. And while you're at it, tell me why *you're* here. You were supposed to land in a field three miles east of here. At which point someone in the reception committee would bring you to your safe house and arrange for us to meet tomorrow.' She had the effrontery to look amused. 'Technically, you're early.'

'Bah,' I said, but a seed of doubt began to grow.

Maybe she was telling the truth. I didn't know details, but I *did* remember hearing that before her arrest last year, Dominique had used her position as an artist to infiltrate the drawing rooms of key Nazis, passing on information to the Resistance. And, odd as it still sounded, a German colonel had worked with Jérôme to help free her.

'Didn't you know this was my house?'

'Of course not,' I snapped. 'Yours was the first house I came to.'

'Good. The Resistance arranged for us live far enough from neighbours so that wounded fighters can come and go unseen. Or when a stray agent walks down the street.' With a mighty heft, she threw me off her, but didn't run or reach for the Colt. Just scooted far enough away to take a deep breath. Wrapping her arms around her knees she said, 'You still fight well.'

'My life depends on it.'

'Yes, I know.' She looked down, her foot pushing the door open so that the moon could illuminate the shed. 'And maybe mine will, too, at some point. Regardless, you're looking well, old friend. And although you may choose not to believe me, I'm glad you're here.'

She stood up and held out her hand.

'Come inside. You have questions. Some I can answer, some . . .' She shook her head and shrugged. Slowly she lowered her hand and stood back a step. 'Come on, Cécile. Let me make a pot of coffee. I suspect this is going to be a long night. Keep hold of the gun, if it makes you feel better.'

That was easy to say, considering I held the weapon. Still, I followed as Dominique led us through the back door and to a kitchen painted bright yellow. Framed charcoal sketches hung on the walls. The lines were bold, confident, telling stories of ordinary people, doing ordinary things. I paused before a drawing of an old woman with a cat. Her face was turned away from the artist, but her posture, the set of her shoulders, the glass of wine on the table . . . This was Madame Renard, the woman who had hosted Dominique when she was in Paris, who had sheltered me when I was recovering from my wounds, and who had later helped me escape. Was it only a year ago? So much had happened, to all of us.

A quick glance confirmed that the subjects of all the portraits had their faces turned away. Some artists did that, to better study the models' backs, but I sensed that she did it to protect friends, in case she was arrested, and the last of my mistrust abated.

33

The smell of coffee brought me back to the present. We moved to the parlour. It wasn't large, but it was warm, decorated in shades of blue and cream. A bookshelf took up one wall, and above the fireplace, on the other long wall, was a painting of two little girls lying on their backs, holding hands. One was dark, the other fair, and in this painting, both girls showed their faces. Each had eyes the same shade of sea green.

In one corner, an easel was set up on top of a paint-splattered drop cloth. It faced a large window now hidden behind blackout curtains.

She set the tray on a low table in the centre of the room, and moved to the sideboard where a gramophone squatted beside a water jug and a pair of crystal decanters.

'My nearest neighbour is quite deaf,' she said, winding it. 'But it never hurts to be cautious.'

As the opening strains of Fauré's 'Après un rêve' were coaxed from the machine, she frowned, selecting instead a recording of something more contemporary. I took off my cap, set it aside and waited for her to pour the coffee.

'You'll have other questions?' she asked.

I did. Several, actually.

'The car?'

'The one that dropped me off? It is gendarme, of course. Most people can't afford one here. Or the petrol to run it, even if they can secure a permit.'

'And they were driving you home, because . . . ?'

'As I said, because they think I work for them.' She dropped a spoonful of saccharine into her coffee. 'You haven't asked what I do for the gendarmes, but let me explain. I suppose you know

34

how many people are betrayed, not because they are guilty of anything, but because someone has a grudge to settle?'

'I do, yes. And the Gestapo acts first, and asks questions later.'

She nodded. 'And then, it rarely matters what the answer is, unless it implicates someone else. When they have someone in their sights, with a name, an address, there isn't much I can do. But the others? Where there's a description, based on a fleeting encounter? One that could be the boy next door or your uncle Claude?' One hand fluttered gracefully. 'Eyewitnesses are often unreliable. Unsettled, they make mistakes. A mole here, a scar there.' She shrugged. 'I do what I can.'

'As what? The person who . . .' The penny dropped, and when I finished the sentence, my voice was flat. 'Creates the police sketch.'

'Yes.'

'Why should they trust you?'

'The gendarmes? Because they believe I'm reliable. So much so, they lend me out to the Germans.'

'And why should *I* believe you?'

She nodded, acknowledging my point, but also, I thought, sensing that the question was academic.

'Because, Cécile, you know me better than almost anyone else.'

She tucked a stray curl behind her ear and looked at me. She dampened a cloth from the water jug, and ran it over her face before holding it out in front of her, thick with make-up. I might not believe her words, but her eyes, with the dark circles around them laid bare, were clear.

35

'I do what I can, Cécile. As I have always done. And I am very glad you're here.'

Any relief I felt dissipated when another engine stopped in front of the house. This time, I'd almost been fearing it.

Chapter Six

I moved towards the window and peered out from behind the blackout curtains just as the car door softly closed.

Where I'd been expecting several, only two men emerged, dressed in civilian clothes instead of uniforms, although that didn't mean much. One was tall and lean, with thick dark hair; the other was wide – muscular rather than fat – and bald. The light was too dim to see their faces, but their body language was tense.

'Relax, Cécile,' Dominique said. 'It's only Jérôme and André.'

She couldn't know that – not from the other side of the room. I didn't think I'd been followed, but had the Boche found me anyway? I moved behind a chair with a view of the parlour door. My fingers tightened on my gun, just in case.

The large man entered the house first, his footfalls heavy on the wooden floors. He stepped through the doorway and stopped suddenly, so that the taller man almost bumped into him.

'We have a guest,' Dom said, her voice casual.

For a few seconds, they stared at me. Then the big man strode forward, grinning.

'Veronica Lake. With a gun. I think I'm in love.'

The man I knew from training as Big André lurched forward, enfolding me in a bear hug. I let him, my mind whirling. Not only Dom and Jérôme, but Big André too. This was an unexpected and completely welcome boon.

'You're here, too!'

'Weapons instructor,' Big André said. 'Not that I'm half the marksman that little Dominique here is. *She* can shoot the balls off a mouse, but me? I still get the job done.' It was said with little modesty, and from experience I knew that he could 'get the job done' with incredible efficiency. 'What are you doing here, Red?'

'I'm not red on this mission,' I said, unable to quell a smile. André had called me Red from the moment we met in training, a reference to my hair's natural colour.

'Fair point, Blondie. I'm guessing you're one of the agents that dropped tonight?'

I nodded.

'Bad orienteering. You missed the landing ground,' he pointed out, his serious tone at odds with his grin, and the companionable arm he slung over my shoulders.

'It wasn't my call. The pilot was in charge of that.' I unfastened the money belt and handed it to him. 'I'm meant to pass this on to the Resistance. I'm sure you'll do.'

He opened it and grinned. 'It's not often a woman hands *me* large sums of money.'

Dominique shook her head. 'No, I imagine it's usually the other way around.'

André put one hand over his heart, pretending to be wounded by the barb.

'They're forgeries, of course, but good ones. I understand our forgers even pinned the stacks together through the watermarks,

38

like the banks here do.' Glad that the money belt was no longer in my custody, I pulled a small silver case from my pocket and lit a cigarette. Inhaled deeply to calm my nerves and directed my question to Jerome. 'You found the canisters?'

He shook his head. 'Not unless the boys found your drop site.'

'And assuming that Jerry didn't get there first.'

'Well, have a look in a field a couple of miles due east of here. The dispatcher must have wanted to lighten the load for the trip home.'

'Couple of miles? That close?' Jérôme signalled André, and the big man dropped another kiss on my cheek. 'Glad to see you again, Red ... er ... Blondie, but that's my cue to go. See what we can rescue from the Boche. We don't have time to hide you, so come up with a story and change into your nightie fast, before Vallentin and his goons come knocking. It's past your bedtime, and the door-to-door searches will have already started.' He slipped the money belt under his shirt and stepped out of the door and into the night.

Jérôme nodded. 'He's right. Where's your case?'

'In your shed. There's a wireless in it.'

'You can borrow something of mine,' Dom said. 'Jérôme will hide the case – there's a trapdoor in the floor of the shed – and bring in your clothes.' She led the way up the stairs. 'We have a spare room that you'll use while you're here. What happened?'

I hovered outside her bedroom as she rifled through a drawer.

'The pilot couldn't find the lights. We jumped blind.'

She paused, and stared at me. 'Blind? Again? How many of you were there this time?'

'Only two of us, and I hope my colleague already found her safe house.'

'I hope so too.' She tossed me a cotton nightgown and dressing gown. 'Get changed. André's right, it's too late to hide you, so far as I'm concerned, you're an old friend who's passing through. At least for tonight. Maybe your house got bombed, or something. We'll make it up as we go along.'

It was as good a reason as any, and I nodded.

'My name here is Anna,' she said. 'Anna Severin.'

'I know. But I'll have to be a *very* old friend.' I took a deep breath, and braced myself. 'My name here is Katrin Hügel, and I'm from Strasbourg.'

'Jesus,' Jérôme groaned from the bottom of the stairs. 'I hope you know what you're doing.'

He met me on the landing, holding out my valise, presumably without the Jed Set.

'If it wasn't dangerous, I wouldn't have been sent.' I kept my voice light, but they knew it was no joke. 'For what it's worth, it'll be good to work with friends again.'

He was about to answer when the third motor car of the night stopped in front of the Severins' home.

The Boche had arrived.

Chapter Seven

I ran into the spare bedroom, quickly changing into Dom's cotton nightgown and rolled under the covers to make it look as if the bed, and my hair, had been slept in. A heavy hand rapped on the front door. I held my breath as Jérôme moved to open it.

'You are up late, Herr Doktor,' an unfamiliar voice said.

'So are you.' Jérôme's voice was weary. 'I just arrived home after being called out to help Madame Houlette deliver her firstborn. What's your excuse, Captain?'

Jérôme knew better than to lie about an event, and the specificity of the lie meant that he really was with Madame Houlette earlier in the evening. A normal person might have asked how she and her child fared, but the Gestapo weren't known for their manners.

'The Resistance were active tonight. Have you seen anything suspicious?'

If Jérôme was going to betray me, it would be now. He could tell them there was a spy upstairs – an agent who'd dropped tonight. Could tell them who I was, what I'd done . . . but when he spoke, his soft voice was firm.

'No,' he said.

My exhalation was loud, even to my own ears, though I hadn't expected him to betray me.

'No strangers?'

'No. None.'

'Then you will not mind if we check?'

I'd expected no less, and closed my eyes, forcing my breathing to even out. Soft footsteps sounded from outside my door.

'Olivier?'

Jérôme's voice softened. 'Nothing to worry about. Captain Vallentin just wants to keep us safe, *ma coeur*.' How he uttered that with a straight face was beyond me.

I joined Dom on the landing. 'What's going on?'

They were on the stairs in a heartbeat, three guns pointed at me.

'Who are you?'

'*Gott im Himmel*,' I muttered, just loud enough. 'Put those away, will you? It's far too late in the night for this nonsense.' Tying a knot in the belt of the borrowed dressing gown, I stomped past the men on the stairs to stand in front of the man I guessed was the captain. 'What's this all about?'

Vallentin was an inch or two shorter than Jérôme, fair-haired, and not unattractive. He met my gaze with a calculating look, although when he spoke, he directed his words to Jérôme.

'You did not tell me you had a house guest.'

Vallentin's words were light enough, but there was a dark, viscous tone that ran underneath them that told me how much danger I put my friends into.

'You didn't ask.' Jérôme tempered his words with a bland smile, and neatly explained my presence. 'I met her at the train station this evening. Madame Hügel is a friend of my wife's.'

'Frau Hügel.' Vallentin's half-smile was just this side of polite. 'You speak German well, almost as if you were a native.'

'I speak German like an Alsatian.' I inclined my head, and allowed my own half-smile to match his. 'Perhaps because I *am* Alsatian.'

'Katrin and I went to school together,' Dom explained. 'What can we do for you?'

His sharp eyes studied us for a few moments. He allowed the silence to build, perhaps hoping that we would break it and incriminate ourselves. We were too well trained for that, and finally he spoke.

'We saw parachutes some miles from here, and came to investigate. We have reason to believe that someone might have landed. You haven't seen any strangers, have you?'

Dom shrugged her shoulders, her green eyes wide and innocent. 'I haven't, no.'

'Herr Doktor? You have been known to treat people regardless of their allegiance.'

'As per the Hippocratic Oath. However, no man came to me tonight, for medical or any other type of assistance.' Jérôme ushered us into the parlour and poured a glass of Calvados for Vallentin, unable to hide his wince as a bang came from down the hall. 'But by all means, have your men search my home. Again.'

Vallentin's smile was humourless.

'You understand we must be certain, don't you?' He took a seat opposite me, his pale eyes boring into mine. 'Where are you from, Frau Hügel?'

'Strasbourg.'

'It's a long way away.'

I shrugged, wishing I hadn't left my cigarettes upstairs.

43

'I suppose so.'

'Why are you here?' When I tilted my head, he added, 'Why have you travelled here? Was it necessary?'

It was the same in England. Given how scarce petrol was, non-essential travel, even by rail, was noteworthy.

'Necessary?' I echoed. 'My house was bombed, my friends have fled, and the last I heard, my husband was in Berlin. There wasn't much left for me in Strasbourg.'

'You think it is safe here?'

'You think it's safe in Strasbourg?' I asked. 'At least here I am with friends.'

He leant forward and placed a hand on my bandaged ankle.

'Ouch!' My cry of pain was real enough, and peppered with shock. A Frenchwoman might have tolerated that, but not a German woman. 'Don't you dare touch me,' I snarled.

'Vallentin!' Jérôme protested. 'She can show you her papers. Her travel documents.'

He ignored Jérôme, and tightened his grip.

'How did you hurt your ankle?'

I yanked my foot out of his reach. 'Running to an air raid shelter. Three days, and it still hurts. And I'll thank you for not putting a hand on me again.'

He inclined his head to the side, almost politely, and sat back. Sniffed the Calvados before taking a small sip.

'Let's see those papers.'

One of Vallentin's men followed me up the stairs. From the way he stared into my bedroom, I guessed it was probably the first time he was close to a woman's bedroom that he hadn't had to pay for. I growled at him at the doorway and he stood back, but his eyes still took in the details: the rumpled bed, the valise in the corner, my handbag on the bedside table. I pulled out the papers. They had the wrong look and feel to be French, but were they good enough to pass for German? Hoping none of my anxiety showed, I handed them over. He stared at my cigarette case and lighter, on the bureau.

'Filthy habit,' he said, although he smelled of nicotine himself.

'Just as filthy for a man,' I agreed and grabbed the case.

The Boche frowned on Frenchwomen smoking, which I assume extended to German women. But the alternative was for them to think the cigarettes belonged to a man hiding nearby. So they'd have to get used to the sight of seeing the tall Alsatian woman smoking. Sighing, I lit one and made a point of blowing the cloud in his direction.

Vallentin's goon grunted and retreated. I followed him down the stairs and back to the parlour. It was going to be a long night, and I only hoped that it didn't end with all of us in the Gestapo's custody.

Chapter Eight

My papers must have held up to Vallentin's scrutiny. We stood at the window, peering out from behind the blackout curtains and counting the men entering the vehicle.

'Remind me to send the boffins back home a case of champagne, when I get back,' I said, once they had departed.

It had been a long night, and tense. First, with Vallentin's questions, then with an exhaustion that didn't preclude sleep. Vallentin's visit brought a challenge: as a wireless operator, I usually had to relocate often to avoid being apprehended. Word would spread about the Severins' German house guest, and while I could now hide in plain sight, I would need to be clever about how and where I transmitted, to keep my friends as well as myself safe. The safe house that had been secured for me in Caen would have to remain vacant for the time being – at least until I was able to purchase a few disguises, not the least of which was a brown wig. At five feet ten, I was already too noticeable. The wig wouldn't solve the problem, but it would help. People, I found, often saw what they wanted to.

Nerves on edge long after Vallentin had departed, Dominque and Jérôme spent the next hour sharing what information they knew about the Germans' defences.

So it was that, after a late rising, under the guise of showing me what sights remained, Dom and I strolled through the town, moving at a pace that didn't strain my ankle. Jérôme, meanwhile, would liaise with Marcel Beaune, one of the Resistance leaders, to update him on my arrival and arrange a meeting.

There wasn't much to see; the town was small, and centred around a stone church with a blockish bell tower. Across the village green, hastily constructed barracks sprouted, with the usual visible security measures of guards, gates and barbed wire.

Bright flowers bloomed in the window boxes of an auberge on the road adjacent to the church, and beside it, a general store, butcher's shop, haberdashery, vintner and a garage. Jérôme's surgery was further along, a lone building standing between two fire-scarred husks.

As we passed a ruined building on the corner, Dom murmured, 'This was the draper. Monsieur survived, but has now left to live with relatives further inland.' She pointed to a building that stood beside it. 'Olivier's surgery, although we use the small room beside the parlour as his home-surgery, in case someone comes to us with an emergency in the evenings or weekends.'

I nodded and she continued.

'That building was once the hairdresser. Madame and her family . . .' She shook her head; they hadn't survived.

There would be a frightening number of stories like this – people who had lost livelihood and loved ones.

'I'm sorry.'

'This is war. We lose people we love, and we make do.'

That stoic statement was echoed in London and Paris, and probably across the world, but something in her voice made me ask, 'Who have you lost?'

She looked around before she answered, her voice low.

'Other than almost losing my life last year?' I nodded, slow-ing my pace to hers as she considered her answer. 'My mother was taking shelter in Marble Arch Tube station when it was bombed in '40. My sister Madeleine died a few months ago.' She shrugged self-consciously. 'Vera sent word.'

When I met Dom in '42, we were told not to speak of our backgrounds, our families, our tragedies. Would she have told me about her mother when I knew her in Paris last year?

No, I thought. Not any more than I would have told her of the loss of my first husband, Philip, sunk off the coast of Greenland in the early months of the war.

'Oh, Dom, I'm so sorry.' The words seemed insignificant, but they were all I could manage.

We walked another few steps before I asked, 'With the Allies bombing us, what sort of support can we expect from the locals?'

She thought about that for a moment.

'Some will hate the Allies for what has been destroyed, but others, many others, hate the Boche more. Hate being second-class citizens in their own country. They will support the Allies, when they come.'

She slanted a glance my way, silently asking if I knew when that would be.

I shrugged; I didn't know, but guessed that it wouldn't be long. Part of my job here was to do what I could to pave their way, including confirming what sort of reception the locals would give them.

We looped around, re-entering the square from the far side. A black staff car was now parked outside the auberge. Captain Vallentin and a black-uniformed man stood beside it, faces animated as they vied for the attention of a young woman in a tight jumper.

'Mademoiselle Raoullin seems to prefer Major Lorenz's men.' Dom's nose flared slightly at the name.

'Lorenz?'

'Vallentin's boss. Local Gestapo. A thug, with a taste for cards and champagne.' She cleared her throat. 'He's more interested in his own pleasures and internal rivalries than in us. He leaves that to his men. But don't let *that* –' she jerked her head at the two men – 'deceive you. They're true believers in Hitler and his Reich. They'll pursue any whiff of resistance as far as they can.'

Vallentin turned towards us. The easy smile he flashed at Mademoiselle Raoullin faded, and he studied us with a clinical detachment.

No, I couldn't underestimate this man. I had to find a way to allay his suspicions, or I'd be forever watching for him over my shoulder. We allowed a reasonable distance to grow before continuing.

'So. These internal rivalries?'

'More or less what you'd expect. The SS hate the Wehrmacht, the Wehrmacht hate the SS.' Dom kept her voice soft, careful not to be overheard. 'There's a new man in town. Former Abwehr, if you listen to rumours.'

'In Portugal, with one or two exceptions, they were more famous for sleeping with their secretaries than they were for accomplishing . . . well, anything.'

'The Abwehr was dissolved because Hitler thought they were working against him, but this man has a reputation. He's dangerous, maybe more so than Vallentin. So far he's only observed.' She smiled politely as two gendarmes passed. 'But it feels as if little escapes him.'

A youth with longish hair and a stack of books under one arm strode towards us. Wedged between the books, the corner of a newspaper peeked out. Uttering a low expletive, Dom crossed the street to intercept him. In moments, the boy had dropped his books; red-faced, he bent to pick them up. His flush deepened when he realised that Dom had stuffed the newspaper into her handbag. I caught a glimpse of *Combat*'s familiar masthead and the leading story, 'LES COMMUNISTES DANS LE GOUVERNEMENT', before it was hidden from sight.

'Have you lost your mind, Guillaume?' Her expression was amiable as she handed him a book, but her voice held enough of a bite to stop the boy from arguing. 'Walking around with that drivel? You know it's banned.'

The lad gritted his teeth, but Dom gave him the sort of soft smile that a fond aunt would give a favourite nephew. It wasn't reflected in her tone.

'With Vallentin around the corner and checkpoints all along the road this morning? You *know* what will happen if they catch you with it.'

I moved between them and the road, doing my best to hide the youth's mutinous expression from view.

'Anything interesting?' I drawled.

The boy's eyes widened as he looked at me. Colour seeped from his face and, with a thin squawk, he grabbed the remaining books and fled.

'So the Resistance's underground newspaper even makes it this far north,' I said.

'Unfortunately, yes. We had an incident here, a few months ago. One of the local boys got hold of a copy. He passed it around until one of them got caught with it. He was only fifteen, but he was arrested.' She looked at the sky; it told me all I needed to know about what had happened to the boy. 'As were eight others. And I couldn't tell you if they were even remotely associated with the Resistance.'

'Stupid boy.'

'Stupid war,' she corrected, keeping her voice low. 'Guillaume's a good lad, and in a better world he would be playing football and reading *Twenty Thousand Leagues Under the Sea*. Maybe he still would be, but his father was rounded up with the Communists.'

Which explained why the boy was interested in the Resistance, and perhaps that issue of *Combat* in particular.

'And,' Dom continued, 'despite having two German soldiers billeted in her home, his mother dabbles with the idea of the Resistance, but the only thing she's ever done is build up that boy's illusions.'

I held up a hand to stop her. 'The soldiers know?'

'I'd be surprised if they hadn't heard her talk,' she said. 'But they're young and homesick, and Guillaume's mother looks after them.' She shrugged. 'She hates the Nazis as a whole, but is fond enough of her two.'

'The lines can blur when you live among them. Speaking of which, how did you avoid having a German lodger?'

'Luck.'

Her tone made it clear that it was nothing of the sort, but that she wouldn't elaborate.

We passed the main street and moved towards a residential area. A distant rumble announced the motorcade.

'Let's go. I have no desire to see this. Not with that paper in your bag.'

Dom's hand held me in place, insisting we stay.

'To leave now will draw attention to us.'

A motorcycle led the way, the man in the sidecar holding an assault rifle. Swastikas flew from the bonnets of the three cars following it. The first two cars carried seasoned soldiers, their uniforms pristine and their faces battle-scarred and wary.

I held my breath, maintaining an expression of polite disinterest as they approached, while my stomach churned. Dom had taken that paper from the boy to keep him safe, but by doing so, had put us at risk. The sort of risk we'd have the devil's own job talking our way out of if we were searched.

The motorcade kicked up a spray of dirt and sand, which the wind blew into my face. My sunglasses did little to avert the small boulders, so that one lodged in my eye, and my first glimpse of the man in the third car was through a veil of tears.

He was slight and balding. Middle-aged. He turned and time slowed.

There was an energy about him. A personality, an intelligence, that was barely contained in his unremarkable frame. A man, spoken well of by men on both sides of the war, including my husband, who had no love for the Nazis.

'Is that . . . ?' I breathed, although I didn't need Dom's answer to know who he was. Everyone in the world did.

If there was a protocol for this sort of situation, it flew from my head, and transfixed, all I could do was stare, listening to my heart beating.

And wonder what Erwin Rommel, the Desert Fox, saw when his eyes met mine.

Chapter Nine

Everyone knew Field Marshal Rommel was stationed here, but I hadn't expected to see him – not so soon. How much his presence here might complicate my mission would remain to be seen.

'Cécile?'

I looked up. The edges of the newspaper browned and began to curl. As Guillaume's issue of *Combat* caught the flame, Dom dropped it into a large ashtray, handed the lighter back to me and opened the kitchen window to let the smoke escape. 'I asked you when you will be seeing Beaune.'

'Oh. Jérôme said he'd confirm with Monsieur Beaune this morning, and assuming Beaune is available, I'll be meeting him this afternoon.' I sighed. 'I hope that with Jérôme and André speaking for me, I won't have to go through the bother of proving myself.'

'You should be fine,' she said. 'And I might go part of the way with you. Jérôme can drop me off at the gendarmes' station.' Her moue of distaste was identical to the one she wore when setting the copy of *Combat* alight. 'If your friend Léonie was picked up, I'd rather find out before Sunday. There is the odd benefit to working for Charles Pomeroy. Very little happens in the area that he doesn't know about, so even if it's the Gestapo who grabbed her, there'll be news.'

'Good plan,' I agreed. 'They won't be suspicious of you asking around?'

'What makes you think I'm going to ask anyone anything?' She raised an eyebrow. 'They're used to me showing up to help, even when I'm not scheduled to work. If people forget to hold their tongues around me, that's not my fault.'

I laughed. She looked unassuming, so people often forgot she was there. It was a damned convenient skill to have, for a courier.

Jérôme arrived within the hour with news that Beaune would see me. We shared a light lunch and drove the fifteen minutes to the gendarmerie where Dom worked. The building would have been unremarkable, but for the air of menace that seemed to surround it.

'Good luck,' I murmured as Dom closed the door and walked up the steps, greeting a young man in a suit smoking nearby. He tipped his hat, but his interest seemed more on the Peugeot. Specifically, on me.

'Lieutenant Courtenay,' Jérôme explained.

I scratched my nose, hiding my lips from sight as I spoke.

'Friend or foe?'

'Not sure.' He guided the Peugeot away from the kerb, and away from Courtenay. 'He's not involved with the Resistance, but I haven't heard of any excesses in the other direction either.'

'A man just doing his job? Diligent?'

He kept his eyes on the road ahead, navigating through the potholes.

'As far as I can tell, yes, but be careful around him.'

It was good advice, albeit unnecessary. Since signing up to work for Special Operations, that advice covered my interactions with everyone. Even old friends like Big André and the Severins.

I turned my attention to the passing countryside. If the fighting was here, our boys would have a challenge: the fields and pastures we passed were all bordered by tall, thick hedgerows that might break the wind but also limited visibility, and would become an ambusher's dream. I was certain they were already aware of this, but made a mental note to include it in my next transmission, just in case.

'Who else will I be meeting today?'

'Just Marcel Beaune. As per your request.'

'I asked to meet the leader in private because the more people who know who I am, the greater the chance that someone will blow my cover. According to London, Jacques Mandeville leads the *réseau*. So why am I meeting this Marcel Beaune?'

'Jacques Mandeville and Alain Sablonnières – you know his name? No? Sablonnières' family settled here when he was a child. He and Mandeville grew up together, and they're still close. So while Jacques is officially in charge, with Alain Sablonnières as his second in command, in practice, the *réseau* defers to Marcel Beaune. Jacques' uncle.'

'Why?'

'Experience.' His voice rose as the engine protested over a gruelling series of holes. 'Beaune was a hero in the Great War. He understands the Germans and their tactics, but he also understands the cost of human lives. He does what he can to ensure that lives are not risked unnecessarily.'

I understood what he was saying.

'There are problems with a few firebrands?'

'The problems are with people who are losing patience. And who forget how many people, including innocents, are rounded up and murdered every time a German is killed.'

'So why isn't Beaune officially the leader?'

'He isn't interested. He'd rather work his farm and help his nephew when needed.'

'And yet, I'm meeting Beaune, and not Mandeville,' I repeated, and then pointed out, 'You still haven't answered the "why?". You, and Mandeville, respect him that much?'

'I do, yes. But don't let that stop you from forming your own opinion.'

I had to laugh. 'As if it would?'

His grin was natural and almost boyish, erasing the small lines on his face.

'As to the "why?". It was his suggestion. The other two have been organising whatever moves we make against the Boche. He offered to handle the communications side of things. It also is another layer of protection for you. The other two are more visible. You'd be seen working with them, which would defeat your request that only one of them knows who you are.'

His smile faded. About 500 metres ahead, a barricade was manned by three soldiers with machine guns. Jérôme slowed the Peugeot, murmuring, 'Routine, I hope. You have nothing incriminating with you?'

Nothing other than the sgian dubh strapped to my thigh as usual. It might take a bit of fast talking to explain it away, but it wasn't impossible. I answered Jérôme with a light shrug.

Of course, it would be a bigger issue if Léonie had been caught, or if someone recognised me from my first trip to France. But at this point, I had to assume that wasn't likely. Yet.

The soldier in the middle stepped forward with authority.

'Papers, please.'

The soldier held out his hand, waiting as Jérôme produced his from an inside pocket of his jacket. Jérôme's face looked completely neutral. The roadblock may well have been a regular occurrence, but with the Boche aware that agents had dropped the other night, they would be more rigorous than usual.

The soldier scowled. 'You are very young for a doctor,' he said, despite the fact that Jérôme looked at least five years older than his thirty years. 'Maquis?' he asked. 'Resistance?'

The other two soldiers raised their weapons. My heart began to pound, but Jérôme remained composed.

'Don't be absurd. My name is Doctor Severin. I believe you'll find my paperwork is in order, including an *Ausweis*, allowing me to drive at any hour.'

'And today's emergency?'

'A farmer's cow is calving.'

The soldier flicked through Jérôme's papers.

'You are not a doctor for animals.'

'No, but I like milk with my coffee, so I help where I can.'

'And the woman?'

I handed Jérôme my papers, watching him pass them over as the other two soldiers advanced.

'A friend of my wife's. In case I need another pair of hands.'

One of the men commented, in German, about where my hands would best be placed. A Frenchwoman might have pretended she

58

didn't understand, but an Alsatian woman would not. I clenched my jaw and snapped the answer my Alsatian grandmother would have made.

'Watch your manners.'

Surprised, he took a step back, his posture straight. I continued in the same tone.

'His wife had more important work this afternoon. For the gendarmes, in case you're curious.'

The soldier in command leant towards me, his eyes dark in the fading light.

'Frau Hügel, your German is excellent.'

'What do you think we speak in Strasbourg?' I handed him my papers, feeling more confident about them, now that they had passed Vallentin's scrutiny. 'Greek?'

'You're German?'

Grand-mère Elisabeth would have corrected him and said 'Alsatian', but as of January '42, the Nazis had declared all German-speaking residents to be German. Now wasn't the time to argue the point.

'Last time I checked.'

'Why are you here?'

'As the doctor said, I'm visiting my friend. And helping her husband with a cow.' I jerked my head at Jérôme. 'Not because I have any skill, before you ask, but simply because I, too, like milk in that wretched swill his wife calls coffee.'

'Your family?'

'Not many remain. My husband is in Berlin, and my brothers were integrated into German troops and sent east. Everyone else was killed in an Allied bombing raid.'

'And yet, you are alive. In a car in Normandy. With a French doctor.'

'Thank you for making it sound sordid.' I gently pried my papers from the soldier's fingers. 'I'm sure you can find many more interesting people to detain, can't you?'

He stared at us for a few moments.

'More interesting? That remains to be seen.'

With a half-smile, he waved at one of his comrades. The second soldier laid down his weapon and picked up a long stick with a mirror at the end.

Jérôme's face was the picture of bored resignation but, in character, I glared at the soldier as they searched the Peugeot.

'Was that entirely necessary?' Jérôme asked after we had driven in silence for a mile or two.

I lit a cigarette. 'They didn't find anything.'

'That doesn't necessarily mean they won't arrest you.' Jérôme parked the car on the fringe of the woods. He looked as if he wanted to slam the door, but thought better of it and closed it softly. His irritation visible, he opened the Peugeot's boot, threw a pair of trousers and my cap at me, along with a pair of boots. 'Or me.'

'Nonsense,' I said. 'Grumpy as you are, you're missing the point. Katrin Hügel is not French. Don't expect her to act like one. *They* don't.'

'French or not French is irrelevant. I haven't seen a German woman – and yes, they are here as well – act like—'

'An aristocrat?' I finished the sentence for him. 'Or the pampered wife of a German officer?'

He leant against the Peugeot and took a deep breath. And then a second one.

'Cécile, your arrogance is going to be the death of us all.'

'It's not arrogance. Look, they'll see what they want to see. Will they remember me? Yes, of course. I'm little short of one metre eighty. They would notice me even if I was quiet as a mouse. Took me a while to realise just how much I stand out in a crowd, so I figure I might as well use that to my advantage.'

'You're not bulletproof.'

'You know I'm not,' I said. 'You dug two bullets out of me yourself, and every time you cringe, it makes them believe in Katrin Hügel a little bit more. Perhaps it's best if Olivier Severin doesn't like his new house guest.'

'You're not making this easy.'

I laughed. 'If it was an easy job, Jérôme, any other mortal could do it.'

'Just remember that you *are* mortal, and it's not just you. Your actions have repercussions on Dominique, on me, on us all.'

'I know.'

'Good. Then put on the trousers, boots and cap. Beaune agreed to your request to meet you alone, and we also agreed that, at least for now, it's best that people think that the radio operator is a man. From here on, we will refer to you as Cecil.'

He pulled a fishing rod from the boot and turned his back.

'Hurry up, *mon ami* Cecil. Marcel Beaune is waiting.'

Chapter Ten

Jérôme led the way into the woods, stepping over brush and following a small stream. At the point where it merged with a larger one, an old man, maybe sixty or seventy, sat on a rock, dangling a line into the water. He looked up, watching us approach with calm eyes. He put down the rod and stood straight and tall, despite his age. He was of average height, but that was the only thing average about him. His steel-grey hair was close-cropped, and his bright black eyes assessed me.

If he was surprised by my appearance, he kept it to himself. He doffed his cap and bowed smartly.

'Good afternoon, Monsieur Cecil. You come in good company, and well disguised.'

It was difficult not to smile.

'Thank you, Monsieur Beaune. I apologise for any confusion, but I think it's best for the *réseau*, and for me, if everyone thinks your new pianist is a man.'

There was no point in adding my suspicion that the Boche already had reason to believe that was the case.

I peered into his pail and added, 'It looks like you've had a productive afternoon.'

'That remains to be seen. Do you fish, Cecil?'

'Not really,' I said, not looking at Jérôme as I added: 'I've been told I lack the patience for it.'

A hint of a smile flitted across his face, as my friend guffawed.

'I see.'

The rod bowed and, for a moment, Beaune was preoccupied with landing the fish. He carefully removed the hook from its mouth and set it free back in the water.

'Too small,' he explained, and focused his attention back on me. 'You've worked together before, I trust?'

'Yes, in Paris last year.'

The two men exchanged a quick glance.

'Before he left in . . . what was it? February?'

If it was a test, it was an easy one.

'April. Just before Easter.'

He exchanged a glance with Jérôme, who nodded.

'I know why he left. Why did you?'

'I turned down a neighbour's invitation for dinner. He didn't take it very well.'

'Informed on you, did he?'

I nodded. 'I was lucky to get out before the Gestapo could catch me.'

'Where did you go?'

'Now that, monsieur, is a long story. Suffice to say, I left Paris for a while.'

I'd left *France* for a while, but he didn't need to know that.

He settled himself back onto the rock and baited the hook, watching me standing above him. If he was trying to make me feel uncomfortable, like a child called into the headmaster's office, then he would be disappointed. I sat, as gracefully as I could, on a fallen log. A small smile twitched under his moustache and he cast the line into the pond.

'Your job now?'

'Working with your *réseau*, although I must warn you, I have other duties as well.'

'Understood.'

Remembering something Vera had said about Virgil – that most likely he was betrayed because he trusted the wrong person, or was connected to someone who trusted the wrong person – I laid out my conditions.

'I have another request, for my protection, and yours. I would rather only Jérôme, Dominique and Big André know who I am, and that you use only them to liaise with me.'

He smiled. 'Big André, indeed. He's only slightly smaller than Versailles.' Still chuckling, he said, 'But yes. That is acceptable. And for drops?'

'As agreed, I'll co-ordinate them with you, and with London, again using only those three as intermediaries. Although I do hope you'll answer a question for me, now?'

He inclined his head, and I asked the question that had been scratching at the back of my mind.

'Our drop was a disaster. The pilot couldn't find your landing zone, so after circling a few times, we jumped blind. He sent the canisters out after us. It meant that the Boche probably arrived first and now have the canisters, as well as a good suspicion that we landed. What happened? And, perhaps more importantly, how did you arrange the drop if your operator had already been compromised?'

Beaune stroked his moustache, nodding his approval.

'Very good questions, Cecil, and my apologies. The drop had been arranged before Pascal was arrested. We were at the right location, the one agreed with London. I do not know why your pilot had different coordinates.'

It happened more often than anyone wanted to admit, but something didn't feel right.

'Who knew about it?'

'The *réseau* knew the day, but the location? Only Pascal, our wireless operator, Alain, Jacques and myself. Pascal is now gone, arrested and executed. Hence our request for a new operator. None of the three of us would know how to use the wireless to change the drop.'

'Right. No one else knows how to use the set?'

'No. We were hoping you'd be able to teach one of our men.'

'I'd need to clear that with London first. Then we can agree who should be trained. Do you still have Pascal's piano? I mean, his wireless set. Maybe a GEE or Eureka beacon as well?'

'Yes. Both his set and a Eureka.'

Good, that could be a spare set, in case something happened to mine. Something else occurred to me.

'If our agreed intermediaries are unavailable and you need to send someone else, I want a code word to know that they really are from you. Do not share it, or my identity, with anyone, including Jacques Mandeville and Alain Sablonnières.'

We agreed the code word, and Jérôme and I returned to the car. I leant against it to change out of the boots, and said, 'Tell me about Pascal.'

'He was incarcerated in the prison near Amiens—'

'No, not that. What was he like as a man, as an agent?'

65

'You mean – did he inform on the *réseau*, only to end up incarcerated himself?'

Jérôme's voice was ironic, although I hadn't hinted that Pascal might have been dodgy. It wouldn't stand to reason that someone who was working with the Germans would then be arrested by them.

'No, I don't think so,' he replied. 'He was quiet and careful. Kept himself to himself.'

'His job?'

'Other than what he did for us, he worked for La Poste, which provided him with a good excuse to move around. He built a hidden compartment for the wireless in his van, so that he could transmit from relative safety and be on his way quickly. We were able to recover it so – as far as I know – there was no incriminating evidence against him, but as you will know, that doesn't always matter.'

'No, it doesn't.' I tossed the boots into the boot and seated myself in the passenger's seat. 'But if he was as careful as you say, how did he get caught?'

He folded himself into the driver's seat and mulled over my question for a few moments.

'The average lifespan for an operator is six weeks – which I hope you will beat. But, Pascal? It could have been anything, Cécile. A rival who wanted him out of the way. Someone who thought they saw him in the wrong place.'

I took a breath and added another possibility – one that increasingly worried me. Jérôme and Beaune had been too quick to agree to my condition of anonymity.

'Or a leak within the *réseau*.' When he didn't refute my theory, I continued. 'Do you know who it is?'

His expression resolute, he started the engine.

'No proof that there is one, or that there isn't.'

'You have suspicions?'

He squinted into the setting sun.

'Nothing to hang my hat on.'

'And the *réseau* is trying to find the leak?'

He frowned, his eyes still on the road. 'We are.'

'And Dom? What does she think?'

Jérôme swerved to avoid a deep crater in the road.

'Bloody Germans are usually good at fixing these.' The car straightened and he continued. 'She hasn't been directly involved with any of this since leaving Paris. As far as they know, or as far as I know they know, she's just my wife. Who *might* pass on a bit of gossip from her work with the gendarmes.'

'And that's the way she wants it?'

'That's the way we both wanted it.' His voice was as strong and implacable as a battleship. 'You didn't see the state she was in when we rescued her last year. The Gestapo tried to break her, and they came damned close.' He hit the brakes, stopping the car in the middle of the road, the canopy of trees darkening his face. 'It took a lot of work, and she's still not quite what she was before. Oh, she'll do what you ask. You know that, but I will not stand by and watch her break again. Don't ask me to.'

I nodded, not wanting her to break either, and wondering how much of this Vera knew.

His expression softened.

'I don't want to lose you either, Cécile. So do whatever it is you need to do, but for the love of God, for all our sakes, be careful, will you?'

Chapter Eleven

The next day dawned, cool but bright. My friends had left the house by the time I padded downstairs. While I had been meeting Beaune, Dom had confirmed that while the Boche had found evidence of two agents landing, they hadn't apprehended either 'man' yet.

That was good. Léonie was still at large, as far as we knew, and the longer they were looking for a pair of men, the better.

I pottered around the house for a bit, then helped myself to Dom's bicycle. She and Jérôme had provided a decent accounting of what troops were based where on that first night, but I wanted to confirm it myself. Pointing the bicycle west, I started pedalling along the side of the gravelled road.

The gravel road turned into a dirt one as I neared the Orne. Easier to cycle, allowing me to focus less on the road and more on my surroundings. The river was about 180 feet or so wide, with houses lining its muddy banks. Sandbags protected muddy trenches that ran parallel along the banks. On the eastern bank a pillbox squatted, its anti-tank and anti-aircraft guns menacing a now-silent sky.

Men milled around, their Wehrmacht uniforms sporting the badges of the 716th Infantry. Dom had mentioned that, but it made little sense; the 716th division was a static division – the sort that usually guarded a garrison, not an important asset like the Orne.

Moreover, the men were mostly older, well into their forties. One of the few young men was bent almost double with a hacking cough, using a light machine gun to prop himself up. It looked like a Browning, but that, too, made no sense. German soldiers didn't use American guns. Unless it was taken from a Yank, or maybe from a country that had copied the design?

Or from one of the drops the Germans got to before the Resistance did?

His was not the only foreign-looking weapon.

Why on earth would someone put a second-rate regiment here, made up of the old or unwell, armed with scavenged weapons. Was this a distraction, or did some idiot really think putting them here was a good idea?

Someone called for me to halt. I braked, rolling to a stop in front of the two battle-scarred men blocking my path.

'*Guten Morgen*,' I said. 'What can I do for you?'

The man on the left's expression remained impassive, but the one on the right flashed a moment of surprise at my easy use of German.

'State your business,' the first man barked, as his comrade raised his weapon.

'Oh, put that away,' I snapped, and handed over my forged papers. 'What is this about needing to look at my papers every five metres, anyway?' Other than the sgian dubh, they were the only incriminating things I carried, and I gave the guard a stern look and held up my hand in a silent warning not to allow his chum to frisk me.

70

The man with the gun shuffled his feet while the other flicked through my papers. He grunted as he saw my travel permit, and handed them back, waving me past.

Along the road connecting the river to the canal, men toiled under the watchful gaze of an armed guard who couldn't have been more than sixteen. Their uniforms were unfamiliar; emaciated, ill and sunburnt, the men's features read like a map of Eurasia. Most likely, they were prisoners of war, forced to toil for the Reich.

They looked away as I cycled past and, even though my heart broke a little more with each man, I knew I had to do the same.

A flash of sun through the leafy canopy caught my eyes, temporarily blinding me. My wheel caught in something and I toppled from the bike. My hands and bad ankle broke my fall and I bit my lip until the pain subsided. One man close by murmured in accented French, 'Are you all right?'

His broad face, features and accents were Eastern European – maybe Russian. His pale eyes widened as the guard strode forward. He didn't cringe, only tensed his body, bracing himself.

The guard swung his rifle, hitting the prisoner behind the knees, and again until he fell to the ground.

'How dare you speak to her?' He raised the rifle again, now aiming for the man's head.

This time, I couldn't look away and shouted, 'Stop!'

The guard's face flushed. 'You dared touch a *German* woman?'

'Stop, I said.'

I glanced at the man at my feet. Muscles bunched under his thin shirt. It wasn't the pose of a defeated foe; he was a caged

71

animal ready to strike. I dusted off my hands, willing the man to stay down.

'He didn't touch me, and no harm was done.' Despite my own anger, my voice was cool, if firm.

The prisoner's white-hot anger was almost palpable, and I forced myself not to take a step back. Didn't the fool know that if he attacked now, both of us were in trouble?

A different guard called out, and the stand-off was broken.

'Get back to work,' the guard ordered the prisoner. He turned to me, the polite smile not mitigating the cruel eyes. 'I am glad you're well, Fräulein. You must be careful. The roads are unsafe, as are these curs.'

I hummed a response, afraid to open my mouth for fear of telling him that *he* was the one making it unsafe – that he was the cur.

My hands shook as I pulled the bicycle from the ground and remounted. I didn't look behind me, concentrated my mind on moving further away and promising myself that before this was done, I'd do something about that guard. Unless one of the prisoners got to him first, and that would be fine by me.

Anger still coursed through my veins, as I reached the rolling lift bridge over the canal at Bénouville. The bridge was raised, and I balanced the bike, noting the gun emplacements as a ship plodded downstream. Guards stood on a small balcony over the canal, and on the far side, a two-storey, red brick café beckoned.

I waited for it to lower and crossed to the café, taking a seat by the window, aware that, aside from the proprietress

72

and a girl I guessed to be her daughter, I was the only woman in the place. I didn't care. I ordered a cup of coffee, and when the ersatz didn't stop my hands from trembling, I lit a cigarette and asked for a glass of white wine and a sandwich.

The wine began to calm my nerves as soon as it reached my bloodstream, and I looked around. The room wasn't large. Against the far wall, two men in uniform sat beside a trio of men in suits. I would have to get closer to hear which language they spoke, but my sense was that they were German. All of them, including the proprietress, watched me.

Of course they would. I was a tall blonde woman, by myself, having a glass of wine and smoking a cigarette. I was at once all the things they feared, and yet were intrigued by.

Most of them probably thought I was one of their agents, and that was fine.

One of the men made the sort of moves that heralded an unwanted advance. I threw down a note and, leaving half the sandwich untouched, headed for the café's exit, in no mood to pretend to be flattered by the fat fool.

As I reached for the door, a boy in an ill-fitting uniform burst through it, knocking me aside. I glared, watching as he relayed his message to the fat officer.

'The railway bridge,' the youth panted. 'It's just blown up.'

'Fucking Resistance,' the fat man growled. 'Casualties?'

I paused, fiddling with my handbag and trying not to look obvious as I listened.

'The munitions train.'

'When?'

'Less than ten minutes ago, sir.'

They bloody blew up a train, and I knew nothing about it. Surely Jérôme had known, and for certain, Beaune had. Why hadn't they told me?

I'd been seen by enough people to establish my alibi, but it was time to return to the Severins' house. There would be a message to London that would need to be sent, and I needed to make it clear to Jérôme, Beaune, and the rest of the *réseau* the importance of keeping me informed of their plans.

Chapter Twelve

Instead of Jérôme, Big André, casually but neatly dressed, sat on the sofa in the parlour. Despite his fresh-scrubbed appearance, a quick glance at Dom told me the seriousness of the situation. I poured a glass of Calvados, while I gathered my still-incandescent thoughts.

'What happened?'

They exchanged a glance, and André spoke.

'We had knowledge of a train due in. Carrying munitions. We didn't want them to get through. Not now.'

'Why not now?'

'Look, we know there's a reason you're here. We know it won't be long before England invades. And the last thing we want is a train full of tanks and mortar shells arriving, and making problems for our lads.'

'But?'

'Things got out of hand,' André said.

That was never good news.

'Just how far out of hand?'

Dom and André exchanged wary glances, and he waited for her to nod before speaking.

'My cousin, Antoine, and Jérôme set the charges before dawn. The bridge, it's heavy, but functional. The river was high, but that wasn't the problem.' He took a deep breath. 'We heard another whistle above the waters. It was too early for the munitions train and the lads clambered over the side. Clung to the supports below.'

I could see it: the water swirling angrily below them; the locomotive lumbering into view, smoke billowing behind it. Two men clutching at the steel beams, staring at their own explosives as the train shook dust and soot onto them.

'This one was a passenger train. So Antoine climbed further up to make sure the explosives didn't go off.'

'But they did?' I asked.

'No, not then. We don't mind blowing up tanks, but passengers? Not our style, Blondie.' André shook his head. 'No – so my cousin climbs and removes the timing pencils. So far so good, right? But then he slips.'

I closed my eyes, seeing the man, legs scissoring as he plunged into the river. Maybe he screamed, his voice lost in the roar of the engine overhead.

'The boys pulled Antoine out of the water. After the train had passed, Jérôme went back up to reset the devices.'

'And your cousin?'

They exchanged another look.

'Broken leg. He's a good-looking lad. We'll tell people he got that jumping out of his girlfriend's window when her husband came home early.'

It wasn't the most believable tale, but stranger things probably happened. I sensed that the story wasn't over, though.

'What then?'

'When Jérôme got off the bridge, he picked up his doctor's bag and went to look after Antoine. The rest of us, we waited for the munitions train.'

'And?'

'And everything worked the way it should. The explosives detonated, the bridge blew, and the train went into the river.'

'So, what got out of hand?'

'The boys, Cécile. The boys got out of hand. There weren't just munitions on the train. Soldiers, too. The boys, they've been on the receiving end for too long. Some of them decided to fight back. To do what the explosion didn't and finish off some of the enemy.'

Feeling ill, I put the glass back on the table.

'Repercussions?'

'There will be, for sure. The Nazis always extract a large human price for any infraction.' André drained his glass and set it firmly on the table between us. 'The only question is *when*.'

'And how severe,' I added. 'Why didn't you tell me this was happening?'

'What do you mean?'

'Blowing up the bridge. I had no idea about it.'

'On the plus side,' Dom said, 'your reaction was authentic to anyone who might have seen you.'

That was true, and while there was a room full of Boche soldiers who saw how shocked I was by the news, they could also attest to how unsettled I was when I arrived.

'That's not the point. Look, there's a difference between keeping my identity secret, and locking me out of what's going on. I'm the liaison between the *réseau* and London. If something is planned, I need to know about it.'

Dom and André exchanged a glance.

'It was arranged weeks ago. Pascal told London and they approved the plan. They didn't tell you?'

77

They didn't. And there was no reason not to tell me of any planned activity. Which, when combined with the pilot being given the wrong co-ordinates for the drop, was beginning to paint a damning picture.

The only question was around the role Pascal had played. Either he didn't know himself, which was unlikely, or he was working with someone else who had a different agenda. But if he was working for the Boche, then why had they arrested him?

Jérôme arrived home well past curfew, shoulders hunched with exhaustion and despair. Dom prepared a cup of tea from a small stash hidden in the kitchen. Contraband, I guessed, dropped from Blighty. The cup and saucer lay untouched at his elbow.

'How many?' Dom asked.

'Seven Germans dead. Four of ours. Nothing short of a miracle,' he said through his hands. 'But scores wounded. Vallentin and his men are moving through the city, rounding up whoever they can find. Young, old, men, women – they don't care if they were involved or not. "An example needs to be made",' he mimicked, and shook his head. 'What rot. The more they crack down on us, the more we'll fight. Even Vallentin knows that.'

It seemed impossible, and yet, his shoulders dropped even further.

'Foolish lads, but can you blame them? How many years have the Krauts been occupying France? How many years have these men been second-class citizens in their own country?

How many of them have watched fathers or brothers or friends deported or executed? Imprisoned?'

At the last word, Dom winced.

'How can I blame them?' he continued, oblivious. 'They see a train full of the bastards bogged down in the river. They have guns in their hands that they've been trained to use. It must have been like shooting fish in a barrel. And the one saving grace is that they were carrying Stens. A few jammed, otherwise it could have been even worse.'

'What about our men?'

His laugh held no humour. 'Let's face it – the Krauts know how to build guns. A couple of bastards let off a burst. Xavier and Christophe were almost cut in half. Luc caught a bullet in his eye. Franc was gut shot. Bled out before we could get him out of there. Aimeri, Marc and Denis, they got off with minor cuts.'

The names held no memories for me, but they were someone's sons, husbands, sweethearts and fathers.

'Did anyone see them?' Dom asked.

'Can't say for sure.'

'They won't ignore it.'

He raised his head and stared at his wife. 'Do you think I don't know that?'

'Of course you do.' Her voice was calm, belying the worry that had had her pacing the floor before his return. 'Who have they arrested?'

'I don't know. We should know by morning.' He looked at me and narrowed his eyes. 'I doubt it'd help, but do you have an alibi?'

'Dom was at the police station, and I was having lunch in plain sight of Germany's proudest, at a café near the canal.' I raised one shoulder in a half-shrug. 'They'll be hunting tonight. I'll transmit at the agreed sched, once we've rendezvoused with Léonie.'

And when we have a better idea of who's been taken.

Chapter Thirteen

The gendarmes, in the form of a fat sergeant called Lenglet, came for Dominique early the next morning. While Dom went to collect her things, Lenglet sat in the parlour, staring at me until I forced a wan smile.

'I understand there was a spot of trouble yesterday. I hope it was nothing serious.'

His chubby face flushed. 'The terrorists had the *unmitigated audacity* to blow up a railway bridge. *Surely* they know those bridges are our *lifeline*. We receive supplies from other cities, and troops who protect us!'

'Yes, of course,' I said, wondering if he believed his own drivel. 'Have you caught them?'

'We have some of the terrorists in custody, yes,' Lenglet said. 'But not all. We found witnesses who we think will help root out the rest of the pack. Madame Severin, she will help, but this I swear to you.' He raised his fat finger and waved it around in circles. 'I will not rest until they are all incarcerated!' That finger now stabbed at the ceiling. 'Or dead!'

It was the sort of melodrama from the old 1920s silent pictures, and I stifled a sigh.

'The world is a safer place with you in it.'

He took the words at face value, and puffed out his chest. His tirade was cut short when Dom appeared, holding her handbag and sketch pad.

She opened the door for him, allowing him to go first. Lenglet was a gendarme, but Vallentin's men had rounded up suspects. Did the gendarmes have suspects of their own, or were they farming Dom out to the Gestapo?

The door closed and I moved to the window, pulling aside the heavy drapes to watch Lenglet try to fold himself into the Citroën.

That was the problem with being a wireless operator. There were moments of heart-stopping danger, but the time between transmissions was ghastly. I knew what was expected. For the next twenty-four hours, until we rendezvoused with Léonie at the church, I should remain as far from trouble as I could. So far, no one was looking for me, and it was best to keep it that way.

With my ankle returned to normal size and function, I opted for a bit of exercise and the need to better familiarise myself with the nearby towns. Borrowing Dom's bicycle again, I passed the neat house with the magnolia trees and deaf neighbour, and began exploring the neighbouring towns, stopping briefly in each one to pick up the odd bits of gossip and an item or two that might help with a disguise, not the least of which was a brown wig.

By two o'clock, with no information more interesting than who was being accused of *collaboration horizontale* that week, I stopped at a restaurant that was still serving lunch. I sat down near the front window, as much for the folded newspaper some-one had left behind, as the need to watch the street traffic. A waitress pointed out the restaurant's meagre offerings chalked onto a board and took my order for a coffee, blinking at my clipped accent. Her friendly smile hardened into granite, and I returned my attention to the menu.

The restaurant's offering was more common to the south: daube Provençal, ratatouille, bouillabaisse, soupe au pistou. Most likely, seasoned with the waitress's spit.

I unfolded the newspaper. It was the morning edition of a local paper, the lead story TERRORISTS BOMB RAILWAY BRIDGE. The accompanying photograph was cleverly taken; snapped from the riverbank, it focused on a passenger carriage below the ruined structure, rather than any destroyed tanks or munitions. The text was designed to exact sympathy and anger.

The waitress banged a cup of ersatz coffee and a basket with chunks of fougasse in front of me. Before I could inspect it for suspect globules, an air-raid siren went off. She bit out a curse and retreated to the kitchens. Gulping down the coffee and grabbing the bread and my packages, I followed her, grabbing the door before she could slam it closed on me. We retreated down a rickety set of stairs into the basement, where a large man with a fleshy face and faintly blue skin was lighting a pair of lanterns. He pulled off his hat and ran his fingers through oily hair before untying his apron. He glanced at me and then at the waitress.

He looked no happier about my presence, but pulled up a third cask as a stool.

'Sit down, it'll be a while.' He placed a third lantern on the table between us. 'Power always goes out in a raid.'

'It's good to be prepared,' I murmured.

'We have a lot of practice.' He peered through the gloom at me. 'You're new here. From where?'

I lit a cigarette and offered him one, smiling slightly when he took one.

'Strasbourg.'

'Germany,' the woman corrected, her tone just shy of antagonistic.

I considered giving her a history lesson. The corridor between France and Germany changed hands with each war, so that most people from the area considered themselves Alsatian, rather than French or German. The Germans didn't see it that way, of course. Strasbourg was evacuated just after the Germans attacked Poland in September '39, and only those who were 'German-minded' were allowed to return ten months later to find possessions confiscated, streets renamed, and French monuments replaced with German ones.

Not to mention the 'introduction' of Nazi values: the Jewish synagogue burnt, citizens sent to work camps, soldiers 'integrated' into the German army and sent to the Eastern front.

Instead, I exhaled a small cloud of smoke and forced a bland smile.

'As you say.'

When she opened her mouth to continue, the chef shook his head.

'Leave it, Sandrine.'

A bomb exploded close by, followed by a second and a third. Dust rained down from the rafters as the ground shook beneath us. Cigarette clamped between my teeth, I hung on to the makeshift table as the bottles rattled on the wall behind me. Another bomb hit nearby, the shock waves knocking the waitress from her seat. She crawled away on all fours, returning with two glasses, which she slammed on the table.

'Why not? It'll be a while.'

The chef opened a bottle of red table wine, diplomatically adding a third glass.

While the waitress was clear in her animosity, the chef watched me with a wary curiosity. I wouldn't be the first 'German' in his restaurant, and while he might hate the Boche as much as his waitress did, if he wanted this place to survive, he couldn't afford to alienate his clientele. I guessed that she hid her feelings somewhat better when she served German men. The chef forced a smile.

'Forgive her manners, madame. It has been a stressful day.'

Given that I was likely to be here for a while, it made sense to put things onto as amicable a footing as possible. At least for as long as we were trapped in the cellar with the bombs falling outside.

'You're right, the only thing we can do is make the best of it,' I said. 'But please, add the wine to my bill.'

One side of the chef's mouth rose; he had planned to do that anyway. He poured the wine and offered me a glass, accepting the silent truce.

'Thank you.'

I lit a cigarette and leant my head back against the rough wall, until a bomb exploded nearby, its reverberations ringing through my ears. For a few moments, all I could hear was a muffled roar, highlighting the terrifying truth that we weren't deep enough. If a bomb fell on us, we'd be dead.

Wordlessly, we scurried to the space under a shelf. I clutched my glass and closed my eyes, holding a picture of my husband in my mind. Focused on the single thought that we both would make it through the war to see a free Europe.

Another explosion shook the earth, sloshing the wine over my hand. Sandrine reached for the lantern before it could topple.

The chef produced a battered copy of Louis-Ferdinand Céline's satire, *Voyage au bout de la nuit* and read aloud. His deep voice made the time pass, but by the time the all-clear sounded, we were all relieved to leave the cellar unbloodied. Still shaking, I followed them up the stairs into the evening light.

The warm air had nothing to do with the season. Three buildings down from the café, a shop was ablaze. Men and women, emerging from their shelters, formed a chain, passing buckets of water along. A young woman screamed and, holding a toddler close to her chest, ran towards the blaze. Two men barred her from trying to force herself into the inferno. I joined the chain, passing a bucket from left to right, trying to block out the woman as her shrieks turned to pleas, then to sobs. She pointed to the remains of the first-floor window, gesticulating wildly. Then she sank to her knees, her keening and the child's shrieks audible over the roar of the fire. Flames bathed her crimson as she held the child to her chest, weeping. A crack sounded and the firefighter pulled her back as the structure threatened to collapse upon itself.

One moment Sandrine was beside me, then she was moving, shouldering a heavyset man out of the way. The prickly woman who couldn't say a civil word to me over the last few hours threw her arms around the weeping woman and pulled both mother and child away from the blaze, using her own body to shelter them from the sparks and falling debris.

'The human cost of war,' an old woman murmured, and nudged me to pass on the pail of water.

We fought the blaze for over two hours. The shop was destroyed, as were the buildings on either side. The old woman in the chain beside me explained that the woman Sandrine had led away was her sister, who'd married the vintner, whose shop we'd tried to save. The vintner himself had been sent to Germany in 1940, and had passed away before the child was born, but his effects, all that was left of his legacy, had remained in that building. The human cost of war, indeed.

I returned to Dom's home, tired, filthy and depressed. With only a half moon to see by, it took longer than expected to find my way. The house was dark, but the smell of cooking food lured me deeper inside. Dom stood by the stove, pushing a pair of eggs around a frying pan. A silver candelabrum was lit on the table, and candles burned throughout the room. It looked strangely romantic.

She looked at my filthy packages and raised a brow.

'Disguises. Hopefully the smoke won't have ruined any of it.'

'It'll be fine.'

She divided the eggs onto two plates, supplementing the meagre meal with bread and cheese, as I washed the ash from my hands and face. Out of the corner of my eye, I saw an envelope with formal German calligraphy on the front. I picked it up and opened it while Dom sat down.

'A reception for the Desert Fox, on Saturday,' I read. 'Seems like a good opportunity to listen in on what they're planning.'

'The local councillors wanted a visible show of support for the field marshal and our German "guests".' She spoke casually, her tone conveying none of the irony I knew she felt.

'As the wife of the town doctor, and the gendarmes' favourite artist, you will be going, won't you?'

She flicked a glance at the portrait of Madame Renard on the wall.

'I don't want to be their favourite artist,' she murmured, and I knew she thought of her own time in Paris, where being the Germans' favourite artist hadn't saved her from arrest. 'I don't think I will. I'd rather not chance meeting any of the Germans I knew in Paris, especially when they think I died.'

For a moment, the shutters behind her eyes opened and I saw the raw fear of being taken back into the Gestapo's custody. I wouldn't force her, but still asked, 'They're in Paris. How probable is that?'

'People move around. The Germans know that an invasion is likely, and most agree that it'll be the northern shores. And so, Rommel builds his Atlantic Wall, and slowly, slowly, more troops are directed here. Maybe some from Paris.' She shook her head. 'No, it's a risk I don't want to take,' she said. 'But Charles Pomeroy, the gendarme captain I work for, has given Jérôme a strong recommendation to attend. So far, he's held them off, but if you want to attend in my place, you'll be doing both of us a favour.'

I nodded, not feeling entirely comfortable stepping out at a social event with her husband.

'If you're certain?'

She laughed. 'I'm not worried about his honour, Cécile. Or yours.' She kissed my cheek and stood up. 'There's a basin of water in your room – you might want to clean yourself up before bed. And don't forget, tomorrow's Sunday. We'll need to leave a fair amount of time if we're going to meet your Léonie at Mass.'

It had only been four days since I landed, but it felt much longer. I nodded and trod towards the stairs, catching my reflection in a looking glass by the door. Dark sooty smudges still decorated my face in some abstract Picasso-like pattern. I grimaced at it, hoping that Léonie had had an easier time with her part of the mission. I had reached the top of the stairs when I turned to look back at Dom.

'Have you heard anything of the Germans' reprisals for the bridge? It's not like them to waste time.'

'No.' Her voice was glum. 'So far I've only heard of arrests. But don't worry, they'll have something planned. They always do.'

Chapter Fourteen

The weather was hot and humid, and my green cotton dress stuck to my back as I followed Dom and Jérôme to the Abbey of Saint-Étienne. If the suburbs had taken a beating, Caen was all but flattened, missing walls on half-destroyed buildings looking like gaping mouths.

In the midst of the ruined city, the Abbaye aux Hommes rose up above the rubble. Its twin spires soaring into the sky continued to pay homage to God. I shaded my eyes to see better, hoping I would have time to walk around the church afterwards.

'It is rather awe-inspiring, isn't it?' Jérôme paused, watching Dom move ahead to greet a trio of old ladies. One side of his mouth rose in a wry smile. 'Some say that the RAF haven't bombed it because William the Conqueror is laid to rest here. If that's the case, I hope his ghost continues to cast a long shadow.'

He anticipated my next question. 'People continue to take refuge here, of course. Physically as well as spiritually. I expect more will continue to do so as time passes.'

Once the invasion begins.

He nodded politely to people who greeted him, introducing me as his house guest, a friend of his wife's. We passed through the ornate doors into the cool depth of the abbey. Despite the turmoil outside, inside there was a sense of light, awe and a quiet serenity, powerful enough to impact even the irreligious.

I was no devotee of architecture, but this abbey, still standing amid ruin, sent chills down my spine. Rows of arches along the nave held up a magnificent vaulted ceiling, and the massive stained-glass windows on the far side of the apse let in a light that seemed magical.

Beside me, Dom moved to light three candles. I moved closer to Jérôme, softly asking, 'Three?'

'One is for her mother, the second is for her sister.'

'The third?'

He shook his head. 'She won't tell me, but I suspect it is for Konrad Becker.'

It took me a moment to make the connection.

'Konrad Becker? The Gestapo officer who tried to kill us last year?' His grim expression confirmed it. Becker was a nasty piece of work by any standard. 'Why would she light a candle for *him*?'

Two old women shuffled by, giving me a dark look. One sniffed loudly in my direction. I ignored her, watching Dom genuflect. Finally, Jérôme sighed.

'He was still a life.'

Because I had never killed someone who wasn't trying to kill me, I wasn't overly inclined to mourn them. But if I had to light a candle for every man I'd killed, I'd probably burn down the whole blasted abbey. Dom was a better person than I was.

She looked over, as if sensing my thoughts. Her expression was unrepentant as she led the way down the aisle, primly taking a seat. André was seated between a young man on crutches, who was probably his cousin, and an older woman with a single silver streak in her dark hair who must have been his aunt.

91

There was no sign of Léonie, and I hoped that she hadn't run into trouble.

The service was infernally long. I kept myself awake watching the congregants, a mixture of German and French, although still no sign of Léonie. Finally we made our way out into the sun, milling around in the hum of inane conversation and the age-old tradition of seeing and being seen.

The rhythmic cadence of hobnailed boots on concrete set off a different sort of hum. Faces went carefully blank, and shoulders pulled in, bracing against the familiar threat. A score of soldiers came into view, barking orders and using their machine rifles to herd us into the square between the church and the school.

There were hundreds of us here. For seven dead Germans?

Oh, God.

'Whatever happens, Blondie,' André murmured as he passed by, '*keep your head down.*'

This was the retribution we'd been waiting for. It was Sunday, after services, and outside a house of God. What irony, that they were searching the countryside for me, only to trap me here, without knowing who I was.

My heart beat double-time and I braced myself against a scream that built deep inside me. *It's not my time!*

Dom elbowed me, a quick jerk of her head indicating where prisoners were being led past the ancient *palais de justice*. My relief at not being their target was short-lived. We would be made to watch this travesty.

The prisoners were lined up, single file against a wall. The first man moved with a pronounced limp and hands manacled behind his back. His shoulders were held back, and his jaw

92

thrust forward with a defiance that made me proud. His eyes scanned the crowd, and mine followed, noticing how many people chose to look at their feet, the trees, the gargoyles, the rubble, rather than the doomed captives.

They deserved better.

The man beside him was slender, with tortoiseshell glasses and the look of an academic. Unlike the first man, he refrained from eye contact, staring into the distance – holding himself remote. The next one was young, the bandage on his arm stained red. He leant to the left as they were lined up. His shoulder touched the woman beside him and she whispered something, tears glistening in her eyes.

Four. Only four? My heart skipped a beat.

Unless they are doing this at other churches, other nearby towns?

Bile raced up the back of my throat, and I knew that would be the case. Four was too small a number for the people they had lost.

Behind the prisoners, two small groups of Nazi officers formed – the green uniforms of the Wehrmacht to one side, the black-clad SS on the other – while their men fanned out among the crowd.

I almost missed her, standing beside a green-clad colonel. Her face was as lovely and remote as a Dresden doll, each blonde hair perfectly in place, her blue-violet silk dress the same colour as her eyes.

Léonie noticed me immediately, raising one pencilled eyebrow.

'*Merde*,' I murmured, and quickly looked around to see if anyone noticed, but all eyes were either on the captives or their feet. I looked back at her, repulsed by her seemingly calm acceptance of whatever spectacle was about to happen.

An SS major strode forward. Stocky, and with pale eyes set too close together, he bellowed out the accusations. They were Maquisards, convicted of the bombing of the bridge and the attack on German soldiers. Their penalty was death.

Dom's face was carefully expressionless and a muscle jumped once in Jérôme's jaw. After the time in Portugal, where the enemy was often the one you didn't see, I had forgotten the blatant brutality this regime could inflict.

I wanted to dull my senses, blind myself to the tragedy playing out in front of me, but these condemned people deserved better. I bit my lip, wishing I could lend them my strength, wishing I could thank them for their bravery and sacrifice.

The second man, the one who seemed a quiet intellectual, screamed '*Vive la France!*' and choked out the first words of the Marseillaise.

The crowd's angry murmur was silenced by the loud bursts from the machine guns. Red stains blossomed on his torso as the bullets pushed him in a macabre dance. Bullets sprayed left and right. The young man lunged in front of the woman, as she cried out. And then she joined him, falling forward, her head coming to rest against his chest in one last embrace.

The first man, the angry man, raised his head. His red, red mouth opened, but any words he uttered were lost in gunfire.

I felt heartsick. Tasted my own blood, but bit harder on my cheek. The pain kept me from crying out, from rushing to the people massacred before me.

Soldiers peppered the crowd, weaving in between the groups of horrified citizens. Maybe they were there to keep the peace. Or maybe to see who betrayed themselves.

Bite harder.

Chills and heat alternated, and I struggled not to be ill.

Finally, the order was given and the guns lowered. It was over, and the crowd dispersed with unprecedented speed and silence. Dom's hand slipped into mine, her soft voice lost in the silent echo of the bullets.

We kept our eyes on our shoes, careful not to look at the bodies. We were nearly at the street when a precise voice cut through the din.

'Frau Hügel.'

I froze, turning slowly to face her. She stood less than five feet away, pale and lovely, her hand lightly resting on the colonel's arm. How could she do that? How could she *touch* him after what we had just seen?

'Frau Hügel,' she repeated. 'I did think that was you. I wasn't aware you were in Caen.'

'I've only recently arrived.'

My voice was higher than I intended. Behind her, the sightless eyes urged me to pull myself together, for them if not for myself.

'It's so good to see you. May I present Colonel Zeit?'

Zeit was more than twenty years older than we were, his sunburnt face made pinker by an explosion of veins across his nose and cheeks. Had he really been so overcome by her beauty to set her up as his mistress after a handful of days?

He misread the source of my horror and inhaled, pulling in a paunch barely contained by his tunic.

'An unfortunate affair,' he said, trying to sound urbane despite his breathless voice. 'This rabble, they cannot be allowed to continue this insurrection.'

Insurrection?

'Your presence is fortuitous, Frau Hügel,' the colonel said. 'Frau Deines was just saying how miserable the French were, and how she would love to see a friendly face.'

Feeling Dom and Jérôme's attention, I murmured, 'Not all French are miserable. In fact, I'm staying with French friends.'

Before I could introduce them, Zeit scowled.

'Are you? Well.' He cleared his throat. 'Well. We will visit the casino on Tuesday. A good group of Germans. You will join us.' A quick glance behind me. 'Your friends as well. As you choose.'

Léonie gave a half-smile that betrayed nothing.

'I'm delighted you're here, dear Frau Hügel. Here, let me write out the address and telephone number.'

I struggled not to let my surprise show. It seemed too . . . . too *normal* for the situation, with the bodies of the four resistance fighters so close. She rummaged in her handbag and took out a piece of paper. Flicked it over, confirming that nothing important was written on it, and jotted down her details.

I glanced left, watching soldiers carry the dead Maquisards away. Those people were strangers, but my knees wobbled, reminding me that that careless brutality would be my fate if I got caught.

'Frau Hügel, you are a gentle soul,' Léonie murmured. 'Please don't even spare a glance at them, they are murderers. Now then, we'll send a car for you on Tuesday. Be ready by seven o'clock.'

She looked at Dom and Jérôme. 'These are your friends? They speak German?'

I nodded, unable to utter a word as she reached out a hand to them.

'I am Frau Lene Deines. You are . . . ?'

Jérôme responded in a subdued voice. The small talk was awkward and we were all relieved when Léonie retreated, arm in arm with Zeit, through the rose-lined path to the main road, the colonel's coven trailing behind.

'You didn't think to warn us that she's German?' Dom hissed the moment we were out of earshot.

'Didn't I?'

I could still see her hand, lightly on the fat colonel's arm. How could she bring herself to do that without burying a knife in his belly?

I silently thanked Vera that she'd chosen Léonie to cosy up to Zeit, and not me.

'You did not.'

The silence became the fourth person walking with us to Jérôme's parked Peugeot. I slid into the back seat, wincing as Dom slammed the door behind her. Waited until Jérôme was seated and the engine started before I spoke.

'Sorry, I thought I had. So, Léonie's German.'

'No bloody kidding.'

I felt the wry smile, despite myself.

'As beautiful as a Dresden doll, and just as German. Her performance was Oscar-worthy, but don't let it fool you. She's more than competent, and hates the Nazis.'

'You believe that?'

'I do. So do Buck and Vera.'

That took a bit of wind out of Dom's sails.

'What's her story?'

'I don't know. Not any more than I know yours. She's not warm, not open. I can't say whether or not she was born that way, but I get the strange feeling that she has closed herself off to survive. But let me tell you what I do know. I know that she excelled at everything she put her mind to in training. I know that while she doesn't trust easily, once you've earned it, you have it. Maybe not the sort of trust where she'll tell you her story, but she doesn't need to.'

I stared out of the window, watching the fields flit past.

'And I know she hates the Nazis. You remember what it's like on the training ground, Dom? Where we were worked harder than the men, and were still the first out of the plane? Now, imagine if we'd had a German accent. It was only a matter of time before someone called her a "Nazi bitch". He was a big chap, a few inches taller than you, Jérôme, and almost as wide as André. Armed to the teeth, as we'd just come off the training ground.'

I shook my head, remembering the sight of Léonie, a pale blur as she disarmed and almost dismembered the man.

'She had him on his back with a Fairbairn Sykes at his throat in less than a minute. Might have slit it, too, if the instructor hadn't pulled her off him. Make up your own minds, of course, but while I might not like her methods, I do trust her.'

They exchanged another look.

'And you know that I don't trust easily,' I added, knowing it wouldn't be enough to win them over. She would have to prove herself to them, but until then, as long as both sides trusted me, we'd make this work.

'Who were they?' I asked. 'The people who died?'

'Were murdered,' Dom corrected under her breath.

'Yes,' I agreed. 'Who were they? Were they Maquisards or civilians?'

'Gilles's girl was a civilian. I think her name was Anne-Marie, but Gilles, Philbert and Jacques? Yes, they were with us.'

His voice hitched on the last name and sent off my internal alarms.

'Jacques? As in Jacques Mandeville?'

His brow lowered and a muscle twitched in his jaw.

'Yes. As in Jacques Mandeville, head of the *réseau*.'

Jérôme parked the Peugeot in front of the house. We moved to the salon, and wound the gramophone before sinking into the armchairs.

'What does this mean?'

'I don't know,' Jérôme said. 'Beaune has already been the unofficial lead. I expect he'll step forward.'

'I can't imagine Alain Sablonnières would let that happen without an argument,' Dom said, although Jérôme was already shaking his head.

'He won't have a choice. The men will follow Beaune.' Then he shrugged. 'Either they'll work it out between themselves, or André and I will step in. Me, I'd prefer them to work it out.' He rested his head back and closed his eyes. They were still shut when he asked, 'What did your friend have to tell you?'

'Damned if I know.' The paper she'd given me still appeared blank on either side, bar the neat address. I flicked it back and forth in my fingers to demonstrate. 'Blank, only I'd bet it isn't. Give me a few minutes and I'll see what I can do with it.' I was halfway up the stairs when something occurred to me. 'What's the problem with Sablonnières?'

They exchanged a guarded look.

'What do you mean?'

'He and Mandeville were supposed to be the joint heads of the *réseau*, yet it was Marcel Beaune that you directed me to. And now that Mandeville is dead, you think people will bypass Sablonnières. Why?'

Dom looked at Jérôme and shrugged.

'I'll let you explain.'

She brushed past me on the stairs, already removing her hatpin.

'Jérôme?'

He took a deep breath, and spoke softly, his words carefully chosen.

'With Jacques, the *réseau* was inclusive. It didn't matter if you were a nationalist, a Jew, a Communist, or anything else. If you wanted the Germans gone, and were willing to roll up your sleeves to make that happen, you were welcome.' His shrug almost matched Dom's. 'Alain is less welcoming. He leans too far to the right, and a little too close to the fire. Too reckless.

Some will follow him, but I think most will turn towards Beaune, who has experience fighting the Germans in the Great War and so far has maintained a perspective not unlike his nephew's.'

Jérôme carefully placed his keys on the small table in the hallway, beside the telephone.

'For all our sakes, I hope I'm not wrong,' he said, almost to himself.

His words followed me up the stairs. I stood on the landing for a moment and asked, 'What was Pascal's relationship to Alain Sablonnières?'

Jérôme's eyebrows rose. 'I imagine the same it was with Jacques. They weren't friends – Pascal kept to himself – but I believe they respected each other. Why do you ask?'

I didn't know myself, and shook off my unease.

'Just wondering.'

The sky was clear, but holding the paper up to the light didn't reveal anything. Frowning, I muttered, 'You're going to make this difficult for me, aren't you, you German lunatic?'

I fished into my handbag for my lighter and ignited it. Waved the flame behind the paper until Léonie's neat script emerged.

Caen primary domain of veteran 21st Panzer Division comprised of the 22nd Panzers, the 200th Sturmgeschutz Battalion, the 125th Panzergrenadiers and the 192nd Panzergrenadiers. Formation intended for rapid response to invasion. Coastal defence 716th Static Infantry Division comprised of 441st Ost Batt. 726th Grenadiers and 736th Grenadiers.

In four days, I'd obtained only a fraction of that information. Her tactics might churn my stomach, but they were effective, and now it was up to me to relay that information to London. I went out into the shed. Pushed aside a few crates and a bit of dirt. Pulled open the trap door and pulled out the wireless. Beneath it was another crate with the familiar markings. Jérôme, the *réseau*'s demolitions expert, took his work home with him. Hid it well enough that Vallentin hadn't found it. Yet.

I drafted the message in my mind, confirming our rendezvous with Léonie and relaying her news, as well as news of the destroyed bridge and its human ramifications. SOE required all operators to be able to transmit at twelve words per minute to have a fighting chance against the Boche. I was a little faster than that, but there was a lot of information to pass on, and I couldn't risk sending an indecipherable.

Threading the silk scarf that contained my codes through the loops of my trousers, I eyed my reflection in the looking glass. As long as no one stopped me or looked too closely, I'd be fine.

Calling a brief adieu to my friends, I put on the brown wig, borrowed Dom's bicycle and rode with the case far enough from the house not to jeopardise my friends. Hiding behind a hedge, I unfurled the scarf and used it to encode the message. Took a deep breath and turned on the wireless and began to transmit.

When I worked in Paris, it was easier. Two regular safe houses and taking rooms when I needed to transmit, moving quickly through the streets as soon as I was done. Once or twice, passing the Boche's Radio Detection Vehicle on my way. It would be more difficult to hide in the countryside, or small towns where everyone knew everyone else.

Caen was the obvious answer. The challenge would be how easy it would be to get in and out of the city without earning the Boche's attention.

Chapter Fifteen

'Uh-oh,' I murmured as the black Mercedes staff car slid to a halt in front of the house like a barracuda.

For a place that complained of petrol shortages, there seemed to be a lot of motor cars around. I took a mental inventory. My wireless had been replaced in the shed with Jérôme's explosives. My weapons were hidden as best they could be in the bedroom.

'Dom?'

Dominique put down her paintbrush and joined me at the window.

A spotty youth emerged from the driver's side, and moved around the car.

'Wehrmacht uniform, not SS,' I said. 'Are you expecting any other Germans?'

'No,' she said as the rear door opened. 'Are you?'

The woman who emerged from the back seat was immaculately clad in a cobalt suit with a matching hat.

'As a matter of fact, I think we both are.'

I allowed the curtains to fall back into place and went to open the door for Léonie. She brushed past me, pulling off her gloves as she entered the house.

'Good afternoon, Frau Hügel,' she said.

I closed the door behind her. 'It's OK. Only Dominique and I are home, and London is aware we've rendezvoused.'

'Did they have any news to report?'

'Just confirmation of a planned drop later this week. I'll set up the beacon for the Resistance so that the next pilot doesn't miss the field.'

She nodded and preceded me into the parlour, where Dom stood in front of her easel. She had composed herself, and watched Léonie with calm green eyes.

'Frau Deines.'

'Frau Severin,' Léonie responded, her mouth twitching as the German formality was appeased. 'However, you are not Anna Severin, any more than I am Lene Deines. I think that when we are alone, you may use my code name. I assume you know it?'

'I didn't expect you to be German,' Dom said, adding with a hint of sarcasm, 'Léonie.'

'Is that a problem?' One fair eyebrow rose, although there was nothing apologetic in Léonie's posture.

Dom met her gaze. She reached for the discarded paintbrush and began to clean it, first swishing it in a glass of murky water, then blotting it with a cloth – all the while, focused on Léonie.

'You come highly recommended. From Cécile, as well as Buck and Vera, I understand.'

'You have not answered my question, Dominique. Do *you* have a problem with me being German?'

Dom put the cloth down. 'I don't have a problem with Germans, Léonie. I have a problem with Nazis.'

Léonie's smile became a shade more genuine.

'Good. Then we have something in common.' She sat on the love seat, and delicately crossed her ankles. 'Cécile has informed you of our mission?'

'She has.'

This was a different side of Dom. When I'd arrived, she'd first gone to brew a pot of coffee. Now she was watching Léonie the way a mongoose would a cobra. Careful not to get paint on the upholstery, she sat in the armchair across from Léonie.

'You've made very powerful friends very quickly, Frau Deines.'

Léonie could have looked offended; instead she maintained her usual cool demeanour.

'Then more fool them.' There it was again – a flash of genuine amusement, quickly suppressed. She leant forward. 'Are you concerned about my commitment, Dominique? My ability to lead this operation?'

Dom's half-smile matched Léonie's. 'Oddly enough, no. Sometimes you need to get close to the enemy in order to defeat them. I understand that. And if someone has to get close to Zeit, I'd much prefer that to be you than me.'

'Then be glad that it's not you. So let us discuss what I *do* require of you.'

When Léonie had departed, I turned to Dom.

'You like her, don't you?'

'It doesn't matter if I like her or not.' Dom was standing at the window, watching the Mercedes take Léonie away. 'I think she knows what she's doing, and I'll do my part.'

Her words had a strange tone, as had the afternoon. There wasn't a budding friendship in the works, but there was a sense of respect between the two, however grudging it was on Dominque's part. And that would have to be good enough.

For now.

Chapter Sixteen

Jérôme arrived home late that evening, with news that Beaune had stepped forward to lead the *réseau*. There was still the fear that Alain Sablonnières would not work as well with Beaune as he had with Jacques Mandeville, but it was a situation Jérôme and André would monitor closely.

Jérôme politely, if firmly, turned down my offer of assistance. Until they could find – and neutralise – the person who had betrayed Pascal, they wouldn't risk me.

The next day passed quickly. I hadn't brought a cocktail dress over from England and didn't have time to acquire one. The best I could do was a black pencil skirt and black silk blouse. My hair was done up in a twist, and the only jewellery I wore was the fake wedding ring, and a simple necklace borrowed from Dominique.

A captain in Zeit's posse knocked on the door at seven o'clock sharp. He was about my height, with receding dark hair, hazel eyes and a mole at the corner of his mouth, that looked like a chocolate smudge.

'Good evening, Frau Hügel,' he said. 'You look lovely. Are you ready?'

As ready as I was likely to be. I avoided his proffered arm and preceded him to the staff car waiting at the kerb.

The driver was waiting and started the engine as soon as the captain closed the door.

'Gambling is all but outlawed in the Fatherland, but here it is acceptable?' I asked.

He pursed his lips, considering his answer.

'For some, it is almost expected.'

The 'some', I guessed, was the officer class, which meant the casino at Ouistreham would be a hotbed of gossip. Hopefully I could glean information that would help London or the *réseau*. Worst case, I was at least establishing my cover story.

The driver followed the river Orne north, the smell of brine getting stronger as we approached the sea. The casino was just beyond the Rive Belle Hotel, looking out over the water. The incoming tide hid the mines and other devices to prevent Allied ships from landing; in that moment, a person could almost pretend the war wasn't going on.

If it weren't for the uniforms, staff cars, and the glimpse of guns peering over the roof.

The driver stopped in front of the entrance, and the captain escorted me to the poker tables, where Léonie sat behind and to the left of Zeit. She looked resplendent in a pale blue Empire-waisted gown, with gold flowers embroidered on the band under her bust. It made her seem both childlike and untouchable. She wasn't playing, and her expression was one of sublime boredom. To Zeit's right, a lieutenant-colonel frowned at his cards. He wasn't much younger than Zeit, but trimmer, and sported a burgundy-clad older woman, draped over his shoulder like a fat stoat. Completing the table was a major from the 726th Grenadiers and a short bald man poured into his dinner jacket.

'Fräulein,' the lieutenant-colonel smiled, standing up and bowing.

I ignored him and addressed Zeit. 'Thank you for the invitation, Colonel.'

He raised his eyes, his gaze assessing. 'Will you play?'

A quick glance confirmed how few women were playing, and I shrugged.

'Maybe later.'

Later being when I had a better understanding of who the men were, and what sort of actions they did when they bluffed.

The man in the dinner jacket opened his mouth to speak, but Léonie was there first.

'Katrin, why don't we leave the men to their game and take a turn around the room.'

'Splendid idea.'

With a small twist of her hips, she neatly avoided Zeit's groping hand. Looping her arm in mine, she steered me deeper into the casino.

'Your friend seems forthright,' she said.

I had to stifle a smile. 'I wouldn't want to be on the wrong side of her, but there's no one I'd rather have at my back.'

Across the room, Zeit bellowed a laugh while the lieutenant-colonel and the bald man smiled politely.

'It would seem that you've landed on your feet with the colonel.'

'So it would seem.' That she was able to say that without choking was a miracle. 'He's taking me with him when he inspects the battery later this week.'

At least her sacrifice wasn't without a benefit.

'Who are the other men at the table?'

'Lieutenant-Colonel Rannulf Kühn of the 716th. I understand he has had dealings with Herr Mönch and invited him to the table.'

Guessing Herr Mönch was the man in the suit, I asked: 'Civilian contractor?'

She slipped something into my hand, her movement slight enough that I barely noticed, before my fingers closed around a canister, an inch or two in length. I dropped it into my bag on the pretext of looking for a lipstick while she continued.

'He is a planner with the Todt Organisation. You do not know them? They built the autobahn before the war, and now they work with fortifications here.'

'And repairing the roads?' I guessed.

She shrugged. 'They build roads in Germany – it would make sense for them to repair the roads here, too. Why?'

'I've seen their people working while I've been cycling around.'

Prisoners of war, pressed into service to the Reich.

A pair of SS captains drew alongside us, blocking our way. Had she seen them coming? I snapped the evening bag closed.

'Good evening, ladies.' The first man grinned, his smile toothy, his eyes cold.

Léonie crossed her arms over her chest, and met his gaze. 'And?'

'And?' he echoed, taking a step closer.

The canister felt like a beacon in my handbag.

'We're not interested,' I drawled.

They didn't move immediately. Paused, as if assessing their chances of success, until the second one jerked his head back, and they melted back into the crowd. They weren't the only ones; most of the room wore either green or black uniforms.

We resumed our stroll.

'The battery?' I prompted.

'In Merville. Not far from here. The Allies have bombed it repeatedly, and the colonel wants to be certain that it can continue to protect us.'

I nodded, realising the canister likely contained a roll of film. I would pass it on to Dom, as agreed. She had the contacts to get it to London.

'I'll tell you how it goes when I see you next,' she said, and then added, 'I understand there will be a reception for Herr Feldmarschall on Saturday. I will secure an invitation for you.'

We wandered towards a large window overlooking the seafront.

'I already have one,' I said, hoping to have surprised her, although it was a good thing I hadn't expected much of a reaction. She raised an eyebrow and I explained. 'I will be accompanying Doctor Severin.'

'His wife?'

If Vera hadn't explained Dom's apprehension of being recognised by the Boche from her time in Paris, then I wasn't about to.

'She asked me to go in her place. I'm not sure those sorts of events are . . .' I paused. The next word should have been 'safe', and I searched for a less telling alternative. 'Enjoyable for her.'

'Very well. It is best the three of us are not seen spending too much time together. I look forward to seeing you there.'

The two SS men were returning, looking determined.

'Shall we return?' Léonie suggested, just loud enough for them to hear. 'I'm sure you're aching to try your hand at cards.'

The stoat woman took on a pinched look as we returned to the table. The fourth chair was empty – the major had left – and this time I accepted Zeit's invitation to play a hand.

I bet low, deliberately losing the first few hands and watching my opponents. Zeit tapped his foot when he was excited. Kühn, the lieutenant-colonel, rubbed his thumb along the side of his forefinger when concerned, and Herr Mönch sweated terribly.

And then, I stopped losing.

Chapter Seventeen

I put my winnings to good use, kitting myself out with a few pieces of jewellery and other accoutrements expected of a wealthy German woman, before Dom took me to see her dressmaker friends. Apparently they had few bolts of fabric, and might be the only chance I had of having a gown ready in time for Saturday, although it would likely come at a large cost.

There were two of them, wearing neat and well-mended clothes. I followed the one called Yvette into the back room to be measured, leaving Dom to chat with the other one. When I undressed, I noticed her staring at the puckered scar on my shoulder.

'Wrong place, and the wrong time,' I said, which was true enough.

That scar, and the one on my side, were visible reminders of an ambush by the Boche, more than a year ago, but that was a story she didn't need to know.

'I was caught in a crossfire,' I added, and hoped that would be sufficient.

She nodded and didn't ask questions. Simply adjusted the fabric she held to lie over my shoulders in such a way as to cover the scar, and added that adjustment to her notes.

I paid the rather steep markup for the gown, ordered a few more dresses to be delivered the following week, and left wearing a new rose-toned hat.

'She noticed my scar,' I murmured to Dom after the door closed behind me.

I didn't have to explain which one. Dominique had been beside me when I was shot.

'You explained it?'

'I think so. Doesn't mean she won't tell anyone.'

'Don't worry. She won't.'

There was something in her voice, that quiet confidence, that made me understand Dom's connection to the dressmakers: they were with the Resistance. And possibly were the contacts that she'd passed Léonie's canister on to, while I was being measured.

We paused one last time, at the post office, so that Dom could collect her mail. I remained outside, perusing the obligatory wanted posters. Most looked weathered, but one was new, warning residents of new terrorists in the area, who had arrived by air last Wednesday. One was possibly injured. They were both probably French-speaking English. There was a modest reward offered for information, but also a reminder: the penalty for helping an Allied terrorist was death.

I hoped Dom was right about her dressmaker friends. For both our sakes. If I was arrested, that would shine the wrong sort of light on Dom and Jérôme. Something I wasn't prepared to risk.

We returned home in time for me to leave my parcels in the bedroom, and change into dark trousers. With my hair tucked into a knitted cap, and wearing a jersey 'borrowed' from Jérôme over my blouse.

'It's almost dark,' Dom noted, poking her head around the parlour door. 'I thought you usually transmitted during the day.'

'I do, yes. This is different. I'm going to set up the homing beacon for tonight's drop, so that the Resistance has a fighting chance to get whatever London sends.'

'Good luck,' she said. 'And be careful. Are you sure it's wise to dress like that, with the Boche looking for men?'

It was something I'd considered as well.

'If someone from the *réseau* happens to see me, it's best they see Cecil and draw no links to Katrin.' I shrugged. 'But if someone sees a woman, then Cecil is compromised and people will start looking for a female agent. It's the lesser of two evils.'

She didn't disagree.

I cycled east, avoiding the main roads, to the Bois de Bavent, not far from the field I'd dropped into.

The suitcase was waiting for me where Jérôme said it would be: a light brown fibreboard child's valise with darker brown leather around each corner, hidden in the brush, beneath a small cluster of trees.

It looked common enough, and rather more unobtrusive than the slimline red case the device was supplied with. It was small, but bloody heavy. I lugged the case further into the woods, until I felt safe enough from the eyes of passers-by, and opened the clasps.

The Eureka device positioned in the centre was a relatively recent model, and padded with felt so that it would be protected. There was no spares box, but the headphones and Morse key were neatly placed to the side of the Eureka. Methodically I began a thorough inspection, hoping there wouldn't be a problem with the power supply or crystals, as those would need to be shipped from London.

It was faulty, but the issue was only a loose connection, and once resolved, the power light flashed on. I shut it off, and repacked the case. Secured it to my bicycle and rode towards the designated area.

I stopped about half a mile from the drop zone on a rise over-looking the zone, shaded by a small copse. Like the field we'd dropped into, this one also boasted a crop of Rommel's wooden 'asparagus'.

There was no need to get closer; I didn't want the Maquisards to see me, and according to the boffins, the beacon was effective until the plane was within two miles. Then its response would overlap the interrogation pulses coming from the plane and both would get confused.

The sky was already darkening. I would wait another hour before setting up the device, and would hide further afield until I could hear the plane's engines, turn off the box and hide it back where I found it for Jérôme or André to pick up.

Or at least that was the plan, until something moved, deeper into the woods.

Even if it was only an animal, I needed to know.

I slipped the PPK into my waistband and pulled the knitted cap further over my forehead. I eased to my feet and, keeping low to the ground, moved as silently as I could from tree to tree. I searched for more than twenty minutes, but there was no sign of anyone.

Had I imagined it? I *knew* I'd heard something – felt some-one's gaze – but if anyone else was there, they were now gone.

I retraced my steps to the Eureka device, and headed towards the area the sound had come from. There was no sign of life, but there were footprints. They were too big to be mine. Almost certainly a man's, and most likely the man was heavier than I was. But why was he here?

Who knew I was here? Jérôme knew I'd be in the area, but not here specifically. Had he or André decided to keep an eye on me to protect me?

No, they would have shown themselves, knowing that if I saw a threat, I'd neutralise it and ask questions later, as we were trained to do.

Then who?

Accepting that I wouldn't find out who it was tonight, I returned to the Eureka, and placed the PPK in easy reach. Did the last few checks, and turned the device on.

It wasn't long after dark when I heard the engines. Silhouetted against the waning moon, a Halifax bomber flew in low from the west, its belly only a couple of hundred feet above the ground. For all I knew it was the same plane that dropped me here.

I turned off the device and disassembled it, glancing up as a long black stream erupted from the plane's bay doors, blossoming into dark flowers as the parachutes opened. Five, ten, twenty. It was hard to see some of the colours, and while I knew what was supposed to drop, what actually arrived wasn't always the same. Red parachutes for weaponry, yellow for medical supplies and blue for food. The white ones were used for anything miscellaneous, including agents, or when the base ran out of other colours.

The Maquisards would be busy loading the crates into wheel-barrows, wagons, and maybe even someone's old lorry, but the Germans would already be on the move. Dressed like this, with a German pistol tucked into my waistband and a Scottish blade fastened to my ankle, I was an easy target.

Clenching my teeth, I pedalled faster, feeling every rut. There was no time to replace the set where I found it, so I hid it as best I could, taking note of the location so that Jérôme or André could retrieve it.

I decided to stay off the main road, cycling just inside the fields, partly hidden by the dense hedgerows. I heard the vehicles before I could see them. Threw the bicycle down and lay flat in the pasture.

It wasn't the Radio Detection Vehicle; it was worse: a pair of Kübelwagens with a big Spandau MG 08 gun mounted at the back. The soldiers in the front held sub-machine guns, indicating that they meant business. I hoped the Maquisards would get away in time.

I breathed through my mouth to suppress any sound, unwilling to take the chance of them hearing me above the noisy engines, but they didn't pause, didn't even slow down.

Once they were gone, I extricated the bicycle and, still shaking, continued on my way. Within ten minutes, I threw myself back into a hedge. Sweat trickled down my back as a pair of armoured cars passed by. In the moonlight I could see the vehicles were French – AMD 178s – but the men standing half-out of the turrets wore German uniforms.

The trip took three times as long as it should have, as I had to hide in the hedges every time a vehicle passed by.

Dom met me at the door. She reached out to pull me inside, then her nose wrinkled.

'Go around to the shed,' she said. 'I'll meet you there.'

'Why?'

'Because you're filthy and smell of cow dung. I'm not having you in the house like that.'

On the other side of the door, Jérôme laughed.

By the time she arrived, a large pail of water in each hand and a towel around her neck, I was already down to my camisole and under-things.

'We'll get the worst off you out here,' she explained. 'Then you can go inside and bathe properly.'

She pulled a bar of strong-smelling soap from her pocket and sat on a crate with her back to me as I scrubbed myself.

'A letter came by courier for you today,' she said. 'A German courier.'

'What did it say?'

'What makes you think I read it?'

'Because it came by German courier.' My voice was half-muffled as I washed my face. Her voice, however, was light enough to convince me that she hadn't waited long before she steamed it open. I didn't mind; there wasn't much I would hide from her. 'Who was it from and what did it say?'

'It's an *Ausweis* – a pass allowing you to be out after curfew.' She cleared her throat. 'Compliments of Lieutenant-Colonel Rannulf Kühn.'

'Compliments of Léonie, more like.'

'Be careful. She's playing a dangerous game. Zeit might fancy her, but that won't stop him from killing her if he realises she's playing him for a fool.'

'I know.'

I rubbed at a stubborn patch of dirt not realising it was a bruise.

'And the next person they'd look at is you.'

'I know,' I repeated. 'I'm not keen on her tactics either, but if I have any complaints about her results, it's that the pass didn't come a few hours earlier.'

We both stared at the pile of filthy and stinking clothing.

'Burn them,' I suggested.

'Don't be daft,' she said. 'If I burned Jérôme's clothes every time he came back like that, he'd have nothing to wear. Close your eyes.'

She dumped a pail of water over my head, and I brushed wet strands of hair out of my face and asked the question I'd spent the last hour or two wondering.

'Who else knew where I would be tonight? Exactly where I'd be?'

Her words confirmed my fears.

'Just Jérôme and André.'

'And they weren't out tonight?'

'Jérôme wasn't, and André was at the drop site. Why?'

'Because we have a problem. Someone else was in those woods tonight. Watching me work.'

Chapter Eighteen

I had only just fallen asleep, when the heavy knocking woke me.

Peering through the curtains, two Kübelwagens were parked at the kerb in front of Jérôme's Peugeot. My heart began to race: what if they found my wet and smelly clothes? Would they think them mine or Jérôme's?

It didn't matter; they'd arrest all three of us and then link me to Léonie.

Damn. Damn, damn, *damn*.

Of course they'd come here. I should have anticipated that.

Jérôme had; he was already walking down the stairs. The door opened, and there were voices, Vallentin's louder than Jérôme's.

I imagined Jérôme rubbing his eyes.

'Do you know what time it is, Captain?'

Vallentin said something about the Resistance being on the move again, and Jérôme's response was lost in the sound of boots on wooden floors. I peered through the door, seeing Dom's pale face on the other side of the hall doing the same. But this time it was my fault – my smelly clothes were hidden outside.

I slipped on a dressing gown and stepped into the hallway.

An angry German voice barked, '*Was ist dies?*' and everyone froze. Eyes pointed up the stairs and I realised the voice was mine. There was only one thing to do, and I stormed down the stairs.

'What is this?' I repeated. 'You come here, in the middle of the night, disturbing our sleep? Again? For what?' I was working myself up to a state of righteous indignation. 'You are here to protect us. And yet, we are still bombed, and disturbed in the middle of the night. You want the Resistance?' My nose was inches from his. 'I saw the plane go east.' My finger jabbed in that general direction. 'Go and bloody follow that and let me sleep.'

His head tilted sideways, calculating.

'You saw the plane?'

'I saw the plane, heard it, too.' I shrugged. 'I'm sure a lot of people did.'

Only they wouldn't admit it.

'What were you doing?'

'Having a drink outside with my friend.' I pointed up the stairs at Dom, who gripped the balustrade with white knuckles. 'And my other friend.' I now pointed to Jérôme, who showed the appropriate amount of horror.

I continued, my voice rising. 'After commissioning a frock for the party this district is throwing for the field marshal. It's not a breach of curfew to sit in the garden after dark, is it? Oh, and if it is, I have a bloody pass!'

The silence was deafening, until one of Vallentin's men asked, 'Do you want us to continue the search, sir?'

I was still nose to nose with Vallentin, could smell his breath hot on my face. Seconds or maybe minutes later, he turned to his man.

122

'No. I think we're done here.'

He faced me again and murmured, 'For now.'

We waited until the Kübelwagens had departed, with all men accounted for.

'What was that?' Dom whispered, echoing my earlier words as she lowered herself to sit on the top step.

Now that they were gone, my hand began to tremble, and I gripped the balustrade harder.

'That, my friend, is how a tired and cranky Alsatian woman, with nothing to hide, would respond. Show fear, and they will pounce. Like a blasted dog.' I climbed the stairs, and as I passed her, rested my hand on her shoulder. 'We will get through this, you know.'

Her head dropped, and once had I closed my bedroom door behind me, my bravado left me. I was in no doubt that that was exactly what an angry Alsatian woman would have done. I could almost hear my grandmother's voice in my own, but there was one key difference: that hypothetical Alsatian woman had nothing to hide. We were three Special Operations Executive agents. A wireless and a crate or two of explosives were hidden in the shed, and the odds were good that if they looked hard enough, they'd find spare sets of papers for each of us, under different names.

We were playing with fire, and the clock was ticking.

Chapter Nineteen

The dressmakers had done an extraordinary job with the gown, and even with a critical view, the woman in the looking glass looked elegant. The dress was a midnight-blue silk with a fitted bodice. Wide straps were positioned, sash-like, on the edges of my shoulders, hiding the puckered scar. The ends were gathered in a rose between my breasts, before pooling at the floor with the A-line skirt.

My hair was secured to the back of my head in a neat chignon, and the only jewellery I wore was a sapphire necklace and the replacement wedding band, hidden underneath long white gloves.

Jérôme's borrowed dinner jacket was too large in the shoulders, but he wore it well. What he wore less well was the grumpy expression that made it clear that his attendance was under duress.

Dominique walked us to the door.

'Good luck,' she said.

For a moment, I wondered if I would miss this – rubbing shoulders with the enemy, looking for an opportunity to outfox them – once the war was over.

'Thank you,' I said, following Jérôme to the Peugeot, adjusting the long skirt around my legs.

'Are you ready?' he asked, starting the engine.

'Why wouldn't I be?' I said. 'It's just a party, after all?'

His smile silently called my bluff. There was always a chance someone from Paris would recognise Jérôme or me, even with my new disguise.

We skirted Caen and headed south to the château, in relative silence. There was still no answer as to who had watched me with the Eureka, and how they knew I was there.

'It was successful, you know,' he finally said.

'What was?'

'The drop. We got the canisters and hid them before the Germans arrived.'

'Jolly good.'

He cast me a level glare, but continued. 'Munitions, mostly. But some medicines, which I'm grateful for, a packet of Earl Grey for Dom, which *she's* grateful for, and a letter for you.'

I blinked, surprised. 'Me? From who?'

He shrugged, keeping his hands on the wheel. The roads were becoming smaller and smaller. Jérôme swerved to avoid a pothole.

'One of the boys dropped it off while you were getting ready. It was initially addressed to me, but there was another envelope inside with a *C* on it, that I'd guess is you.'

Which meant that if Dom hadn't had time to steam it open before we left, she'd certainly have read it by the time we arrived back.

'Whatever it is, it'll have to wait a few hours.'

Staring out of the window, I heard again the snap of the twig, saw the big footprints. If the man was part of the *réseau*, Jérôme should have known. Everyone repeated 'protect the wireless operator', but when the time came, who did?

Well, *this* wireless operator could bloody well take care of herself.

We were driving further away.

'I thought the reception would be at the Château du Heaume.' As far as I knew, it was the nearest stately home, nearby in Ranville.

'No such luck.'

We turned off onto a long straight road. In the distance, the lights of the château twinkled.

'Do they think they're not a target?' I asked.

Jérôme shrugged. 'We're far enough from any city that the château is probably safe enough.'

He slowed down as we approached a small hut midway down the drive. Further on, I could see a small building, flanked by a pair of towers, with other turrets peering from behind.

'A folly?'

'The *châtelet*,' he said. 'The château is behind it.'

A guard gestured for us to halt outside the gatehouse. As his colleague trained his gun on us, he approached the vehicle.

'Name?'

It was less of a checkpoint than the usual ones on the road, although the château was a jolly good target – for the Resistance, as well as the RAF. With little more than a cursory glance at our papers, the guard waved us through.

We passed through the gatehouse and I gaped.

'A moat? A bloody moat? Seriously?'

'More of a folly than the *châtelet*,' Jérôme said.

'I don't like it. There's no way to get out quickly if we need to.'

'I'm sure there's a dungeon, if there's a raid.'

That wasn't what I'd referred to, but there was no need to debate the matter. It had been already settled for us. A valet waited for us to vacate the Peugeot, and took custody of it as soon as Jérôme had helped me from the vehicle.

'Relax,' Jérôme murmured as we stepped onto the bridge over the moat.

I nodded, wondering why he had suddenly become more relaxed about the situation than I had. The windows on the ground floor were small, and open in the heat. The larger windows were on the first floor.

The château was solidly built in red brick with a dark slate roof, rather than the native Caen stone, and despite not favouring straight lines, the design was less opulent than the folly. I held my breath as we crossed under a faux portcullis into the courtyard.

The organisers of the evening might have wanted people to be on the first floor, but crowds congregated in the cooler air of the courtyard.

Jérôme took two glasses of chilled champagne from a passing waiter and handed me one.

'We stay until we're seen,' he said. 'Once Rommel arrives, we go.'

I nodded, although we had different agendas. His priority was to minimise his risk, but I needed the information that would flow along with the champagne. Surely he had to know that?

Around us, fine crystal clinked in bejewelled hands. The men wore uniforms, green and blue and black, decorated with gold epaulettes and campaign ribbons. Women wore silks and satins of every imaginable colour, and despite their opulence, Léonie stood out, shimmering in a low-cut gown of the palest blue. As usual, she stood surrounded by the colonel and his posse, an expression of sublime boredom on her face.

'I hate this.'

Jérôme's voice was almost conversational. He could have been referring to Léonie, the Germans, or our own presence here. There was no point in asking him to elaborate. His shoulders drooped as an older couple made their way towards us.

'Ah, Dr Severin!' The man's oily voice preceded his bow. His wife, an older woman with steel-grey hair tortured into an elaborate pile of curls and feathers, stood at his side. 'I'm so pleased you decided to grace us with your presence, it is so very far to travel.' It was less than an hour, but Jérôme didn't bother correcting him. 'And where is the lovely Madame Severin?'

'Indisposed, I'm afraid.'

'Ah.' He turned to me. 'You must be the lovely Madame Hügel. I have heard so much about you.'

'I do hope it's all flattering,' I murmured, pulling my hand from his, under the guise of pulling a folding fan from my evening bag and snapping it open.

Face tight, Jérôme introduced Captain Charles Pomeroy, and his wife. I recognised the name; Pomeroy was the gendarme who Dom worked for.

At the first break in the stilted conversation, I excused myself. I didn't like Pomeroy any more than Zeit, but at least Zeit didn't pretend to be anything other than the fat, lazy creep he was.

Jérôme's eyes issued a silent warning: *Be careful.*

I gave him a small nod and crossed the courtyard towards an octagonal tower in the corner, stopping short when Zeit, hands clasped behind his back, threw his paunch forward and boomed, 'Calais!' Taking no notice of me, he continued, 'And with Patton in charge at that. There is no other alternative. Mark my words – it will be Calais. Don't you agree, Kühn?'

That an invasion was coming was no surprise to anyone. Almost everyone in England last spring could see the build-up of troops, and General Patton, a force unto himself, had been overheard telling another general that he'd see them in Calais. How likely was it that Zeit would have heard of that?

'Of course, sir,' Rannulf Kühn responded, his eyes raking me. 'Good evening, Frau Hügel. You look splendid.'

'Thank you,' I replied, stifling a sigh and pasting on a friendly smile. 'What's this about Calais?'

'Our colonel thinks that is where the Allies will invade next,' Kühn explained.

'It is only logical! The Allies are amassing troops. Those in Edinburgh will make for Norway, and those in the south, the Pas de Calais.'

I tapped a fingernail against the crystal flute.

'Not that I wouldn't be delighted to avoid more fighting, but why Calais, Colonel?'

'It's the shortest crossing point, isn't it?' Léonie answered, stopping short of rolling her eyes. 'And isn't it the fastest way into Germany? The colonel is quite right – it makes sense.'

'Ah, but my lovely Frau Deines, do not forget about our Atlantic Wall. It's quite impenetrable. You are perfectly safe here. Perfectly safe.'

'Certainly, with all these lights blazing,' she murmured.

'Nonsense. We're perfectly safe here,' Zeit repeated.

'As long as you stay away from Merville,' Kühn said. 'I heard it was bombed again last night. How extensive was the damage, sir?'

'Nothing that can't be fixed,' Zeit said.

'I am certain Hauptmann Wolter would disagree.' Kühn seemed to remember I was there, and cleared his throat. 'Perhaps you would be so kind as to allow me to show you the château, Frau Hügel?'

'Of course.' I placed my hand on his arm and the lieutenant-colonel smiled. 'What was that about Hautpmann Wolter? I don't think I've met him yet.'

'And you won't. He was the commander of the Merville battery, until an Allied shell found him last night.'

'Ah.' I looked at the blazing first-floor windows, wondering what the best way was to play Kühn. Decided on the direct approach. 'You think the colonel is wrong, don't you?'

He shrugged and led me past a gaggle of gaily dressed German women, nodding politely to them without breaking his easy pace.

'He knows more than I do, and our analysts agree on Calais.'

Their analysts . . . or our agents?

Kühn glanced at Zeit and again changed the subject.

'You must be bored with all this war talk.'

'Not at all.'

I wanted him to talk, to tell me his order of battle. Which regiments would be sent to fight, how many would be held in reserve and where the cracks were in this Atlantic Wall.

He wouldn't, of course, even if he knew the answers. I managed a polite laugh, and paused when I saw Jérôme approach, his normally amiable face looking harried. Kühn greeted him with a slight bow, and then straightened far more stiffly than the situation warranted. I looked over my shoulder towards the entrance into the courtyard.

Erwin Rommel, the Desert Fox, strode through the faux portcullis with an easy grace. He had a strong nose and chin, high cheekbones, and eyes that held more humanity than one would expect. He wasn't tall, but he was a giant – backed up by the medals on his chest and the Knight's Cross at his throat.

Before the rest of his entourage could funnel into the courtyard, Rommel turned to speak with General Hans Speidel, his chief of staff, and one of the other staff officers. Like the field marshal and general, the third man also wore an iron necktie and a chest full of ribbons. He towered above Rommel, but didn't disrespect the field marshal by stooping.

The air was punched out of my lungs. I didn't need to see his face to know that his nose was a breath too long, that his dark deep-set eyes crinkled at the corners when he laughed.

'Katrin?' Jérôme's voice seemed to come from miles away.

Unable to answer, every sense urged me to run, but I could no more run away from him than I could run to him. Fear, longing, and a few hundred watching eyes rooted me to the spot. When his gaze found mine, his almost-black eyes widened and his polite smile melted away.

He managed two steps towards me before the crowd barred his way.

Every cell in my body shrieked.

'Excuse me,' I choked to Kühn, amazed at how normal my voice sounded.

There was an art to moving fast without looking like you were moving fast. Every instinct urged me to stop and turn, but I couldn't. Couldn't even look over my shoulder. Just focused on putting one foot in front of the other as I crossed along the back of the courtyard towards the powder room.

I couldn't do it. Couldn't feign nonchalance much longer. And the fewer people who witnessed my façade crumbling, the better. I closed the door and leant back against it, taking a steadying breath, and then a second one. A woman stood at the looking glass, touching up her make-up. She applied another coat of lipstick and glanced my way.

The door was yanked open, almost toppling me. With one hand, Léonie pushed me forward.

'*Raus!*' she barked at the other woman, and jerked her head towards the door.

The woman gave her a nasty look, threw her lipstick into her bag and stalked to the door, muttering, '*Boche* bitch.'

Léonie locked it after her and leant back against it.

'What's wrong?' she demanded. 'You staggered from the room like a drunkard.'

The looking glass confirmed her assessment. My eyes were enormous and glassy; I looked dazed.

I leant out of the window, pulling off one long glove and drinking in the cool air and the smell of summer. Looked down at the bloody moat. I couldn't drop from here, without going for a swim.

132

'I need to go.'

'You can't use the front door like everyone else?' She narrowed her eyes at me and guessed: 'You saw someone you know.' She muttered a curse under her breath. 'Someone knows who you really are? Or who you were supposed to be . . .' She fluttered her hand. 'At some other time?'

I used the glove to secure my shoes to the strap of my evening bag, and handed it to Léonie.

'Hold this.'

I climbed onto the windowsill and looked down. It really wasn't an option.

I looked up, and sighed. There was a touch of ivy crawling up the walls. It wouldn't be stable, but it would have to hold. I pulled off my stockings and, recovering my bag from Léonie, stuffed them inside.

'Someone who knows who I really am.'

On every possible level.

'*Scheisse*,' she muttered.

We both knew that a compromised agent could risk the mission, and the team with it. The options were simple: abort the mission (impossible), or hide me while she eliminated the threat. Also unacceptable.

'Just buy me a few moments, Léonie. He won't betray me, but I need to talk to him first, and I can't do it with an audience.'

'You can't be sure of that.'

A heavy hand pounded on the door, and I knew it was him. My foot was already seeking purchase on the ivy below.

'Of all the things I am sure of in this life, that's it.'

He might make my life hell, but he would never betray me.

'Angel?' The voice on the other side of the door was as ragged as my breathing. 'Are you in there?'

I steeled myself. 'Buy me time, Léonie.'

'Who is he?' she asked.

There was no sense in lying; she could find out easily enough. I stared at the sky above the manor, and whispered the name I'd been too afraid to speak for months.

'Major Eduard Graf.'

My husband.

Chapter Twenty

Careful not to snag my dress, I reached for the ivy. My fingers searched for purchase on the walls. Toehold, toehold, foothold. One move at a time, until the texture changed and I reached the first-floor window. Bright light was coming from within and, unwilling to chance being seen, I edged to the side, ignoring my screaming muscles, and my breaking heart, until I reached the next window.

This one was dark, and I pulled myself into a tiny room that must have served as an office once upon a time. I quickly replaced my stockings and shoes, and flopped into a sixteenth-century chair. Allowed myself a few moments to calm my heartbeat.

Eduard Graf. Here.

What were the chances?

He wasn't supposed to be here. He was stationed in Lisbon before he was summoned to Berlin last January. Nothing I'd seen indicated that he'd be in France.

But the Fox is here.

Every nerve in my body urged me to run to him, and for that reason, I had to make it past him, out of the château. No one who saw us together would believe that Katrin Hügel didn't know Eduard Graf, and I couldn't afford to blow my own cover. Not without compromising myself, my friends, and *Eduard*.

I opened the door, blinking at the hallway's bright light.

'What are you doing in there? You shouldn't be there.'

A man was moving towards me, his expression irate. I summoned a facsimile of a careless shrug.

'I was curious, and someone said I was free to explore the château.'

His firm hand on my arm escorted me to the next room, with carved inlaid walls, hung with portraits of previous counts and countesses. One of them, looking as sublimely bored as Léonie had only moments ago, made me smile.

'She's rather beautiful, isn't she?'

A short, stocky man rubbed his hands together. It was the gesture rather than his face that I recognised. The planner from Organisation Todt – Herr Mönch. I nodded and inclined my head towards the woman in the portrait.

'Who was she?'

'The Countess Catherine, painted in the early 1600s, I imagine.' He clapped his hands together. 'I see we share the same interest in this magnificent château. Parts of it date back to the fourteenth century!'

If I expected to last longer than the next fourteen minutes, I had to be seen by just enough people to establish an alibi. Without anyone noticing that my heart was racing, and that I was perspiring more than the spring heat could account for.

Mönch offered me his arm.

'Come, Frau Hügel. You must see – each room is different. Some have painted walls, others carved, still others, exposed brick. It is simply stunning!'

'I'm sure it is,' I said. 'Perhaps later.'

I moved on before he could stop me. One room after another. Portraits on walls of the château's counts and countesses, interspersed with dead kings and queens, moving to the far side of the corridor while downstairs, Eduard Graf searched for me.

I paused at the top of a stairwell of exposed brick. Hoped that Eduard was still seeking entry to the ladies' lavatory, and glided down the steps.

He wasn't. He stood in the middle of the room, craning his neck. The neutral expression expected of an officer had dropped, and he looked desperate. He was in pain, and it was my fault.

I felt my heart break. Backed into the shadows, hoping that the crowds would hide me as I edged towards the portcullis.

The last time I'd seen him was that January. He'd been summoned to Germany in the wake of the arrests after Johanna Solf's party. When I returned to England, I harassed an acquaintance of mine in MI6, until he provided a list of the men arrested in conjunction with both events. Eduard's name wasn't on it, and I'd rejoiced that he was still free and, as far as I knew, alive in Berlin. What in heaven's name had brought him to Normandy?

I nodded in turn at Pomeroy and Kühn as I moved closer, murmuring senseless excuses. Nausea assaulted me as I passed through the gate and staggered over the bridge, hoping anyone who saw me would attribute it to an excess of champagne.

I passed the wall to the area where the valets had parked the car. Leant against a Mercedes and tried not to crumble.

An engine revved, and I looked up, half-expecting to see the little sports car Eduard used to drive.

Instead, it was Jérôme's Peugeot.

The passenger's door was pushed open and Jérôme ordered, 'Get in.'

I did, closing the door behind me with trembling fingers.

Jérôme put the car into gear.

'There's a flask of Calvados under the seat.' He waited for me to take a sip from it and asked, 'What happened?'

He was lucky I didn't spray Calvados all over the car.

'Why are you here?'

'Léonie figured you'd need to escape. What happened?'

'I hope she told everyone else she saw me on my way to the gardens,' I muttered.

A gulp of Calvados radiated out from my belly, giving me the Dutch courage to withstand the interrogation that Jérôme was within his rights to give me.

'Yes, and that you were complaining of a headache. Would you care to divulge the reason an Abwehr colonel was so keen to find you that he kicked down a door?'

'Colonel?'

My voice came out in a high squeak. Eduard was a major in January. How had he risen two ranks in four months?

He kicked down the door?

Bloody hell.

'Stop stalling, Cécile,' Jérôme snapped. 'Who is he, and how does he know you?'

I grasped on a minor point, playing for time.

'There is no Abwehr anymore. Not since Hitler sacked Canaris.'

'Thank you for the history lesson, Cécile. But you still haven't answered my question.'

'Well enough.' I glumly stared out of the window.

'Since you're so forthcoming with your information, let me tell you what I know about him. Colonel Graf is a veteran of the Ghost Division, with a Knight's Cross earned during the Battle of France. And a protégé of the Desert Fox.'

It was nothing I didn't already know.

'Yes.'

'He transferred back to Rommel's staff at the field marshal's request last February, with the rank of lieutenant-colonel. Now why would a Panzer commander transfer into the Abwehr, and then back under Rommel as a staff officer, instead of transferring to whatever the Abwehr turned into?'

'The *Reichssicherheitshauptamt*? I have no idea.'

Jérôme continued as if I hadn't spoken. 'The consensus, after seeing his reaction to you, was that he mistook you for his wife. Apparently, you bear a striking resemblance to Solange Graf. However, Frau Graf is brunette, not blonde – a Frenchwoman who was kidnapped earlier this year, some months after they wed.'

'How tragic.'

Nausea rose and I opened the window, drinking in the cool air and fighting back tears.

'Isn't it just? Rumour has it that he walked out of a meeting with Schellenberg when he learnt of her disappearance, and did everything he could to find her. But there was no trace of the new Frau Graf.'

'He wasn't . . .' My voice was croaky and unfamiliar. I cleared my throat and tried again. 'He wasn't supposed to be here.'

'I expect he's saying the same about you. Assuming, of course, that you are Solange Graf.' Jérôme's voice was hard.

'Solange Graf doesn't exist.'

Technically.

'Of course she doesn't,' he growled. 'Will he betray you?'

'No.'

He heard something in my voice and braked hard, jerking the car to a stop before staring at me.

'You care for him? A Nazi?'

It wasn't easy to maintain a level tone.

'Eduard Graf is a lot of things, including a loyal German,' I finally said. 'But he's no Nazi.'

While I had my share of suspicions as to the work Eduard was doing, those were secrets that weren't mine to tell. I wouldn't betray Eduard any more than he would betray me. Even to Jérôme.

'There are good and bad men on both sides of this war. You know that.'

An angry silence pulsed between us as the miles flitted past.

'We need to get you out of here,' he finally said as we passed the deaf neighbour's house.

My response came from every fibre of my being.

'No.'

His expression didn't change. 'He will jeopardise everything – your mission, you, and the rest of us.'

I shook my head. 'He won't jeopardise anything.'

'You can't know that.'

'Yes, Jérôme, I can.' It had been a long night and I knew it would prove longer still. I hated having to defend Eduard, as much as he would hate me having to. 'Trust me on this.'

'You ask me to trust you – to trust your Boche boyfriend – with all our lives? Think again.'

Jérôme parked the car and stalked into the house. Grateful for a few moments alone to sift through my feelings, I leant against the house and lit a cigarette. Had Vera known Eduard would be here when she sent me? Would she have done that deliberately, the way she hadn't told me about the Resistance's plan to blow up the bridge?

What did it mean that he was here?

No one who saw us together would think us strangers. How on earth was I supposed to pretend?

Jérôme was right: it wasn't just me anymore. I could risk my own neck, but couldn't place my friends in jeopardy.

Dom opened the door and sat down beside me.

'You're back early. What happened?'

I could hear Jérôme storming up the stairs.

'Didn't Jérôme tell you?'

'He wasn't making sense.' Dom shrugged and handed me an envelope. 'Come inside. By the way, this arrived for you earlier. And before you ask, I didn't steam it open.'

I wasn't sure I believed her, but followed her inside. My energy depleted, I sat on the bottom stair and ripped it open. Instead of the letter I'd expected, a single photograph slipped out. Four men, walking through a battered fort.

A string of low curses erupted, and I wanted to cry. The photograph was taken from a distance of about twenty feet. It couldn't have been from the roll of film Léonie had passed on; there was no way that had made it to London in time. I mentally noted a probable second photographer operating in the area, and looked at his work.

Four men, each familiar: the man walking just behind Rommel was the fat Todt planner. Not surprising if he was accompanying the architect of the Atlantic Wall on an inspection, but it was the two men trailing behind him, almost cut off from the picture, who arrested my attention: Hans Speidel, Rommel's Chief of Staff, rapt in conversation with Eduard Graf.

Vera's warning had come too late.

Chapter Twenty-one

My fingers were white against the glossy paper. I needed to find him, but how could I do that when I didn't know where he lived? Léonie. Léonie would know. She could find him for me.

But would she? Or would she use that information to neutralise Eduard?

What about Eduard's man, Lieutenant Neumann? He was hard to miss in any crowd, and if I could find Andreas Neumann, I'd find Eduard.

He'll find you. He'll learn that you arrived with Olivier Severin, and in looking for Severin will find you.

The thought was as comforting as it was terrifying.

How would he react? As a German officer, it would be his duty to inform on me. Would he do that? Stand by while I was arrested and incarcerated? He hadn't last year, but a lot had changed since then. Would he now?

I didn't think so. Not even after four months of separation.

'Cécile?' Dom sat on the step beside me. 'Are you all right? What happened?'

I couldn't talk. Opened my mouth a few times, but only a single squeak emerged. I should have let him catch me; I could have brazened it out.

Who are you fooling? You would have fallen into his arms, and every Kraut there would wonder how Solange Graf had become Katrin Hügel. And then *they'd arrest all of you.*

Dom's hand squeezed my shoulder. I was dimly aware of her moving into the kitchen and setting the kettle to boil. She returned some minutes later with two steaming cups, and pressed one into my hand. I felt the vapour under my chin and smelled the steeping herbs.

'It'll take more than chamomile . . .' Nonetheless, I took a dutiful sip. 'Go upstairs, Dom. I'll be fine.'

'What? Sitting on the stairs in a gown, with shoes in your lap and leaves in your hair? You look like some sort of demented Cinderella. You do have both shoes, don't you?'

'Sod off, Dom.'

She smiled. 'That's good. Come into the parlour, at least it's more comfortable.' I allowed her to guide me to the settee, and placed my gloves and shoes neatly beside me. 'So, what happened?' Her eyes widened at the high-pitched roar outside. 'The Gestapo?'

'Worse,' I muttered, my heart beating a furious tattoo. 'Much worse.'

The door buckled under the first kick; the colour in Dom's face ebbed away. I braced myself, and it burst open on the second kick.

'Elisabeth!' Eduard Graf bellowed.

That wasn't good. He only called me by my first name when he was truly angry, and he should have known better than to use my real name.

Dom's hand held me in the chair. Her eyes narrowed as she went into the hall. Given what she'd been through last year with the Gestapo, she must have been terrified, but her voice was calm.

'May I help you?'

That was odd. In her place, I would have asked what the hell he'd done to the door. Still, she must have been racked with terror for Jérôme, and maybe even for herself, yet her voice was calm.

'Frau Hügel, *bitte*,' his voice barked.

'I'm Anna Severin.' A hint of steel lurked in her polite tone. 'Can I help you?' At his glare, she translated her question into German.

'You cannot,' he said, stepping further into the foyer. His harsh voice echoed up the stairwell. 'Katrin? Solange?' And then it broke. 'Angel?'

A wealth of pain was conveyed in my name, releasing me from my near-paralysis, and I lurched to the door.

My eyes drank in the sight of him; clad in his uniform and his fury, he'd never looked so good. Several inches taller than Jérôme, Eduard towered over Dom. His dark eyes blazed, and he ran his fingers through his dark hair, now with a few silver strands at his temples that weren't there before.

For a moment, there was an option. Katrin could deny being Solange, deny being *Elisabeth*. It was what was expected. It was the right thing to do, but he wouldn't believe it. Not for a second, even if I was able to create that illusion.

'My name is Katrin,' I said, coming forward.

It wasn't the right thing to say. I realised that as soon as the words were out. Eduard's face darkened and Dom danced out of his way, her head moving quickly back and forth between us, trying to understand.

'What the blazes are you doing here? You disappeared. You were gone without a trace, and I looked. Everywhere. And now I find you here, living with some French doctor! Who the devil is Severin?'

He was now nose to nose with me, his voice low but intense.

There was another option, one no one would believe, but that might protect my friends.

'I think you confuse me for someone else. Olivier and Anna Severin are my friends. My name is Katrin Hügel.'

'Good Lord,' Dom murmured.

Her wide eyes made her resemble a small animal that wasn't sure if it wanted to freeze or flee.

For a moment, Eduard's face sagged, and then it hardened.

I placed a shaking hand on his forearm and steered him out of the door, relieved to see the hinges hadn't broken.

'Come, walk with me, Colonel.' Under my breath, I added, 'I'd rather we didn't have an audience.'

He nodded, following me from the house. My bare feet squelched in the dewy grass as I led him to a table at the back of the garden.

'What are you playing at, Elisabeth?'

'Keep your voice down,' I hissed.

He pulled me into the shadow of the shed. I rose to my toes to meet him, terrified and intoxicated by his presence.

'Eduard.'

I breathed his name into his mouth, revelling in the closeness, the feel and taste of him.

He pulled away from me.

'Please explain to me, Elisabeth ...' His voice rasped and he took a deep breath. 'Please explain to me how my wife disappears from Portugal and then ends up in Normandy, with another name and another life.'

I leant against the shed to steady myself.

'You knew what I was when you married me,' I reminded him. 'But what happened last January – leaving Portugal, leaving you – that was not my doing. I was attacked on the street. They chloroformed me, and the next thing I knew, I was being put on a plane. It wasn't something I asked for, or was in favour of, in case you're wondering.'

'You did not think to send word? To let me know that you were alive?'

'You think I didn't try?' I blinked. 'I didn't know where you were. The last time I saw you, you were boarding a ship bound for Germany. Then I hear that anyone connected to Johanna Solf and her blasted indiscreet circle is arrested. Do I know if you're connected? No. But I do know that you were once friendly with Erich Vermehren, and that people were arrested and questioned after his defection in February. And the next thing I hear is that the Abwehr is disbanded. So I did what I could. I wrote to "Solange" in Portugal, in case you'd gone home. And Matthew promised to let you know what had happened.'

He snorted at my godfather's name. 'I had been in Berlin for less than two hours when I was informed that you had been kidnapped off the streets. I left the meeting and returned to Portugal.'

That was not a good sign.

'They let you?'

147

'If I had asked, my request would have been denied. So I did not ask.'

He had gone AWOL. For an officer to go absent without leave . . . Someone must have protected him. Who?

'I found nothing, no evidence in Portugal. Your pet thug and I scoured the streets of Lisbon looking for you.'

'Bertie? You worked with *Bertie*?'

Hubert Jones was another SOE operative, and while I counted him as a friend, there was no love lost between him and Eduard.

'He is fond of you. And for the first few days, he seemed almost as upset as I was. Then something changed.'

'He spoke to Matthew,' I guessed, grimacing.

While my godfather, a British diplomat, however grudgingly owed Eduard his life, he wasn't above using us as pawns in some great chess game.

'One of these days, I will kill that godforsaken creature.'

I understood Eduard's position.

'He didn't tell you that I was alive?'

'He did not. So I returned to Germany. And yes, I was questioned. For my absence, as well as my acquaintance to Erich.' He sighed and shook his head. 'Idealistic fool.'

I wasn't sure if he was referring to Vermehren, me, or himself.

'Erich also claimed to be "kidnapped by the British".' He gave me a dark look. 'They seem to have been very busy last January, Elisabeth.'

Despite his anger, I felt a warm glow, For so long I'd been answering to aliases and code names. Only with Eduard was I

Elisabeth. And it wouldn't serve my case to split hairs and point out that Erich Vermehren had defected in February, not January.

'Do the Severins know who you are?'

I was walking a fine line. He would do his own research, but whatever I said had to ring true.

'Anna Severin is an old school friend.' It wasn't exactly a lie: we'd once referred to the stately home where we trained together as 'the school for spies'. 'A good enough friend not to ask too many questions about why I'm now blonde, and with a different name, and what I'm doing. But for what it's worth, neither she nor her husband are involved with what I'm doing.'

It was splitting hairs, but as neither of them was a wireless operator, it wasn't *exactly* a lie.

His expression made it clear he didn't believe my explanation. 'Why are you here, Eduard? And as a colonel?'

His lips twisted. 'The first promotion was waiting for me when I arrived in Berlin. They did not strip me of it when I left to look for you. The second was because I stayed alive when others did not. Now I am part of Rommel's staff.'

He tried again. 'Why are you in Normandy?'

This time, I shrugged. 'I go where I'm told. The same way you do.'

He shook his head. 'You are the least compliant person I know. I do not want to know what you are doing – just promise me that you will be careful. And swear to me that if or when the fighting starts, you will be far away from it. I thought you were dead once. I cannot go through that again.'

He had to know that was a promise I couldn't make. I met his gaze.

'Eduard, all I can do is promise that I will take no unnecessary chances, but I expect you to do the same. I'm too young to be a widow again. Now, will you bloody kiss me?'

Eduard sighed, his arms going around me. I leant into it, to the familiar feel of him, the sense of security that I always had in his presence.

'Angel, what am I going to do with you?'

Slowly, sweetly, he lowered his lips to mine. The kiss wasn't gentle. He tasted of Calvados and despair. I probably did, too. Far too soon he pulled away.

'Prepare yourself, Frau Graf,' he said, and answered his own question. 'I am going to court you again.'

'Katrin,' I corrected. 'Katrin Hügel. And beware – Frau Hügel is quite devoted to her husband.'

He leant back, eyes telling me the challenge was accepted.

'Good.'

Chapter Twenty-two

I watched Eduard disappear into the Mercedes' driver's seat. At least he hadn't had his adjutant Andreas Neumann or someone else chauffeur him. As grateful as I was to know he was alive, his presence complicated an already complex situation. A leak in the Resistance, someone watching me with the Eureka beacon, and now Eduard, who would no doubt be keeping a close eye on me. And my friends.

Dom was waiting for me in the hallway.

'Angel? He calls *you* Angel?'

I sent her a filthy look. 'So?'

'Apparently love really is blind.'

An arch look that didn't soften the waspish tone.

I held my tongue and followed her to the kitchen, where Jérôme leant against a counter, coffee cup in hand. The casual posture didn't fool me, and I braced myself for the questions.

'Does he know who you really are? *What* you are?'

She didn't start with the easy questions, and I knew I had to be careful. My friends were trained to spot lies and half-truths, and Eduard presented a very big risk to them.

'He thinks he does.'

'And is he right? And more importantly, do we have to worry about the Gestapo showing up here any time soon?'

'The Gestapo seem to be regular callers here anyway, but if they come back, it won't be because of Eduard Graf.'

'How can you be sure?'

'What is it with you and Germans?' Dom asked.

'Not every German is a Nazi,' I pointed out. 'And not every Frenchman is an ally. Eduard Graf is a lot of things, and as angry as he might be with me for turning up where he thinks I shouldn't be, he won't set the Gestapo on me, and he won't set them on you.'

I looked around the kitchen, but there was no third cup of coffee for me.

'And why are you so certain that even you are safe?' Dom added.

'He knows I'm more than I seem, which would be hard to deny when the last time he saw me was in Lisbon.' I glanced at Dom. 'By the way, my alias when I met him was Solange Verin, which could explain why he might have reacted badly when he learnt I attended the reception with Dr Severin.' I felt a corner of my mouth twitch and added wryly, 'And from Solange, he got Angel.'

'I'll assume he's under no misconceptions there. Does he know you're English?'

'Clip the claws, kitten. You're angry, and you have a right to be. If you want me to move out and find another place, I'm happy to do so, but as long as you pose no threat to Eduard Graf – or me – then he will pose no threat to you.' I hoped I wasn't lying.

I took a deep breath. 'But let me be clear – he's off limits. I don't care who else the Resistance targets, as long as it's not him.'

Dom raised her hands and stepped between Jérôme and me.

'Fine. Let's see how this works out. Keep him out of the house, if you can, Cécile.' She rinsed out her cup and turned back to me, watching me for a few seconds. 'Perhaps stepping out with him can be useful, for London and for the *réseau*, not to mention all three of us.' She shook her head. 'Four of us. I assume Léonie knows?'

I nodded, a sick feeling beginning in my belly. The moment Léonie thought he was a threat, she'd eliminate him. I'd have to find a way to make certain she understood not to harm him. I thought through Dom's logic aloud.

'Because a Maquisard wouldn't be dating a German, or because if a Wehrmacht officer, formerly an Abwehr officer, is spending time here, the Gestapo might leave us alone?' I raised my shoulders in a tired shrug. 'But that's not necessarily the case. The Wehrmacht and Gestapo hate each other.'

'We'll have to see how this plays out.' She made a point of looking at her wristwatch. 'Now then. We have exactly six hours before we need to get up. I'd suggest we sleep on this and discuss it further in the morning.'

'What's in six hours?'

'It's Sunday, Cécile. Even in this remote corner of hell, church attendance is expected, and you have a scheduled transmission to London then.'

The parish church was somewhat less impressive than Saint-Étienne, but the simple stone church and high bell tower had a reassuring solidity and, despite the warmth outside, inside it was pleasantly cool. Dom lit her three candles as Jérôme and I

153

waited, and then led the way to the pew. As we passed, hushed voices rose and fell and, when I turned, several people quickly looked away.

'People are staring at me,' I muttered.

'People always stare at you,' she replied, keeping her voice low. 'Some are curious because they have heard that an old school friend is visiting me and they haven't met you. Others will have heard about how a German colonel mistook you for his wife.'

'Already?'

Her smile held no humour. 'News travels fast here.'

The service provided me with the opportunity to sit still and sift through these new developments, and try to figure out how to keep the various parts of my life from destroying one another.

Eduard's presence was a complication, and yet, my soul sang at the thought of having him here. Having stolen hours together in this madness.

Dom elbowed me, and I followed her into the queue to take communion. I wasn't Catholic, but after a year of masquerading as other people with different backgrounds, I'd come to my own terms with religion, deciding that a few prayers in a different language was better than standing out any more than necessary.

I ignored the curious glances and allowed my friends to usher me through the lines, stopping sporadically to greet acquaintances. When we had left the crowd behind, Dom murmured, 'We have a problem.'

'Bigger than the one our guest brought home last night?' Jérôme asked.

'André,' Dom said. 'A friend of mine from the gendarmerie just told me that someone had come to the station last night. They said they saw him near the bridge just after the explosion.'

'André, or someone who looks like him?'

'Someone who looks like him. They've already put together the sketch.' She looked at Jérôme, and I could hear the unspoken words: *was he also betrayed from within? Like Pascal?* 'Do you know where he is?'

'I don't know. Maybe.' Jérôme pulled his car keys from his pocket. 'You go on ahead, I'll see if I can find him before they do.' He turned back to look at me. 'Your sched? The transmission to London?'

I nodded, confirming it would go ahead as planned.

'And I'll let them know. I'd like to use Pascal's wireless this time. Can you arrange for one of the Maquisards to hide it? That way I don't have to trot about the countryside with my device.'

Jérôme nodded. 'That shouldn't be a problem, but I can't get that set up in time for today's sched. Will you be able to risk one more trip with your own?'

'Why don't you take her in the car?' Dom asked Jérôme. 'I'll take the bike and warn André.'

I nodded, relieved. 'Thank you. But I think it makes sense after this to stash the case in Caen, where it's easier to move about with a case and not be noticed.'

Chapter Twenty-three

We didn't travel far. Two villages over, there was a disused warehouse at the edge of town. Leo Marks, SOE's head of agent codes, had once told me about an agent who transmitted from a field while disguised as a cow, complete with the aerial wired into the cow's tail. Crouching in the brush, between the warehouse and a dense hedgerow, I envied that agent their innovation, and would move the piano to Caen at the next opportunity.

I was reasonably certain we hadn't been followed, and felt more comfortable putting the headset on, knowing Jérôme watched my back. I kept the message to London as short as possible, confirming successful receipt of the items dropped, sharing the intelligence Léonie and I had gathered, thanking Vera for the warning – even though it had come too late – and relaying our fears about André.

On impulse, I also asked how much knowledge they had of the Resistance blowing up the bridge, or any sense that there was a betrayer from within the *réseau*.

I coded the message and set up the wireless. Checked the PPK and set it carefully next to the piano. Took a deep breath and turned it on. Tapped out the message as quickly as I could, hoping that it wasn't indecipherable. Hoping they wouldn't need me to repeat the message if it was.

I signed off and turned off the device. We hid the case in the boot, and began the careful trip home, zigzagging to make sure no one followed.

We were nearing the house when Jérôme asked, 'Have you decided what to do about your German?'

There were options?

'I'll see him, of course, when he comes to call on me. But if you aren't comfortable with that, I'll find another accommodation.' I repeated the offer, hoping that Jérôme wouldn't take me up on it. 'Which might be easier if I start transmitting from Caen.'

'No,' he said. 'People already know you're our guest. Let Graf court you – he's no worse than others you might pass time with. But just remember, your first obligation is to London. Second and third is your team, and my *réseau*. Clear?'

'That was always the case.'

I was offended that he felt the need to point it out.

'Good. Trust Graf as much as you need to, but no more. He's still a German, Nazi or no. Don't expect him to protect your back, if it's at the expense of his own.'

There was no point in contradicting him, so I nodded.

'And finally, for the sake of respectability, you must keep him . . . How do I say this? You must keep him at arm's length for as long as you can. Whoever else he thinks you are, here and now, you're Katrin Hügel. He must be seen to court her. Make it too easy for him,' Jérôme concluded, 'and you've given us all up.'

Chapter Twenty-four

Léonie was waiting for me in the parlour when I arrived home. The gramophone played a whimsical song by Josephine Baker, and a tea service sat in the middle of the table, with two cups already poured. As social as it looked, the mood in the room was sombre.

There could be only one reason she was here, and after hearing Jérôme's perspective, I wasn't overly keen to hear hers. The longest Sunday ever looked set to get even longer.

Jérôme offered an abbreviated greeting, took a book from the shelf, and closed the parlour door softly after himself.

'Good to see you, Léonie. I thought we weren't meeting until tomorrow.' I lit a cigarette. Trying to take control of the encounter, I turned to Dom and asked, 'Any luck with André?'

'I found him in time. He's going to stay at the Bois with Beaune's men, and his aunt is prepared to tell the Boche that he's away for business. If I know Madame de la Hay, she'll send them to Cherbourg or Rouen. Your transmission went well?'

I nodded, my eyes straying back to Léonie. She sat straight-backed at the edge of an armchair, ankles crossed. On any-one else, her pose might have looked uncomfortable. Her cool gaze met mine and when she spoke, she didn't mince her words.

'Eduard Graf. How much of a risk is he?'

A quick glance at Dom confirmed that she'd already relayed the details of Eduard's visit last night. I wasn't sure how I felt about that. Being the only conduit between them meant that I could finesse the story for the situation, but with the two legs of the triangle now linked, they'd outfoxed me.

'He isn't.'

Léonie took a delicate sip of tea, watching me over the rim of the teacup.

'He has a reputation for loyalty, bravery and diligence. How much does he know?'

The subtext to her question was: *why wouldn't a loyal German officer turn you in?*

I didn't have to lie. 'Of our mission, nothing. And as I've already said to you – both of you – he won't betray me. Won't betray us.'

I hoped she wouldn't ask too many questions as to the reason.

'You're certain of this?'

'Without a doubt.'

She nodded. 'Who else knows who you are?'

It was a jolly good question.

'With regards to what? That I'm SOE? Only you two, Jérôme, André and Marcel Beaune. Although Graf may suspect, he doesn't know for certain.'

'That's not quite true, is it?' Dom said.

She might have a point, but it was best not to answer that question.

'His adjutant is probably here, but he will say nothing. He is loyal to Eduard, and would see any betrayal of me as betraying him.'

'His name?' Léonie asked.

'Lieutenant Neumann. Andreas. He wasn't at the party yesterday,' I explained. 'He's scarred, injured during the Battle of France. I don't know what he was like before the war, but now he all but shuns social gatherings.'

For a moment, it looked like Léonie was going to ask another question, but she shook her head and murmured to herself, 'How small this world is.'

'And not always conveniently so,' Dominique said, dropping her brush in a glass of water and coming out from behind the easel. 'But that's not who I was referring to. There's the small matter of the man you think was watching you when you set up the Eureka device for the last drop.'

Léonie took a deep breath. 'Have you identified who it is?'

'Not yet.'

She turned to Dom. 'What is the *réseau* doing to find out?'

'They know there's a leak. Sablonnières and Beaune are trying to find out who it is—'

'What are they doing?' she repeated.

Dom held her ground. 'I don't know the details. But I'll find out.'

'Good.' Léonie turned her attention back to me. 'Take whatever precautions you need to protect yourself and our mission, but let the *réseau* handle this problem. If Katrin Hügel starts to ask questions, people will wonder why the Severins' German guest asks these questions, and what else she knows. And you will become a greater target.'

As much as I hated to admit it, she was right.

'However, once we find out who it is . . .'

Her lips curled in a small smile. 'You will eliminate the threat. I would expect no less. You and I will still meet tomorrow, Cécile.

We need to make sure certain people hear Katrin Hügel's tale of mistaken identity, before too much doubt sets in. Now, if you'll excuse me, I'm off to inspect the battery.'

Léonie departed in Zeit's staff car and Dominique exchanged the Josephine Baker recording for one of Charles Trenet's.

'She's right, you know. If you look too hard, you'll paint a target on more than just yourself.'

'I know.' I poured myself a drink. Poured a second one for her. 'I might not be able to go hunting, but if he gets close enough, he's mine.'

'As Léonie said, she – and I – would expect no less. What will you do?'

I shrugged. 'I don't know yet, but everything points to Pascal, and this watcher, being part of a wider plot. I don't like it.'

'I don't either.'

We prepared a light supper of bread and cheese, none of us having much appetite to eat. Just as Jérôme sat down, I pounced.

'What's the *réseau* doing to find the chap who was watching me?'

'I don't want you involved, Cécile.'

'I'm already involved. It was me he was watching!'

He rubbed his fingers through his already tousled hair.

'Cécile, the best thing we can do is to protect you. I want you as far away from this as you can be.'

'Then tell me what's happening. If you have it under control, fine. I'll leave you to do what you need to.'

It seemed a perfectly reasonably arrangement, but Dom still rolled her eyes.

If Jérôme noticed, he ignored her, leaning forward.

'Fine. We're trying to smoke him out. Different rumours as to where "Cecil" will be, different messages he's supposed to send. We'll have people watching when Fake Cecil transmits, and we'll have people watching out for which messages the Boche hear about.'

I didn't know what I expected, but somehow I hoped there would be more. Or at least a fighting chance for me to be able to work without having to watch my back for the rogue Resistance fighter, as well as the Boche.

I would give them a few days to sort it out, and then I would take matters into my own hands.

We wound the gramophone and tuned the radio for the nightly BBC news broadcast. The newsreader began with the Allied progress in Italy, and moved neatly on to the special messages from London. Within the nonsensical phrases were the odd line or two of poetry. So many of us waited for the lines of Verlaine's poem 'Chanson d'automne', the signal that the invasion would commence within a fortnight, but the lines the newsreader spoke were the final ones from the *Aeneid*.

'*And with a groan for that indignity / His spirit fled into the gloom below.*'

I started. I'd been expecting it, but it was still a blow. It was Buck's message to me, confirming that Virgil had been betrayed and was dead.

The ghastly end to a ghastly day. Complaining of heat and a headache, I went to bed early. Had Buck and Vera found the person who'd betrayed Virgil? Or, like the traitor here, was that person still at large?

Who would tell Virgil's wife? Could they even let her know how brave he was? The work he had sacrificed himself for? How much did she even know, when everything we did was in secret?

I closed my eyes and could see him again, listen to him singing Welsh lullabies as he transmitted, so that they could fly on the same waves to his baby daughter across the Channel.

'Rest well, my friend,' I whispered.

Chapter Twenty-five

M y headache abated overnight; the temperature had not. Still feeling disorientated from the last few days' events, I dressed and padded downstairs to find both Jérôme and Dom already gone. My footfalls echoed through the empty house until I could bear it no longer. Pulling Dom's bicycle from the shed, I pointed it west. A ride would burn off a bit of energy.

The 'volunteers' from Organisation Todt were already at work on either side of the road, about twenty men to one SS overseer, clearing rubble and filling potholes. The overseers leered as I passed, but to a man the 'volunteers' looked down or away. They weren't going to make the same mistake as the man who'd tried to help me when I fell.

The injustice of this burned in my blood. What sort of world did we live in when people were beaten for helping others?

The same one that shoots people for fighting those injustices.

My bicycle wobbled, and I righted it, holding on with an iron grip.

The closer I got to Caen, the more difficult it was to ride. The city, already in ruins, had taken further damage in a recent raid, although the abbey's spires were still visible. I had time to spare, and dismounted. Walking the bicycle through the streets, I took a mental inventory of what remained standing, and where there were likely places to transmit from.

Bombed buildings and broken people. Was that all that would be left once the war was over?

I pushed the thought aside and made my way to the restaurant for my rendezvous with Léonie. It was a small affair, rustic and more modest than I expected. Watercolours decorated the walls, and wild flowers brightened the tables. Léonie waited in the far corner, impeccably clad in a cornflower-blue silk dress, and surrounded by a few bags and parcels. I weaved past tables of fat German women, and a few wealthy Frenchwomen.

'You're late,' Léonie said without preamble. Her face was calm, but her fingers traced the rim of the water glass.

I shrugged, allowing the maître d' to pull my chair out for me.

'I haven't seen you since you took ill at the reception. Your headache is better now, I trust?'

She spoke more for the tables around us – the women with their children, the nannies and the old biddies.

'Much better, thank you.'

'Colonel Graf seemed quite determined to find you.'

My cringe was all too real. 'Yes, I've been told he made quite a spectacle, although it would seem I missed all the excitement.'

A single raised eyebrow was less of a response than I expected, and she continued, 'Did he eventually find you?'

'Why, yes. He did. Apparently, I bear some resemblance to his missing wife.' I raised one shoulder in a half-shrug. 'I was sorry to disappoint him.'

'Will he call on you?' she asked, her cool eyes assessing me.

I opened my mouth to feign a denial, as Katrin would, and surprised myself at a quiet wave of fury I felt at the idea of my husband calling on another woman. Even if that other woman was still me.

'He's married, and so am I,' I snapped.

Two tables away, a trio of women watched us. One finally nodded, approving. Unlike the German women attached to their forces here, these women weren't in uniform, and I guessed they were wives. If they were relieved by my morality, they should see the way Zeit followed Léonie around.

'My dear Frau Hügel,' Léonie purred, not for a moment taken in by my indignation, 'I would expect no less of you.'

She waited for the waiter to pour our wine before placing a gaily wrapped package on the table and pushing it across to me.

'Something that reminded me of you.'

It was too small to be a Bible, a book of morals, or the SOE handbook which, I was certain, would advise against cavorting with the enemy. Watching her from under my lashes, I opened the box. Pushing aside the tissue paper, my fingers caught on something hard and round. I stared up at Léonie in surprise but, while her eyes were serious, she flipped her hand for me to continue. Nestled in the wrapping was a beautiful scarf, a dark forest green silk with cream and russet flowers. Underneath, a small canister lay hidden in a furl of paper: the film from her trip to the Merville battery.

'The colours will suit you. I do hope you'll put it to good use.'

'Thank you, it's perfect.'

I'd decrypt whatever she'd written on the paper, and Dom would have to find a way to pass the film on to the dressmakers, or whoever would get it to London.

We didn't linger. Léonie gathered her parcels as I went to the bathroom to transfer the film and the wrapping paper into my handbag, and tie the scarf around my neck. I refreshed my lipstick and left the box on the table for the staff to clear.

We walked in a strangely companionable silence towards the Château de Caen. Léonie stilled, sensing the danger before I did. I followed her gaze, the food I'd picked at over lunch threatened to rise. Just outside the imposing *porte des champs*, a small group of men surrounded a woman, pushing her from one to another.

She stood in the centre of the circle, fair hair tied back, black eyes snapping at them. She was encircled, but she raged. Her shoulders were back, her chin forward. Trying to reason with them. These men hadn't defeated her . . . yet.

It wasn't the first time I'd seen a pack of SS men terrorise a lone woman. Last time, I had braced myself to stand by, as my training had directed, to protect myself and my mission. Someone else had risked his life to try to save hers. She was dead before he could reach her, and he, too, died for his efforts. Their souls weighed on my conscience, and every fibre of my being revolted. Anything I did to save this woman would be foolish, especially with Léonie's note and roll of film hidden in my bag, but I couldn't let this happen again. I just couldn't.

My good intentions of the morning disappeared, and I only realised that Léonie held my arm when her hand fell away. We moved as one, Léonie's throaty voice cutting through their laughs.

'For heaven's sake leave her alone.'

Blue-violet eyes blazed as she pushed into the circle. She was almost a foot shorter than the shortest man, but one by one, she made eye contact with each man. And one by one, they stood back.

'We are not animals.'

No one seeing Léonie in this moment could doubt her courage.

I moved, adding my size to her fury. Asked the woman, 'Are you all right?'

Her eyes met mine; they were the angry eyes of a wounded animal. She didn't seem to understand me, and I repeated the question in French.

'*Sie ist untermenschlich*,' one of the men said.

Subhuman. The filthy term the Nazis used for anyone who wasn't Aryan stoked my anger.

I ignored him and repeated my question to her again, this time more softly.

'I don't need your help,' she hissed, but when I turned to leave, she reached for my hand, and her eyes dropped, looking at her scuffed shoes.

'We are not animals.' I repeated Léonie's words, drawing the woman between Léonie and me. 'You have mothers. Maybe sisters or wives or daughters. What if they were here? What if they were this woman, bullied because . . . what? Because you don't know her? Because you can? You should be ashamed of yourselves.'

I pushed my way out of the circle, pulling the woman with me, feeling the waves of hostility emanating from them.

'Thank you,' the woman said.

My anger-fuelled bravery ebbed, and I moved a step or two away. She followed.

'Why did you do that? You didn't have to.'

Her German was flawless, but the SS man was right: she had the hint of an accent. Not English, but not French either.

I stopped and turned, almost expecting to see the brown curly hair of the girl I had seen kicked to death. On the far side of the street something caught my eye: another soldier, this one wearing Wehrmacht green. His peaked cap was tilted over a face as beautiful as a Botticelli angel, but I knew that the other side was horribly scarred. Eduard's adjutant, Lieutenant Andreas Neumann nodded, acknowledging my presence, but the sidearm in his hand was a clear warning to the SS men to stand down.

'We are not animals,' he echoed.

Like a pack of hyenas, they retreated from his challenge. If I had to be followed, I didn't mind if it was Andreas Neumann. Eduard's adjutant was a good man, and loyal to Eduard.

And with his maimed left leg, I wouldn't have much of a problem losing him if I needed to. I was less certain of the man who'd watched me with the Eureka device. Sighing, I thanked him. When I turned back, I realised Léonie had taken advantage of the confusion, and was gone.

My attention returned to the woman beside me. Scuffed shoes were the least of her problems. Her clothes were thin. Threadbare. I couldn't watch her die, but I wasn't in a position to keep her alive either. I pulled a ring from my finger, part of my winnings from my trip to the casino. It was ugly, garish, but big, and worth a fair amount. I pressed it into her hand.

'Sell it if you need to. Use it to bribe someone to take you away, I don't care. But this place, it's not safe for you.'

She blinked, fingers closing around the ring.

'You do know that, don't you?' I asked.

Black eyes softened, and when she spoke, her voice was low and pleading.

'I have a safe conduct pass. I must get to Portugal.'

Portugal?

I closed my eyes, and for a second remembered the refugees sitting in cafés in the Rossio, sharing their stories. Some spoke of Portuguese officials who helped them. Maybe she was being helped as well, but I didn't know her, and couldn't afford to endanger Dom and Jérôme by taking her to their home.

But knew I had to do something.

Clad in a tattered dress and the remnants of her pride, the woman raised her chin further. Even with the strongest will, she wouldn't last a day longer on her own.

Following a hunch, I took a chance. 'Come with me,' I said.

Chapter Twenty-six

We walked through the rubbled ruins of a once-beautiful city, while questions bubbled and burst in my mind: who had given her the pass? Why? How had she got this far alone? Presumably unarmed? We had moved from the populated area into a wasteland when the woman began to talk.

'My name is Felícian,' she said.

It was a different name from the one she'd given the SS, and her pronunciation was slightly off, neither French nor German. Hopefully she had told the Boche the truth, or at least given them one that matched her papers and the safe conduct, assuming it was real. But she didn't trust me, and that was good – the less I knew, the safer it was for us both – but she would need to be consistent in her story if she was to survive.

'I am not your friend, but if you must use that name, pronounce it *Felícienne* while you're in France.' I switched from German to French. 'You do speak French, don't you?'

A shutter fell behind her eyes; she understood that I knew what she was. 'Fluently. Why are you helping me?'

'Don't thank me yet. If those men find you again, you won't escape.'

As harsh as it sounded, it was the truth. I backed up a few feet. Whatever she had gone through, she had done the best she could to clean herself up, but it was still there: an insidious stench. Of fear, but also something rather more human.

As if she sensed my reaction, those proud shoulders went back again.

'I've made it this far, and I thank you for your help. You can go now.'

She meant to be rude, to make me walk away. She had called on every last reserve for that speech, and I didn't believe it for a moment.

'So you still have your pride,' I said. 'Jolly good. Don't let that go, but don't be a fool. I'm trying to help you.'

'Why?'

'Goodness of my heart.'

She looked sceptical, and it was my turn to look away, unable to explain it to myself. Maybe it was her posture, her bearing in the face of adversity. She had clearly been through hell. Maybe lost someone she loved, and still moved forward. She wouldn't tell me her story, even if I asked, but I understood it anyway: it was clear in her expression. An expression I'd seen more than once in the looking glass.

'You remind me of someone,' I admitted. I couldn't tell her it was me she reminded me of, fleeing France and the Gestapo. One year ago, making my way first to Spain, and then to Portugal. 'You said you have a visa for Portugal?'

She nodded.

'Good. Well, if you make it there, you must go to the Pastelaria Suíça on Rossio Square in Lisbon. And if you find the ugliest man there, scarred, burnt and battered, give him my regards.'

She nodded, but remained standing still.

A woman manhandling a pram trundled into sight, dark hair barely trapped under a tattered hat. At the corner behind her, two men waited. Their suits didn't hide what they were.

'Damn,' I muttered.

Holding on to her arm, I led Felícienne down another street, doubling back twice to be certain no one followed. When we neared our destination, I drew Felícienne closer to the side of a building.

'I wish you luck,' I said and pushed open the door.

Felícienne's horror compounded with the ringing bell, but my hand on her arm prevented her from running.

'Hello?' I called out.

I repeated the word again until one of Dom's dressmaker friends scurried forward. She was the one who'd measured me. Yvette.

'Good afternoon, Frau Hügel,' she murmured. 'The blue dress?'

'Was exceptional. Thank you.' I pulled the woman forward. 'This is Felícienne. She's had a bit of bad luck. She lost her papers – and her belongings – in last night's raid.'

Yvette made a sympathetic sound.

'And I have, unfortunately, caused some damage to her skirt and have offered to pay for its replacement. The blouse as well.'

The dressmaker blinked, her eyes moving back and forth between Felícienne and me.

'Of course,' she said, although her voice was anything but certain.

'Today,' I stipulated.

173

Both women paled. Felícienne opened her hand; the ugly ring I had just given her rested in her palm.

'Oh, put that away,' I snapped. 'The rip was my fault, and I will pay for it to be replaced.'

Black eyes swam with an emotion that I wasn't prepared to deal with. I addressed Yvette.

'See that she has what she needs, and add the cost to my account.'

The dressmaker raised her eyes to mine, and it was as if an entire conversation had passed. She pushed her wire-rimmed spectacles further up her nose.

'Leave her with me, madame. I will take care of her.'

And that was all I needed to know.

On the walk back to the restaurant where I'd left my bicycle, I reviewed everything I'd said – to Felícienne, and to the dress-maker. The only thing that *could* incriminate me, if Felícienne was caught, would be the comment about Portugal, but a wealthy woman like Katrin would be well travelled, may have visited Lisbon and recommended a favourite watering hole.

Maybe, just maybe, I'd avoid being arrested for my part in saving the girl.

Chapter Twenty-seven

Each nerve ending felt exposed. I was mentally exhausted, and the bicycle ride from Caen hadn't helped. I turned north, hoping to take comfort in the gentle lapping of sea, and across the water, the Allies positioning themselves to liberate us.

I left the bicycle leaning against a building and took a deep breath, drinking in the briny air and allowing the sea breeze to cool my face. Hotels, businesses and homes lined one side of the esplanade. On the other side, mines peppered the beaches. Gun emplacements were at regular intervals, clearly prioritising fire-power and leaving cover to the surrounding terrain. The design was awkward, as if battered tanks had sunk deep into the mud, and instead of trying to free them, the Germans had left them in place while allowing the turrets to rotate on a 360-degree traverse. I couldn't see within, but from the outside, they looked barely large enough for the soldiers to man their guns.

'What the devil sort of thing is that?'

'*Die Panzerstellung.*'

A curt voice startled me, and I jumped, one hand rising to my throat, grateful that if I was stupid enough to talk to myself, at least I kept it to German.

The man wore the grey-green uniform of the Gestapo, the braid on his shoulder boards and four silver squares on his collar marking him as a major. I had seen him outside the abbey, the day the four Resistance fighters had been slaughtered. We hadn't been introduced, but I could guess who he was.

'What exactly is a *Panzerstellung*?'

The major clasped his hands behind his back.

'A Renault 35 turret mounted on a Tobruk-type emplacement.'

Which meant an anti-tank gun, pilfered from a tank and plonked on top of a static emplacement. Maybe with a machine gun or two stashed away.

'Renault?' I asked, feigning ignorance.

He flashed a devilish grin. 'Oh, yes. Compliments of the former French army. I am sure they are delighted their tanks still defend their shores.'

'No doubt.'

He inclined his head, and puffed out his chest.

'I am Major Lorenz. And you must be Frau Hügel.'

'I suppose I must, yes. I don't think I've had the pleasure to meet you, Major.' I forced a smile and looked beyond him to his black-clad entourage. My stomach churning, I added, 'However, I have met Captain Vallentin.'

Leaning against a car, Vallentin casually saluted me. How long had he been standing there? Was he following me? He couldn't have heard about Felícienne this quickly.

'May I ask what you're doing, nosing around an area clearly marked as restricted?' Lorenz asked with a deceptively even tone.

If they searched me, and found Léonie's film, I could say that I had it as a favour for a friend, getting the film developed. But if they developed the film, it would implicate both of us, so not an option. If they arrested me, I'd have to get rid of it, and hope that whatever was on it could be replaced.

'Is it?' It wasn't a bluff; in my exhaustion, I genuinely hadn't noticed the sign. 'My apologies. I didn't see the signs. I'm afraid that I didn't sleep well last night, and I've obviously not been paying attention.'

He raised an eyebrow and waited for me to continue. When I didn't answer, he shook his head, bemused.

'You aristocrats, you never think the rules apply to you.'

The conversation had veered in a direction I hadn't expected.

'What makes you think I am an aristocrat?'

He answered with a glare, and I understood. People like Lorenz used their insecurities to progress within the SS's ranks, where they had carte blanche to settle imagined scores.

I shook my head. 'I'm flattered, Major, but whatever you think, I'm well aware that these rules are for my – our – safety. I really didn't see the sign.'

Lorenz rocked back on his heels and pursed his lips in a reasonable facsimile of Benito Mussolini. I tried to focus on the screeching seagulls and the surf accompanying the rising tide. One minute. Two minutes.

At the third minute, he held out his elbow.

'Come and walk with me, Frau Hügel, and perhaps you would explain why you decided to intervene earlier when my men were questioning a member of the Resistance.'

He had heard about that. How? Had I been wrong about the dressmakers? Had Felícienne already been apprehended? Would they arrest me?

He jerked his elbow impatiently. If Lorenz wanted to maintain a façade of civility, I could play along. I linked my arm in his, and smiled at him with all the charm I could muster.

'Again, my apologies for any confusion, Major. I hadn't realised they were questioning her.'

'Your naïveté is surprising, Frau Hügel.' The lower lip jutted out again. 'What did you think it was?'

Bullying. Terrorising. I kept my thoughts to myself and gave him a half-shrug.

'Frau Hügel?' he prompted.

Any misstep, and he would arrest me. He was Gestapo – he didn't even need an excuse. So I opted for honesty.

'I don't know. It didn't look like an arrest, it looked like men picking on a woman and that poor woman looked terrified.'

'Perhaps she was right to be. We have been tracking her. Sometimes we get close, but she has always evaded us.'

Impressive.

'So, why didn't they arrest her when they found her?'

His flat look told me that was the order he had given them. They had just decided to have fun first.

Which meant there was a chance they hadn't apprehended her yet.

'Who is she?'

'An enemy of the Reich. That is all you need to know.'

A seagull screamed my protest for me, diving within a foot of Lorenz's head. He gritted his teeth and hissed, 'Stinking scavenger!'

Behind him one of the men palmed his sidearm.

'Sir?'

He was going to shoot a seagull? For doing whatever dive-bombing antics that seagulls did? Or was this seagull, too, an enemy of the Reich? Lorenz looked like he wanted to order his man to kill it, but perhaps something he saw in my expression had him gesture his minion to put the gun away.

He took a step back and bowed formally.

'Good day, Frau Hügel.' He straightened and stepped closer. 'I am certain we will meet again soon.'

I felt sick by the time I returned home. I uttered the barest of greetings to Dom and retreated to my bedroom. Took off my shoes and flopped on the bed, curling my body around the pillow and willing the tremors to subside.

It might have been the right thing to do, but it was stupid to risk myself, my friends, my husband and my mission for a woman I didn't know. But there was nothing I could do to change it now. With any luck, Felícienne was still alive, and Dom's friends would hide her until the Resistance could spirit her out of the area.

When the shaking eased, I got out of bed. As far as I knew, invisible ink was not a favoured method of communication by anyone other than Léonie. Most inks were old, insecure, and left a residue on the paper that would scream 'Hidden Message!' To be fair to Léonie, it was a useful way of passing information in plain sight, and no one looking at her paper would think it had been tampered with.

A roughly drawn map appeared, its pentagonal shape instantly familiar. I ran downstairs, and rummaged in the parlour. If they had an atlas, it wasn't on the shelf, nor in any of the drawers. Frustrated, I knelt on the floor and peered into a lower drawer.

'What are you looking for?'

179

Startled, I looked up. Dom stood in the doorway, securing her hat with a long pin.

'Going out?'

'Yes. And I'll need the bicycle.'

The words were out before I could stop them: 'What do you expect me to use?'

'The bus?'

She read my expression and burst into laughter, the first genuine laugh I had heard from her since I'd got here.

'You're priceless, Cécile. Everyone takes the bus. It's the best way to hear what other people are talking about. No? Well, then go out and buy your own bicycle – you certainly made enough money at the casino to be able to afford one. Or you can do what the other Maquisards do, and steal someone else's. Just leave mine alone. Today, at least.'

The hat firmly in place, she crossed her arms over her chest.

'What are you looking for?'

'A map. Léonie sent through a bit more information on the troops, and I thought it would make sense to track it on a map.'

Her heels clicked on the parquet floor as she moved to the table in the foyer. Returned with a folded map and a pencil.

'We need to be careful with this. Hide it when you're done.'

I nodded, and marked the *Panzerstellung* emplacements and the defences I had seen around the countryside and at the Ranville and Bénouville bridges. Transcribed the details Léonie noted of the Merville battery: a five-foot high barbed wire fence

180

and a 100-yard-deep minefield. There were two barbed wire obstacles, each about fifteen feet thick, and an anti-tank ditch running along the north-west side, protecting the battery from any coastal attack.

Inside were four casemates, a 20mm anti-aircraft gun, and machine guns in fifteen positions. She'd drawn the command bunker, and several other outbuildings which I presumed were barracks and ammunition stores, and had noted that all four casemates were complete. She had also indicated that there were approximately eighty artillery men, and fifty engineers from the 1st Battery Artillery Regiment 1716, part of the 716th, stationed there.

At the bottom, she had two names. 'Hauptmann Karl Heinrich Wolter' had been crossed out, and above it was 'Oberleutnant Raimund Steiner'. Wolter. The man whom Kühn had mentioned at Rommel's reception.

Dom tapped one long finger against the first name.

'I'd heard he died, along with his mistress, when Merville was bombed last Friday. I don't know this Steiner.'

'They replaced a Hauptmann, a captain, with a lieutenant? For such an important asset, it makes no sense. Why would they do that?'

She shrugged and shook her head. 'I don't know. Why are the decrepit 716th stationed here?'

'Fine. I'll transmit what we know to London. Can you get the map to them?'

She took the pencil from my hand, added a few more details, and folded the map and tucked it in her purse.

'Yes.'

'It feels wrong. Like a decoy or something,' I muttered to myself. 'Hold on, there's one more thing.' I reached into a pocket and then handed her the film canister. 'But be careful. The Gestapo are out looking for trouble.'

'The Gestapo are always out looking for trouble.'

'More than usual, Dom. Be careful.'

Chapter Twenty-eight

I hadn't seen Eduard since Saturday night, and while I missed him, it was better that he wasn't seen to be too involved with me. Not when I was neck-deep in trouble, with a leak in the Resistance, and the Gestapo watching my every move.

However, as far as anyone knew, Katrin Hügel had nothing to hide, so I selected a novel from the shelf and took the bus into Ranville. Paid a handsome price for a well-used bicycle, and then had to wait for the vendor to realign the damned thing so that it didn't keep urging me to go left. It was battered, and ugly enough that there was a chance it wouldn't be stolen. Or so the vendor joked.

From there, I crossed the Orne and followed the canal to the café near the Bénouville bridge.

I took a small table by the window and placed the book on it in front of me. Four men were seated to my right, a sergeant and three enlisted men from the 125th Panzergrenadiers. The sergeant looked weathered and weary, his men little more than boys.

They sat about as far away as they could from the pair of SS goons perched near the back of the room, watching me like a couple of malevolent crows.

For a change, the only incriminating thing on me was the sgian dubh by my thigh, and it was something that wouldn't be immediately obvious if there was an unexpected search.

A young woman came to take my order. She was returning with my coffee when one of the SS goons fondled her behind. Surprised, she jerked, and a long spray of hot coffee arched towards my lap.

Yelping, I jumped to my feet, holding the steaming skirt away from my legs. The proprietor came running out with a towel. I snatched it and dabbed at the hot coffee.

'Madame, I am so sorry,' he repeated. 'Please. Come into the back and my wife will see to your skirt.'

One large hand pressed at the small of my back, allowing me seconds to snatch my handbag before guiding me through the tables. One or two Panzergrenadiers looked at me sympathetically, but the rest just stared where my skirt clung to my legs.

'Idiots,' I muttered.

Madame stood by the stove, an apron wrapped around her waist. A second daughter was folded into a chair, her nose in a book. Monsieur closed the kitchen door behind us.

'An accident,' I explained. 'One of the SS men surprised your daughter.'

The other girl stifled a giggle. Madame shooed Monsieur from the kitchen and looked critically at my skirt.

'Fortunately, madame,' she said, 'your skirt is dark and I do not think the coffee will stain. You weren't burned, were you?'

'No.'

We dried the skirt as best we could and returned to the dining room, just as the door swung open to let in the field marshal and his entourage. The room instantly became smaller, the air thick and electric.

Eduard Graf saw me immediately. The flash of surprise that crossed his face was replaced by a wide smile. He took off his cap, and tucked it under an arm.

'Frau Hügel,' he said. 'What a pleasant surprise.'

The space between us was far too great, but I remained rooted to the spot. Standing beside him, the field marshal's gaze assessed me.

'So this is the woman who looks like your wife, Colonel?'

'Less so close up, sir,' Eduard said, his voice carefully neutral. 'Field Marshal, General, may I present Frau Hügel. From Strasbourg.'

And with that, wearing a soiled skirt, I was introduced to Erwin Rommel, the Desert Fox, and his chief of staff, Hans Speidel.

'Sir,' I inclined my head and strove to hide my shock. 'It ... I am honoured to meet you.'

'Ah, you caused the colonel rather a lot of distress the other night,' the Desert Fox said. There didn't appear to be any malice in his tone as he glanced at Eduard. 'I do hope no offence was given?'

'Not at all,' I said and, unable to resist teasing Eduard, added, 'He called on me the other day to apologise.'

Speidel, taller than Rommel but not as tall as Eduard, with spectacles and a serious face, executed a small bow.

'A pleasure, Frau Hügel,' he said.

Unsure if he was greeting or dismissing me, I took a step back.

'I shan't delay you further. It was a pleasure to meet you, gentlemen. Good afternoon.'

Rommel kissed my hand and I moved outside, past Rommel's Horch staff car. There was a determined crunch of boots on gravel before Eduard's hand closed on my arm.

'Wait.'

He reached for my bicycle, holding it between us.

'I'm sorry for sending you away Saturday night,' I said, careful to keep my voice from carrying. 'But for you to stay would have shattered Katrin's cover. I'm sorry.'

'I know,' he said, but the upset still lingered in his eyes.

'Do you?' I kicked at a pebble. 'Sometimes I'm not so sure I do.'

He laughed, his eyes crinkling at the corners.

'You are the least uncertain person I know. Sometimes your certainty is ill-conceived. However, I never doubt the conviction of your beliefs.'

It wasn't quite the same thing.

'I missed you,' he added, his words cutting my heart and catching my breath.

Striving for a blasé tone, I smiled.

'I can tell. Your incessant attention has become quite tedious.'

'Ah.' He leant back, unable to hide the ghost of a smile. 'You missed me, too?'

'Of course I did,' I snapped, not sure why I was being irritated by something I was happy to admit.

The edges of his mouth quirked into a not-quite-suppressed smile.

'Good. Then I will pick you up tomorrow evening at eight o'clock.'

'For what?'

'For the cinema. There is one in Bayeux, and Graf would like to spend more time with the woman who reminds him of his wife.'

'What would the field marshal think? His love for his wife is legendary.'

It wasn't really as if I cared; Eduard and I would find a way to meet, regardless. He smiled, acknowledging the point.

'Indeed it is. He hopes to return to see her for her birthday next month.'

His eyes briefly searched mine, a silent query that could neither be asked nor answered: would there be Resistance activity before then?

Yes, probably.

But I didn't know the specifics, and wouldn't share them if I did. Besides, that was more of a problem for the SS and the gendarmerie, than for Rommel.

The deeper question Eduard silently asked was whether the invasion would be before Frau Rommel's birthday, and prevent her husband's return. The truth was, I didn't know that either. London hadn't yet sent the message to let us know.

He must have read this in my expression. He stood back, and like Speidel, executed a formal bow.

'Eight o'clock,' he said, turning abruptly.

There was no question in his voice, just the hard expectation of a senior officer that his order would be executed.

Chapter Twenty-nine

Time plays a funny game, sometimes elongating, other times, flying. Thirty-six hours passed, and I couldn't remember a single thing I did.

From the other side of the easel, Dom responded with a long-suffering sigh.

I cleared my throat. 'I'll go upstairs to get ready.'

'That's a good idea.' Her bland tone made it clear that she was losing patience.

I hurried up the stairs and stared at the dress I'd laid out on the bed: it was a deep forest green in a lightweight wool batiste. It wasn't evening attire, but was perfectly suitable for dinner and the pictures. The fabric flowed from the cap sleeves, crossing at the décolletage into a bow at the back. Dom's dressmakers had suggested a full skirt, despite the scarcity of fabric. Although I preferred the cleaner pencil lines, I acquiesced, but only because the full skirt and deep pockets could hide my sgian dubh.

I shouldn't need it tonight, but the days I didn't think I would need it often turned out to be the days I needed it most.

I bathed and washed my hair. Towelled it dry and then twisted it, still damp, into a chignon. The look was as severe as it was striking, and I pulled loose a few tendrils on one side to better frame my face.

The bracelet and earrings were small and simple. Good quality, but understated. I left my neck and chest bare, unadorned by anything more than a spray of Chanel No. 5.

I studied myself in the looking glass and frowned. Added a touch of red lipstick and smiled, pleased with the result.

Tonight felt as much like a first date as our actual first date had, almost a year ago. On that night he'd promised to take me to hear the queen of *fado*, Amália Rodrigues, perform. I'd convinced myself that I only agreed because my alias was a French woman with German sympathies, and stepping out with an Abwehr officer reinforced my cover story. It was also playing with fire, not least because Eduard Graf intrigued me.

That evening he took me first for a drink at the Avenida hotel, where he left me in the company of his adjutant while he conducted an 'unavoidable' meeting that I still knew no details about. I'd used the time with Andreas Neumann to better understand Graf, learning of his bravery during the Battle of France, and how he'd saved Neumann's life when their tank had been destroyed.

And I'd spotted a Gestapo agent who came frightfully close to killing us both. I hoped tonight would be less eventful.

A tank commander who'd moved to the Abwehr and who now sat on Rommel's staff. Eduard Graf was a 'good' German who hated the Nazis, and while on several levels he was a man of contradictions, he was also one of the bravest and most honourable men I knew.

I picked up my wrap and descended the stairs, just as Eduard's car stopped outside the house.

'Do you think he'll want to come inside?' Dom asked, stepping out from behind her easel.

'Why? To ask Jérôme for his permission to take me out?'

From behind his newspaper, Jérôme asked, 'Can I answer honestly?'

'No.'

My high heels clicked on the wooden floors as I went to answer the door. Eduard was freshly shaven, looking smart in his uniform, complete with the Knight's Cross at his throat. With oak leaves, I noticed.

'When did your *Ritterkreuz* get upgraded?'

'Shortly after my wife disappeared,' he said. 'It was poor consolation. You look beautiful tonight.'

Feeling a blush heating my cheeks, I struggled to maintain my composure.

'Thank you. And you look quite dashing. Are those for me?' I gestured to the roses in his hand and box of chocolate truffles under his arm

'The flowers are, yes. But the chocolates are for Madame Severin.' He smiled and followed me down the short hallway towards the parlour.

Dom's heart-shaped face peered out from the parlour.

'Me?'

'In apology for your door, and my poor manners when last we met.'

He would need to do more than that to get into Dom's good graces.

'You didn't need to do that, Colonel,' she said, her voice studiously cool.

'Perhaps not, but please accept them anyway.'

Dom stopped short of rolling her eyes, but accepted his offering. Visibly struggling to stifle a smile, she shooed us out of the door.

'How did you explain this to your friends?' he asked as soon as we were far enough from the door.

'I told them that, despite the mistaken identity, I found you fascinating.'

He looked surprised. 'Did they believe you?'

'No. Not after how long we spoke in the garden, but they won't ask. And they won't cause problems.' I settled myself into the little sports car. 'So, what do you have planned?'

He looked like he wasn't about to finish the conversation about the Severins yet, but shrugged.

'I had hoped to arrange a viewing of the Bayeux Tapestry before seeing the film. However, I have since learnt that it has been removed.'

I cleared my throat but held my tongue.

'Yes. It is no secret that Himmler covets the tapestry.' This time he cleared his throat. 'However, to my knowledge it was not taken by us.'

'I've seen it,' I murmured. 'Years ago. Yard after yard of embroidery depicting the Norman Conquest. It's magnificent and quite priceless. I assume that's why Himmler wants it?'

'He claims it is important for our glorious and cultured Germanic history.'

'But neither King Harold nor King William was German.' And then, sighing, I held up my hand. 'Yes, I know the Angles and the Saxons were Germanic tribes, but Harold lost to the Norman duke.'

He glanced over at me in warning.

'I do not recommend trying to educate the *Reichsführer* of the SS on these matters, Angel.'

'I doubt I'll have that opportunity.'

And if I got that close, it wouldn't be his pride, or lack of education, that I'd attack. Eduard remained silent, navigating the little sports car past craters in the road that hadn't yet been repaired.

'I was thinking,' I said. 'It's a beautiful evening. Instead of the cinema, why don't we go somewhere in Caen, where maybe someone who recognises us can see you courting me, so there won't be questions later. Maybe dinner, and a stroll along the seaside? I do love the smell of the sea.'

And if I could get a better look at the defences at the same time, well then, that was fine, wasn't it?

Eduard chose a restaurant far enough from the shore to avoid random Boche soldiers and their French girlfriends or rent-a-dates, yet close enough for us to still smell the sea air. After a brief conversation, the maître d' escorted us through the restaurant and up a set of stairs to the first floor, where we were accosted by a middle-aged German Frau with a bosom like a battleship's prow.

'Herr Oberst,' she cooed at Eduard, ignoring me. 'What a surprise to see you here.'

I looked beyond her to the table she'd emerged from, to see a portly man who stared at his plate of canard à la Rouennaise, and a teenage girl, overdressed for the venue. I gave her a sympathetic smile, understanding the situation.

The maître d' also seemed to understand, and ushered us outside and down two steps onto a rooftop terrace-type patio, raised one storey above the street. The table was at the edge, bordered on two sides by a wrought-iron lace barrier and lit by candles. Eduard must have tipped the maître d' generously to take over this table, clearly set up for someone else.

'I hope it's not too cool outside for you?' he asked.

I glanced behind us, unable to see through the blackout curtains to the glare the battleship was probably sending me.

'This is perfect,' I said.

Three other tables were occupied, mostly older German officers, some with younger women. The maître d' brought us a menu that featured local cuisine: seafood, duck and pork, cooked in cream, Camembert or cider. Eduard sent me a wry glance.

'There is a place, Frau Hügel,' he said, just loud enough. 'A beautiful place. Another city – another country – on another coast. Sea air and cuisine that is cooked in spices rather than sauces. It is a beautiful place. I think you would like it.'

'I'm certain I would, Colonel.' I leant forward, and placed my hand on the table, beside my wine glass. 'Where is it?'

His left hand covered mine, the gold wedding band that was the wrong colour glowing in the candlelight.

'In—'

He was interrupted by gunfire. We automatically looked up, but it wasn't coming from the sky. We lunged to the wall. A small, crumpled body was curled on the street below, as a woman wailed. A pack of uniformed thugs stood in the doorway, laughing. When the woman rushed towards the body, they shot her in the back.

'*Verdammt*,' Eduard muttered, bolting for the door.

I followed behind him, my right hand reaching through green wool folds to close over the sgian dubh's hilt.

We clattered down the stairs and through the restaurant to the street. A crowd was already forming, but Eduard pushed through. He assessed first one body, then the second one. Turned his angry black glare on the Gestapo officer.

'What is the meaning of this?'

'Colonel,' the officer said, barely giving me a glance. 'What is your interest here?'

'I heard gunfire.'

The fair-haired officer shrugged. 'This is not a Wehrmacht issue. That boy . . . ' He gestured towards the small body. 'He is a Jew. We had been informed – reliably – that he masqueraded as an altar boy every Sunday.'

'He was a child. Shot in the back.' Eduard drew a ragged breath. 'And the woman?'

'She was hiding him. You do understand, Colonel, that we cannot allow this insurrection to continue?'

A Jewish boy, hiding to save his life? What threat could he possibly be? Or the woman who'd risked her life to save him? How the bloody hell was that insurrection?

The moon was barely past the new moon, a tiny sliver in the sky. But when the Gestapo man turned, I saw the fair hair, the pale and handsome features. Recognised that smug smile. He clapped Eduard on the shoulder.

'Come, Herr Oberst. Why do you concern yourself with these *Untermenschen*? When you know it is our responsibility, as good Germans, to root out this evil?'

Evil? If there was any evil here, it stood boldly in front of us, in a grey-green uniform and hobnailed boots. There was no regret in his mien, no empathy, no feeling. He'd killed a child in cold blood, and a woman who had tried to protect the boy.

And he took pleasure in it.

He was sick – a sickness that was propagated by the Nazi regime.

In that moment, standing across from the man who'd hunted me as he had that child, I made a promise to myself. One day, Eugene Vallentin would pay for those innocent deaths.

Preferably, at my hand.

Chapter Thirty

I slept badly and woke late, and set off towards the village where I could catch the bus into Caen. Jérôme had gone on ahead, leaving my wireless in the safe house that had originally been earmarked for me.

The brown wig was at the bottom of my shoulder bag, the identity that matched it hidden in the lining. I would have preferred to cycle in, but the wonky bike had a wonkier tyre and I couldn't find a bicycle pump.

At least it made it easier to identify my tail: a wiry man two rows behind me. He wore civvies, but bore a striking resemblance to Lorenz's goons.

Mentally I rehearsed the lines to excuse away the wig, in case I was stopped. The matching set of documents hidden in my bag's lining would be more difficult, and I didn't want to imagine what they'd think about the silk scarf with my codes printed on it, currently being used to belt my skirt.

The bus bumped along the route. I hated buses. Hated the way you were packed in. The windows were open, but it still felt airless. And someone had eaten too many onions.

It stopped at Ranville. Outside the window, a smartly dressed man stood with a case in his hand. He wore a toupee, of good enough quality that it almost looked real, and a beard, that might have looked piratical, but instead seemed distinguished.

His eyes met mine through the open window. One Atlas-like shoulder shrugged and he took a step back.

I understood.

'Oh no!' I grabbed my bag, and shimmied past a woman with a pram. 'I forgot something at home.'

I stepped off the bus and into the crowd before Vallentin's man could follow.

The bus drove off, the man's angry face pressed against the window. I followed André's wide shoulders as he weaved in and out, the way we'd been trained to lose someone tailing us. He almost lost me once or twice, and I was relieved to find him in the driver's seat of a small Renault.

'Get in,' he said.

I didn't think twice. The situation must be dire for André to come out of hiding.

'What's wrong?' I asked, sliding into the passenger seat.

He leant forward the way a cheeky lover would, but his voice was serious.

'Too many Boche in Caen.' Wide hazel eyes stared into mine. 'Not safe for you there, not when everyone is looking for a single woman.'

A single woman. Felícienne? Or me?

He put the Renault into gear and grinned in a distinctly avuncular way.

'I heard you had a date last night. How did it go?'

'Well enough,' I said. 'Until the Gestapo had to go and ruin it. Where are we going? My set is in Caen.'

'We have another one,' he said. 'What we don't have is someone else who knows how to use it.'

197

That wasn't my biggest worry.

'Other than Dom, Jérôme and apparently you, who else knew I'd be heading into Caen today?' I asked. 'And are they looking for Cecil – or me?'

André shrugged again. 'Six of one, Blondie. They're looking for an operator . . . and the Kellen girl. Best you stay away for a while.'

I assumed 'the Kellen Girl' was Felícienne, or one of her aliases.

'There's clothes on the floor. Don't want people to see German Katrin with me.'

Privacy would have been nice, but it wouldn't be the first time I had changed clothing in front of my comrades without compromising my modesty. I shimmied into the trousers. Tucked my skirt in, and buttoned the shirt over my blouse. One detail at a time, until a bulky Cecil appeared.

André glanced at me.

'You're a damned pretty bloke,' he said.

'Too pretty for you,' I said.

'Ha. Listen, I know a boy. Good kid. Beaune wonders if you might be willing to train him? He's sharp. His dad was a Communist, sent east in one of the first round-ups. His mum spouts a lot of drivel, but has nothing to do with the Resistance. The boy is smart, but angry. Needs a bit of focus. Might not be so good with a gun, but you should see him with a crossword puzzle.'

I blinked, guessing that the boy André referred to was the youth Dom had caught with a copy of *Combat*.

'He's only a kid.'

'He's sixteen. He's old enough to fight, and would if we'd let him.'

The boy Vallentin had killed last night was much younger. Sixteen wasn't too young to fight in the Resistance.

'What's wrong with him?'

'Nothing. Couldn't stop my cousin Antoine. Can stop this one. Or, at least, redirect him.'

I was already shaking my head. 'You know this isn't safe. Come on, André. On our first day of training, the major in charge told us that only half of us were expected to return. The pianists are the hardest hit.'

'You're still alive. You can teach him how to survive. We can't have only one, as good as you are, Blondie.'

I could have told him how many near misses I'd had, but I didn't have the time, or the inclination, to relive them.

'No. Absolutely not. I can't do this, it's too risky. The SS don't care if anyone has actually *done* something once they decide on their guilt. The last protégé I had was betrayed and killed. No, I don't want the responsibility of training someone else, only to have them caught by the Boche.'

And to have a finger pointed at me when they're questioned.

'In Paris we had fifteen minutes, from the start of the transmission, before the Boche pinpointed us. Do you want me to tell you how many operators were lost?' I had been too afraid to ask for the exact number, but I knew it was high. Especially after the Boche began infiltrating the *réseaux* over the past year. 'The SS won't look the other way just because he's a kid.'

'We need a second pianist. Call it succession planning, Blondie.'

'I'm not planning on dying.'

'And I hope you don't. Ever. But you have your other work, and we, the *réseau*, need our own man. Not today, maybe not tomorrow, but think of it this way – if the boy is transmitting while you're hobnobbing with the Krauts, won't it take the heat off you? Give you an alibi, in case, despite the good colonel's attentions, they start looking at you?'

Which might already be the case, after Léonie and I tried to help Felícienne. André had a good point, but I still wasn't comfortable with the idea.

'I'll think about it.'

He nodded, and parked the car. Led the way to the shrubbery my wireless was hidden in. Pulled out the case and a Sten, and led the way from the forest. We crossed a hedge, André waiting patiently while I freed my trousers from the branches and then crouched low to minimise my silhouette.

'How long do you need?' André asked. 'I don't want anyone to see the car and start looking for us. But I'll be close by.'

I understood: having the Renault available meant we could be out of the area before the Radio Detection Vehicle arrived.

'Give me a few minutes to craft and code the message, but not more than ten from the time I start transmitting. I'll keep it short.'

He left the Sten with me. Positioning it within reach, I started to craft the message.

LÉONIES PACKAGE EN ROUTE.

I followed it with information she'd passed on about the Merville battery. Bit my lip and considered whether or not to relay the titbit Eduard had accidentally given me, before deciding that if he hadn't wanted me to know, he wouldn't have mentioned it. My pencil scratched out:

ROMMEL PLANS TO SEE WIFE FOR HER BIRTHDAY.

Chances were that the invasion would come near a full moon to facilitate any air support. The next one was 6 June, but would the troops be ready then? The weather and tides accommodating? I couldn't know, but found myself hoping that Rommel got the chance to see his wife.

I coded the message, assembled the device and, glancing every now and again to make sure André was keeping an eye out for strangers, put on my headphones. Tuned the set to the right frequency, and began to tap.

Once the message was sent, I disassembled the transmitter.

And paused. Something was in the brush, further away from the road than I was.

Part of me wanted to investigate; the other knew the RDV would already be on its way here. I picked up the case and returned to the road, just as André arrived. I put the case in the back seat, threw a windcheater over it and closed the Renault's door behind me. Looked at André and said, 'We have a problem.'

Chapter Thirty-one

'Whoever it was, followed you to get to me,' I concluded.
'Did you see him?' André said. His voice was calm, but his fingers had tightened on the steering wheel.

'No. With the Boche looking for an operator, I didn't think it wise to linger. I figured if they wanted me dead, they would have taken a shot when I had the headphones on and was transmitting.'

I wriggled out of the trousers and smoothed down my skirt. Removed the shirt and threw the discarded clothing into the back seat.

'I'll go back later and see if I can find anything. Cécile, I'm so sorry. I did what I could to lose a tail. Don't know where he picked me up.'

'He was probably waiting to see who would get Pascal's wireless, and followed you until you hid it. After that, all they had to do was wait.'

'I didn't see a tail on the road, or in Ranville. Did you?'

'No, but that doesn't mean that someone else wasn't watching.'

Damn. And if they were, they would know that Cecil was Katrin Hügel.

He pulled the car to the side of the road.

'I'll let you off here. There's a bike in the boot. Make sure Katrin is seen, without a case. I'll hide the set and head back. See what I can find.'

'Hide it well, André. If they can get their hands on it, they may try to tamper with it. And give the Boche enough time to be done with the area before you get close. They're already looking for you.'

André retrieved the bicycle and kissed my cheek. Raised one hand in farewell as I began to pedal.

I cycled for a good twenty minutes before stopping at a café. Three tables were occupied, mostly by old men, and given the proximity to curfew, they probably lived within the town. Ignoring their hostile looks, I encroached within their all-male domain, took a seat and ordered a Pernod. Dug a novel out from the bottom of my bag, and settled in.

I didn't have long to wait. The commotion of the old men by the window was enough of a warning that the Boche had arrived.

It wasn't accompanied by a Radio Detection Vehicle, but this long after the transmission ended, it'd be next to useless. Six men alighted from the transport, gripping assault rifles. They fanned out and began moving from door to door. I was grateful not to have my case, but hoped André had managed to avoid them.

'*Merde*,' an old man muttered just before two soldiers entered the café.

'Your papers!' one soldier demanded.

Conscious of the wig and London's response in my bag, I took a chance. If they thought I was accommodating, maybe they wouldn't look too close. I stood, and smoothed down my trim pencil skirt. Handed them my documents and asked in German, 'What's this all about?'

The soldier straightened, surprised.

'Looking for a Resistance fighter. Have you seen anyone suspicious?'

'Oh.' I raised a hand to my mouth, trying to look frightened. 'No. What does he look like?'

'Average height and of medium build. Somewhere in his twenties. Unsure about hair colour as he often wears a cap. He may be carrying a valise. He may be travelling with another terrorist or may be alone. Have you seen him?'

The soldier repeated the description in French and waited for each of us to shake our heads. He handed back my papers, noting Kühn's signature on the *Ausweis*.

'You may go.'

I took my time gathering my belongings, so that I didn't look in too much of a hurry. Mounted the bicycle and pedalled past the transport, although it wasn't until the town was out of sight that I allowed myself to relax. The soldier's description was vague, and could have fitted half the population – if most of the men in their twenties hadn't been deported to Germany.

Which raised a problem. Whoever had seen me had given the Boche a rough description. The only saving grace was that they were still looking for a man, which meant that there was a chance they hadn't seen Katrin.

So who was he? A plant within the Resistance, yes. But was he the same person who'd betrayed Pascal? And, more importantly, was he acting alone?

With more questions than answers, I glided the few remaining yards to Dom's house and stored André's bicycle in the shed.

Gathering my resolve around myself like a cashmere shawl, I shared the news with Dom and Jérôme.

'André's no green recruit to have been followed so easily,' Dom said, worry furrowing her brow.

'No. That's concerning.' I looked up from the table, where I'd decrypted London's response. 'I don't know how they knew that I'd transmit from there, rather than Caen. And it was me, or rather Cecil, the Boche was looking for. Which means that this person may know André is working with the Resistance, but saw the pianist as the greater threat. Why?'

I tapped the pencil on the paper, staring at London's message. Things had just become even more complicated.

'What's wrong?'

I leant back and closed my eyes, trying to make sense of this.

'Cécile?' Jérôme prompted.

'It would appear that London didn't know the Resistance planned to blow up that railway bridge. Why would Pascal not have told them?'

Chapter Thirty-two

Each vehicle had a slightly different sound, and I was learning to differentiate between them. The little Mercedes that Eduard parked at the kerb almost purred.

'Someone's keen,' Dom murmured, moving to the window. 'Are you going to tell him?'

'That someone was watching me transmit this morning? No. I'd rather he not find out what I'm doing.'

Not because I didn't trust him. He knew I was part of Special Operations; he just didn't know *exactly* what I did for them.

She drew the curtains. 'I don't know if that makes me feel better or not.'

Neither did I. If he knew that I was in danger from the Resistance as well as the Boche, he'd try to get me out of Normandy, whether I agreed to leave or not.

'He has a dog with him,' Dom said.

'Knut?'

I joined her at the window, watching the Alsatian shepherd bound down the walkway ahead of Eduard. I tried not to laugh when Dom cringed at the dog's claws on the front door.

'What that door has gone through,' she said, shaking her head.

Smothering a grin, I let him in, stepping back as the dog danced around my legs, and when that wasn't sufficient, he jumped. His paws hit my shoulders; the force of his leap sent me crashing to the floor.

When Dom and Eduard reached me, I was flat on my back, with six stone of happy dog licking my face.

'He's missed you,' Eduard told me, fighting back a smile.

'With that sort of reaction, you're right,' Dom commented from a safe position around the parlour door. 'It's better that he saw you here first, rather than out in public.'

'My thoughts exactly, Frau Severin,' Eduard said. 'Enough, Knut.'

With one last lick across my face, Knut returned to Eduard's side. My husband helped me to my feet, looking chagrined when I ruffled the fur on the dog's head before greeting him.

Dom held out her hand in a loose fist for the dog to sniff. He obliged, tail wagging, and thrust his snout into her crotch.

'Quite enough of that,' she scolded, red-faced. 'How are you going to fit both Katrin and your dog in that little car, Colonel?'

Eduard appeared to consider that for a moment.

'I suppose Knut could stay with you, Frau Severin?'

Dom cleared her throat. 'I'm sure you'll make it work.'

With her back straight, she returned to the parlour, closing the door firmly behind her.

Eduard managed to wait until we were halfway down the path to his Mercedes before commenting, 'Your friend doesn't like dogs, does she?'

'She likes them fine. Just prefers cats, I think.'

'Then it must be me.'

He allowed the ghost of a smile to emerge, and half-surprised, I asked: 'You like her, don't you?'

'She cares for you, Angel. And she will watch your back. For that alone, I am grateful to her.'

He opened the door, allowing Knut in first. The dog posed in the passenger seat, tongue lolling in a canine smile, moving to the almost non-existent back seat only at Eduard's command. It was the same configuration we'd used many times before, and a fierce love, for this man and his dog, rose to choke me.

'Are you all right?' he asked, starting the motor.

I nodded and placed my hand above his on the gear lever.

As we drove, the problem of the watcher refused to leave my thoughts. I rested my head against the seat, watching Knut enjoy the drive, his face turned into the wind, alternating between gurning and sneezing. Absently, I wiped dog saliva from my cheek and wondered whether the *réseau* had made any progress in finding the person hunting me, and if not, how I could address the problem myself.

'You are quiet,' Eduard observed.

I shook my head. 'Just enjoying the ride.'

His sideways glance told me he didn't believe me.

'What mischief are you planning, Angel?'

There was no point in compounding his fears with mine. I smiled and slid a bit closer to him.

'Why can't I just be quiet?'

His smile was touched with worry. 'It is, quite simply, not your nature.'

'Where are we going?'

'The countryside.' He glanced over at me. 'Have you told them?'

He wasn't asking about the person who waited to betray me. He wanted to know if I'd told the Severins that I really had married him. I wasn't ready for that conversation.

'Told who what?'

Trees flitted past, one field and then another. Eduard Graf kept his eyes on the road, allowing me the time to incriminate myself. It wasn't an unusual technique, and despite knowing his game, I'd usually succumb.

Not this time.

By the time we approached the next town, his brow had lowered.

'Well, she did comment on my blonde hair.' I forced a laugh and a teasing tone. 'She's convinced I'm hiding from a difficult husband.'

The look he gave me told me how flat the joke had fallen.

'Look, if I were hiding from you, you wouldn't find me.' His glare reminded me of the four months he'd searched for me, without any luck. With full knowledge that I was digging myself deeper into a pit, I sighed. It was tiresome protecting the three people I loved best from each other, especially when there was a greater threat. 'As I told you, they will not ask questions.'

A muscle flexed in Eduard's jaw.

'They are willing to risk their lives for you? You, and they, are aware that the penalty for harbouring an Englishman, or woman, is death?'

'They know.' I rubbed my thumb over the back of his hand. 'And they accept the risk.'

'And the other matter?' He shifted his hand away from mine.

'What you're doing here? I'm not sure *I* know. Besides, it's your secret to tell. Not mine.'

'That was not my question, Angel.'

No, it wasn't. And while he knew the answer, he wouldn't wait much longer for me to admit it.

'She knows we were involved. Knows we're likely to be involved again.'

'But not that you truly are my wife,' he finished. His tone made it clear how much he hated that.

Bracing myself, I told him the truth.

'No.'

'Why on earth, Angel . . . ?' he ground out, accelerating into a turn. We were already driving too fast, and I hung on as the Mercedes screamed. 'Why would you allow your friend to think you are my whore instead of my wife?'

'Don't be absurd,' I snapped. 'Slow down, will you? Killing us both won't fix the situation.'

The car slowed marginally, but the muscle jumping at his jaw was a good indication of the level of his fury.

'Don't let your pride get in the way of this, Eduard. You know I'm your wife, and I know I'm your wife. What do you think would be accomplished if the Severins knew? They have known me for *years*. They know I'm English. And they know that I wouldn't, couldn't, marry a Nazi.'

'I'm not a Nazi,' he snapped.

'No, Eduard, but you are a highly decorated German officer who has commanded a tank brigade, was awarded the Knight's Cross – which was pinned on your chest by Rommel himself – worked in the Abwehr, and are now part of the

Desert Fox's general staff.' I enumerated each point on my fingers. 'Have I missed anything?'

He waved that away as if it were inconsequential.

'Do they know who you work for?'

We were now treading on thin ice.

'They know I'm here, with a name they don't recognise. They won't ask questions they don't want to know the answers to. Not as long as I don't bring trouble to their doorstep.'

'You bring trouble with you whether it is your intention or not.'

He didn't ask whether Dom and Jérôme were part of it as well, but he would, and then, I'd have to lie to him. I hated lying to Eduard Graf.

Anger I hadn't realised I carried dissipated and I looked away, pretending to watch the Todt men toiling at the side of the road. Did he really think I didn't understand the consequences of my actions? Of *all* our actions?

'How long have we known each other, Angel?'

I sensed he wasn't changing the subject, and answered.

'Almost one full year.'

His near-perfect profile betrayed little.

'And in that time, have I ever asked you what you do for your country?'

'No more than I've asked you what you're doing for yours.'

Eduard's head dipped in the smallest of nods.

'And yet I ask you, countless times, to be careful. Because I do know what will happen – to you, your friends, and to me – should you get caught.'

My voice was subdued. 'I know.'

'Then understand this – the Allies will invade. I do not know when, and I do not know where, but it is inevitable. When it happens, you must leave. Take your friends with you if you can, but this place . . .' His free hand indicated more than just the Caen area. 'This place will not be safe. Not for any of us.'

He swerved to avoid a pothole, and was silent as he guided the Mercedes in a careful slalom past several more.

'I will ask Lieutenant Neumann to make the arrangements.'

'What arrangements?'

'I want you away from this war, Elisabeth. I want you safe.'

'Nowhere is safe.'

'No, but some places are safer than others.' He took a deep breath and made the suggestion I half-expected, half-dreaded. 'Let me send you back to Lisbon.'

Lisbon, dangerous in its own way, albeit without the immediate threat of imminent, outright war.

It was an enticing dream, but one that remained beyond my grasp.

'You know I can't leave.'

'Can't or won't?'

Eduard accelerated through Hérouvillette, reaching the junction before an approaching convoy of canopied lorries, heading north. The sight of it further deflated my spirits.

'Eduard, let's not spoil the day with an argument.'

'Just remember your promise.'

The muscle in his jaw jumped again, but he put his arm around me and allowed me to rest my head on his shoulder. Knut, not one to be left out, rested his jaw on my ear.

We drove like that past Escoville, and the fields of 'Rommel's asparagus'. Eduard stopped near an inn on the border of the forest, not far from where I'd transmitted less than twenty-four hours ago. As the hound bounded from the vehicle, I looked at the trees, wondering how deep into the Bois we would go; there would be little that would dampen the day more than coming face to face with an armed and opportunistic Maquisard.

Eduard waved to the innkeeper and pulled a hamper and an old army-issue blanket from the boot. We didn't go far, stopping at the first clearing. I spread the blanket on the ground and took off my shoes while Eduard poured two glasses of pommeau.

He touched his glass to mine. '*Prost.* To having my wife to myself. If only for a day.'

'Almost,' I corrected, smiling as Knut chased a butterfly.

Eduard stretched out beside me. A stray breeze toyed with the edges of my scarf, and he placed a kiss in the hollow of my collar. I leant into it – into him.

'It's a strange thing to say, but I'm glad I found you. Glad you're here.'

'I would be happier if you were safe,' he muttered, but pulled me closer. 'And I do not know how to accomplish that.'

It was ridiculous, given the situation – the pending invasion, the fool who wanted to get rid of me. But in that moment, with Eduard's arms around me, I couldn't have felt safer.

'If I hadn't . . . If I hadn't been recalled last January, would you . . . ?'

'Still be here?' I felt him shrug. 'As you say, Angel. I am a soldier – I go where I am ordered. But yes, I think I would be here. Rommel is here.'

I pulled back to watch him. We were at the edge of the minefield, and I wasn't sure how far I could go – how far I wanted to go. My next question was tentative.

'He's the crux, isn't he? To whatever you're doing?'

Eduard considered his answer. 'How can I explain? We are Germans. We love our country, despite what Hitler has done to the Fatherland. But to rid ourselves of him, we have to fight our countrymen. To be patriots, we risk being seen as traitors.'

'How can you be a traitor when you're ridding your country of a despot – a madman?'

'It is not that simple. If everything goes to plan, things will conclude swiftly. A new government, then we sue for peace.'

It was the most candid he'd ever been about the topic, but who else could he talk to? Need overcame reticence, and in that remote copse, I wasn't an English spy; I was simply his wife. I stroked the broad expanse of his back, unsure of how to answer.

'The same as Italy, last summer.'

'Yes. Rommel . . .' Eduard took a deep breath, still looking away from me. 'Rommel opposes an assassination, fearing Hitler will become a martyr. Instead, they will push for his arrest and a trial for war crimes. The risk, my Angel, is that if the Führer remains alive, there will be attempts to free him. If Skorzeny could "liberate" Mussolini from Gran Sasso, what would he do for Hitler? There would be new uprisings. Constant unrest.'

In the wrong ears, his words would result in him – and Rommel – being tortured and strung up with piano wire. I'd long suspected he was involved in a plot to rid Germany of the Nazis, but until he spoke the words aloud, it hadn't seemed real. Now cold shivers swept through me. Every single plot against Hitler had failed. But even if this *coup d'état* succeeded, what then?

'Civil war.' I answered my own question.

'That is the one thing we cannot find our way around. We hope to organise a peace with the Allies that will – as much as possible – allow us to handle such matters without their intervention. Without allowing them to carve up Germany for their own purposes.'

'And that's where you come in?'

'Me?' He seemed surprised. 'I am only a go-between. I am not a field marshal or a general. I do not make the policies or the decisions, but I try to negotiate on their behalf. Where I can. And I fear that without intervention, we will be annihilated.' He shook his head. 'We cannot win this war. The Allies are taking back Africa, Italy . . . Before long, it will be France. Defeat is a certainty, but after how much damage? What more can we afford to lose? The Japanese woke a sleeping dragon when they bombed Pearl Harbor. The Americans have limitless resources – they can fight forever. Their soldiers, their guns, their tanks and their planes will continue long after Germany has become rubble. I cannot let that happen, Angel.' He turned to face me, his beloved visage haggard. 'I cannot allow that to happen. Not while there is breath in my body.'

I caressed his jaw, staring into his eyes. Hated the shadows that lived within them. Hated even more the thought of what would happen should he fail.

'I am sorry, Angel,' he said, raising his hand to cover mine. 'I have been indiscreet. I did not mean to burden you with this.'

He pulled me close to him, comforting me with his strength. If anyone could accomplish this, it was Eduard, but his window of opportunity was closing. The more territory the Allies claimed, the less inclined they would be to deal generously with the enemy. Roosevelt and Churchill had issued a statement calling for Germany's 'unconditional surrender' during the Casablanca conference last year. I understood the statement of purpose – Nazism had to be eradicated. So much death and destruction . . . for what? The megalomania of a nasty Austrian wallpaper-hanger? But unconditional surrender had wide-reaching repercussions that included the creation of the very same conditions that had led to this blasted war.

But as long as there was a chance of success, of surviving this madness and being together in a world without Hitler and his Nazi goons, there was hope.

Chapter Thirty-three

Desperation tinged Eduard's lovemaking. It was as if a clock was winding down.

'Eduard?' I asked. My fingers were tracing patterns on his chest, but my mind was still on the work he was doing, and what could happen if he was unsuccessful. And what could happen even if he *was* successful. 'Do you remember what you said when you proposed to me?'

'What?' He brushed a strand of hair behind my ear. 'That you drink too much, smoke too much and keep bad company? You still do.'

I raised myself on one elbow and placed a finger over his lips.

'That wasn't what I was talking about.' I felt the earth shift and the tables turn. 'You warned me that I was a danger to myself and thus to you, should anything happen to me. Don't you realise, Eduard, that it is the same for me?' My breath stuck in my throat, but he had to know the truth. 'If you die, Eduard . . .'

That thought brought an almost physical pain. His arm tightened and I staved off tears.

'If you die, you will kill me.'

His smile didn't reach his eyes. 'Come, my Angel. It's not like you to be maudlin.'

'I'm not.'

Knut whined, and nudged Eduard. Eduard absently scratched the dog behind his ears and continued.

'You are. You're stronger than you realise, and so, perhaps am I.'

His body went still, hearing the same sounds that had upset Knut, but were still too faint for me. He lunged for the pile of clothes and tossed my blouse to me. It bounced off my breasts and fell to the ground. He shrugged into his trousers and flicked the corner of the blanket over the detritus of the picnic.

'What's wrong?'

'Bombers, Angel!'

I slipped the blouse over my head, already running as I fastened my skirt.

As the planes neared, the Pratt & Whitney engines shook the ground. We raced to the edge of the clearing. Cowered in the brush, while a phalanx of B-17s flew overhead in a tight box formation. Eduard reached around, shielding me with his body.

'They will not waste ammunition by strafing the trees,' he said, ever logical, but pressing my cheek against his bare chest. 'They will be heading for Chartres or Le Mans.'

'Not Paris?'

'I do not think so,' he whispered. 'Stay still.'

I was awe-struck. The planes were indeed flying fortresses. Two massive engines thundered from each wing. They were flying high, but my imagination filled in the details. The bombers' noses were glazed, allowing the gunners to fire forwards. Top gunners, tail gunners, belly gunners, chin and waist emplacements.

'They say the glory is with the fighters, but those . . . Those are terrifying,' I whispered, although it wasn't likely the airmen could hear us over the engines.

'Fighters?' he murmured, trying to distract me.

It didn't work, and I waited for the last bomber to fade from sight before I spoke.

'My younger brothers are pilots. One flies a Spit, the other a Mossie.' I looked down, watched an ant crawl over a twig. 'Or they did. I haven't spoken to either in years. You know that.'

I had tried to look up Will, my youngest brother, when I was training with the Jeds. I 'borrowed' a car and drove to RAF Hunsdon, but Will was already airborne. I sat, half-frozen, in the car all night and a good part of the next day waiting for his return.

Will landed just after lunchtime. He alighted from the Mosquito, his auburn hair as bright as his smile, and clapped his navigator on the shoulder. The boyish grin was gone, as was the last of the baby fat. In the last five years, Will had become a man. And that man's place was with his wing.

I choked down the lump in my throat and, without speaking a word to him, drove back to Milton Hall.

That was last February. The 19th. It wasn't until the papers reported on it that I learnt about 140 Wing's raid on the prison in Amiens. Two hundred and twenty-five prisoners escaped that day. Most were Resistance members, maybe even someone I'd trained with or crossed paths with on my first trip to France.

Eduard was surprised enough to raise his head.

'You told me you have three brothers. The third . . . ?'

I was surprised he remembered; I'd only mentioned them once before.

'I have two full brothers, and one half-brother – George.' Five years older, with an unfathomable dislike for me. 'He was a barrister before the war, and is now with the Inns of Court Regiment. Infantry, of course. Because George Wright has to have both feet planted on the ground.'

He ignored the sarcasm in my voice.

'You're back in touch with them?'

I blinked. If my mother hadn't liked my first husband, she'd be incandescent that I was now married to a German officer.

'What? No. Good heavens, no. Why do you ask?'

'You told me once that you were forced to choose – your first husband or your family – yet you still know what they're doing?'

'Defy my mother and divorce the family,' I muttered, remembering. Shrugged, as if the decision didn't matter, but while the pain no longer burned, it remained a dull ache. 'No. My godfather is the only one to still acknowledge me. But these circles I now run with? Sometimes they intersect, and I hear things.'

Eduard, who hadn't quite been able to hide the twitch at the mention of my godfather, continued.

'Then they have heard of you as well. They know what you are doing?'

'Probably. Matthew would have told them, considering I spent the better part of last year working for him, but I don't see how that would matter.' I flicked my fingers at the ant, watched it scramble under a leaf. 'They won't claim me. You are my family. You and the Severins. Anna and Olivier are more like my siblings than my own brothers.'

He stared off in the direction the bombers had travelled, braced as if he expected to see explosions nearby. When it

220

became clear the targets really were further afield, he stood and helped me to my feet. He kissed the top of my head and his fingers brushed the side of my neck. His smile didn't hide the worry.

'I will repeat to you what I said this morning, my Angel. For that, for their loyalty to you, I am grateful.'

Chapter Thirty-four

Night was falling by the time we arrived back at the Severins' house. The Mercedes slid to a halt and Eduard cut the engine.

Fully aware that if I didn't leave quickly, I wouldn't leave at all, I reached for the door handle. His hand stopped me.

'I'd feel more comfortable if you stayed with me tonight.'

It wasn't the first time he'd asked and, despite every instinct telling me to agree, I stepped out into the cool evening. Folded my arms on the rolled-down window and leant in.

'After only two dates? As much as I'd love to, for now, it's best to maintain Katrin Hügel's morality and keep up appearances.'

He nodded. His words were slow and considered.

'Remember your promise, Angel. Be careful. I worry for you, but it is not just you that your actions impact. Please remember that.' He shook his head. 'You will do what you think is right – you always do. Do you know how to find me, should you need to?'

He gave me the address where he was staying and had me repeat it back to him twice so that I would remember it, but reminded me to be careful. The old women who owned the house must have deliberately given him the first-floor apartment to keep track of his comings and goings.

On the doorstep, I paused and waved, mouthing the words I still had problems saying aloud. Eduard revved the engine and drove from sight.

Inside, the radio trilled the soft sounds of Lucienne Delyle singing *Mon amant de Saint-Jean*. The evening news report was long over, but the volume indicated an interesting conversation happening within. The window was open, but the words were muffled by the blackout curtains.

With a chance that the loud music had hidden the sound of Eduard's Mercedes, I leant forward, listening.

'You see how ... awkward it is for Monsieur Sablonnières, don't you, Madame Severin?'

If the voice was unfamiliar, the tone wasn't. Condescending, patriarchal. Jérôme must not be home; he wouldn't have allowed anyone to talk down to his wife, ever.

'Awkward?'

The tone of Dom's voice told me she didn't need her husband to stand up for her. She had already read him, and I imagined her wide green eyes looking up at the stranger. People unfamiliar with her would be drawn in, eager to trust her, eager to help. Dominique was a human Venus flytrap.

'But of course. Monsieur Beaune, he seeks to consolidate power for himself. To *exclude* Monsieur Sablonnières. He is the only one to know the identity of our cell's wireless operator, when Monsieur Sablonnières is the leader? It is madness. It is a blatant power grab, Madame Severin, I assure you.'

Dom didn't appreciate a pompous man any more than I did, but her voice betrayed none of her feelings.

'I'm sure that's how it looks to you, monsieur, but may I remind you that I am not involved in the *réseau*? You are, of course, welcome to wait for my husband. I can make you a cup of tea – chamomile from my garden, or coffee from last week's drop?'

'No, madame. I do not want tea, or coffee. I want answers!'

He punctuated this with a bang, on a table or the arm of a chair. This sort of theatrics was worthy of a third-rate barrister, and I could hear Dom's heavy sigh.

'Answers that I do not have. The only Cecil I know is Cecil Gardinier, the chemist. As to why Monsieur Sablonnières does not know Cecil's identity, I'm afraid you must ask him yourself. I cannot answer your questions, monsieur.'

A hint of steel entered her voice in the last sentence – my cue to enter – and I clattered through the front door.

'*Guten Abend, bon soir!* Anna? Olivier? Is anyone home?'

She responded, 'In the parlour, Katrin.'

I entered, my eyes going to the man sitting across from Dom. He was utterly nondescript. Maybe thirty or so years old. Medium brown hair, medium brown eyes, medium features, and an exceptional disregard for my friend.

'My guest, Katrin Hügel.'

Dom introduced me, her shuttered green eyes still on the man. He studied me as I studied him, and after a few moments, made longer by awkwardness, he rose.

'Good evening, Madame Severin.'

'Would you like to leave that message with me, monsieur? For my husband?'

'I will give it to him myself,' he said.

He didn't wait for her to rise, to escort him from the house. When the door slammed, I went to the window, peering from the edge of the curtains as he stormed to the street.

'What was that all about?' I asked.

'Can I get you a drink?' she said, adding, 'I could do with one myself.' She splashed Calvados into two glasses, and handed one to me. 'When we arrived here, two men ran the *réseau* – Jacques Mandeville and Alain Sablonnières. Friends, and good organisers who balanced each other.' Her glass of Calvados was cradled between her hands, untouched. 'Sablonnières was a war hawk, his approach supported by the younger men, men without wives and children. Mandeville and his uncle, Marcel Beaune, were more measured, balancing risk against reward. But you know this.'

I nodded, but gestured for her to continue.

'That bridge? That was Sablonnières' doing. It held little benefit really, and the engineers rebuilt it within three days. What was gained?' She shrugged, not expecting an answer. 'But what was lost? Fifteen members of the *réseau* in total, including Mandeville himself. So to balance Sablonnières, Beaune took a more active role. Does he want to?' Another shrug. 'Most likely not. He fought during the Great War, saw the carnage, the needless death there. If he can save lives, French lives, he will do so.'

'And it was this ideology that caused the rift? The reason Beaune – and both Jérôme and André – agreed so easily to keep my identity a secret. Is this because . . . ?'

'Yes and no.' A small sip, followed by a delicate moue. 'For a start, it is good practice. Keep the pianist protected. You'll have seen that elsewhere, maybe?'

It was my turn to shrug. 'The only other *réseau* I worked with was the one with you and Jérôme in Paris. They said the same, too, but you'll remember that I was standing beside you when the Boche arrived.'

She nodded. 'It's one that Beaune and Mandeville supported. Your predecessor, Pascal? Few people knew of his work, and it was a surprise to everyone when he was arrested. Few knew he was involved with the Resistance.'

I hedged a guess. 'So how did it happen?'

She looked away in silent confirmation. 'They say that he gave himself away. Maybe he was lonely, and bragged. Maybe he wanted to impress a girl.'

'You don't believe either story.'

The radio played an old song by Maurice Chevalier. Dom's shoulders moved, almost involuntarily, with the beat as she stared into her drink.

'No. It didn't seem the sort of person Pascal was.'

This was the first time anyone had shared any information about Pascal, and I wasn't about to lose the opportunity.

'What was he like?'

'Careful. Reserved. Private.' A wry smile. 'Perfect traits for a pianist, you'd think.'

'You would,' I echoed. 'What do you think happened?'

'He was betrayed.' She didn't pause to consider her answer. 'But by whom? Why? I do not know. People were betraying each other every day, for money, to right a perceived wrong, and sometimes maybe for no reason at all. I think that the "why" is perhaps less important than the "who".'

The clock in the corner ticked the hour, and she frowned.

Why betray the pianist, a man who kept to himself, when they could have betrayed someone more central? The penny dropped.

'You think it is someone connected to Sablonnières? What would he have to gain?'

'*Lex parsimoniae*,' she said. 'The simplest solution is usually the correct one. As to why? I would guess to wrest control of the *réseau* from his friends Jacques Mandeville and Marcel Beaune.'

'I still have a problem with the railway bridge. If destroying the bridge was Sablonnières' idea, and agreed to by Mandeville, then someone would have instructed Pascal to notify London. London supplies them. Helps to co-ordinate their activities with what's happening further afield. Why cut out Pascal? Why cut off London?'

'And why get rid of Pascal? I don't know. Maybe London was telling them something they didn't want to hear. Or maybe they don't want to take direction from the British, and saw Pascal as London's mouthpiece. I just don't know!'

I swished the last dregs of Calvados around in my glass, surprised to see it almost empty. Something else was bothering me: how the Boche had obtained a rough description of me so quickly after the person in the bushes saw me.

'There's another theory, Dom – what if someone saw Pascal as an asset. And maybe to prove themselves to the enemy, they sacrificed that asset?'

Her shoulders dropped. 'I don't want to believe that.'

'But?'

'But the man who was here when you arrived wanted me to pass on an "urgent" message to Cecil. They know Jérôme is one of the links between Marcel Beaune and the new pianist. I don't know what's in that message, but I am convinced it's a trap.'

Chapter Thirty-five

Of course it was a trap. Just as I wanted to draw my watcher into the open, they wanted to do the same to me. They would watch who Jérôme would pass the message on to, and then we all would be arrested.

Eduard had reminded me that I wasn't alone anymore – that my actions had consequences – but there was a flip side of that coin: *I wasn't* alone *and I had people I trusted who could help.*

I lay in bed, staring at the ceiling and listening to the morning birdsong. One by one, options presented themselves, only to be discarded. Only one made sense. Muffled voices from downstairs confirmed that Dom and Jérôme were already awake, and probably discussing last night's visitor. I dressed quickly and went down the stairs to join them.

Accepting the cup of coffee Dominique was making, I sat down at the table across from Jérôme.

'You heard?'

Pushing an envelope across to me, he nodded.

'Pierre was waiting for me last night.'

I flicked the envelope between my fingers for a second, noting the unsealed flap.

'You steamed it open?' I asked Dom, before answering, 'Of course you did.' I would have done the same. 'And?'

Dom spooned saccharine into her coffee and stirred it. A silent conversation was underway between them, broken only when Jérôme murmured, 'Read it for yourself.'

I skimmed the note, shaking my head.

'It's not coded, in any way. Your man . . . Pierre, was it? Well, Pierre must have been pretty confident to travel through town with this. Pretty confident that he wouldn't be searched.'

'What code would he have, Cécile?' Dom said. 'We try to pass on messages verbally. Less chance of getting caught red-handed if you're searched by the Boche. Besides, why bother coding a message before giving it to someone who has to understand it enough to code it again before transmitting it?'

It was a fair point.

'What else?' Jérôme prompted.

'The information isn't wrong, per se. It's just old. I sent London almost exactly the same message when I first arrived. What's the urgency in repeating the same intelligence to them?'

'Unless . . . ?'

'Oh, for heaven's sake, Jérôme. This is not a final exam, and you are not the schoolmaster. We all know the only reason he gave you this old bit of duff' – I was holding the note, flapping it in front of my friend – 'is to follow you to Cecil.'

I slapped it back on the table, and leant back, crossing my arms.

'And I say we let him.'

Jérôme spent the morning at a makeshift surgery in Colombelles. He had lunch with two men in a restaurant with a view of the Orne in Mondeville. I drew alongside an artist mixing her oil paints along the riverbank.

'And?' I murmured, leaning close to admire Dom's work.

'He's with two local councillors, one more pompous than the other. They're determined to figure out whether Jérôme supports the Boche or the Resistance.' She wrinkled her nose and rubbed it with the back of her paint-dappled hand. 'This is a regular luncheon. I think he enjoys keeping them guessing.'

She hadn't answered my question.

'And?' I prompted.

'I haven't seen Pierre. Nor any of the men he associates with, but that doesn't mean they're not watching.' She dabbed her brush in a glob of green paint. 'And they wouldn't be the only ones.'

'The only ones who . . . ?'

She leant into her brush cup as she murmured, 'There are patrols out, more than usual. I don't know if they're hunting Cecil, but they're hunting someone. Be careful. By the way, Vallentin will not be amused at how quickly you keep "losing" his men.'

I shook my head. 'It's not my fault he couldn't find me in a crowd.' She gave me an arch look. 'All right, so it was. Look, don't worry. I'll allow him to follow me to church tomorrow, and maybe on a tedious shopping trip next week.'

Jérôme finished his luncheon and said goodbye to the fat councillors. I straightened the brown wig, and started after him as he began his rounds. Dom and I had the advantage over Pierre; we alternated watching, knowing where Jérôme came from, and where he would go next.

Once or twice, I would glimpse Pierre, but he disappeared quickly. Unfortunately the patrols became more frequent as we neared the centre of Caen, and it only took a brief pause near the post office to realise why. Two new wanted posters were pinned to the board outside. Unlike the usual ones, these did not describe a local Frenchman, or a suspected English agent. Under an artist's representation of a darkly handsome man, the description provided height, weight, eye colour and rank – Captain – along with a warning that he had been wounded, attempting to assassinate a high-ranking Nazi officer in Frankfurt.

The other image was of a fair-haired woman with intense dark eyes, presumably his wife. Her expression on the sketch alternated between confidence and insecurity, depending on which way I looked at it. The name didn't match the one she'd given the Gestapo, or the one she'd given me, but it did explain why André had referred to the woman Léonie and I rescued as 'the Kellen Girl'. Silke Kellen, and her husband, Tomas.

The posters warned they might be travelling either separately or together. I had sensed a loss in the woman named Felícienne, and hoped that she'd found her husband, and that they'd both survived.

As Jérôme left one patient's home and moved to the next, it was now Dom's turn. I eased out of my disguise and sat at a table outside a nearby café. My coffee hadn't even been delivered before the SS appeared.

'*Papiere!*'

'*Ja*,' I answered, grateful that my appearance now matched my documents, and handed them over. One eyebrow rose at the sight of the double-headed eagle. His colleague took a step back.

'*Spionin?*' he murmured.

Why did the Boche always think that a German woman, moving around independently in France, had to be a spy? What fools.

'What do you think?' I asked, letting every iota of anger I had permeate it.

The second man recognised danger; his left foot raised as if it wanted to retreat. It edged backwards, then thrust forward, close enough that I could almost see the weave on his black trousers. I glared.

'What?'

'What, what?' he barked. 'Give me your papers.'

I could feel the ghost of my grandmother marching her way up my backbone.

'Don't you take that tone with me!' I surprised myself when I stood, irate, thrusting my finger in his chest. 'You want my papers? I gave them to your man. You have a question for me? Fine. Ask it.' Scowling, I moved closer. 'But you *will* ask it with respect.'

'Or what?'

Grand-mère Elisabeth wasn't done with them yet. We raised a single eyebrow, narrowing our eyes until the man with my papers threw them onto the ground and moved to the next table.

'*Or'var,*' I muttered under my breath. When the waitress met my eyes, I raised my voice. 'My coffee?' I reminded her; traces of anger were still laced through my tone. 'And bring me a piece of that plum tart while you're at it!'

'What were you thinking?' Dom hissed at the next handover.

I was less embarrassed to admit that I wasn't thinking, than that I was following my dead grandmother's lead. So

232

I shrugged, hoping my bad mood would prevent further questions.

'It worked, didn't it?'

'They'll remember you, Cécile.'

'As a foul-tempered Alsatian? Probably. Maybe even as a German spy, which could be fun.'

Dom's eyes were flat. 'You're playing a dangerous game, my friend.'

Jérôme had complained about the same thing, but this was perhaps the first time Dominique saw it first-hand. It was dangerous, yes, but I sensed that I was on the right path.

'My grandmother used to say, *si tu ne sais pas où tu vas, tu risques de te perdre*. If you start out without knowing where you're going, then you're probably going to end up somewhere else. Well, I know where I'm going, my friend. Just damned if I know how I'm going to get myself there.'

'Where you're going?' she echoed. 'You're going to get yourself arrested, and you're going to wind up in Fresnes or Amiens – or dead – if you keep this up.'

Dominique rolled her eyes and waved me on to follow Jérôme to the next patient.

The trail of patients brought us closer to the centre of Caen. Jérôme had dinner in a square near the Château de Caen. The name of the site made it sound elegant, but the structure that William the Conqueror had once called home was a fortress, imposingly solid despite the Allied bombs, and for me would now hold the memory of the SS circling Felícienne . . . no. Kellen. Silke Kellen.

Heavy raindrops began to fall, and I sheltered in the doorway of a ruined building.

From Jérôme's agenda, I knew the man sitting across from him was a deacon from a nearby church. The man didn't look like a deacon. He was young-ish. Certainly young for a church officer. And his generous waistline made it clear that he liked his food and drink – an observation borne out by the amount he ordered.

As far as I knew, rationing also applied to Church officials. Would he allow Jérôme to pay the bill, or did he have a comfortable enough income to support his tastes, something not many Frenchmen had, unless they were in the Boche's pockets?

The evening wore on, with an increasing number of patrols. Finally, I spotted Pierre moving away, his face inscrutable.

He wouldn't have seen Jérôme pass on an envelope, because the envelope had been burnt, but what would he relay back to Sablonnières?

They might hunt for my wireless set, but I trusted Jérôme when he said the 'safe hands' who had custody of it wouldn't betray me.

I stepped back quickly, pressing myself flat against a wall to avoid another patrol. Fat raindrops began to pelt down, bouncing off the street. I passed the château, and followed Pierre down the smaller backstreets.

He moved with ease, just another man going about his business. There was nothing furtive in his movements, until he reached the restaurant. He didn't push open the front door; instead he went around to the back. He knocked on the door until a man appeared. It was too dim to make out any features, but the man was broad, maybe about my height.

A few words were passed between them before Pierre stood back. I hid in an alley, holding my breath as Pierre doubled back the way he came, passing within feet of me.

I eased out of the alley, and around to the front. Blackout curtains blocked any customers from view, but there was a good chance that the man inside had ordered Pierre after me, or at least worked with him. I had to know.

Returning around to the back, I took the PPK from my handbag and eased the door open. Moved silently past crates of vegetables and through a deserted kitchen that had stopped serving food.

Light shone from under the door to the restaurant itself. Crouching low, I edged the door open, peering into the room. The tables had been set up for the next service, all empty, save for two men sitting against a wall, a half-empty bottle of Calvados between them. One was Eugene Vallentin, and the other was the chef I had met my first week in France.

I realised the restaurant was Avignon, the same one I had sheltered in all those weeks ago. I didn't know if the grumpy waitress was involved in Pierre's plot, but for sure, the chef was. The question remained: was Sablonnières was calling the shots himself, or was one of his men acting independently on his behalf?

Heavy rain made it difficult to see more than a few feet ahead. I wouldn't make it all the way back to the Severins' house in this weather. The only other option would come with its own challenges, ones I wasn't keen to address, but fate had outmanoeuvred me.

Navigating by instinct, I moved from one district to another until I found the affluent suburb, still relatively intact. I passed homes hidden behind ivy, jasmine, and fences until I reached the two-storey building, covered by heavy wisteria vines.

A drainpipe, almost hidden by the foliage, spouted out water at ankle height. It didn't look secure enough to hold my weight, even if scaling it in this rain was possible. Hoping no one noticed me, I took hold of the vines. I tried to heave myself up; they were slippery and I kept sliding, achieving nothing more than scratched hands. Picking up a couple of pebbles, I lobbed one at a first-floor window, hoping it was Eduard's – and that the sound wasn't lost in the pounding rain.

The pebble hit the wooden frame and bounced into darkness. The second and third ones pinged against a pane, but yielded no response. At the fourth one, the curtains were pushed aside, revealing Eduard's irritated gaze.

I raised one hand in a tentative wave, brushed the rainwater out of my face, and tried to smile.

He rubbed his eyes and stepped away, allowing the curtains to hide him from view.

If he left me out in the downpour, I'd kill him. I was reaching for more gravel when I heard an old woman raise her voice in question.

'I am letting out the dog, madame,' Eduard called back in very bad French.

Moments later, wearing a vest and trousers, he thrust a baulking Knut into the rain. Slipping under his arm, I kissed his jaw and tiptoed up the stairs. His footfalls were heavier as he followed, and he locked the door before crossing his arms over his chest.

'What are you doing here, Angel?'

His voice was low, indicating that he wasn't sure whether to trust his landladies.

'Hoping to seduce my husband.' I brushed a sodden strand of hair from my forehead. 'I didn't take the rain into consideration.'

'Ah. At . . .' He checked his wristwatch. 'At 12:37 a.m., soaking wet, most likely with a PPK tucked into your waistband?'

Levity was the only option.

'The gun is in my handbag, and I was helping a friend out,' I said. 'Do you have a towel?'

'You do know that it is illegal for a Frenchman to carry a weapon, much less a concealed weapon?'

'I'm Alsatian.'

'You are English.' He sighed. 'How long did it take you to break your promise?'

Water pooled at my feet, but I held his gaze until he broke away. I followed him into the bathroom, conscious of the need to keep my voice down.

'I didn't. No unnecessary chances were taken.' I sat on the edge of the bath as he applied the towel to my hair, his hands less than gentle. 'No shots were fired, no bombs detonated, and no one was stabbed.'

I took hold of the towel and tossed it onto the countertop. 'However, if my company offends you, I can return to the Severins', and you can take responsibility for the *unnecessary chance*.'

He draped the wadded towel over a rack and waited for me to continue. I hated it when he did that; I'd been trained to withstand interrogation, but Eduard didn't ask questions. He allowed me to incriminate myself. He remained still, save for a muscle twitching in his jaw.

'You are aware of the patrols?'

'Why do you think I'm here?' I snapped.

Damn. He'd done it again. I tried to backtrack.

'I missed you.'

'Of course you did.' He crossed his hands over his chest and waited.

'I have an *Ausweis*,' I reminded him. 'I'm allowed out after curfew.'

'Yes, and I'm quite certain it's valid. But did the fool who issued it know what you would use it for?'

There was a chance he might see the funny side of the situation. I allowed a small smile.

'God, I hope not.'

His expression remained neutral. 'And if you were stopped by a patrol?'

'I wasn't doing anything wrong, Eduard.' At least not this time. I hoped he heard the honesty in my reply and hazarded a careful question. 'Who are they hunting?'

'A German couple. He was dressed in a Wehrmacht uniform, but none of the witnesses was certain which regiment. He shot . . .' Eduard was about to say the name, but gave me a dark glance and paused. 'An official.'

'Did he kill him?'

'No. Not then, at least. And the shooter and the woman he was travelling with – we assume it is his wife, as they travelled under the same name – disappeared. The SS think they came this way.'

'Did they?'

His expression darkened. 'We know the woman has.'

He knows, I realised. Of course he knew. Lieutenant Neumann had been watching me.

Eduard continued, 'We know she made it to Caen. She was about to be picked up by the SS, but for some misbegotten reason, two German women stepped in to "rescue" her.'

I kept my eyes fixed on his, resisting the urge to clear my throat.

'Misbegotten? Is it misbegotten to save someone's life?'

He sighed. 'It is always a brave thing, albeit a foolish one, when the cost of saving them might be the forfeit of your own life, or the lives of people you care about. The Gestapo are frustrated. They do not hunt you tonight, but how long before they question you, wondering if you knew who she was – what she did?'

'But I didn't!'

'And you think that will stop them from questioning you? Or your friend, Frau Deines?' His deep breath was intended to calm him down; from the look of it, it wasn't working. He strove for a calm tone, but each syllable vibrated with anger. 'They will then look further. To the Severins. To me.' Another deep breath. 'And maybe to others connected to me.'

'Fine. I'll go now, then, shall I?'

He closed the distance between us.

'And risk further peril to yourself?' His hand gripped my arm. 'You will not.'

'Fine. Then I'll stay here.'

My fingers clumsy from cold and anger, I shook off his grip, peeled my shirt off and threw it into a corner. I stepped out of my trousers and, clad in my camisole and knickers, slid between still-warm sheets that smelled of Eduard. Turned my back to him and stared at the wall.

The bed sagged as he lay beside me. He didn't touch me and it was several long minutes before he spoke.

'Angel, I do not know what more I can do.' His deep voice, usually so comforting, now made me feel like an irrational child throwing a tantrum. 'You refuse to keep yourself safe, and will not allow me to do so. Before you arrived, I did not know where you were or who had taken you. I could only hope that, with no request for ransom, with no proof of death, whoever had you was keeping you safe.'

He took a ragged breath, and tears pricked my eyes.

Rolling over, I laid my head over his heart. I had written to tell him I was safe – but never received a reply. Had assumed he was angry, or that my letters hadn't reached him. I'd never fully appreciated before what he'd gone through.

His hand rose to stroke my back. 'Now you appear in the heart of the storm. At first, I worried that your association with me would get you killed, but now, I think you will get yourself shot long before my actions spill over onto you. I could send you away, but you would only return. So I must hope that your friends in London will keep you away from the worst of the fighting. And pray that you survive.'

I didn't have the eloquence to sway him, or the strength to lie to him. I just lay there, in his arms, with his vest soaking up my silent tears.

The rain passed during the night and the day dawned warm and bright. Wrapped in a towel, I stared at my damp clothing lying on the floor, prodding it with my toe.

'There's a skirt and jumper in my closet,' Eduard said from the bed, his voice husky with sleep. He rolled onto his side, his eyes serious as he watched me.

'What are you doing with a woman's skirt in your closet?'

'Lieutenant Neumann acquired the clothes when we saw you here, in case you would need them.'

I stifled a smile. From the moment my relationship with Eduard became serious, his adjutant had extended his scope – and his loyalty – to include me. But it was more than that, more than his thoughtfulness. I genuinely liked Eduard's lieutenant.

'Ah.' I leant over and kissed him. 'I really don't deserve you. Either of you.'

'No, you do not.'

His anger had receded into a wariness. He sat up and stretched. Despite having made love twice during the night, my mouth went dry.

'You'll be going to church with the Severins today. Plan on coming with me next week.'

He walked to the bathroom and closed the door behind him.

I rummaged through his closet, pulling out a chocolate brown pencil skirt that fitted surprisingly well. The jumper was beautiful, dark green with short sleeves and a leaf design around the scooped neck, but I didn't need to try it on to know it wouldn't fit. I tried to stretch it with arms, knees and brute determination. The jumper was equally determined.

'Andreas, old boy,' I sighed, 'if Eduard sees me in this, he'll kill you.'

With my own blouse a sodden wreck, it was either the tight jumper or one of Eduard's shirts. Grateful that he didn't see Andreas's handiwork, I whispered a farewell through the door and, careful to avoid the old women, crept down the stairs.

A rusty bicycle, marginally more disreputable than mine, was discarded on a front lawn. It provided my transportation to my own bicycle, which was miraculously where I'd left it. After that, the ride to the Severins' house passed without incident. Dom opened the door before I'd dismounted.

'We were worried you had been picked up by the SS. Any problems?'

'Too many patrols,' I replied. 'I'm fine. Any news?'

'No. Not yet. Nice jumper, by the way.'

I didn't feel bad for the councillors or the deacon, if that's who Pierre thought Cecil was, but there was no guarantee. No indication that the trap had sprung, and who might lie in its clutches.

Dom pressed my shoulder as I passed her and climbed the stairs. I changed into a silk dress her friends had sewn, but even respectably clad, with white kid gloves hiding the scratches on my hands, I knew nothing would still the gossip that Anna Severin's married schoolfriend was stepping out with an equally married German colonel.

My reputation with the prim church ladies would be in tatters.

Chapter Thirty-six

Snide whispers and sideways looks that slid away when I glared at them.

'You'd think that in a house of God, the biddies would have tempered their cattiness?' I muttered.

'What did you expect?' Dom shrugged, adjusting the tilt of her hat. 'Carrying on with a married man . . . tsk.'

'Stop,' I grumbled. 'Stop it now.'

Leaving the church would be like running a gauntlet, dodging between one curious biddy and the next, each keen to find the tastiest morsel of gossip.

By the time the third woman sidled towards us, I felt my eyes narrow, considering the best way to scare her off. I opened my mouth to speak, but Dom pinched me. Jérôme flanked my other side, escorting me from the church.

'I'd recommend keeping the air of mystique,' Dom suggested when we were far enough from the church. 'There's no need to alienate them.'

'There's also no reason for bad behaviour,' I pointed out.

Jérôme laughed, looking away when Dom glared at him.

'There isn't, but isn't it better to be considered a tart than to be shot as a spy?'

Why the devil did everyone think that not only was I going to get caught, but that it would be by my own carelessness? I raised my chin, pausing to light a cigarette. The reflection in my gold lighter didn't look right. Despite the cross looks of my friends, I stopped, burrowed into my handbag for my compact and lipstick, angling the mirror to show the area behind me.

'We're being followed,' I murmured.

'Who?'

'I don't know the man. About my height, medium weight, around forty. Balding.'

'Not surprising,' Jérôme said. 'They didn't see anything yesterday, so they're still watching.'

'Fantastic.' Under normal circumstances, I would have lost him. Maybe doubled back and asked him a few questions, but for the fact that everyone knew that Katrin Hügel was staying with the Severins, and where the doctor lived. I glanced behind me. 'Not one of Pierre's men. That chap is one of Vallentin's.'

'Aren't you the popular one,' Dom noted. 'And look, your colonel is here, too.'

Eduard's little Mercedes was parked outside, and if he'd come here to give me grief for leaving his rooms without his permission, he was in for a surprise. I'd squared my shoulders, when Dom's soft voice broke through my ire.

'Don't forget your follower.' Louder, she added, 'It looks like you have company. We'll give you your privacy.'

She linked her arm in Jérôme's and entered the house, closing the door firmly behind her.

Eduard emerged from the Mercedes. There was no sign of Knut, which was not a good sign.

'What's happened?' I asked.

'What makes you think something is wrong, Angel?'

'I only saw you a few hours ago.' I stopped to light another cigarette. 'And you would have brought Knut with you if this was a social call.'

He managed a tired smile. 'It's not that type of call either, Angel. Let's go for a walk.'

Aware that Vallentin's man was moving behind, not in sight, but likely not too far from it, I kept my voice low.

'What's happened, Eduard? Something's bothering you. Something that wasn't there this morning. Tell me.'

He looked over my shoulder at the house, and I wanted to point out that the threat came from another direction, but there was no point in causing him further worry.

'If you can,' I added.

'It is nothing you do not already know,' Eduard said, pausing as a field mouse cut in front of us. 'With all the talk of invasion, I've been ordered to inspect the fortifications.'

'Where?'

He hesitated before answering. 'Calais.'

I wasn't sure I believed him, and it was on the tip of my tongue to ask him if he wanted company on the trip. I stifled the urge, knowing that he would decline. Even if 'the inspection' was a ruse.

'How long will you be gone?'

'I should be back on Wednesday.'

A dutiful German wife might not question her man, but as Eduard was quick to point out, I was neither dutiful, nor German.

'There's something you're not telling me.'

He raised one eyebrow. *Quid pro quo.*

'Fine.' I tried not to feel hurt. 'Just be careful. When do you leave?'

'First thing in the morning.'

'Ah.'

I stared down the road as a Radio Detection Vehicle rumbled towards us, its antennae making it look like a large green cockroach. I held myself still, assembling my face into an expression of bland interest as the vehicle came abreast of us. The driver saluted Eduard but didn't slow.

Eduard read my expression as only he could. 'Cat and mouse. I almost think you enjoy it.' He shook his head, as if that would dispel the thought. 'I will be gone for three days, Angel.' He glanced in the general area of Vallentin's man. 'Please endeavour not to get yourself caught and shot by the Gestapo in the interim.'

'That promise you keep reminding me of, Eduard? It works in both directions. Remember that.'

Chapter Thirty-seven

The house started moving earlier than usual. Curious, I padded downstairs in my dressing gown.

'What's happening?'

'Today's the 29th,' Jérôme said, as if that was supposed to mean something to me.

Dom explained. 'With all the talk of invasion, the Civil Defence is ramping up their efforts. They've run a number of practice exercises in the case of a full-on air assault, but today we're running a full-scale rehearsal, across all areas of Civil Defence.'

As medically adept members of the community, of course Dr Severin and his wife were included. They would need to be on hand to treat any wounded. I, on the other hand, wasn't medically trained, and wasn't yet certain what my role would be once the invasion happened, but was confident I could add *something*. Or at least something more productive than trying to figure out how to contain the situation with Pierre and the chef. Or worrying about Eduard.

'Would you like me to come with you? London will want to know how well the Civil Defence can operate, and it's always better if I have first-hand knowledge.'

They exchanged a glance, not buying my beatific smile.

'No one would expect you to go, Cécile,' Jérôme said. 'As far as anyone knows, you're our guest here, and might not be around when the Allies invade.'

'We both know I might well be. And unless London or Léonie directs me to be on my set, I'm sure an extra pair of hands would be welcome.' As we walked to the bus stop, I asked, 'But why Caen, and not the village here?'

Jérôme shook his head, and raised his shoulders.

'I am the doctor here, my surgery is here – but in Caen? They will need all the help they can get. I can do more good there.'

It still amazed me that a demolitions expert could also be a doctor.

We caught the bus into Caen. We walked in silence past the Palais de Justice, towards the abbey. It was the first time I had been near it since the day the Germans had shot Jacques Mandeville and the other Resistance fighters.

Jérôme went to check in with the mayor, while Dom left me in the charge of Sister Anne, an aged battleaxe of a nun.

'What can you do?' she demanded.

Dominique, smothering a smirk, sidled away.

I wasn't about to confess my wireless or weapons skills to the nun, and I cleared my throat.

'Not a lot, I'm afraid.' Her brow lowered and I added, 'But I'm happy to help.'

She turned and trudged a few steps. Looked over her shoulder.

'Are you coming?'

'Oh, yes.'

She was a foot shorter than me, and decades older, with the rough shape of a mostly clean-shaven walrus, and yet, I had to struggle to keep up with her.

'Can you cook?'

'Uhmmm.'

'Fine.' She didn't *quite* roll her eyes. 'How are you with blood?'

'Mine or someone else's?'

It was a valid question, but she whirled, glaring at me.

'Look, madame. We are barely able to cope with the bombs the Allies drop on us, but if they attack by air as part of an invasion, it will be far worse than we've seen. This . . .' She stabbed her finger at the long four-storey building in front of us, perpendicular to the abbey. 'This is the Lycée Malherbe. We are a school, but we expect people to gravitate here, and to the Abbaye aux Hommes, once the air attack begins in earnest.' She pointed to the abbey. 'We are the fourth of the five reception centres for people seeking refuge. We will need to feed them, give them shelter. A safe place to sleep, or as safe as we can make it. We will need to triage and treat their wounds. And' – here she narrowed her eyes – 'to deal with the city's administrative services.'

Triage. What did it take to make that life-or-death decision if it was someone they knew?

'Madame?'

'I can do whatever you need me to do. Just tell me what it is, and if I haven't done it before, have someone explain it to me. They won't need to repeat themselves a second time.'

'Good, we will not have time for that. Come with me.'

Sister Walrus was a sergeant-major at heart, barking orders as the exercise commenced. Like any new recruit, I was convinced I was hopeless at the tasks at hand, until, her jowls raised slightly, 'You are passable, madame. Should your services be required, please make certain you report in to me.'

I wasn't sure what she was thinking when our eyes met, but figured it was the same thing I was: 'And when that time comes, heaven help us all.'

I sneaked away mid-afternoon. Vallentin's man, who had followed us into Caen, was no longer visible. Taking pains to make sure he hadn't been replaced by anyone else, I moved to the safe house to collect my wireless set. Took advantage of the Civil Defence exercises to blend into crowds. Disguised with the wig, I checked into a hotel, paying cash in advance. Set up the wireless, dangling the aerial out the window and transmitted:

In the case of invasion, Caen is prepared with 5 reception centres. Almost 10,000 beds organised, in reception centres or in private homes. Canteens ready, with stores containing beans, pasta and canned goods. Teams of volunteers organised to go to the surrounding villages to resupply Caen with vegetables, meat, milk and other necessities. Resupply drops near the abbey would be welcomed.

I added my observation that, despite Caen's preparations, the consensus from Germans and Frenchmen alike was that when invasion came, it would be further east. On the matter of my watcher, I noted my suspicions about Sablonnières and his men and that, because Jérôme and André's efforts to confirm and neutralise the threat had proven fruitless so far, I would have to take the situation into my own hands.

London would need time to decrypt my message, so I had a few days to resolve the situation before Buck approved the plan, but they had a message for us in return: to liaise with the train unions; that a general strike would be useful to keep the Germans from fully mobilising once the invasion began.

I disassembled the device and slipped out of the hotel through the garden in the rear of the building. Replaced the case in the safe house and, as Katrin Hügel, made my way back to the Lycée Malherbe, slipping past Vallentin's man, who was having a beer at a bistro not far from the abbey.

I'd expected better from Vallentin. Expected him to assign someone to me who would at least be subtle enough for me not to notice.

Unless he had? Unless the man I'd seen – kept seeing – was a decoy.

Chapter Thirty-eight

By Wednesday I still hadn't heard from Eduard which, while not unexpected, was certainly disappointing. I woke early, opting to cycle into Caen rather than taking the bus for my weekly meeting with Léonie. She had arrived first, emerging from the back of a staff car in front of the bistro as I neared. She smoothed the invisible wrinkles from the cornflower blue silk dress. I'd seen her wear the dress once before, but this time she paired it with matching high heels, and a beige hat with dark purple ribbons tilted over one eye.

'Frau Hügel.' Her voice was as friendly as I'd ever heard it. 'We have not seen you for a week. Has Colonel Graf locked you up somewhere?'

'The colonel has been summoned away to inspect the fortifications, but I shall tell him you asked after him.'

'Walk with me, Frau Hügel.' She smiled and waved the driver away. Linking her arm in mine, she was close enough that I could smell the iris, violet and vanilla of her perfume. L'Heure Bleue. I'd heard somewhere that when Jacques Guerlain created it, he wanted it to evoke the 'suspended hour when the night had not found its star'. The complex scent suited her, although I believed she'd already found her star; her purpose. 'Your courtship with your colonel seems to be going well,' she said.

'Courtship?'

'You have another word for it?'

'It'll do. And I'm enjoying his company.' If she was amused by my dry tone, she refrained from showing it. 'Although I haven't seen him for a few days.'

'Yes, well. I'm certain he'll be back in touch when he returns.'

A pair of women pushed their prams towards us, preventing me from asking whether she knew where he was, and what he was doing. They were well dressed, and only when they neared could I detect the frayed hems and worn shoes. They sized us up as well, and briskly crossed to the other side of the street.

In the brief moments we were out of earshot of passers-by, I updated her about the situation in the *réseau*, and the orders from London.

'I don't like the leak within the *réseau*.'

'I can handle it,' I said.

She didn't look convinced, but nodded.

'The rail workers' union will expect a Frenchman to negotiate with – someone within the *réseau*,' she pointed out. 'Is Dominique capable?'

'Yes,' I said. 'I assume you'll still focus on the military intelligence?'

When she didn't reply, I followed her gaze to the far side of the street – not to the women who'd passed us, but to a trio of SS thugs. They were older than the ones who'd accosted Felícienne, well into their forties, with hard faces and dead eyes. I was about to say something to Léonie, but her eyes were focused on one of the thugs. His face had been ravaged by acne and battered by fights. A triangular scar blossomed where his jaw met his neck, and his ear looked as if it had been ripped off.

253

Whoever he was, she knew him, but the moment passed and she pushed through the door of a jeweller's shop.

I had to ask: 'Are you all right?'

'Quite,' she lied.

Her expression was guarded, but standing beside her was like being near a tuning fork. Léonie had been chosen to lead this mission for her cold, rational decision-making while I, who might have more experience, was considered too 'emotional'. Seeing Léonie in the grip of some powerful emotion was not just surprising; for the split second it lasted, it was almost terrifying.

'Frau Deines?' I asked.

'Yes?' Léonie's distracted word was as good as a snapped, *I'm fine.*

She gestured to the shop girl, putting a clear halt to any attempt I would make to probe. If she wasn't inclined to confide in me, then I couldn't force her. I had to trust that Buck hadn't misjudged her, and that whatever it was wouldn't spill into our mission. Nonetheless, this man presented a risk, and I would also need to let London know what I'd seen.

'Never mind.'

Pretending to believe her, I leant over the case, admiring the jeweller's collection. Léonie's finger traced the edge of a sapphire earring, set in antique gold. She held them to her ears and gestured for the girl to wrap them, and a second set as well, this one with diamonds and rubies.

'They will go with your red dress for tomorrow,' she said, neatly changing the subject.

'What's tomorrow?' I asked. 'And what red dress?'

254

'I thought we'd return to the casino. You seemed to have such luck last time.' She told the girl to send the bill to Zeit and handed me the second box. 'Wear them in good health, Frau Hügel.'

For a moment we were alone on the street.

'Who are they?' I asked again.

She sighed and came as close as she could to rolling her eyes.

'I don't know what you're talking about.'

The tone of her voice was light and open, and perhaps I imagined it: the barely discernible undertone that made it clear that the matter was not open for discussion.

We walked for a few minutes in silence.

'Has there been any word about that refugee?'

I didn't need to ask which one she referred to.

'No.'

'They are still looking for her.'

'Yes, I've seen the broadsheets.'

'Be careful, Frau Hügel.' She turned to face me, those blue-violet eyes wide and serious. 'There are people who know who we are, and that we intervened. They await our smallest misstep. It is prudent to be seen with our countrymen. You agree?'

I did, although her tone left me with little other option.

'Of course.'

'Good.' She stood back and signalled for her driver to approach. 'Then I look forward to seeing you at the casino in Ouistreham tomorrow evening.'

'You want me to do what?' Dom's voice was almost pleasant from the other side of her easel. That wasn't a good sign.

'You're the courier, Dom,' I pointed out.

The brush swished around in water. She peered around the canvas, one elegant eyebrow lifted.

'Your idea?'

'London's, Dom, but Léonie agrees.' I changed the record on the gramophone to something livelier, hoping that it would have a positive impact on Dom's mood. 'If we can stop the trains from running during the invasion, we'll prevent – in part – German reinforcements from arriving.'

She didn't look convinced, tapping her finger on the shaft of the brush.

'And when are we supposed to have this arranged by?'

I wandered over, hoping for a glimpse of what she was painting.

'Everything will need to be ready once the invasion is underway.'

She blocked me. 'Which is when, exactly?'

'You know as much as I do. We have to wait for the BBC to start quoting Verlaine, just like everyone else.'

She replaced the brush in the glass, set it on the small shelf below the canvas. She took off her smock and, after a quick glance to confirm that she hadn't splodged paint on her clothes, joined me on the settee.

'Everyone else,' she said. 'Do you think the Germans know?'

It was a good question.

'They know something's happening, that there will be an Allied invasion.'

'I heard that the First US Army Group is ready. That General Patton is in charge of it, and that it's even bigger than Monty's 21st Army Group.'

I'd heard the same from the Germans at Rommel's reception.

'How the devil did you hear that?'

'People talk.' She shrugged. 'And I listen. I'm not the only one who doesn't think it'll be long before it happens.' She picked up the teacup from the table, frowning at the first sip. 'What will you do?'

'When invasion happens?'

'No. Yes.' She sighed. 'I don't know. Yes, I'll work with the rail unions. Most of the people I need to speak to are in Caen, which means I should be able to continue to pass on whatever you and Léonie need me to.'

'Well, that's good. Because there is something else I need.'

Chapter Thirty-nine

On the one foray I had made to Baker Street's archives, I'd found a file that outlined the many attempts that had been made on Hitler's life. I'd thought there were ten, maybe twelve.

There were ten attempts in 1933 alone. Yes, that far back. And all had failed.

I didn't know what number Eduard's plot was, but it had to be time for Hitler's luck to run out. The alternative was too horrible to bear thinking about.

In the week and a half that he was gone, I'd only received a single letter, indicating a delay but not the reason for it. Not that Eduard would be foolish enough to put anything incriminating in writing. He knew as well as I that if the Gestapo could infiltrate the Resistance, they could infiltrate the cabal working to bring down the Führer.

With little to distract me, I passed the days in a frustrating monotony. There had been no sign of Pierre since seeing him enter Avignon, nor any indication that anyone else was following me. I had also not yet been able to confirm how much of it was at Sablonnières' direction, rather than his minions acting independently.

Trips to the casino in Ouistreham added to my finances, but yielded little intelligence, and did less to stave off my anxiety.

In the evenings, we huddled around the radio listening to the BBC, with the gramophone blaring to cloak the sound.

The British 8th Army was moving up the boot, and had taken Frosinone. Great news, but what about France?

The newsreader moved to the coded messages, relaying in a dry, Home Counties accent, the usual nonsense: the tea is bitter, my grandmother wears pink, the dog has fleas. But on Thursday, the first day of June, he droned the opening lines of Paul Verlaine's 'Chanson d'automne':

'*Les sanglots longs / Des violons / De l'automne.*'

At first, I thought I'd imagined it, but the stunned looks on the Severins' faces told me the message was real. We'd waited what felt like a lifetime to hear those words, but when they were spoken, they came as a shock. Dom raised her hands to her mouth, but no sound came out. Jérôme sank into a chair.

'That's it,' I whispered, finding my own breath and repeating the words. '"*The long sobs of autumn violins.*" The alert message.' I groped for their hands, feeling tears streak down my face. 'It's finally come.'

'Invasion,' Jérôme agreed. 'Within a fortnight. Finally. We need to get to Beaune's.'

I wanted to go, more than anything. To be part of the Resistance, part of something bigger than I was, bigger than we all were.

Jérôme picked up his keys. Tossed them into the air, and then caught them.

'Hurry up.'

It didn't make sense to blow Katrin's cover story yet, and there were elements within the *réseau* who still hunted Cecil. But could I miss the opportunity to find out who they were, when they all gathered in one place?

One thing worried me.

'Vallentin's man?'

Dom grinned. 'He has not been outside for the past two nights. For some reason, they appear to be more concerned with what you're doing during daylight hours.'

Daylight. When a pianist transmits. Had Vallentin already connected Cecil to Katrin?

'It's safe?'

'Safe? No. Nothing is safe these days, but would you really want to miss out on this?'

'No. Give me a few minutes, I need to change.'

I ran up the stairs. Instead of raiding Jérôme's wardrobe for a jumper, I reached for a shirt and jacket. Slipped the rubber pads inside my cheeks and darkened my jawline with powder to simulate a five o'clock shadow. With my breasts bound, and my hair hidden under Jérôme's grey felt fedora, I had to admit: the man who looked back from the looking glass wasn't unattractive.

The only flaw was my shoes, which looked a touch feminine. Chances were slim that anyone would notice, but I didn't want to take that chance tonight, and stuffed a handkerchief in the toes of Jérôme's shoes.

With confidence surging through my veins, I swaggered down the steps, hoping I wouldn't trip.

'If anyone asks, I'm someone you met, negotiating with the unions. Go ahead,' I said, nodding. 'I'll meet you there.'

'Do you know where to go?' Dom called. I nodded, already moving.

*

André hadn't collected the bicycle he lent me after our last outing together. It was even less distinctive than mine, and added to the disguise. After confirming that no one was nearby watching the house, I pointed it east and began to cycle and rode to the farm uninterrupted. The Germans would feel it, too – the buzz in the air. Would they know why? And what the devil would they do – could they do – to prevent it from happening?

I turned up the dirt road leading to the Beaune farm, surprised to see it lit up like a Christmas tree. Men clustered in small groups, whispering, and waiting, the air humming with an almost tangible excitement. Dom and Jérôme stood on one side; André and his cousin on the other. Between them, a sea of men and women I didn't know.

That wasn't quite true. I recognised the waitress from Avignon, Sandrine, leaning against a battered lorry, not far from Dom's dressmakers. I'd been right about them; they were part of the Resistance. Perhaps, then, Félicienne was safe?

Silence fell as Marcel Beaune and another man stepped from the house onto the veranda. The second man would be Alain Sablonnières, and I understood they were both here together to present a united front to the *réseau*. I squinted to see his features, but from the distance, with the man cloaked in shadows, it was impossible.

Beaune took his time, filling and lighting his pipe. His first words came on a fragrant cloud of smoke.

'When I was a young man,' he began. His voice, soft as it was, carried through the clearing. '. . . I was privileged to hear the American president, Theodore Roosevelt, address the Sorbonne.'

A titter raced through the crowd. Marcel raised a hand for silence.

'Yes, yes. I was perhaps not the youngest student at the time.'

His smile was self-deprecating, but his eyes were bright.

'He spoke of material gain, and how, for a man or a nation, it is only of value as a foundation. That it must be complemented by the devotion to loftier ideals.'

'*Liberté, Egalité, Fraternité!*' someone cried out.

'Exactly.' Marcel nodded. 'He spoke of individual citizenship. Under the rule of one man or very few men, the quality of the leaders is all-important. If it is high enough, then the nation adds to the sum of world achievement, no matter how low the quality of average citizen – because the average citizen will follow on their path to national greatness.'

'Americans,' someone grumbled beside me. 'What do they know?'

Marcel Beaune smiled, but held out a hand, asking us to give him time to finish.

'We do not have that strong government in our country here. We are ruled by Germany. We have become negligible citizens in our own country. We exist in a situation that we have tolerated for far too long. Do we need the ghost of Monsieur le President Roosevelt to tell us that it is time to be both strong and brave?'

'No!' the crowd answered.

'To fight?'

'No!' the crowd screamed.

'To serve our country as soldiers? Well, I tell you, that time is now!'

'We've fought back!' a man yelled, his identity lost in the crowd.

'We have!' The man beside Beaune pushed forward, his voice loud and angry, his hand raised, fingers folded into a fist. 'It is our time now, my friends! Now it is time to fight, with the flag of righteousness carried before us! Across the channel our allies are poised to invade.'

Everyone knew it, but there was still a communal gasp upon hearing the words. I still couldn't see his face clearly, but there was something about his voice.

He waited for the noise to die down, looking out over the men and women who *were* strong and brave and ready to fight for their country – for de Gaulle, leading the French government from London.

He took another step forward, his face finally illuminated by the moon. I felt the air punched out of me. For weeks I'd thought Sablonnières had set his dogs on me for his own gains, that it wasn't personal – couldn't be personal, because I hadn't met him.

I was partially right. It wasn't personal, but I *had* met him. Pierre hadn't gone to Avignon that night to pass on information to the chef; he had passed it on to *Alain Sablonnières*. The chef *was* Alain Sablonnières.

He ran his hand though greasy hair.

'Invasion,' he said. 'Some say it is an ugly word. *Some* will remind us of when we were invaded five years ago.'

I picked up the inflection, although many others might not have. I glanced left to Beaune, whose demeanour hadn't changed.

'They will bleat about casualties, about death. About another master.' Sablonnières' hand slashed through the air, dismissing the claims. 'It is nonsense!'

Beaune interjected, 'Our friends are now poised to help us win back our freedom!'

Sablonnières' voice was louder. 'We are Frenchmen. *We have no master!*'

The cheers were deafening.

'The general!' One of the men challenged Beaune. 'He said that France does not have friends, only interests!'

Dom bristled, and responded. 'Is it not in France's – and the rest of the world's – *interest* to push the Boche back into Germany?'

When the titters died down, Marcel answered.

'Madame Severin is correct. Every country has its own interests, and right now our interests are aligned. Will they always be? I do not know, and forgive me, I do not care! It is time to shoulder our weapons, to fight for our freedom!'

The crowd went mad, ecstatic to see Marcel Beaune and Alain Sablonnières finally in agreement.

'It will not be an easy road, my friends,' Beaune said. 'More death, more devastation. Some caused by the Germans, others by the Allies. It will be hard to stay the course. I know this. So now, I too will quote the general: "*Soyons fermes, purs et fidèles!*"' The cheer thundered, and Marcel had to raise his voice to be heard. '"At the end of our sorrow, there is the greatest glory of the world – that of the men who did not give in!" It is a sacrifice we make, my friends. One we make for our freedom, for our rights!' He took a deep breath and, with bright eyes, looked around. 'It is one that I made back in '14. And one that I offer again now, gladly, thirty years later.'

An incomprehensible cheer rose. Marcel's voice broke as he continued.

'Join with me, my friends. Join with me and let us liberate France!'

People cheered and screamed, tears streaking down their faces. Sablonnières pushed forward to bask in adulation. Corks began to pop.

A year and a half ago, Winston Churchill had spoken of the end of the beginning. Perhaps we were now at the beginning of the end.

As the crowd began to sing the Marseillaise, a man, standing nearby, looked at me and murmured, his voice grim.

'And may its first casualty not be Normandy.'

Chapter Forty

The last words of the Marseillaise flowed into the Chant des Partisans, the unofficial anthem of the Resistance, and I took my leave. I rode home, feeling intoxicated by more than the pending invasion. Dom had been right; it had been useful watching the crowd – the cliques operating within themselves, rarely mixing. Pierre had been there, never far from his boss.

The chef. The bloody chef was the one causing all these problems. Why? What did he have to gain?

Power.

Having forsaken Beaune's champagne, I poured myself a glass of Calvados once I arrived home, and tried to sift through my thoughts as I waited for my friends.

Invasion was coming, and the *réseau* was baying for blood.

The news hadn't mended the rifts in the *réseau*; it had exposed them. They should be aligning to fight the Germans, but even the leaders jockeyed for position.

If the Germans knew something was happening, they would mobilise. How much information had Sablonnières passed on to them?

The Severins had a telephone, as was expected of the village doctor. I availed myself of it the next morning, asking the operator to connect me to the number Léonie had given me.

She answered the phone on the second ring; her voice gave nothing away as she accepted my invitation to lunch, but not for that day as she already had an engagement – for the next day, Saturday. She named the restaurant, on a bluff overlooking the sea, and rang off before I could protest the distance.

And yet, the next day I managed to arrive ahead of Léonie.

The waiter led me to a table with a view. I ordered a cup of coffee, lit a cigarette and looked out over the sea, imagining what it would look like when landing craft arrived from England. The *Panzerstellen* and other defences would come to life, and the battle for the beachheads would be long and bloody. We hadn't done so well on the Dieppe raid, but a lot had changed in two years.

Léonie arrived half an hour later, immaculately dressed in her usual shades of blue.

'Good afternoon, Frau Hügel,' she said, slipping into the chair across from me. 'I see you put your winnings to good use.' She indicated my new jade and gold earrings.

'I believe in investing in the local economy,' I said, picking up my cup of cold coffee.

I waited for her attention, and then tapped out *Verlaine* in slow Morse against the porcelain. It was the only way I could think of to ask her in public.

She appeared not to notice, and I began to tap again. Her heel dug into mine before I could tap the second dot of the letter V.

'I was sorry to have missed your birthday, my dear,' she said without inflection, and pushed a gaily wrapped parcel across the table.

My birthday, and Katrin's birthday, had come and gone months before, but I slowly peeled back the paper and opened the box.

A beautiful Leica camera sat on top of a book, *Der Fall Wagner* by Friedrich Nietzsche, where, if I remembered correctly, Nietzsche blasted Wagner as a person and as a musician. While Wagner was too heavy for my taste, he was a firm favourite with the Nazis. But then, so was Nietzsche. Today, at least. Still, interesting gifts.

'There cannot be too many photographs of this beautiful countryside,' she said. 'And perhaps of you and your colonel.'

I understood: whatever photographs we took now would likely help the planning efforts in London. I wrapped it back in the paper and stuffed it into my bag.

'Thank you.'

Indicating to the waiter that Zeit would pay the bill, she looped her arm in mine.

'Let us go for a walk, Frau Hügel.'

We wandered above the bluffs. The sky was the colour of a battleship, and as heavy. Wind kicked up our skirts and threw dust into our eyes. I would have the devil's own luck if I got home before it rained, but this was important.

'You heard the message?' I asked.

Léonie took her time responding, her eyes on the sea.

'Yes. Invasion within the next fortnight. How is Dominique getting on with the train unions?'

'She's been carrying messages between the *réseau* and the union bosses, and the rail barons that Beaune deems "friendly". They're willing, but it will be difficult to co-ordinate without letting the Germans know what's afoot.'

'No guarantees,' she said, without inflection.

'No guarantees, especially when we have a window that invasion will happen within, but no fixed date. The good news is that they want to be on the right side when the invasion happens. The men who did not give in. The men who fought for their country.'

She rolled her eyes, and I continued. 'There's another problem – the leak in the *réseau*? I believe Alain Sablonnières may be giving the Germans information.'

'You think, or you know?'

'No proof, but it looks likely. The problem is that he has a large following.'

She uttered a low curse. 'Can you neutralise him?'

I was hoping she'd suggest that; I'd already been planning for it.

'I'll do my best. In the interim, Beaune remains our point person. He'll try to keep Sablonnières away from anything sensitive. What have you heard? Do the Germans know about the invasion?'

'They know something is pending and are still convinced it will begin in Calais.' Léonie's head tilted to the side, violet-blue eyes staring at the darkening sky. 'I am not sure I agree.'

'Why?' That wasn't the more important question. 'When?'

'It is only speculation – a combination of tides and weather. The consensus is July. With General Patton and the First US Army Group at its head.' Those blue eyes turned on me, holding me still. 'What do you think?'

'Rommel is confident enough to visit his wife for her birthday, although the two-week warning suggests otherwise. It could be Patton at its head. I don't know.'

'And your colonel?'

'Is still out inspecting fortifications.'

Her clever eyes narrowed. 'Make sure his absence, or his presence, does not become a distraction, Cécile. The job must come first, you understand?'

I did.

'Good. Relay everything to Baker Street. I will try to find out what I can about Sablonnières. Good work,' she said, and taking a deep breath, added, 'And good luck.'

I arrived home as the skies opened up. But it wasn't the rain that made my blood run cold. A Mercedes was parked outside, larger than Eduard's convertible, with a man slouched in the driver's seat, cap pulled low over his face. *Gestapo!* flashed in my mind. I ducked into a hedge and swiftly ran through my checklist. My wireless was still hidden in Caen, and while I had Léonie's book, at a glance, there was no message within the pages. My sidearm was German, and while my knives were British, I could explain them away. If anyone went through my things, they'd think I was an agent, sure. But a German one.

I hoped.

The man stirred and I glimpsed the hideous scars. There was no one in the back seat, and Andreas Neumann would never leave Eduard.

I raced to the Mercedes, fear pulsing with each step.

Please don't let it be bad news, I prayed. *Not when we're so close . . .*

I slammed my hands on the rolled-down window, and bellowed 'Where is he?', not caring that I woke the lieutenant.

Andreas Neumann jerked upright and straightened his cap.

'Frau G—Hügel.'

'Where is he?' I repeated. 'What's happened? Where's Eduard?'

I grabbed at the lapels of his tunic, yelling the words into his face until he looked as panicked as I felt.

'C-Caen,' he stuttered, trying to free himself. 'We've just returned.'

My fingers loosened and my knees threatened to dump me onto the grass. Neumann stepped from the car, awkwardly, yet held out a hand to steady me.

'Well, why didn't you bloody say that instead of scaring me half to death?' I ignored his hand, and leant against the car. Took a deep breath and glared at him. Eduard's adjutant had never been on the wrong side of my temper, and I was instantly contrite. 'I'm sorry, Lieutenant. I didn't mean to snap at you.'

A spark of amusement flared in his eyes.

'You were worried.' He spoke as if that were an excuse. I answered it as if it were a question.

'Yes. He's all right? He wasn't wounded?'

'No, madame. Just tired. He wanted to refresh himself before . . . It was a long trip, but he hoped you would join him for a late dinner tonight. In Caen.' The beautiful side of his face flushed. 'The weather is poor, and I will drive you, if you are amenable.'

Relief left me exhausted, but still his words made me smile.

'Did he really think I wouldn't be amenable?'

It wasn't fair to tease the quiet and proper Andreas Neumann, but as relief surged through me, I found I couldn't help myself. The unscarred half of his face went a darker shade of red.

'Ah . . .'

271

'Did he ask you to persuade me if I wasn't?' Grinning, I spared the man the pain of answering. 'Consider me amenable. I just need a moment to freshen up. Come inside while you wait.' I held up a hand to still his protests. There was no sign of Jérôme's Peugeot, and I hazarded a guess. 'The Severins aren't at home, and this weather is foul.'

As horrible as his scars were, the other side of his face was beautiful. Once, I'd asked Eduard what he'd been like before them.

'Not much different,' Eduard had said. 'Quiet and efficient. More interested in reading history than going out with the girls who followed after him.'

'Is he in love with someone, then?' I'd asked.

Eduard had smiled. 'He would not tell me if he was.'

I'd thought that strange, then. There was clearly no one Andreas Neumann respected more, but as I got to know him, it was less about respect, and more that Andreas was just incredibly self-contained.

He followed me into the house, trying to hold an umbrella over my head. I left him in the parlour with his dignity and a glass of Jérôme's Calvados, and ran upstairs to get ready.

The dress was a gold silk sheath reminiscent of the one I'd worn on my first date with Eduard, and like that night, my hands trembled. I sat down, placed my head in my hands and willed the shaking to stop. Twisted the sodden mass of my hair at the back of my head into a neat chignon and sighed.

It's because it's almost over.

And the fear for what I suspected he was involved in. And the worry about what was happening within the *réseau*. And the irritation of having Vallentin's men watch me. On that point, I hoped the man had seen me welcome Andreas into the Severins' home. And would see me stepping out with Eduard.

Like the good Alsatian girl that Katrin was.

I made my way down the stairs to the waiting lieutenant. This time I allowed Andreas to hold the umbrella over me as he escorted me to the Mercedes.

'It was a good trip?' I asked.

The words escaped before I could censor them, but to my surprise, Andreas answered.

'Reasonably. Although there is still a lot of work to do.'

Something about his answer triggered a nerve, and I asked, 'Are you involved as well?'

He glanced at me. 'In what, Frau Hügel?'

Andreas was ever-polite but his voice didn't invite me to answer. I did, anyway.

'In what Eduard is doing.'

His bright blue eyes assessed me, and he nodded.

'Yes, of course. I, too, inspect the defences.'

It was the correct answer, but I wasn't certain it was entirely accurate. Or maybe it was. Maybe Andreas, with a keen interest in military history, inspected the defences while Eduard did . . . what?

Maybe I was overcomplicating things. Maybe they were both doing what they said. Only I didn't believe that. Not for a second.

We drove the rest of the way in silence, until Andreas double-parked outside a small restaurant with views of the angry sea, not far from the restaurant where I'd met Léonie at lunchtime.

273

Time was running out. In two weeks . . . No. In twelve days, if not before, the Allies would invade. Normandy would be over-run, caught in the cross-currents between the invaders and . . . the previous invaders. How would it – they – *we* – cope?

In one corner, a waiter fussed over a middle-aged officer and his smartly dressed companion. At the other table, a group of young men had finished dinner and an after-dinner spirit was being poured. Did they know that we were all on borrowed time?

I found Eduard standing under the awning on the almost empty terrace, staring through the rain, past the coastal defences. His back was straight, and his dark hair glistened as he raised a glass to his lips.

Half a head taller than anyone else, he looked more lonely than alone.

A lump rose in my throat as I placed my clutch-bag on an empty table and slipped my arms around his slim waist. He didn't move and I rested my cheek against his back, breathing in his scent.

'I've missed you.'

He turned, drawing me closer and kissing the top of my head. I felt his sigh more than heard it.

'Are you all right, Eduard?'

'Of course.'

He was lying; dark circles shadowed his eyes, and he looked gaunt. When Lieutenant Neumann said Eduard was tired, he wasn't lying, but he wasn't telling the full truth. Eduard was haunted. And I would have done anything, *anything*, to allevi-ate his worries. I bit back a smart remark and held his hand firmly in mine as the maître d' led us to a table. He looked at our linked fingers and smiled.

'I'm not going anywhere, Angel.'

'I won't ask if it was a good trip.' I reached out to trace his jaw. 'But if you want to talk about it, I'll listen.' *Without passing on the information to anyone.* 'I was worried.' *I love you!*

It was hard enough to say the words in private, but it wasn't something Katrin Hügel would say. Not yet.

He pressed a kiss on my palm. 'I know, and I'm sorry. Promise me something, Angel?'

'Anything,' I said, knowing what he wanted. 'As long as you make me the same promise.'

He batted away my answer. 'Let me send you to Estoril.'

Live, and betray my orders, my country. Stay, and remain on borrowed time until a bullet takes one of us. I stared down at my hands, at the ring that was the wrong colour gold.

'No,' I said. 'No. I can't.'

'The house . . .' He cleared his throat. 'The house is as you left it. You will be safe there.'

I couldn't leave any more than he could, and my heart began to pound, as I understood the words he hadn't spoken aloud.

He doesn't expect to survive.

'Eduard, no.'

'Angel.' Exhaustion and worry made his voice sharp, but it was still difficult not to take his tone personally.

'Fine.' My low voice didn't hide my fury. 'You want me to go to Estoril? OK.'

His eyes narrowed, focusing on my face. Looking for the loophole.

'You will?'

'Of course. I'll go, but on your arm. Let me know when you'll be ready to leave.'

He sighed his frustration. 'You know I cannot.'

'And you know that *I* cannot.' I softened my tone. He was only trying to protect me, and I would do the same in his place. 'But I know this – we'll go back. One day, both of us. When this is over. I'll go on your arm, Eduard Graf. Or I won't go at all.'

The sommelier presented a bottle for inspection. Eduard didn't even glance at it, just waved with his free hand.

'Pour it.'

He waited until we were alone again before speaking.

'You're being stubborn. Foolish.'

I was no more stubborn than he was, but with so little time left, I didn't want to argue, so Uncomfortable Silence became the third person at our table until he pushed his glass away.

'I am sorry, Angel. I'm not good company this evening. Finish your meal and I will drive you home.'

Eduard was a lot of things, but petulant wasn't one of them. Whatever had happened over the past few days had scared him.

'Don't be daft, Eduard. You'll drink your wine. You'll feed me. And then the home you'll drive me to will be yours. It seems Katrin Hügel can't resist the colonel's charms. However lacking they may be at the moment.'

'You don't need to do this, Angel.'

'If I had to, I wouldn't, you dolt.' I leant close, and kissed his lips. 'But if you think we're going to spend whatever time we have left apart, think again.'

The shadows were still in his eyes, but his hand squeezed mine.

'Dinner be damned,' I whispered. 'Take me home now, Eduard.'

Chapter Forty-one

In my haste to meet Eduard at the restaurant, I hadn't thought to pack a bag, and Andreas hadn't replaced the skirt and blouse he kept for me at Eduard's apartment. So when, for the first time for five months, I went to church on my husband's arm, I was wearing a water-stained gold cocktail dress and matching jacket that telegraphed to all of Caen where I'd spent the previous night.

To make matters worse, he took me to Saint-Etienne's Abbey, where the four Maquisards had been murdered, and next door to the Lycée Malherbe where I'd volunteered to help as part of the Civil Defence.

With a proprietary hand at the small of my back, Eduard escorted me down the vaulted corridor of the nave towards the rose-windowed apse and the monument to William the Conqueror.

Léonie sat two pews ahead and across the aisle from us, wearing a smart suit and a bland smile on her Dresden-doll face. She hid a lot behind that, but her patience had to be waning. It couldn't be long before she buried a knife in the fat colonel's belly.

I inched closer to Eduard. I had missed him. The feel of him beside me, the way he breathed, the smell of his cologne. His hand closed over mine, warm and reassuring. With my free hand I traced the edges of the gold band on his fourth finger.

He leant close, his breath warm against my cheek.

'I will replace yours. And cement it on.'

I laughed, but kept my voice low. A husky edge crept in.

'I don't need a ring to remind me I'm yours.' I grinned and moved closer.

'Shall we give them something to talk about?'

Since everyone thought I was already his mistress, there was no point in not having fun with it.

'Hush, Angel. We're in church.'

An old woman to our left gave us a filthy look. Eduard cleared his throat and stared at her until she ducked her head.

Service over, we went outside, and immediately Lorenz and his grey-green clique angled towards us. Even though Lorenz might be lazy, his men were not. The way they dressed, the way they moved, was designed to intimidate.

They passed close enough by that I could smell Vallentin's expensive cologne. Remembering that small boy, dead in the street, and the man he'd sent to watch me, I plastered a polite smile on my face and inclined my head in greeting, hoping they couldn't tell that I was holding my breath. When they left the churchyard, I exhaled with a small whoosh.

'What are your plans for the day?'

'I was hoping that you could drive me to Roland Garros for the tennis?'

When he shook his head, bemused, I winked at him.

'Jokes aside, Olivier will be seeing patients nearby, and Anna will be with him. Perhaps ...' I held my breath for a second time. 'Perhaps you'd like to join us for a stroll later?'

He took a deep breath to answer, which came out as a soft *whoof*. I followed his eyes and my heart fell as Andreas

Neumann approached, accompanied by Knut on the lead. The lieutenant's face was impassive, but there was something apologetic in his mien.

'I would, yes,' Eduard said. 'But I fear that may have to wait for another time.'

Chapter Forty-two

I spent Monday at home with the Severins, planning my next move, only leaving the house when we heard the aircraft engines.

'A little warning would be nice,' I panted, sprinting after them into the line of trees.

Dom and Jérôme ignored me, knowing I didn't require an answer; the house was too far from the town to hear the sirens. The bombers came from the east, heading into the setting sun, towards Caen.

Just because the house wasn't a good target, didn't mean a bomb wouldn't be dropped on it.

We crouched low, ignoring the drizzle, watching the underside of one plane after another. When they all seemed to have passed, we returned to the house.

Dom and I quickly changed into darker clothes, with Dom muttering, 'Another message to another union representative. Have they agreed? Yes, in principle. Do they want details? Yes, of course. Only we don't have those details, do we?'

'You couldn't talk to them during the day?'

She rolled her eyes. 'They are *uncomfortable* discussing these tactics in their office, so I am to meet them, at their convenience, of course.' She glanced at the door and lowered her voice so Jérôme wouldn't hear. 'Which means that often I need to explain that I myself am not part of the bargain. What about you? Don't you usually transmit during the day?'

'Yep. Easier to see what I'm doing, and that's when the operators at Norgeby House are listening. But not everyone knows that.'

'So, tonight?'

'Tonight?' I patted the camera Léonie had given me, slung on its strap diagonally across my chest, over my shoulder bag. 'I'm just going out to take photographs.'

She glanced at the window. 'In this weather?'

'It's atmospheric. And I have the *Ausweis*, if anyone wants to stop me.'

Which would help, considering the PPK was in my bag, and the sgian dubh on my thigh, accessible via a slit in my trouser pocket.

'Is that sensible? Going out with no one to protect your back?'

My skirt, instead of being bunched around my waist to bulk me out, was neatly folded in my shoulder bag with the rubber cheek pads and knitted cap, in case I needed different disguises. The ensemble was completed with Jérôme's water-proof jacket.

'I'm safe enough. Are you?'

She studied me for a few seconds, then crossed to her dresser and pulled a Fairbairn Sykes knife from between two jumpers, and slipped the sheathed blade into her garter.

'Don't say I haven't taught you anything,' I joked.

She smoothed the skirt of her chocolate-brown dress over the knife.

'Do I want to know what you're up to?'

'Probably not.'

'And Léonie knows what you're planning?'

'She does. The *réseau* has had enough time to sort out Sablonnières. For whatever reason, they haven't. So tonight, it's my turn.' I held out a hand. 'I can't keep looking over my shoulder for his men as well as the Boche. It's that simple.'

She didn't pause. 'Do you need help?'

'No, but thank you. You have your own job to do.'

The rain had tapered off by the time we separated at Hérouville. Dom raised her hand and turned north. I backtracked through the streets until I found the house. Sablonnières' restaurant, Avignon, was in Caen, but his home was nearby. According to André, he wasn't expected at any *réseau* meeting this evening, so unless he was having another meeting with Eugene Vallentin, there was a good chance he would be home.

I hid the bicycle and the camera in the neighbour's bushes, and edged closer. The stone house was dark. The windows were open to let in the cooler evening air; any light from within was hidden by heavy blackout curtains. I drew my blade and circled to the back. Twitched a curtain to find the room behind it dark. Eased myself over the sill, and shimmied as far to the right as I could to avoid the desk.

I took off my shoes to avoid the wet leather squelching on the wooden floor and eased out of Sablonnières' office, and moved from one room to the next. The house was simple, and although the kitchen was well stocked, it was very much a bachelor's home. With the resident bachelor away.

That was fine – I could wait. I grabbed a tea towel and retraced my steps to his office, making certain I had left no puddles to alert him to my presence.

I flicked on the desk lamp. The papers in plain sight were mostly receipts. I replaced each one exactly as I'd found it – in case they were positioned in such a way to let Alain Sablonnières know if anyone had invaded his space.

The drawers revealed more receipts and ledgers from the restaurant. The cabinet beside the desk opened to reveal a safe. I rolled a piece of paper into a makeshift stethoscope and went to work.

The mechanism wasn't sophisticated, and the heavy metal door opened.

Cash. Piles of cash. Far more than the small restaurant could have yielded. The cash was separated into francs and Reichmarks. Were the francs the same ones I had brought with me? Or was it from the Boche, payment for delivering the *réseau* to the Nazis? This was a small town. What did he think he could buy without neighbours wondering about his bounty?

I closed the safe, and waited.

Until the air raid sirens sounded. It was nearing curfew, and if Alain Sablonnières was going home, he would have already done so. He must have had another place to go to.

And I would find it.

Swearing under my breath, I waited for a crowd of people to pass before rescuing the bicycle and camera. Following them towards the church, I clattered down the stairs.

The crypt was already crowded, and in the corner, a baby began to cry. The last person fastened the door and lit a lantern, its feeble glow oddly comforting. I hid in the shadows, my eyes fastened on the flame, while avoiding its revealing light.

Moments later, someone banged against the door. Pounded harder until they were let in. Filthy, bedraggled and sporting a torn blouse, Dom stormed down the stairs. Her eyes passed over me, as if I were a stranger, and she sat leaning against a tomb, opposite me.

'Madame Severin!' someone nearby gasped.

'I fell off my bicycle,' she said.

It was plausible enough, for anyone who didn't know that Dom rode a bicycle with the easy confidence of someone born in the Netherlands. I would have to wait until the raid was finished before learning how well her conversation with the union representative had gone.

The familiar sound of Rolls-Royce Merlin engines was quickly overshadowed by the explosion. The earth rocked, and Dom fell forward. Dust fell from the rafters, making me cough. Mothers wrapped their bodies around their children, while someone commented on the increasing frequency of the bombings. We moved closer to the walls, making ourselves as small as we could, even though we knew – on some level, at least – that we were just as much of a target as if we had stretched out.

My wristwatch would say it was only minutes, but it felt like hours. Blasts shook us. Glass shattered. Candles extinguished. Someone prayed aloud and others sang.

The crypt wasn't deep enough to protect us. Maybe the others knew it, too. So I joined them, mumbling the words to the hymn because it was expected, rather than for any hope of salvation.

A deep bass sang a forceful solo, tentative voices weaving in and out, until the all-clear sounded. It was pitch-black in the crypt, but we moved as one towards the stairs. Dom paused at the base of the nave, turned to the altar and genuflected. The cuff of her blouse was spotted with blood, yet she appeared unhurt.

Once outside, we retrieved our bicycles and rendezvoused at the edge of the town.

'What happened?' I asked as we cleared the village. 'The union man?'

'No. A pair of youths.'

It was the blasé way she said it that told me that those youths would wake up with equal amounts of pain and embarrassment.

'And your evening? Was it successful?'

'Not entirely, no.'

Although I did now understand part of the incentive Sablonnières had to betray the *réseau*, the man himself was still at large. I couldn't allow that situation to continue. If I couldn't find him today, I'd have to find another way.

The explosion cut through the night. The earth protested, and we wobbled on our bicycles. A second blast wave threw me into the hedge. Brambles scratched at my face as I grabbed a branch for support.

'Jesus Christ! What the hell just happened?' Behind us, a building was in flames, but the sky was clear. 'The Maquis?'

'Nothing I know about.'

She pulled a pebble from her palm and threw it to the side.

Nor was it something I knew about. Another unsanctioned demolition. Hopefully they'd at least gone after a decent target.

Someone was screaming, and people began to flood onto the streets, trying to save the building. Before long, the gendarmes would show up.

'We have to go. Now.' I pulled Dom after me.

'We can try to fit in, pretend to help . . .'

'You looked like you'd been brawling even before the bombing raid,' I reminded her.

I removed a twig from her hair and threw it into the bushes.

'*Merde*,' she muttered. 'I am tired of all this blood.'

She frowned at the almost-full moon as the sirens blared. The engines wouldn't be far away.

I shrugged out of my jumper. 'Put this on. You're about to fall out of your blouse. We don't want anyone to get the wrong idea.'

She shook her head but slipped it on. 'With the company you keep?' She held up one hand as it poked through the sleeve. 'Don't worry, Cécile. As long as your German does not come after me or mine, he's safe from me. You have my word, you know that.'

I hated trusting his safety to anyone, even Dom, but I had no choice but to believe her, as the Boche arrived.

Chapter Forty-three

The almost-full moon was all but obscured, and the wind was picking up as the SS and gendarmes moved along the street in twos and threes. Officers smoked cigarettes and observed from their position halfway down. Whoever had detonated the explosives was long gone, but the Boche were looking for information – and retribution. There was always retribution, and it wasn't safe to linger.

Firmly grasping Dom's arm, I pulled her into the shadows and down an alley. At the next street, Dom let out a small gasp as a youth was pulled from a house. He couldn't have been more than fourteen, more a child than a man.

'Oh no,' she murmured. 'Philippe . . .'

The boy's mother tried to grab at him and was pushed to the ground. She ran after the gendarmes, her protests turning to pleas, until they were too far away. Another gendarme restrained her, holding her back. Her legs gave out, and she sank to the ground, her face buried in her hands.

It was a replay of Vallentin's men killing the Jewish boy and the woman who had sheltered him. Was this boy involved? Maybe. He was not much younger than Guillaume – but that didn't matter. The SS would have their scapegoat, whether it was the right man or not, and I didn't want to be caught in their net.

'Dom, we *need* to go.' I pulled her forward and wondered aloud, 'What will happen when they find your house empty?'

'They'll assume Jérôme and I are out seeing patients, or that I'm en route to gendarme headquarters.' Her voice went from wry to sour. 'Of course, they'll assume you're in your colonel's bed.'

Assuming he's returned from this last trip.

She seemed to consider our options and veered off, leading the way with a feline grace. We backtracked along the way we'd come, flitting down alleys and always just shy of the moonlight. Black cats on a moon that wasn't quite full, we passed by barracks, protected by guards and barbed wire, and through a little gate into ornate gardens that I recognised.

'Another church?' I struggled not to sigh. 'You think now's the time to pray?'

'Can you think of a better time?'

She pushed through the heavy wooden doors and genuflected, this time in a way that signalled habit rather than piety.

'Churches don't provide sanctuary the way they did a few hundred years ago.'

I followed her into the nave, empty but for the old priest on his knees at the altar. When he saw Dominique, he rose to his feet.

'It doesn't need to.'

She met the priest halfway.

'You received the message, then.' He closed his eyes and uttered a small prayer.

We exchanged a glance. Between the air raid and explosion, we hadn't had either time or opportunity to receive anything.

'The message, Father?'

He motioned us towards an alcove.

'The broadcast, maybe a quarter of an hour ago.'

My surprise that the priest listened to the BBC, banned as it was, was supplanted by shock as he recited:

'*Blessent mon cœur / D'une langueur / Monotone.*'

They were the third and fourth lines of Verlaine's poem – the Action Message. The invasion would start within the next forty-eight hours. I couldn't breathe, in a way that had nothing to do with the yards of linen binding my breasts.

'Is that not why you're here?'

The priest looked from Dom to me. Her face remained cool, but emotion overwhelmed me and I sagged on to the nearest pew. This was what we'd been waiting for. Since I'd returned to England in January. Since joining Special Operations. Since the bloody Boche had rolled over France back in 1940, and my first husband, Philip de Mornay, had buggered off to join the Royal Navy. And since I'd received a telegram, not long after that day, informing me of his death when his ship was torpedoed off the coast of Greenland.

My eyes met Dom's. There had been no orders given for our recall, and now the die was cast. We would fight. Here. Together.

'Of course it is.' Dom could have been answering me as well as the priest. Her gaze was as steady as her hands; she had accepted this mission. 'Please, lead the way, Father.'

The priest pushed aside a tapestry to reveal a door set into the stone. He reached into the neckline of his cassock and pulled out a piece of twine. At the end of it was a small key that unlocked the door. He held it open while Dom rummaged in the small closet behind it. She emerged a few moments later, wearing a clean jumper over her dress and a scarf at her throat. A rucksack was slung over one shoulder, and she held a long leather case, the sort architects use for their drawings. She tossed my jumper back to me.

The priest put a hand on her shoulder, his eyes watering.

'Stay here as long as you need to, my children.'

Dom opened the case, inspecting its contents.

I stared at her. 'You hid armaments in a church?'

'*Si vis pacem . . .*' she murmured.

'*Para bellum.*' I completed the quotation. 'He who seeks peace should prepare for war. I get that, but *here*?'

There was a holdall as well as the case, containing ammunition and a pair of Zeiss binoculars. Sniper's tools. For a woman who, as André said, could shoot the balls off a mouse.

'It was only a matter of time, Cécile,' she said. 'Before we were called upon to deliver violence to the enemy. I wanted it to be on my terms, with equipment I trust.'

I looked down and saw something that looked like a bicycle pump. I hadn't had the chance to handle one, but I knew it was the ultimate assassin's gun – utterly silent, and without markings that would indicate who had manufactured it, or where.

'How the devil did you get your hands on a Welrod?'

I picked it up and turned it around in my hand. It was light – lighter than I expected. I opened it up and checked the rubber wipe – the gun hadn't been fired before.

'We received exploding rats from London as well. Which we're supposed to throw into the coal, to blow up a train engine. Would you like one?'

Her hand hovered over a box, but one eyebrow was raised, as if she had an explosive rat in the bag.

'No.' I stared over my shoulder. The door was closed, but it was the strip of buildings on the other side that held the potential. 'But I'll take the Welrod. Dom, the barracks we passed . . . Those are the Todt "volunteers", right?'

She paused, repacking a rifle into the case.

'Yes – why?' She slung the holdall over her shoulder. 'Where are you going?'

'To deliver the possibility of a bit more violence to the enemy.' I tucked the assassin's gun into my waistband, and slipped back into the discarded jumper, hiding the gun under the heavy knit. 'And maybe our way out. If I'm not back in half an hour, do whatever you need to.'

Chapter Forty-four

The barbed wire barricade was designed to keep people in, not out. A guard patrolled past the gate, moving to the end of a small parade ground that was likely used for roll call and the public displays of brutality that the Nazis loved.

He was young, part of the 716th. A cigarette hung from the corner of his mouth as he ambled back and forth in front of the gate. As he turned, he struck the sort of pose that a movie star might have done. I looked around to see who he was trying to impress, but the courtyard was empty, and the only people on the street were gendarmes. The hordes of adoring women cheered in his head. With his attention away from me, I slipped past.

The barracks weren't big, but they were unfamiliar. I had little time, and there was no point in picking the lock on a door if the room was empty. I eased through the shadows, peering through windows until I found what I was looking for.

The door was locked from the outside. I reached under my cap and removed a hairpin. I slowly worked with the lock, holding my breath when another guard passed close by. I eased the door open and slipped inside, leaving the door slightly ajar behind me.

Inside were row after row of double-decker bunks where men slept. As I went from bunk to bunk, some began to wake, sitting up. A few got to their feet, staring at me with a defiant fury.

'The Russian,' I said.

I didn't have his name – wasn't even certain he was Russian – but it was the best I could do. I mimed his general size and shape, hoping they would know who I meant.

Whispers raced down the wings of the barracks, chased quickly by silence; more moved towards me. The growing crowd began to part and a shadow emerged. As he moved closer, moonlight from outside illuminated his face. He stopped six feet from me and remained silent, watching. He held out both arms, as if expecting to be bound.

I shook my head and drew him to the side. There was no way to hide from the rest of the men, but I didn't want to be seen by a passing guard. The Russian stared at me through the dark, assessing me. He gestured the men back to their bunks.

'What do you want?' His voice was rough, his German heavily accented.

I transferred my PPK to my left hand, and extracted the Welrod from my waistband. Offered it to him butt first.

'What is this?'

'It's your ticket out of here.'

It was an uncomplicated gun – it didn't take long to show him how to use it.

'Why?' he asked.

In the dark, dressed as a man with the rubber strips in my cheek, he wouldn't recognise me, and that was fine; it was best that he didn't.

'Let's just say, I owe you.'

'Not good enough. Why?'

293

'I owe you,' I repeated. 'And you deserve your freedom. Maybe you'll fight when the time comes. Maybe you'll decide to go home, wherever that is. That choice is yours, as it should be.'

He seemed to consider that for a moment.

'When?'

Jolly good question, and there was no answer I could give him.

'I don't know. Soon, I think. There will be a commotion. Take advantage of it. This gun will fire one bullet, but it will be completely silent. Use it wisely. Get out of here. I'd suggest you use it to get into an armoury, there must be one in the compound, but that's up to you.'

We spoke softly, but I knew these men, these 'volunteers' who were treated as slaves, listened from their bunks. Maybe tomorrow one of them would inform on the Russian, on me. It was a foolish chance to take, but it was the right one.

'Friend?' he said, and waited for me to turn back to him. 'Thank you.'

I nodded. 'If you caused a bit of mayhem on your way out, I wouldn't fault you.' I raised a hand in farewell. 'Good luck.'

Chapter Forty-five

It was almost midnight when I re-entered the church. The priest was waiting, his silent finger indicating that Dom had climbed the bell tower.

A bell tower. Dom had planned for this, but I held on to the hope that we would be gone before dawn, without a shot fired, if for no reason other than getting out of this place, surrounded as we were by the enemy, would be a nightmare. Slowly, I began climbing the stairs.

The space at the top was cool and fresh. Gusts of wind buffeted the bell hanging from the ceiling, but not enough to cause it to toll. On each wall was a large arch. From this height, there should have been a clear view of the town, but with the rain, I could just about see the blazes engulfing the bombed building.

'Careful,' Dom said. 'I don't want anyone to know we're here.'

I sat on the floor beside the arch, flinching as a gust of wind sprayed rain into the room. Absently I wiped it off with my sleeve, and peered around the edge, careful to minimise my silhouette.

'Do you know what blew up?'

'The communications centre,' Dom said. 'I don't know who co-ordinated that attack, but at least they chose a target that will hinder the Germans' response.'

My eyes were on the barracks when I muttered, 'Assuming they don't fix it before the invasion.'

More people flooded the streets in twos and threes. I reached for the pair of Zeiss binoculars that Dom had laid out, and focused them on the street. Some of the 'men' were women, and they were all cutting down the telephone poles, further challenging German communications. It was working; the Maquis was now working as a single entity, doing what it had to do to keep the Germans at a disadvantage.

Dom's bell tower was the perfect vantage point.

'Jolly good planning.' I waggled the binoculars. 'But aren't we a bit early, and a bit high up for the party? The wind is picking up. The weather is expected to be gale force. I don't care what your priest heard – I don't see how any invasion can be launched with this sort of weather.'

'I don't know, Cécile. Maybe you're right, and we'll be out of here within the hour.'

'Good.' I sat down and stretched my legs out in front of me. 'Your priest condones this?'

'What's to condone? We're only hiding here while there's so much activity out on the street.' Her innocent tone didn't fool me. 'And despite your *Ausweis*, you're armed and I'm armed. I'd rather not answer awkward questions.'

'Why all this?'

She pulled a rag out of the bag.

'Why all what? If we're up here, we may as well make sure everything is clean. It's been here for a while.'

It was plausible, but not the truth; at least not the full truth.

'Dom.'

'Look, it's nothing more than a bad feeling, but something is telling me not to be out on the street right now, and I've learnt to listen to that instinct.'

That, I believed.

'And the priest? He knows what you're doing?'

'Cleaning my weapons?' She shrugged. 'He's aware of what might be required. Will he sanction a shot fired on church ground? Probably not, but the Germans haven't asked him for permission either.'

The sin of omission. Not one I was inclined to quibble over. The Hail Marys would be on her head, not mine.

Dom unpacked the case, used a rag to clean the equipment.

'One day you'll have to tell me how you got your hands on half this kit.'

She smiled, more relaxed than she had any right to be.

'I'll tell you now. Léonie gave me the binoculars, and the rest of it came in one drop or another from London. Here.'

She handed me a lump of wax and pointed at the bell and her wrist. I stuffed the wax in my ears and the world became muffled. I scooted to a corner and pressed myself flat against the floor, just as the bell swung, narrowly missing me. Vibrations rattled every bone in my body, and by the third *bong*, I dropped the binoculars and pressed my hands over my ears, willing it to stop.

Twelve bells. Twelve fucking bells.

The worst had passed, but I'd need to remember to watch the time. Removing the wax, I crawled back to the arch and peered over its edge. The streets were still crawling with people, the gendarmes clashing with the Maquisards.

A break in the heavy clouds allowed a brief glimpse of the moon. Beneath it a dark shadow crossed, and then a second and a third, coasting above the Orne. I grabbed the Leica and pressed the shutter before I realised what I'd seen: in total, six bombers had flown west along the coastline, but now turned north, towards England.

That made no sense; there were no bombs I could see. What had happened?

I put the camera down, hoping it wouldn't be too dark. Reached again for the binoculars, scanning west to east. Rubbed my eyes, unsure if my eyes were telling me what I wanted to see rather than what was there. Looked again, but my eyes weren't deceiving me. The shadows moved in a sweeping circle towards the ground.

'Oh shit.'

'What?'

'I ... ah ... I think there might be another little diversion planned for the evening.'

She put down the oiled cloth and the rifle.

'What *are* you wittering on about?'

'Halifax bombers. Gliders. Six of them. Separated.' I pointed.

'You're not making sense.' She held out her hand for the binoculars.

'The bombers were towing gliders. Let them loose by the bridges, I think. Six of them. I don't know how many men are in each glider. It's not enough to take Normandy, but maybe it's enough to keep the Boche looking here.' My heart began to pound. 'Forty-eight hours, my—'

'It's only six, Cécile, and don't forget the weather. It's probably a distraction, while they focus on Calais, or maybe Brittany. I don't know.'

'It's the start of it, Dom. I feel it.' I pointed again. 'Look there – to the east. Along the river.'

Her reserve crumbled. The binoculars hid her eyes, but her smile was wide and her voice cracked when she spoke.

'The bridges? Of course! Well, if it's a decoy, it's a jolly good one. And you know what, Cécile? I don't care. Let Calais be the first to be freed. You're right. It's starting. It really is starting!'

'They're wired, aren't they? The bridges?'

'Not by us. And the Boche won't blow them too quickly. Not until they're sure of what's happening.' She grinned. 'There would be hell to pay for the man who destroyed the bridges for a handful of paratroopers.'

'Good. Good! Let's go.'

But I didn't move, just pressed the binoculars to my face and trained them on the Orne and the Caen Canal.

The first glider came in fast, a huge parachute billowing behind it before its nose drove into the field. Two more landed beside it. Gunfire flashed on the canal bridge, and a larger explosion. I pointed at the tremendous ball of fire.

'The gun emplacement on the bridge?'

'Oh my God,' she murmured, transfixed. 'Every moment we keep the soldiers busy here,' she whispered, the sound almost inaudible, 'we buy our boys a bit of time.'

This was what we had trained for: to pave the way for the invasion. Even if it meant a controlled suicide. I closed my eyes, but that didn't stop the vertigo.

'Good thing you oiled the rifles.'

My gaze returned to the river. Light flashed. It was too low to be lightning; it had to be our paras. I cursed the night; it was too dark to determine who was winning.

'I'll need you to spot for me. When the time comes.'

'Yes. Of course.'

I reluctantly trained the Zeiss glasses on the barracks across the way.

Footsteps sounded on the stairs, moving up the tower. I exchanged a look with Dom and pressed my ear to the trapdoor. Held up one finger, indicating one man, and eased the PPK from my waistband.

Was this an advance guard, used to lure us out? Regardless, it was still a threat. Dominique would have to monitor the situation outside the church on her own, while I took care of the intruder.

The weight of the pistol was familiar, but my blood surged as the man neared. I slipped through the trapdoor, resenting every moment that took me away from the scene playing out in the street.

Breath wheezing, the intruder stopped one flight below me.

'My God,' he was muttering. 'Help me, and help them.'

The priest. He sounded alone, but I waited for him to clear the corner, to make sure it wasn't a ruse. He had climbed without the benefit of a torch, relying on the scant moonlight shining through the thin windows. And when he came into sight, alone, there was no sign he had been coerced.

'I am getting old,' he puffed, holding a sack out to me. 'You'll need sustenance. It's just bread and cheese. A little meat.'

'It's the middle of the night,' I hissed. 'Get back downstairs before you get shot.' He raised one eyebrow in the silent chastise common to clergymen and schoolteachers. Feeling rebuked,

I added, 'Thank you, Father. It's kind of you. But you still shouldn't be here.'

'I know.' He braced his hand against the wall. 'But I heard something.'

And he wanted to see what was happening. Maybe even wanted to help. The brave, foolish man ... I couldn't blame him, but Dom did.

From the landing, she commanded, 'Go back downstairs, Father. It's dangerous up here.'

He looked crestfallen. It was history in the making, but she was right. Once the Boche knew we were here, they'd come for us. The old priest didn't have the stamina to run, and his religion prevented him from defending himself, even if he could.

'Go back downstairs, Father. I'm sorry, it's not safe.'

He forced a sad smile and patted my arm.

'Tell Madame Severin that she is doing God's work. She'll need to remember that when this is over.'

I nodded.

'As are you, my child.'

He sketched the sign of the cross in front of me.

'I'm Anglican, Father.'

'That doesn't matter, child,' he corrected. 'We are all children of God, and may He bless you. You and all the others fighting for our freedom.'

'Thank you.'

He smiled and retraced his steps down the tower.

'The priest,' I said, closing the door behind me. 'He sent food and words of redemption.'

Dom blushed. Devout woman that she was, his words meant a lot to her. She composed herself and refocused the field glasses.

'I expected more activity. More troops rushing to the river. To the beaches.'

'Be grateful they're not.' I pulled a hunk of bread and the cheese out of the sack, made a rough sandwich and gave Dom half. 'Eat while you can. We might not have time later.'

She put it on the ledge and, pressing the binoculars to her eyes, surveyed the situation below, and over by the river. Another set of bombers dropped their bombs and Caen was again in flames, with more flashes of light to the east.

'Oh, dear God,' she breathed.

Patience gone, I snatched the binoculars from her and scanned along the coast. It was a sight I would never forget.

Searchlights had found something, and the sky erupted with tracers. Flashes of light illuminated the wall of planes storming through the air. They were no longer shadows under the moon; they were part of a wave – a dark wave of bravery and hope, death and freedom. It was an armada, an airborne armada.

'Jesus Christ,' I breathed.

The planes cleared the coast and wave upon wave of parachutes dropped from them, pale against the sky.

'One thing about Rommel's Atlantic Wall, Dom.'

I passed her the field glasses and pointed to the west.

She looked through them, tears rolling down her cheeks.

'It has no roof.'

'It has no roof.'

I reached for the Leica and took photograph after photograph. It didn't matter if any of the pictures came out. There had never been anything so awe-inspiring.

The invasion had begun, and we were in the middle of it.

Chapter Forty-six

Parachutes blossomed on the night sky – puffs of white interspersed with bursts of flak from the anti-aircraft guns. In good weather, it took fifteen seconds between leaving the plane and landing. On the practice fields that was terrifying enough, but so much more when you were dropping into action. What if you were dropped in the wrong place? What if you had a bad landing? Broke a leg? What if the reception committee had been infiltrated? And what if the wind blew you into the next parish?

The 'what ifs' that haunted an agent were worse for a paratrooper. They would be shot at. They could well expect to be surrounded when they landed. The sky was heavy with paratroopers, but how many would reach the ground alive, much less survive the day?

An alert sounded and Dom picked up her rifle. The Zeiss field glasses stared back at me, and I picked them up. I hated what I had to do, but there was no other choice.

'There,' I said. 'In front of the wine shop. There's a Kübelwagen coming this way. Looks like a captain . . . no, wait.' I focused the lenses on his shoulder insignia, the rose-pink braid. 'Get the major, Dom.'

Her Winchester bucked as she squeezed the trigger. She didn't hit the major, or the driver. She hit the wheel. The vehicle screamed and twisted, bursting the gate of the Todt barracks before it stopped, perpendicular to the road.

Within moments, the guard was nose to nose with the driver while the major dabbed at a small blood trail weaving down his face.

I stared at Dom in shock. 'You missed.'

A small smile began to grow on her face. 'No, I didn't.'

Did she know something I didn't?

'There are paratroopers dropping in by the bridges,' I reminded her.

'I know. And right now, there's a vehicle blocking the road, and a lot of shouting. They're not going anywhere. Nor have they realised we're here. Yet.'

Mayhem reigned. The major, a white handkerchief pressed to his forehead, barked instructions to clear the block. Passing gendarmes were pressed into helping push the Kübelwagen out of the way.

'No Todt "volunteers",' Dom noted, sighting down the barrel of the Winchester.

'No,' I said, not surprised that she'd guessed whom I would take the Welrod to. 'Not yet.'

We waited for the advancing troops. For the next few hours Dom held them at bay, shooting neat holes here and there, preventing troops from advancing to the coast – without a death on her record, and without them spotting where the shots were fired from.

A line of tanks appeared, bypassing the road and moving over gardens and lawns, led by a cannon that meant business.

'What now?' I asked Dom, handing her a freshly loaded rifle.

'Now we give your Todt friends the distraction they need.'

She aimed at the jerricans in the back of the Kübelwagen. Smiled her satisfaction when the vehicle exploded.

It was almost 0400 and the sky was brightening, despite the cloud cover. Footsteps echoed on the stairs, faster and heavier than the old priest's.

'Someone's in!'

'How many?'

I paused, trying to listen. There were too many thuds, from outside as well as the stairwell.

'I don't know,' I whispered. 'More than one. How the hell did they get in? I didn't see them! Dom, *I didn't see them*!'

'It doesn't matter.'

But it did. I'd messed up, and it was now up to me to fix the situation. I pulled my pistol from my waistband and checked the ammunition.

'I'll keep anyone else from coming in.' Dom's attention was focused down the Winchester's sight. 'Can you take them?'

'I'll have to, won't I?'

I slipped through the trapdoor onto the landing and took a deep breath. My options were limited. The men were two floors below and moving fast. The dim light from the windows gleamed dully off three shadows, wearing steel helmets and holding machine guns. They were fast, but not careless. And with the stair serving as both cover and obstacle, it would not be easy.

Three against one wasn't favourable odds, and without armour, my only hope was to surprise them. The first man paused at a landing, under a window. The echo from my pistol was deafening in the small space, and he jerked backwards. The bullet missed, hitting the wooden balustrade in a small explosion of splinters. Cursing, the men dropped back a few steps, taking cover in the turn of the stairs.

The change in their breathing was a signal that one was about to lunge forward. I fired again. This time a man screamed; his shrieks were punctuated by thuds as he fell down a few steps.

Silence pulsed with menace. One man was down, maybe dead, maybe just wounded. Two snicks as guns were set to automatic fire. If they had been hoping to take me alive before, they weren't now.

Gunfire stuttered, loud in the tower stairwell. The spray hit the wall above my head and I raised my left arm to protect myself.

Braced on one knee, I fired. The bullet grazed his shoulder but he kept coming.

They were almost on me, strong and angry. But I was, too. The moment the lead man moved into the watery light, I fired twice at his face. The back of his head exploded, spraying gore onto the man behind him. He brushed his cheek with his shoulder and fired, hitting the wall, where I had been moments before.

Taking aim, I squeezed the trigger. This time the PPK clicked on an empty chamber.

'Damn!'

No time for tears or frustration. No time to reload. The Fairbairn Sykes was still in my pocket but the blade, nasty as it was, was no match for a machine gun.

The first soldier I hit still hadn't moved. And he had a gun that he clearly didn't need anymore. I just had to get it. And that meant getting past the last remaining man.

I threw the Fairbairn Sykes, not expecting it to find its mark, but the soldier retreated a few feet, tripping over his comrade's corpse and taking cover behind a bend in the stairs. It wasn't much, but it allowed me to dart forward and snatch the dead man's machine rifle.

If there were more soldiers behind him, they would have come forward, which meant that there were only two of us left. We were now equally armed and equally angry, but half-hidden by the stairs, it could become an impasse.

I looked down at the stairwell, and up at the trapdoor. A rope snaked from the ceiling, dangling like a lifeline down the stairwell. It was like the confidence course at Milton Hall, only without the safety harness, in the dark, and with someone trying to shoot me.

It was a desperate idea, but maybe unexpected enough to surprise him, and lend us an advantage.

The last soldier was still hidden behind the stairs. I shot at him, knowing I'd miss, but hoping to buy myself a few seconds. I slung the machine gun's strap across my chest, braced my foot on the top of the balustrade, and leapt.

My body stretched forward, arching as my fingers reached for the rope. It ripped into my hand as I slid down a few feet. My stifled cry was lost in the deafening chime as my weight pulled on the bell, dropping me below the soldier. I rotated, rising as the bell struggled to right itself.

The soldier gaped as I came abreast of him. My finger found the trigger and bullets peppered his chest as he fell forward. The second time I descended, the bell didn't right itself. I slipped on the safety and released the gun, letting it settle against my back.

Swung on the rope until I could reach the railing and scrambled over it, landing on the stairs behind the dead men. The bell rang a final time as the rope was loosed, but no one moved.

I shot each of them again, a double-tap to make certain they were dead, and retrieved my Fairbairn Sykes from the wall. Moved up the stairs to the body closest to the top. Opened the trapdoor, and pushed the dead man through.

'What are you doing?' Dom asked as I climbed over the corpse. I asked her to repeat herself, my ears still ringing from the bell's clang as I descended.

'I have fought that good fight.' I quoted the motto immortalised in stained glass at St Bart's, the church we'd all worshipped in when we'd trained. 'And I bloody won it.'

'Bully for you. What are you doing with that?' Her tone was laced with distaste.

'I'm stripping it.' Wasn't that obvious? 'I want his ammunition. I want his armour. And if he has a grenade or anything else interesting, I want that too.'

I tossed her the machine pistol, still breathing hard. The soldier had not been small, and death had made him unwieldy.

She placed it beside her and fingered his sidearm.

'See what you can get from the others. So far, your friends are keeping Jerry busy. I'll help them if need be.'

She tried to jam it into her waistband, until she remembered she was still wearing a dress. She slipped the Luger into the garter alongside her knife.

Slick with sweat, I returned to the bell room with a small arsenal. Dom stood at the open arch, her face pale. Her mouth moved but she had no voice.

'Dom?'

Eyes wide, she pointed out across the countryside. Artillery was being fired into the city, but not from above. The coast was too far away to see, but one thing was certain: we weren't the only one keeping the Germans busy.

The Allied fleet had arrived.

Chapter Forty-seven

The sun rose as bombs exploded on the beaches. Mortars were fired and small boats launched. Coastal defences retaliated and planes roared across the skies. The sheer scale was phenomenal. On the street below us, the Todt 'volunteers' entered the fray. They must have found the barracks arsenal, because armed with years of festered anger and stolen weapons, they attacked the Germans.

Chaos reigned. It was the perfect time – perhaps the only time – to escape.

'It's as much cover fire as we're going to get. Still going to be a nightmare.'

Dominique hesitated. 'Unless they let us go.' Her steady gaze assured me that she hadn't taken leave of her senses. 'Put on your skirt. If anyone sees those trousers, they'll know you were up to no good.'

She was right: the rope had ripped the seams, and there was a hole near the ankle that looked like a bullet had passed through. I wadded them up and threw them on the corpse. Stepped into my skirt and smoothed it over the sgian dubh. Considered sliding the Fairbairn Sykes beside it, but opted instead for the left side.

Dom transferred the German's ammunition into her rucksack and stood.

'Help me position him,' she said, pointing at a corpse.

'Why?'

'No reason for them to think the snipers have left. Let them continue worrying.'

There was a certain symmetry to her plan: moments before, that man was trying to kill me. Now, he might just save our lives.

We positioned him in the window, a Winchester in his arms. From this height, the risk of someone noticing his German uniform was slim. I couldn't fit both the field glasses and the Leica in the bag, so I put the PPK on the bottom, the field glasses on top of it, and slung the Leica over my shoulder, hoping there was nothing suspect about a German woman carrying a German camera.

'Give it to me,' Dom said. 'I'll carry the camera in my bag.'

My cardigan was just long enough to hide the soldier's Luger, tucked in my waistband at the small of my back; it was too good a gun to lose. I hadn't been armed like this since training at Milton Hall with the Jeds, although back then, I had the equipment to carry a small arsenal. Now, I had to rely on men seeing only what they wanted to see. I pulled a pair of white kid gloves from the front pocket of my bag and slipped them on.

'A lady never leaves home without her gloves.' Dom grinned. 'At least they'll hide your rope burns. You should have worn them before.'

'Best I can do.'

We rigged the door with the dead soldiers' grenades and began our descent. Dom led the way down the stairs, ignoring the pools of blood, black in the half-light, but there was no

312

avoiding the stench of copper and cordite. Of death, fresh and cloying. I held my breath, refusing to feel any guilt. I had never killed anyone not trying to kill me, and these men were not exceptions.

A sliver of light illuminated the last man's face. The trickle of blood at the corner of his mouth had dried and he stared at me with sightless dark eyes.

I was only doing my job, he seemed to protest.

So was I.

And yet, I leant down to close his eyes – a courtesy from one combatant to another.

Orders were barked from the street, loud over the sounds of shouts and gunfire. Dom pulled me into a pew halfway down the nave. She dropped to her knees and adjusted her scarf over her head, motioning for me to do the same.

The doors burst open. Heavily armed soldiers stormed in. Instinct had my hand twitch towards the Luger, and it took every ounce of willpower to stop it. We were outnumbered and out-armed.

Dom's wails were as loud as a siren. She was right – our best defence was in our vulnerability. I could do this; I was certainly scared enough. I screamed and covered my head with my hands.

Within seconds, we were surrounded, half a dozen guns trained on us. The enlisted men were young, and maybe as frightened as we were. But their lieutenant seemed carved from granite, but with blue eyes that burned with a zealot-like eagerness.

Tears trembled on Dominique's lower lashes. 'Please don't hurt us,' she whimpered, looking tiny and helpless. How much of that obvious terror was an act, was anyone's guess.

'What are you doing here?' the lieutenant barked.

Beneath the pew, her heel dug into my ankle.

'We took refuge.' I allowed the very real tremor into my voice. 'When the shooting began.'

'Did you see anyone pass by?'

'Three men,' Dom whispered. 'But that was ages ago.'

'We heard the bell ring,' he said. 'It was twenty-one minutes past the hour. Tell me – why did the bell ring?'

'I don't know,' she snivelled.

The lieutenant pointed and a pair of men moved towards the bell tower.

'Be careful,' I called after them.

The sergeant finished searching the nave and joined the lieutenant.

'No sign of the priest,' he reported, barely glancing at us. And then his gaze returned and he stared at me. 'You're Colonel Graf's woman.'

I managed a wobbly smile, my relief genuine. He had not only just confirmed me as sympathetic to the Germans, but might be able to tell me where Eduard was.

'And you . . .' The man turned to Dom. 'Your husband is the doctor. He helped me once, when I was shot.' He turned to the lieutenant. 'Maybe we should let them go, sir. It's not safe for them here.'

The lieutenant's critical eye swept over us. Dom radiated innocence. Knowing that expression would seem ludicrous on me, I met his gaze calmly.

He took his time deciding, unaware that each second he wasted brought us closer to the grenades exploding in the tower.

'Do you have a safe place to go?' he finally said. 'Until we push the invaders back into the Channel?'

'I . . . I don't know,' Dom stammered.

'We will go to her sister's place in Lisieux,' I improvised, taking her hand. 'Can one of your men take us to the train station?'

It was the wrong thing to say, and the lieutenant's face darkened.

'It's not running.'

Dom's work had borne fruit. Without communications – and transport – the Germans would be, at least temporarily, disadvantaged. I looked down so they couldn't see my jubilation. Schooled my features to feign a greater fear than I had.

I asked, 'Can you take us as far as Madame Severin's home? We can pack a bag and cycle from there.'

Precious seconds passed, until he gestured to the sergeant.

'Get them out of here, Knapp.'

We were almost through the heavy wood doors when the grenades exploded. The church shuddered, throwing us against the flagstones. The sergeant shielded us with his body. Seconds turned into minutes, but only silence issued from the tower.

The lieutenant ran towards the stairs.

'Move, Sergeant!'

He pulled us to our feet and, with his rifle held in front of him, eased out of the door. We sprinted behind him to the motor pool and climbed into the last remaining Kübelwagen. It was filthy, but functional. The sergeant hit the ignition, stomped on the accelerator.

'Wait,' Dom said. 'Our bicycles!'

'Have probably already been stolen,' he said, and blasted past the single man guarding the now-defunct gate.

The Todt men had dispersed, but blood and bodies remained on the street. The sergeant swerved to the hard shoulder as another column of Panzers approached. They were enormous, relentless. The time for parades was done; now the hatches atop the turrets were closed, protecting the men inside from Allied fire and, maybe, from missiles dropped from windows by opportunistic Frenchmen.

I held my breath as the turret swivelled and the long barrel turned to point at us.

'*Scheisse*,' I muttered, one hand fumbling for the Luger, even as I knew that its 9 mm bullets would bounce off the tank.

For a moment, the sergeant seemed indecisive. Then he slowly stood. Took off his helmet and handed it to me. I didn't think twice, just rammed it on my head. Uniform still clean and pressed, Knapp raised his hand in the Nazi salute to the Panzers.

The second and third tanks in the column now focused on us. Sitting behind me, Dom slid into the wheel well, which would have been as effective a prevention as my Luger was as an offensive. If they fired on us, we were dead.

But if they were going to fire on us, wouldn't they have already done so?

They moved closer relentlessly – approaching doom. Time was measured in heartbeats until their turrets straightened. They plodded past, one after another in a single file through the street. At the end of the road, beyond the Todt barracks, they turned.

'Heading to the beaches,' Dom guessed.

'They go to defend us against the invaders,' Knapp corrected, without irony. 'I will join them once I have taken you to safety.'

I didn't bother to point out that with the tanks on the streets and bombers in the air, nowhere was safe.

'Thank you, Sergeant.'

He nodded, sinking back into his seat. Drew in a deep breath and held it for a few seconds. Then, with a shaking hand, he put the Kübelwagen into gear. He navigated through streets littered with the remnants of the communications network; telephone poles were chopped down, the cables stretched across the road and tangled into trees.

Sergeant Knapp cursed, low and voluble, but his hands still shook. He followed Dom's directions to an address not far from her house. Knapp helped me from the vehicle, raising an eyebrow at the weight of my bulging shoulder bag.

'I'm sure Colonel Graf will be fine,' he said.

'He has to be.' There was, quite simply, no other option.

Knapp seemed a good man, and I was grateful to him for helping us get this far. It made what I had to do next regrettable, no matter how necessary.

Taking a deep breath, I swung my heavy bag like a cricket bat. It clipped the base of his skull, and he went down hard. I checked for Knapp's pulse, relieved to find it slow but strong.

'I'm sorry,' I whispered.

Dom stared at me.

'He might be a Nazi, but he was kind to us,' I said, unembarrassed. Léonie would have pointed out that my mercy meant one more man fighting against us, but this was a life I couldn't

317

take. 'By the time he wakes up, it won't matter, we'll be long gone.'

Dom slid behind the wheel of the Kübelwagen and drove the short distance to her home. She parked at the kerb.

'Get your set and pack whatever you need. I don't think we'll be back any time soon.'

'My set is still in Caen.'

She paused. 'And Pascal's?'

'André has it.'

'Good enough.'

I changed into clean clothes, maybe for the last time in heaven knew how long. Packed the frocks Dominique's dressmakers had fashioned for me in a suitcase my friend provided. Added in the metal tin containing the jewellery and cash I'd won at the casino. It would be useful for bribes, if I got myself into trouble. Then moved it into the shoulder bag. If I had to jettison the case, I wanted to still have it with me.

With the room it freed in the case, I placed the folded midnight-blue gown that I'd worn to the Desert Fox's reception. It had miraculously survived the climb up the château's wall. It was a survivor, that dress. I took that as a good sign and buckled the suitcase closed over it.

I met Dominique on the landing. She had a suitcase in either hand, her leather sketchbook tucked under her arm.

'We go to Beaune's farm for now,' she said, thumping down the stairs behind me.

She deposited her things in the Kübelwagen and went back inside, returning with a large box of medical supplies from Jérôme's surgery.

318

She turned and looked back into the house. She and Jérôme had made a home here, and I couldn't imagine what she must have felt to leave, knowing how likely it was that it would be destroyed.

Bright green eyes clouded over and she bit her lip. Looked away and sighed.

'There's nothing in there that can't be recreated, once this mess is over.' She forced a watery smile. 'Let's go'

She climbed into the passenger seat and leant her head back, then rolled her neck to the side and blinked at me.

'Maybe it's time for the *réseau* to know who Cecil is. What do you think?'

It would effectively blow my cover story. If the invasion failed, or I was unable to neutralise Sablonnières in time, he would see to it that the Germans wouldn't be the only ones to hunt me, but we'd run out of options.

Engaging first gear, I accelerated the Kübelwagen into the first turn.

Chapter Forty-eight

The German beast was all but impossible to control on the dirt path leading to Beaune's farm. The steering wheel burned my chafed hands, and with the incessant threat of planes overhead, I was close to tears when I cut the engine in front of Beaune's stone farmhouse and rubbed the dust from my eyes. The last time I was here, the place had been filled with Maquisards celebrating the coming invasion, with Beaune and Sablonnières standing on a veranda that in daylight almost looked incongruous.

Now it was here – the bombers overhead, and men crawling through the surf to the beaches. There would be tanks and infantry as well, fighting in the hedges and fields, cities and villages. The time for quietude was over.

All eyes were on me.

'She's German!'

I recognised that voice, followed it to the sulky features of the waitress from Avignon, Sandrine, carrying crates from one of the barns to the two American jeeps parked nearby. She had worked with Sablonnières in the restaurant, and maybe in his coup as well. I would have to keep an eye on her.

Mutterings became louder, people moved closer until Dom stood on her seat, her voice booming.

'She's with me, and she's one of us. Any questions?'

There was something about Dom when she was like this that frightened people. The waitress and her pack of friends looked away. They continued to heft the crates from the barn, moving them towards parked vehicles.

I took a moment to gather the strength to climb from the Kübelwagen. Ignoring the angry voices that came from within the farmhouse, we crossed to where André and another man had mounted a Bren on one jeep. A pair of feet stuck out from beneath the second as someone laboured underneath it. Even the battered lorry had been fitted with a gun, although whether it could be relied on to drive was a different question.

With a wide grin, André wiped his hands on a rag and sauntered over to meet us, giving Dom a kiss on both cheeks, and me a bear hug that lifted me off my feet.

'Hoy, Sandrine!' he yelled over my shoulder. 'Be careful! The Boche aren't going to let us steal replacements!'

Sandrine gave me a filthy look, but tightened her grip on the crate in her arms.

Reluctant to waste time, I asked, 'What do you need done? We're at your disposal.'

'Jérôme left about an hour ago. He and the lads will destroy the tracks and bridges, and then he'll head to the refugee centre at the Lycée Malherbe. Caen's badly hit and the school will begin to fill up.'

The angry voices within the farmhouse reached a crescendo.

'What's happening inside?'

André shrugged. 'Beaune – he wants to find a way to meet with the Allied commanders.'

321

'Because there's more intelligence to pass on than what I was transmitting?'

'Local knowledge. And the situation will be changing as the Kraut troops are moved to attack and defend.'

'OK. So what's the problem?'

'Some of the other men. They think it's too dangerous, that the old man should stay here.'

'Why? So they can be the ones to liaise with the Allies?' I leant in closer. 'What about Sablonnières?'

'Beaune confronted him. Alain, he didn't take it well.'

'I wouldn't expect him to. He denied it, of course.' André's shrug was a good enough answer. 'What's the result?'

'Beaune kicked him out.'

I was stunned.

'Kicked him out? That's it? Instead of killing him? But that means that he's still out there, ready to betray us. He knows where we are, how we operate!'

He didn't look any happier than I felt.

'Beaune knows that, too. But we've lived and worked along-side each other for years. In good faith. I think he's not prepared to kill the man he once called "friend".'

He wouldn't call him 'friend' if he had seen the blood money in Sablonnières' safe.

Anger and bitterness surged through my veins. How could Beaune be that weak, that foolish?

'And so that friend might end up killing him, instead,' I said. 'Or me.'

Beaune might choose leniency, but if Sablonnières crossed my path, he would get none of it from me. I looked over my shoulder towards Sandrine. Sablonnières had been evicted from the *réseau*, but she'd stayed. Did that mean that she wasn't involved, or that she remained as Sablonnières' eyes within the Resistance?

'What's the second vehicle for?'

'That one I'm taking. Reinforcements.'

'I'll go with you.' I spoke without thinking, my words horrifying me as much as they did André.

He looked thunderous, but his friend under the jeep was more sanguine.

'If you know how to fire a Bren, you're more than welcome,' he called out.

'Better than you can.'

It wasn't quite a lie; I *could* fire a Bren, although I lacked the physical strength to control it for any length of time. But if I had to use it, I would find the strength.

'Shut up, Jean-Claude.' André flushed; his chest puffed out and he stepped in front of me. 'No. Absolutely not. I am not taking her to the front lines. There's action happening there, and both sides are out looking for trouble. And Blondie here is a magnet for trouble.'

I couldn't argue with that, but the lieutenant in the church was right: nowhere was safe. I tapped him on the back to regain his attention.

'I'm a magnet who knows how to play the piano. Do you have another wireless operator who's willing to ride along?'

'No, but as you mention it, we don't have another wireless operator. Full stop.' His hard face softened, and he rested one massive hand on my shoulder. 'I know you can handle yourself, and I'd rather you cover my back than almost anyone else, but I'm not going to risk your life. Not when we need you here.'

It was a point I couldn't dispute, even if I wanted to.

Jean-Claude emerged from under the jeep and joined us, a reedy man with sharp, black eyes behind grease-smudged spectacles. He studied me, lips pursed, then said, 'These paras, they're dropping off course. We need to help them, but we don't know where they are. It's not like the telephones are working. And while they have radios, we don't.'

'Except yours, Blondie.'

'We have men and arms here to defend the place, in case Jerry comes this way.'

Or if Sablonnières returns.

'Which they will.'

'Of course they will.'

'All right,' André said, now that the matter was settled. 'Guillaume, get Pascal's wireless case,' he called out, then turned back to me. 'Paul and I will take your Kübelwagen as soon as we can fit it with a gun.' He looked past my shoulder. 'Hoy, Dominique. Where do you think you're going?'

She was crossing towards the American jeep without the Bren, the box of supplies she'd taken from the house in her arms.

'I'm going to the Lycée Malherbe with the medical supplies. I wish I had a Red Cross flag, but I hope they'll see that we don't look like combatants.'

'I'm not sure anyone will wait for you to get close enough to see that before firing,' I said.

Dom raised her hand against the protests. 'I have to get through. They'll need me there. They'll need the supplies.'

'It won't be pretty, Dom.'

'I'm not expecting it to be.'

She placed the box on the floor and was about to climb into the jeep.

'Wait, Dom!'

I didn't know what I was going to say – what I wanted to say. Just knew I couldn't let her leave without saying *something*.

She understood. Of course she did. She met me halfway and hugged me.

'It's not goodbye, Cécile. It's *au revoir*. We will survive, and we will meet again. All of us.' Her smile was bright when she added, 'Trust me.'

Chapter Forty-nine

Dominique turned and waved as her jeep passed behind the trees. I lowered my own arm, finding it difficult to swallow over the lump in my throat. She and Jérôme were family to me, and the chances of *any* of us making it through this mess were shrinking by the minute.

I walked up the steps of the veranda, past my suitcase, which someone had moved from the Kübelwagen, whispers of 'Boche bitch' echoing behind me.

'She's our pianist!' André boomed. 'Regardless of the cover story she's maintained, she's been working for us. If anyone has a problem, they can take it up with me.'

I didn't need his or Dom's help, but was grateful for it nonetheless. The crowd might not be convinced, but with members of Beaune's inner circle vouching for me, they weren't going to attack either. Yet.

I entered the room, and made a beeline for Beaune.

'You knew Sablonnières betrayed Pascal and was trying to get rid of me. And you let him go? Why?'

He took my arm and led me away from the others. At the window, he banged the tobacco out of his pipe. Took his time cleaning and refilling it.

'That was my decision to make.'

'It wasn't you he was trying to kill.' I shook my head. 'Eugene Vallentin. I saw them together at Avignon, after it had closed for the night. Only I didn't realise at the time that the restaurant's chef was Alain Sablonnières.'

Beaune lit the pipe, inhaling deeply. His exhalation was more of a sigh, tempered with fragrant smoke.

'He has left. He won't return.'

'You're wrong, Monsieur Beaune. He's angry. And he has made quite a lot of money by betraying the Resistance. It is in his interests for the Germans to win this war. He will come after us, either with his German friends, or with the men who are loyal to him. You should have killed him when you had the chance.'

I set up the wireless on the kitchen table, only after assurances that there were enough armed men outside to handle the Radio Detection Vehicle when it came.

'And it will come, you know.' I paused and held up a finger at Beaune. 'Despite the invasion, they'll come for me. Whether Sablonnières points them in our direction or not.'

'This time we will be ready for it. We have your back this time, madame.'

'Maybe.'

Outside, vehicles came and went as the Resistance ferried Allied paratroopers who had landed in the wrong place to the front lines. Rain-soaked drivers poked their heads into the house to update Beaune. At first they were surprised to see me sitting beside him, and then word spread.

Guillaume sat quietly on a chair in a corner, watching me until I sighed.

'All right, then. Get me a Sten. One that works, please. Then come over here and I'll show you what I'm doing.'

The boy did as he was told, and he knew Morse code; André had taught him well.

'What's your code name?' I asked, more to amuse myself. He looked taken aback.

'I don't understand, madame.'

'My code name is Cécile. It's not the name my parents gave me, but it's what London calls me. Never mind,' I said, an idea coming to my mind as I remembered Dom saying he should be reading *Twenty Thousand Leagues Under the Sea* instead of the banned *Combat* rag. 'Your code name is Jules. Unless you'd prefer Verne? Nemo? Nautilus?'

'Jules is fine, madame.'

Guillaume struggled to contain his excitement and flashed a wide toothy grin. Dimples. The boy had dimples. The Allies had to rout the Germans quickly. If anything happened to this boy because of me, I'd never forgive myself.

'Fine. I'll let London know that I'm training a new chap called Jules. Now, this is a one-time pad,' I held up the pad, explaining how it was used. 'When we transmit, we need to be fast. Over the years the Germans have got far too good at finding us—'

'Madame?'

I held up a finger, while a plan began to emerge.

'Wait here, I need to check on something,' I said, leaving him to practise tapping out his new name in Morse on Beaune's scarred wooden table.

Chapter Fifty

Half a dozen men milled around on the veranda, close enough to the wall not to be assaulted by the rain. An energy vibrated around them, as if they wanted to do something, but weren't sure what. I didn't know which faction they belonged to, but they were still here, so maybe it was Beaune's. I took a chance and addressed a man with the sort of intensity about him that made him a leader, even if he wasn't the biggest or the strongest.

'Fancy a bit of *quid pro quo*?' I asked.

He looked me up and down while his friends sniggered.

I rolled my eyes. That wasn't the sort of *quid pro quo* I had in mind.

'Don't be daft,' I snapped. 'I'm not offering anything more than a chance to get back at the Boche.'

'What do you have in mind?'

'What if I can guarantee a set of Germans turning up to a place I determine, at a time I dictate?'

'Are you a witch?' Smartarse rolled his shoulders and swaggered closer. 'A *German* witch?'

I'd been called worse.

'If I'm a witch, I'm an English one. Are you up for it or not? A chance to get back at the men who took Pascal?' I had no idea if he'd been rounded up after a transmission, or if he'd been set up in some other way. So I added the one thing I did know. 'The ones who shot Jacques Mandeville and his friends against the wall of the Abbaye aux Hommes?'

'You heard about that?' Smartarse asked.

'I wasn't here when Pascal was taken, but I saw what the Boche did to Mandeville. And I've seen what they've done to a country that I love. I've been fighting the Germans, one way or another, since May 1940. What about you?'

They were young and angry, fit from years of manual labour. I was offering them the excuse they'd been looking for.

'What do you know of us?' another man said.

'You're not the first *réseau* I've worked with. You're young enough to have been shipped off to work in Germany, if the Boche had been fast enough to catch you. I'm guessing you've been hiding in the forest, sniping at the enemy when you can. Hiding, to save yourselves and your families. I think you want to fight, but someone told you to guard Marcel Beaune.' I didn't bother to hide a tight smile. 'And you resent that.'

'And your proposition?'

'We set a trap. I'll even bait it for you. When the Boche come for me – and they will – we spring it.'

'You have a plan?'

I nodded. 'I always have a plan.'

And, drawing a rough map in the wet earth with the end of a stick, I laid it out for him. Even the smartarse was quiet while they considered my proposal.

'Bernard?' one said, turning to him.

'Do we have enough vehicles for this to work?' Bernard asked me.

330

I looked around, taking inventory of the vehicles currently parked around us and made a quick calculation. What I planned might slow the ferry service, but it would keep the Boche from us a little longer which in my mind was worth the risk. 'Yes.'

He stood back, arms crossed over his chest. His lips pursed as he stared at my rough drawings. 'And you're willing to do this?'

It would mean breaking a promise I had once made, but it was the only thing I could do. To save my own life, once again I had to risk it. I nodded.

Bernard nodded.

'Very well,' he said. 'Then may I suggest a few modifications to your plan?'

The men decided that I wasn't a witch – I was a madwoman. The plan was brave enough and ballsy enough to just work.

We would keep the foray small. Bernard would drive one jeep, one of his chums another. Beaune wasn't pleased with my plan, but reluctantly agreed that if successful, it would buy us time.

I walked down the steps, looking up as bombers flew overhead.

'They won't bomb us,' Bernard said. 'Not yet. We're not a good enough target. It's the Germans we need to worry about. Are you sure?'

I shrugged. I wasn't sure, didn't like making myself a target, but it was time to take a stand.

'Are you afraid?'

331

His back straightened as if I had attacked his pride.

'I am not frightened.'

That was good – because a cold finger of sweat was tracing down my spine. As scared as I was, I was more terrified of the alternative. I gestured for Bernard to start the jeep.

Guillaume clattered down the steps after me. He was about to get in the jeep when I asked him, 'Where do you think you're going?'

'With you.'

'No.'

'Why not? I can fight!'

'Guillaume, I am not taking you into this. If anything happens to me, Bernard will bring back the set and you will need to let London know. I need you to be here.'

To survive. I couldn't let him make a target of himself unnecessarily.

Bernard started the engine, and I looked back at the youth's crestfallen face, knowing I'd kept him as safe as I could, but there were no guarantees.

We drove until it felt like we were far enough from Beaune's farm. I looked down the road, studded with craters. I hoped I was right, and that when the Boche came, it would be along this stretch of road.

The sky was grey, the rain making it difficult to see. Evening would come in a few hours and with it, more rain. I slid from the jeep. Adjusted the Sten that was slung across my body, and grabbed the wireless. Stood back to allow Bernard's jeep and the other one to back up and position themselves on either side of the road, under the cover of the hedgerows.

The engines cut and I took a deep breath. This was the best protected I'd ever been when I transmitted, but the first time I'd used it to set a trap. It would be fine.

I would be fine.

'Stay alive, lady,' Bernard said. 'What you said to the kid? About not wanting to lose the operator? We can't lose you, not yet.'

I nodded and walked through the maize field. He was right, of course. Guillaume wouldn't be able to use the wireless, not yet. So I had to make sure I survived. I set up the machine, slipped on the headphones and said a little prayer. For Pascal. For Virgil. For all the other operators who had been caught by the Boche.

Turned it on and began a detailed sitrep to London.

The operator on the other side had a familiar 'fist'. Eileen. The woman who had sat beside me when we learnt that Virgil had been compromised. She confirmed receipt and wished me luck, on behalf of all the operators in Norgeby House.

I closed the case around the wireless and cradled the Sten.

We didn't have long to wait.

The Radio Detection Vehicle led the way, followed by a Kübelwagen armed with a heavy machine gun, and a troop transport. This was more than I anticipated, but they were taking no chances.

The vehicles stopped, men erupting from the RDV and transport. I pressed myself low against the muddy ground, waiting for the gunfire to cease, biting my lip until I tasted blood. At my signal, Bernard's men fired on the Germans.

The sound was deafening. Something exploded.

I wasn't sure if it was ours or theirs. Cautiously, I raised my head above the green fronds and found my bearings. Caught between our jeeps, the Germans didn't have a chance.

The jeeps moved forward, trapping the Kübelwagen. The transport burned and the only movement in the field seemed to be me. I called to Bernard, who strafed the area in front of me. It was as safe as they could make it.

I held my breath, expecting to feel the punch of a bullet, the blossoming of pain.

Instead, I made it to the road and held up a hand. One hand on the Sten's trigger, I walked up to the RDV and checked for signs of life. I ripped a strip of cotton from a dead man's tunic and walked down the vehicle, searching for the fuel tank. Fed the cotton strip into it and lit the tip with my lighter.

Ran to the jeep, skidding behind it as the petrol in the RDV exploded.

There were no other sounds, save for our ragged breathing and the crackle of fire.

'Get in, I'll get you back to Beaune's.'

I was halfway to the jeep, but Fate moved me in a different direction. I walked closer to the burning RDV, remembering every time it had hunted me, threatened my friends. And because I couldn't kick it, whispered: 'May you rot in hell.'

'Feel better?' Bernard asked, his voice patronising.

How could he understand what it was like, having the RDVs hunt me every time I did my job?

'As a matter of fact, yes,' I said. 'They'll send another one, but maybe we'll have a bit of time before they do. Who knows?'

'And then?'

'And then?' I echoed, not knowing the answer.

Maybe they'd come searching for a wireless operator, or because the battle lines had brought them there.

But they would come. And nowhere was safe.

Chapter Fifty-one

Beaune was gone by the time we returned to the farmhouse. Only an hour before, it had been a hive of activity. Now all that remained was the battered lorry, now with a Browning set up in the back, and a handful of women. Even Guillaume was gone.

I didn't need to ask where they'd gone; they'd gone to fight.

Bernard revved the engine, eager to join them. I held up a hand to stop him.

'You can't leave with all three vehicles,' I said. 'Go if you must, but give us a fighting chance to defend ourselves if we need to.' Or flee, if we couldn't. 'That lorry won't carry all of us, if it even still drives.'

Bernard studied me. 'You don't lack nerve, girl. You know how to drive?'

'Yes. And I know how to use the Bren. A Browning, too.'

At his nod, the men from the Kübelwagen crammed into the first jeep. If I had been given the choice, I would have kept the Kübelwagen. Not because it was a better vehicle, but because a Kübelwagen and a jeep would do more to confuse anyone who saw them on the road.

'Good luck then,' he said, raising a hand in farewell.

The jeep set up a spray of gravel and water that barely missed me.

The women stood on the veranda, staring at me, some with apprehension, others with outright hostility.

I pushed past them and into the house, pushing rain-sodden hair from my eyes. With no message to transmit, no patrols to coordinate, and no one willing to talk me, I sat down and willed myself not to think too hard about having made myself a target.

'Car!' one of the women called out.

I joined them, towelling my hair dry with a flannel I'd found in the house.

'Where?'

She pointed, and through the rain I could see a small BMW. It braked in front of the house, and two women emerged, sprinting into the cover of the veranda. Léonie's hair was neatly contained by a silk scarf and, despite the storm, she looked as cool as Marlene bloody Dietrich. In contrast, Dom looked windstrewn and filthy.

I handed my flannel to Dom and turned to face Léonie.

'What's happened?'

'Vallentin is gathering his men. They're coming here.'

'Here?' I echoed.

Her face hardened. 'He received intelligence that the *réseau* is grouping here.'

There were no questions as to who had provided that intelligence. I was furious – with him, and myself. I should have tried to neutralise him earlier. Removed him myself at the first hint that he was involved. My eyes met Sandrine's across the porch.

'Sablonnières told them.'

'You don't know that,' she whispered, going white.

337

'Yes, I do.' She shook her head, but I pressed on. 'What I don't know is how involved you were in it.'

'Me?' Her back straightened. 'Of all the—'

'He met Eugene Vallentin at the restaurant where you both worked. How could you *not* know?'

'I never saw them together.' She looked away. 'These last months, he sent me on errands. Or sent me home early. I thought he was being kind.'

'Now is not the time for this,' Léonie said. With one hand on my arm, she turned to Sandrine. 'You and any one of your friends who is unwilling to fight must leave now.'

One of the women said, 'If the Boche bitches can fight the Germans, so can I. So can *we*.' She jerked her head behind her, towards the pack of women who'd been carrying crates earlier. 'I've trained on the range with the men. We all have. We're not here to run away.'

'Good,' Léonie said, waving the women to get closer as she laid out her plan.

We were outgunned, our armaments limited to the Kübelwagen's mounted Mauser MG 34 machine gun, the lorry's Browning, a few Stens, a box of landmines, another with the exploding rats that Dom had mentioned, and two American tommy guns.

We left the rats, but took everything else, Dom going into Beaune's house and returning with a pair of Lee–Enfield rifles and a box of ammunition.

Sandrine drove the Kübelwagen, with Léonie's sharp eyes on her from the passenger seat. Dom and I rode in the back, while the other women travelled in the lorry.

'What happened?' I asked Dom. 'I thought you were heading into Caen.'

'Couldn't get there,' she said, bracing herself as we bumped along. 'We got caught in the fighting.'

'I found her on the road!' Léonie shouted over the rain and the Kübelwagen's engine. 'The jeep she was in was disabled, the driver dead. Dominique was doing her best to hold off her attackers. Alone.'

'She had a grenade,' Dom said.

'Two,' Léonie corrected.

'I don't know how she got her hands on it, and don't know what she did to Zeit to get his car, but I'm grateful.'

And given how closed-mouth Léonie could be, I wasn't sure any of us would know what she'd done to Zeit.

'How did you find out about Vallentin?' I shouted to Léonie.

The Kübelwagen hit a rut, jerking us into the spray of water kicked up by the front tyres.

'I saw Vallentin get the message. Got close enough to hear the details as he ordered his lieutenant to requisition vehicles.'

'How many?'

'I do not know.'

'How long do we have?'

She raised one shoulder in an oddly Gallic shrug.

'I do not know that either. It will depend on how much resistance they meet between here and Caen.'

And yet, we were driving into it.

Chapter Fifty-two

We reached the site, not far from the destroyed RDV and troop transport. Dom was our lookout, climbing a tree, with a pair of field glasses and the rifles. We hid our vehicles as best we could and mined the road, taking advantage of puddles and potholes to hide the devices.

They came in a convoy of three Demag half-tracks, each with a mounted MG 34 machine gun and four men riding in the back. No Radio Detection Vehicle, but Vallentin was after bigger fish, and he didn't need an RDV to find Beaune's farm.

Thanks to Alain Sablonnières.

The half-tracks came into view. I couldn't see who rode behind the armoured front seats, but knew that one of them held Eugene Vallentin. This was his coup, and he wouldn't miss it. That said, he was taking no chances.

I put down the field glasses and grasped the machine gun, hoping that the Mauser behaved more or less like its British equivalent. Or better. Taking a deep breath, I forced my hands to stop shaking. The kid gloves I wore were scant padding for my chafed palms, but were better than nothing. Yvette, the dressmaker, was hidden on the other side of the road, with the Browning, and more guts than I had given her credit for.

With a mental map in my head, I watched Vallentin's convoy approach the mines. The second vehicle triggered a mine. The initial explosion was followed almost immediately by a second one, when the petrol tank blew.

The other two half-tracks halted. The gunner in the back sprayed the bushes with a volley of bullets that reached scant yards from where we hid. Léonie raised her left hand, palm down, urging patience, while my instincts screamed for action.

Vallentin's men fanned out like a murder of crows. One man called out, 'Sir, I think it's just a random mine.'

The response was lost in the rain and wind, but as the men returned to the vehicles, another mine exploded, felling a pair of Vallentin's men, wounding others.

They were angry now. Machine-gun fire again sprayed the hedges, again too far away.

Léonie repeated her silent demand for patience.

A half-track veered off the road, attempting to use a combination of artillery and the power of the ten belted rear tyres to clear the hedge. A tank might have bullied its way through, but the half-track couldn't breach the thicket.

Vallentin would be cursing by now, I guessed.

Most of his foot soldiers walked behind the vehicles, cradling their weapons. They moved slowly at first, then faster as the half-tracks accelerated, their confidence growing.

I felt, rather than saw, Léonie's half-smile.

Another landmine exploded, but the half-tracks continued forward. They were now almost within our range.

'Wait,' Léonie murmured.

The signal she gave wasn't to me. The bang of Dom's rifle was lost in the rain, but the shot was true, punching through the windscreen on the driver's side. The half-track veered, crashing into the embankment.

'Now!'

He turned then, his handsome face in the window, looking at me even though I knew it wasn't possible for him to see me.

Léonie's voice sounded like it came through the end of a tunnel. I pulled the Mauser's trigger, screaming Vallentin's name and hanging on while it rained a hail of bullets on the half-track. Bullets were coming from Yvette's gun, from Vallentin's men, when the women's army swarmed out.

The ambush was over in minutes. Filthy, soaked, blood-stained, *angry* women sloshing through the rain to make sure every last man was dead.

Reaching up, I flicked the Mauser's safety on, and used the gun to steady myself. The trembling subsided until I felt able to move. I left the Kübelwagen with the Luger in my hand, just in case. Careful of the mines, I moved across the field to where I had last seen Vallentin.

The once-handsome face was twisted in hatred, pale eyes beginning to cloud over. Bullets riddled his body; maybe some of them were mine. I felt no regret, but no joy either. He and his men would have killed me. It wouldn't bring Virgil or Pascal back, but it was one less person who wanted to kill me.

Chapter Fifty-three

We left the remaining mines in place, hoping the destroyed half-track and dead SS men would serve as enough of a warning. We also left the remaining Demags, uncertain we would be able to get them out of the minefield without further casualties, and headed back to Beaune's for lack of any other plan.

Léonie and I rode in the Kübelwagen, just behind the battered lorry with the Browning. It stopped, and one of the women sprinted back to us.

'Another vehicle coming towards us!' she shouted.

'Who?' Léonie snapped.

'They're coming from the north. Painted black.'

That wasn't a good sign, and Léonie and I exchanged a glance.

'Probably German,' I murmured, 'but if they see a bunch of women in German vehicles, they'll know we've done something. If they're Allies, they'll see us as the enemy and fire on us.'

The woman nodded. Sweat was forming on her forehead and she bit her lip.

'Should we hide?'

'No,' Léonie said, already shimmying out of her underskirt. 'Tell the others – anyone wearing a white petticoat, or blouse, anything white, hang it from an aerial. Stand out so that they can see we mean no harm.'

Something exploded nearby, and the lorry's Browning began to turn.

'No!'

Keeping myself low, I sprinted towards it and pulled the woman from her position.

'Idiot! If you fire on them, we're dead! Anything white is to be hung from the highest point. Then hold up your hands! Move!'

I signalled to Léonie. 'I'm going to talk to them,' I said.

If I don't die first.

'Cécile, no,' Dom whispered.

A second shell was fired.

'Cover!' I screamed, but instead of moving into the hedges, I moved forward, dropping to one knee, my hands over my head as the shell whistled over my head.

The blast threw me to the ground before I could even hear it. Waves of heat surged over my back. I closed the sounds from my mind. Hands held high, one step in front of another, towards the approaching vehicles. There were three of them, led by a Daimler armoured car. It took a split second to realise that the device painted on its grille wasn't a swastika. I wanted to exhale my relief, but with the barrel of an anti-tank gun aimed in our direction, we weren't out of trouble yet.

'Friends!' I shouted, not knowing if they could hear me. 'We're friends!'

The Daimler was a hundred yards away. Seventy-five. Fifty. I stopped and stared down its barrel, expecting it to fire.

'I'm English! We're friends.'

The hatch opened with a clang, and I was looking down the business end of a Webley.

'Yeah?' The man's face was painted and bits of twigs and rags were fastened to his helmet. He flicked off the safety. 'Then what the fuck are you doing here?'

'Helping you. My friends and I . . .' I gestured backwards. 'We're with the Resistance!'

He was chewing something. Continued for a few seconds as he stared at me, occasionally glancing over my shoulder.

'Why should I believe you?'

'My name is Elisabeth de Mornay. I know it sounds French, but it's English.' I realised I was babbling and tried to slow down. 'I'm a Special Operations Executive agent. So are two of them.'

I waved towards the women behind me, noting that some of the white flags flying were bloomers, others were blouses. Wasn't sure if I wanted to laugh or cringe.

I returned my attention to the soldier, trying to gauge his expression, but his face was inscrutable underneath the grime and paint.

'Please.'

'Fuck,' he muttered.

Then he retreated back into the Daimler's belly. A different man emerged. Climbed out of the vehicle and jumped to the ground.

A man from the second vehicle, a smaller Daimler Dingo scout car, joined him.

'My name is Elisabeth de Mornay,' I repeated. 'My code name is Cécile, and I'm part of Special Operations Executive.'

'I know who the fuck you are,' he said, storming up to me. 'What I don't know is why the fuck you're here, Elisabeth.'

His filthy face was almost unrecognisable, but his whisky-coloured eyes were familiar. As was the fury emanating from him as he strode towards me.

'Fuck,' I echoed, wondering why the universe hated me so much.

I looked away, not needing to see the embroidered devil on the beret badge to know that these men were from the Inns of Court Regiment – the Devil's Own.

'I asked you a question!' he shouted in my face, spittle dotting my face.

He wasn't much taller than me, but this was a stand-off I felt suddenly unprepared for. Something moved at the edge of my vision, but I couldn't deal with it. Not yet, when decades of impulses ignited. From experience, I knew it was the wrong way to deal with him, but I still moved forward until my nose was inches from his.

'I gave you the answer, you arse! I'm part of Special Operations Executive. I'm *supposed* to be here!'

The figure at the edge of my vision was moving faster, but whoever it was wasn't a threat. The tanks' barrels were still pointed at me.

So was George Wright's angry face. His voice rose.

'What are you? Fucking stupid? You think war is a game? People die here, Elisabeth. Don't you have any fucking sense to keep yourself out of this shit?'

'I'm serving my country, the same as you. You can either take my help or you can shove it—'

'Watch your language, girl. You sound like one of them.' He jerked his head towards his men, now gathering behind him.

'I am one of them, George. What are you going to do? Tell Lady Anne?'

He looked at the sky, and exhaled loudly.

'Will you stop fucking calling her that?'

'What do you want me to call her? Mummy?' My own voice raised itself a decibel or two.

Dom, panting and sweaty, stopped beside me.

'My name is Genevieve Bishop. I'm a Special Operations Executive agent, code name Dominique, and I'm glad you're here. Please don't kill us,' she asked and, noting the aggression between us, added, 'Please don't kill Cécile.'

'Fuck,' he said, glaring at me.

'Fuck,' I echoed. I kept my eyes on George, but spoke to Dom and the other officer. 'He's not going to kill me, as much as he might want to.' I took a deep breath. 'Dominique, let me introduce you to my half-brother, George Wright.'

Chapter Fifty-four

'Fuck,' George said again. He looked over his shoulder and bellowed, 'Patterson, give me your flag!'

'But, sir!'

'Now, Patterson! Take one of their "white flags" as a fucking trophy if you want.' His voice lowered. 'Closest you'll get to a woman's knickers without paying for it,' he muttered.

'What news?' Dom asked.

If she'd been shocked by his language, she opted to let it pass, holding herself unflinching under his scrutiny.

He nodded, but when he spoke it was to me.

'First French town to be liberated was Ranville. Luard's 13th 'Chutes took it this morning. Took the bridge there and the one at Bénouville. Set up a base at the Château du Heaume.'

After two years of service, I wasn't sure how much I believed in a benevolent God, but this . . . this was what I'd been working for. This wasn't the end, but bloody hell! It was one very big step towards it.

'Has the front already moved this far south?'

'No,' George said.

He didn't need to elaborate. His was one of three fast-moving vehicles, and the Dingo was a scout's car. And I'd bet anything the half-track following them was loaded to the gills with explosives.

'The bridges?' I guessed. 'Destroy the bridges and you'll destroy the Boche's exit route, and its ability to resupply.'

For three small and not-very-well-armed vehicles, filled with barristers, to blast behind the lines on that sort of mission was madness. To succeed they really would need the Devil's own luck, but if anyone could accomplish that, it was George Wright.

He nodded, but his eyes were focused behind me as Léonie strode down the road, her dark blue suit jacket was now stained with grime. Her once-smart shoes were caked with mud, and while the silk scarf covering her hair was still in place, blonde tendrils now escaped, curling around her face. Yet she held herself with the same grace as she did when she attended the Desert Fox's reception.

'Shit.'

A man – Patterson, I guessed – flung a Union flag our way and sprinted down the road, goggling at Léonie.

'Fuck,' George said again. 'Why the fuck are there women in the middle of a war?'

'Because war affects us too,' Dom said.

'Fuck's sake, George. Look, whatever you're doing ...' I spoke quickly, knowing that for his mission, as with ours, every moment mattered. 'Just make it home. L—Um ... Anne will be upset to lose you.'

'Whether you believe it or not, Mum would be upset to lose you, too,' he said, and cocked a rare grin. 'Stay alive, Elisabeth, and I'll see you on the other side. You're mad as a March hare, and maybe just daft enough to survive.'

It might have been the only compliment he ever gave me, but for sure, it was by far the best one. I watched him climb back into the Daimler, and raised a hand in a salute.

'Stay alive!' he mouthed, his expression serious.

Léonie reached me as the last of George's three vehicles passed by.

'News?'

Dom answered. 'Cécile isn't the only lunatic in her family.'

Chapter Fifty-five

Feeling the weight of history on my shoulders, I put the Kübelwagen into gear.

'So,' Dom said, 'that's your brother.'

'Half-brother,' I clarified.

'That explains it.'

'Explains what?'

I hit the brakes hard to avoid a crater.

Dom let it go, holding on in silence while I navigated around several potholes, until she said, 'Did you hear that?'

'Hear what?'

I glanced her way, wondering how she could hear anything over the winds and the Kübelwagen's engine. She tilted her head to the side and frowned.

'There it is again. You didn't hear it?'

'You're going mad, Dom.'

But there was something in her voice that gave me pause. I stepped on the brake and cut the engine.

I closed my eyes and concentrated. Isolated, identified and named each sound: the wind whistling through the trees; rain throwing itself against the Kübelwagen; the dilapidated lorry backfiring; distant gunfire and the sound of planes. And then, so faint I almost missed the dog's bark.

But it wasn't just a dog. It was *the* dog. Eduard's dog, Knut. What the devil was he doing here? I pulled hard on the wheel, taking the Kübelwagen off the road. Ignored their questions and yells, I restarted the vehicle and drove as fast as the Kübelwagen would let me. My heart pounded in a way it hadn't when I stared down the barrel of George's gun. Even when I'd been shot at by the RDV or Eugene Vallentin's men.

Because this time, the fear wasn't for myself.

He came running at us before we got far, six stone of black and tan anger, growling and snapping.

I launched myself from the vehicle. He came to me, whimpering. Blood matted the fur on the left side of his head, but he didn't let me touch it. Howling, he raced at me, only to race away.

Sandrine, standing in the Kübelwagen behind me, raised a Sten, pointing it at the dog.

'Don't!' I yelled, glaring until she lowered her arm. 'Don't touch a single hair on him.'

I dropped to one knee.

'What happened?' I asked the dog, as if he could speak.

He did, in his own way. He nipped at my skirt and tugged. He'd take me.

'Fine.'

Climbing back into the Kübelwagen, I put it into gear, following Knut down the track.

'Calm down, Cécile! You'll kill us!'

What did it matter? If Eduard were dead . . .

'He's not!'

I wasn't sure which one of us said the words, but I gripped on to them, holding them close to my heart.

Eduard isn't dead. If he were dead, I would know it. Feel the loss of him.

I didn't feel that. Not yet. Didn't feel anything, other than an all-encompassing fear.

The dog must have been exhausted, but he ran like a greyhound, untiring.

We didn't have far to go. A Renault blocked the road, a man's body half out of the open driver's door, his head resting in a pool of his own blood. In the ditch beside it, a black Mercedes staff car with a shattered windscreen. Knut circled between them, howling.

I fell as I left the Kübelwagen. Righted myself and stumbled to the staff car. Yanked open the door, and stared inside, dumb. Mute. A siren went off in my head.

Someone pushed me aside. Leant in front of me.

A sharp stinging slap on my cheek, and the siren ceased.

'Will you stop that infernal caterwauling?'

I'd expected the voice to have a German accent, but it was Dom who'd slapped me.

'He's not there. Look around, Cécile. The car was attacked, there was a scuffle. Whoever was in the back of the car – they're gone.'

A second slap.

'Stop screaming, Cécile. We don't know he's dead. We don't know if it was even Graf in the car.'

'The dog?'

'It was Graf,' a soft, broken voice said. It wasn't mine.

Dry as her blue-violet eyes were, they contained a soul that I hadn't known existed. Léonie stood aside so we could see the driver's face. The heaven-and-hell of a Botticelli angel, scarred by the fires of a burning Panzer. A new indignity had been dealt to the quietly proud man: a single hole in the centre of his brow, like a third eye, as sightless as the other two.

Her shaking hand cupped his face gently, and drew his eyes closed. She kissed the top of his head, and dropped to one knee, silent tears streaming down her face.

'Go in peace,' she whispered in German, her voice desolate.

Dom went beside her and put a comforting hand on her back.

'You knew him.'

'In another life,' Léonie said, her impeccable façade cracking.

One of the other women pointed to the broken windscreen, and back at a tree over her shoulder.

'Sniper,' she said. 'A rifle, I think. Like Madame Severin's.'

'Who would take Eduard? Why take him instead of ...' I didn't want to say the word aloud. 'Killing him?'

As one, we all looked at Sandrine. Alain Sablonnières' grumpy waitress had paled.

'He would only be killed if they thought he was of no use to them.' Her eyes met mine, pleading. 'I didn't know. I am so sorry.'

And I understood.

'Sablonnières went hunting for Eduard. He knows who I am. He took Eduard to lure me out.'

'I don't know,' she said. 'But yes, I think so. Why else take him and kill the others?'

Léonie answered by addressing another question to Sandrine.

'Where do we find Sablonnières?'

Chapter Fifty-six

'You take the lorry, all of you. I won't risk your lives any more than I have. This isn't your fight.'

'Do you know where he is?' Léonie repeated.

In my mind's eye, I could see them sitting across the table from each other – Eugene Vallentin and Alain Sablonnières, like a pair of old chums. Sablonnières might not know that Vallentin was dead, negating whatever deal he had made. Would it still matter?

Yes, because it was now personal.

The rain was getting heavier, and I pushed my sodden hair out of my face. I knew who to go after, and would start at the logical place: his restaurant, Avignon.

'He said the new operator was a double agent.'

I almost missed Sandrine's whisper.

'What?'

'Alain said that he had proof you were a double agent, and that we needed to get rid of you – of Cecil – before you betrayed the Resistance to the Germans.'

'Only it wasn't me that betrayed them, was it?' I snapped, striding towards her. 'What else do you know? Where is he? Where he's taken Graf?'

'Stop,' Léonie said, her quiet word stopping me in my tracks. She turned and pointed to Dominique. 'Take the women, and return to Beaune's. Take Herr Neumann with you.' She may have struggled to say the words, but they were no less a command. 'And see that he is given a respectful burial. Andreas Neumann was a good man.'

'I'm going with you,' Dom said.

'You're the only one among them with training. They will not make it back on their own. Get them back, if you can. Set up a first aid station there, and when it is safe, join your husband in Caen, or whatever you planned. As far as I am concerned, Madame Severin, you have done your job for me. For us. And you have done it well.'

'Why don't you take them?'

Léonie's smile was tight, and humourless.

'Because I owe a debt to Herr Graf.'

I didn't like the sound of that.

I almost wanted Dom to protest, but she looked between Léonie and me, and slowly said, 'Good luck.'

Back rigid, she walked towards the battered lorry.

Léonie's cold eyes turned on Sandrine.

'Where has he taken Herr Graf?'

Sandrine met her eyes, and then mine. She shook her head.

'I'll show you.'

'Like hell you will,' I said.

Having her at my side when we fought the Germans was one thing. Having her as a wild card when I went up against her friend, one of the heads of the Resistance, traitor as he may be, was a different story.

The Frenchwoman stared, head tilted to the side and gaze challenging.

'You won't find him on your own.'

'Fine,' Léonie said, checking her handgun. 'I do not trust you, but we have no choice. I do not recommend crossing us, madame.'

Léonie was several inches shorter than Sandrine, and garbed like a filthy fashion doll rather than a commando, but there was a quiet menace in her voice that Sandrine couldn't have ignored.

Yvette, the dressmaker, took the Union flag down from the lorry's antenna, folded it, and put it in the Kübelwagen.

'You may need this, I think,' she said.

Sandrine climbed into the driver's seat, waiting for us to hoist ourselves into the vehicle. Knut leapt in after us, putting his head in my lap, and emitting a long, high whine that echoed in my soul.

Sandrine drove in silence while Léonie and I took inventory of our armaments: the Mauser MG 34, mounted next to Léonie; a pair of Stens, and one Thompson; handguns and knives.

It would not be enough if Sablonnières' hideaway was well defended.

With Léonie's gun trained on her back, Sandrine drove past half-derelict houses on streets that were indistinguishable from one another. With each passing mile, I became more certain we were heading into a trap. She knew Sablonnières, cared for him. Why on earth would she take us to him, knowing how likely it was that we would kill him?

For that matter, what debt did Léonie owe Eduard? I leant forward and asked her.

'That is between him and me.'

Her expression was closed again, but something flickered in her eyes, and I guessed.

'Because of Andreas? Because he saved Lieutenant Neumann back in '40? Did you know him then?'

She looked away, her silence a clear answer. It explained why she had been so quick to leave that day we had confronted the SS to save the girl, Felícienne. Andreas had been poised to intervene, and I thought it had been me he was keeping an eye on. What if it was Léonie?

She wouldn't tell me, and I wasn't sure it mattered. What mattered was that she'd chosen to be at my side now.

Sandrine stopped the Kübelwagen at the end of the street. Dahlias bloomed along a neat path to the front door, and behind the house was the forest. The windows were shot out and a dead man lay on the doorstep, reaching for his pistol through the begonias. From a distance, it was impossible to tell which side the man had fought on.

Sandrine gestured for me to get out of the vehicle.

'We'll go the rest of the way on foot.'

Léonie studied her for a moment, the pistol still in her hand.

'Betray us' – her voice was soft, but undercut with steel – 'and it'll be the last thing you do.'

And if Léonie didn't take care of that, I would.

Chapter Fifty-seven

A flash of white light, followed by an explosion. A man appeared in a window of one of the houses, bare-headed but black-faced. The face was replaced by a gun's muzzle.

'Gun,' I warned, as loud as I dared.

I crouched low, and glanced behind me.

Léonie was fingering a slash in her sleeve, where a bullet had passed harmlessly. She muttered something under her breath, but gestured for me to keep moving.

Bullets whizzed overhead and I flattened myself to the ground. I wanted to close my eyes – to look away – but such foolishness put my life at risk, so with shaking hands, I checked my weapon, but the shooting was over in minutes. Unsure if that was a good sign, we inched forward, following Sandrine towards the line of trees, my left hand tight on Knut's collar as he tried to drag me forward.

Behind us, someone bellowed at the house, 'Come out before you burn!'

The blaze crackled, sending waves of heat our way. Whoever might have been in there wasn't likely to survive, but I couldn't look back. I had to move forward – following a woman I didn't trust, with only Léonie to back me up.

You've won against worse odds, I reminded myself.

But then why did it feel like a clock was running down?

The sun had set, and the weather was so foul that there was barely enough light to see an empty American jeep was parked in front of a small cabin, well hidden by trees, and far enough from the road to be safe enough.

For now.

A man dozed on the porch, his feet up on the railing, Sten nearby.

'Even if that cabin is empty, how the devil can he sleep with gunfire so close?'

Sandrine shook her head. 'He's not asleep.'

He didn't look dead, either; there was someone in the cabin, who wanted us to think the lookout was lazy.

But that didn't mean that Eduard was here, either.

'Are you ready?' Léonie asked. Waited for our nods, and signalled us to move.

I peeled to the right while she went left. The brush was over-grown, with the earthy smell of soil that had been overwatered. Sticks and brush pulled at me. The distant gunfire had ceased and Knut looked ready to strike.

'Stop that,' I muttered to him. 'And no barking. Wait for my command.'

His big brown eyes gave me a doleful glare, as if he under-stood what his role was, but I just wasn't moving fast enough. He was probably right.

Ahead, a guard moved towards the brush. He unfastened his flies. His face became almost blissful as he began to urinate, scant feet in front of me. I halted, wanting to look away, but his privacy came at the cost of my safety.

I watched the final shake before he tidied himself and, whistling a tune, took a few steps towards the cabin. I gave Knut the command to stay. Trusting that he would obey it, I rolled from the brush, coming up on one knee, with the Fairbairn Sykes in my hand. Three steps, and it was against his throat.

'What . . .? What do you want?'

'Is Sablonnières inside?' I whispered into his ear.

He didn't answer right away, and I allowed the ugly blade to tease the loose skin at his neck. It caught on a fold, and I knew the man felt his own blood well and drip.

'Yes,' he whimpered.

'And the prisoner?'

'Inside,' he said. 'Please don't hurt me.'

'Why?'

I'd meant 'why shouldn't I hurt him', but he answered the bigger question.

'He was a good target. And Sablonnières, he wants to draw out the double agent. She accused him to deflect attention from her own actions. This is her man. Proof that she's in bed with the Boche. Alain is only trying to do right for us, to protect us from the Boche.'

He was babbling. And a fool for believing Sablonnières' drivel, but he didn't deserve to die for it. I brought the butt of the knife against the side of the guard's head, holding on to his weight as his body sagged against me – one less combatant. He was heavy, and I eased him down to the ground.

'I am sorry you chose the wrong side,' I murmured, my finger on his pulse. He was alive, but wasn't likely to stir for a while.

'You'll have a glory of a headache when you wake up, but that'll be your problem, not mine.'

I gestured to Knut to follow me, and he fell into step, slinking low beside me as we eased closer to the cabin.

Ahead, Sandrine approached the porch.

'Good evening, Simon.' When the sleepy man challenged her, she asked, 'Is Alain here?'

Trusting that Sandrine would do what she was told – if not of her own volition, then out of fear of Léonie's gun – I continued moving around the cabin to the first window. It was darkened, the panes opened to let in the night air.

Léonie was on the far side of the cabin. If Sandrine hadn't lied to us, the two windows we could see led to two bedrooms. She gave me the thumbs up and I moved towards the closest window and peered inside.

And cringed at the sight that greeted me. A man lay on a cot, eyes closed, lying in a state of *déshabille* atop crumpled bed sheets, preoccupied with himself.

Seriously? While France was finally being liberated, he was in a dark room, wanking? What happened to the *Liberté, égalité, fraternité* spirit? What happened to doing your bloody part when the time came to free your country from an invader?

Cursing myself for giving away the silent Welrod, I took advantage of his preoccupation. Hiking up my skirt a few inches gave me enough leeway to vault myself through the open window. He looked up. He should have reached for the gun on the bedside table, but instead, he stared at me, his hand moving faster on himself.

The butt of the Fairbairn Sykes struck a second time.

I left him as he was. Glanced down at the magazine at the foot of the bed, opened to a large photograph of a busty blonde pin-up.

The dog whined and I gave him the low command, standing back as he leapt through the window.

I eased the door open and stepped into the hallway. There was no one there, which meant Léonie was still in the other room, or had moved ahead, but I couldn't waste the time to check.

Around the corner was a large room, a combination of living room and dining room. Eduard Graf sat in an upright chair in the centre, bound and bloodied. And from the anger snapping in his eyes, not only was he still alive, he was *furious*.

That was a good sign. I retreated a step, exhaling with my back against the wall, trying not to allow my relief to make me careless. He was here and he was alive, but we still needed to free him – and get out of the area before it became a battlefield.

I peered around the corner a second time, assessing the threat levels. Five men, none of whom was Sablonnières. One was standing at the front door, chatting with Sandrine and the guard, Simon. Two were focused on Eduard, while the last man stood in front of the fireplace.

Despite the June heat, a fire blazed in the hearth; two pokers pointed into the blaze.

Hell, they were going to *burn* him? This wasn't a lure to draw out a possible double agent, this was torture.

The man picked up a flannel, wrapping it around his hand, and a white-hot fury coursed through me.

Over my dead body.

I sheathed the Fairbairn Sykes and reached for the Luger. Released my grip on Knut's collar and gave him the order to attack. He provided the element of surprise, leaping at one of the men beside Eduard.

The other one reached for a gun.

I bent to the side, feeling the breath of the bullet as it passed. Squeezed the trigger of my gun, watching red blossom on the man's forehead. The man by the fire turned and I squeezed the trigger again. As the pistol's knee joint flexed, ejecting the spent cartridge and chambering the next round, I felt nothing but disgust for the man who fell, dead, into the fire.

On the other side of the open window, the man turned. He raised his weapon. The Luger's slide recoiled, the knee joint dancing three more times. The man fell before he could fire his own weapon, blood flowing from his chest.

I knocked the guns away from the bodies, just in case, as I heard the last man outside scream in pain.

Whatever Eduard was yelling was muffled by the scarf stuffed into his mouth, but I had a feeling it wasn't complimentary. I released the gag and stepped back.

'What the hell are you doing here, Katrin?'

'Freeing you. Hold still and I'll cut the ropes.'

Still bound, he tried to lunge in front of me. I turned to see Alain Sablonnières in the doorway. Tall and broad; dark hair that had been slicked back from his forehead now draped across it in oily tendrils. He had a gun held to Sandrine's head. The grumpy waitress was bloodstained, but it didn't look to be hers and I guessed that she had killed the other man outside.

Sablonnières looked dispassionately at the bodies strewn around the room and frowned.

'Why?' I asked.

He tilted his head, questioning. 'Why what?'

'Why get into bed with the Boche? Money? How much did they pay you to betray your own men, your country?'

'I don't know what you mean.' He jerked his head towards Eduard. 'Look, I've captured a German!'

'I saw the contents of your safe,' I said. 'And I saw you with Eugene Vallentin. He's dead, by the way. Killed by a group of women this afternoon. You'll need to find someone else to collaborate with.'

He snarled, pushing Sandrine towards me.

I lunged to the side to avoid her. Squeezed the trigger as she knocked into me. As I fell, I saw the bullet sail past Sablonnières. The Luger's knee remained up; the cartridge was empty.

Scheisse.

I rolled for one of the dead men's pistols. Before I could grab it, two shots were fired. I wanted to look to Eduard, to reassure myself that he was still alive, but forced my gaze to Sablonnières. Watched him crumble, bleeding from the chest and the side of his head.

Léonie lowered her gun.

'Always reload your gun first,' she said and tossed me a spare cartridge for the Luger. I slammed it into place and crawled the few feet to Eduard. His eyes had gone black with fury. That was good, I could deal with his anger; it was his death that was unacceptable.

'Hurry up,' she said and held a hand out to help Sandrine to her feet.

She was right. Careful not to cut Eduard, I used the Fairbairn Sykes to saw through his bonds. The ropes dropped to my feet, and Eduard brought his arms in front of him, rubbing his wrists.

A shell hit nearby, shaking the ground.

Eduard didn't hesitate.

'We need to get out of here.'

He grabbed my arm and pulled me to the door.

Chapter Fifty-eight

Sablonnières and Vallentin were dead, but the tides of war were about to crash over us.

'Who was the man in the other car?' I yelled, partly because it was the only way to be heard over the Kübelwagen's engine. Partly because Eduard, well over six feet tall and the only man in the vehicle, rode in the back, hanging on to the mounted MG 34 machine gun, crouched low so as not to present too much of a target.

'Who?' he asked, glancing at Sandrine.

'There was another car near the one we found Andreas in. Another man. Who was he?'

'I don't know – he was already there.'

I didn't believe him. I wondered if it was someone he'd worked with. A contact who would help bring a swift end to the war.

The road was barely visible. I was about to turn off and drive towards Beaune's farm, when a better idea came to me. I turned the vehicle around, ignoring the cries from behind me as they hung on.

'Where are you going?'

'You're going straight into the war zone!' Sandrine said. 'Are you completely mad?'

It was crazy, but the battle lines would roll over us sooner or later. If Ranville was already liberated, we might be able to slip through those lines.

'Tanks,' Léonie said to me, pointing. 'Panzers. Through the trees.'

She had the eyes of an eagle. I hadn't seen them. At least the Union flag was still on the floor at her feet, rather than flying from the antenna. As we got closer, I could see them, hiding in the hedges – big, ugly tanks, their guns pointing north. A tank in an open field was a bomber's dream target, but camouflaged by the hedges, these machines were the perfect tools for an ambush.

The turrets began to turn to us, slowly.

Eduard raised his hand in greeting, calling out to them. Still dressed in his uniform, the Knight's Cross at his neck, they thought we were one of them.

Despite three out of the four of us being women.

We passed them, driving as fast as I could make the Kübelwagen go. No idea how many more enemy tanks were ahead of us. Or how many Allied tanks, who would think we were the enemy.

'There should be more of them,' I muttered.

'The 21st Panzers are on manoeuvres,' Léonie said.

How long before they were recalled? Were they already en route?

Planes flew overhead, low enough that I could see three white stripes painted on each wing and the fuselage. If they were regimental markings, it was a squadron I had never heard of.

'Get the flag up!' I screamed.

Léonie was already bracing herself to tie the Union flag to the antenna. Behind me, Eduard stuffed his medal in his pocket and removed his tunic.

Allied vehicles approached. Léonie stood again in the Kübel-wagen, barely clearing the bonnet, smiling and waving at them. Sandrine followed suit. The men in the vehicles waved back as they passed us.

'Fools,' I muttered.

We could have been riding into their midst as a bloody Trojan Horse, but they saw a pretty girl and couldn't believe we were a threat. Despite the vehicle we drove. Despite Eduard Graf in the back.

Astonishing.

We were stopped at the gate outside the château.

'My name is Elisabeth de Mornay, and I'm an agent with Special Operations Executive. I'm here to see . . .' I cast about for the name George had mentioned. 'Luard. Lieutenant-Colonel Luard.'

'Who are they?' The guard gestured to the others.

'My comrades. Luard will want to talk to them.'

'And the German vehicle?'

'The previous owners aren't alive to complain.'

I looked beyond him. The château was set back from the road across a wide expanse of green, torn up by bomb craters. Built of pale Caen stone, under a dark slate roof, with long windows marching sideways from an imposing entrance. So that was what safety looked like.

The guard snorted his amusement, then assumed his serious mien.

'Your name again?'

Relief made my voice light.

'Elisabeth – with an *S* – de Mornay.' *Graf*, I added silently, careful not to look at Eduard. *With an* F *instead of a* PH. 'My code name is Cécile. Check with Baker Street if you want proof.'

He nodded and waved over two comrades.

'They'll escort the three of you inside,' he explained.

Three? I looked around. Eduard was beside me, Sandrine on his other side, but there was no sign of Léonie. She was gone.

Chapter Fifty-nine

Lieutenant-Colonel Peter Luard was somewhere in his early thirties, with the rugged looks of a paratrooper. Despite the late hour, he still wore his battledress and beret. The commander of the 13th Parachute Battalion stood in front of an empty chimney, stroking his moustache as we explained who we were.

'I understand who they are.' Luard waved at Sandrine and me. He crossed his arms over his chest, secure that the armed guards by the door would prevent any attack. 'But who are you?' he asked Eduard.

'I am Colonel Eduard Graf,' my husband said. 'And I am authorised to speak on behalf of a number of senior German officers. However, I have one stipulation.'

Luard raised an eyebrow, his expression a cross between incredulity and amusement.

'You are in no position to make demands to me.'

Eduard inclined his head. 'Perhaps not. A request, then.' He didn't meet my eye as he said, 'This is no place for a woman. They need to be sent to safety. Send Elisabeth de Mornay back to Baker Street. Her friend as well, if she is willing to go to England. Then, and only then, we'll talk.'

'*No!*'

They ignored my protest, and it was as if a silent conversation passed between Eduard and Luard – men of similar rank, similar age, similar determination. Knut whined and lay down on the floor, his eyes bouncing between the men and me. Sandrine meandered over to the floor-to-ceiling windows, looking out into the night.

'I'm not going back to England,' I said, furious that Eduard thought he could send me away. 'Not unless and until I'm recalled by Special Operations Executive.'

'You *want* to stay here? Get caught up in the fighting?' Luard said, moustache twitching.

Did I want to be in the middle of a battle? No, of course not. I didn't want to be on the receiving side of an air attack either, but I had a job to do, and it wasn't for either Eduard or Peter Luard to dictate what that job was.

'It's not for me to decide. If Colonel Buckmaster orders me home, I'll go. Not before.' Buck wasn't one to waste a resource. If he agreed, it was only because he could use me elsewhere.

Luard gestured to one of his men.

'Get word to Baker Street.'

The room they put me in must have once been servants' quarters on the second floor. The wallpaper showed dark spots on the wall where pictures or paintings had once hung, but the furniture was utilitarian; the Boche had used it as an office.

The window overlooked the muddy lawn where tree branches had been blown, either by weather or bombs, during recent hours.

One of Luard's men sat outside the door. I didn't need a babysitter, and I wasn't about to escape, simply because there was nowhere to go.

Sandrine was in the room next door, but I was less worried about her. Léonie was one of the most self-reliant people I knew, but how far could she get on foot, in bad weather, when the Germans, the Allies and the French were out looking for battle?

What did she hope to accomplish? And didn't she know that I would have helped her, had she asked?

It was late afternoon when the guard knocked on the door and called out, 'Visitor.'

If it was Eduard, he'd better have a damn good reason for doing what he did.

But it wasn't Eduard. It was Dominique, carrying my suitcase, with the Leica Léonie had given me slung on its strap from her shoulder.

'I thought you'd need clean clothing,' she said.

'How did you know where to find me?'

'I didn't.' She put the suitcase near the door, and the camera on the desk. 'There was fighting by the farm this morning. The Allies pushed the Germans back, but we took what we could and travelled north. Beaune wanted to engage with the Allied troops anyway. Give them whatever local knowledge we can.'

'And you?'

'I'm still an SOE operative, Cécile.' She tempered the sharp retort with a tired smile. 'I assume you managed to rescue Graf?'

I nodded.

'Sablonnières?'

'Dead.'

'Then why the long face?'

'Eduard is trying to get me recalled to London,' I grumbled.

She shrugged. 'You heard Léonie. We did what we needed to do here, but there's still plenty of work to do.' She sat on the camp bed and took a deep breath. 'About Léonie . . .'

'I don't know where she is. We made it here, but she slipped away when we were stopped at the gate. I hope she's all right.'

Dom took a deep breath, and let it out in a long *whoosh*. She got up and started pacing. Looked out of the window, and then at me.

'Cécile . . . Léonie . . . She isn't . . .'

I didn't want to hear her. Knew it wasn't going to be good. And as long as I didn't have confirmation, I could pretend that Léonie was still out there. Maybe lost, maybe wreaking havoc on the Boche. But alive.

'She's not dead,' I said aloud. 'She can't be. I only saw her a few hours ago.'

Dom's shoulders hunched, and she rubbed her arms as if she was cold.

'What happened?'

'I wasn't there, don't know exactly how it came about.'

'*What* came about, Dom?'

'André heard it from one of the POWs. When she left you, she made her way west, towards Caen. Don't ask me how, I have no idea.'

It wasn't the *how* that bothered me.

'Why? Why would she do that? Did she want to go after Zeit?'

'No. I heard he was killed near the beaches. No. But you do know what she did the night of the invasion? While we were in the bell tower?'

I didn't. There had been no time to ask her.

'The paratroopers we saw land attacked the Bénouville and Ranville bridges. The guards notified their commanding officer, and when the CO realised what was happening and woke Zeit for his orders, Léonie insisted that he first drive her to her apartment before doing anything else. She bought those boys as much time as she could.'

'But she was living with him!'

'She was, within days of her landing. But she had also taken rooms further inland. Always have a safe house.'

Her voice was ironic; it was one of the first lessons we'd been taught, but if Dom had a safe house, I hadn't heard about it in all the time I'd been living with her.

'How did you learn all this?'

'She told me, when we were driving to meet you at Beaune's farm.'

I sensed she had worse news.

'Do you know where she is, Dom?'

'She's dead. One of the POWs told André. There was a gun emplacement on the coast. It couldn't have been the first one she found, but armed with only a Sten and a handgun, she attacked it. By herself.'

'What?' I gasped. 'Why would she do something daft like that?'

'You knew her better than I did, Cécile. Why *would* she do that?'

I shook my head, unable to explain what I didn't understand, even if I had the words. And then a face I'd seen only once flashed in my mind – the SS man with the triangular scar and the missing ear, whom we had seen in Caen. Whoever he was, he'd affected her. I could see her again, brushing it away, but she'd known him. And whoever he was, whatever he'd done, was bad enough that she'd sacrificed herself to kill him.

I had no doubt he was the reason she'd slipped away as soon as we reached the safe haven here.

'Léonie wouldn't have seen it as throwing her life away,' I whispered.

Because she was already broken. And if the man with the missing ear had a role to play in that, then she would consider it a fair exchange, sacrificing her life to take his.

It wasn't likely I would ever know.

'Ah, Léonie.' I brushed away a tear and looked up at the sky. 'May you – and Andreas – rest in peace.'

Chapter Sixty

The guard stuck his head around the door.

'Ma'am? London approved your ride home. Plane will be here within the hour.' He opened the door for me. 'Colonel says you can see the Kraut if you want to. He's been asking about you.'

The guard carried my suitcase downstairs, and escorted me into the back of the château, where Eduard waited. The guard stood some feet away. We wouldn't be given time alone. Luard and his men didn't know our situation; they only knew what we'd told them: that I was Elisabeth de Mornay, SOE agent who'd rescued a German colonel and brought him here so that he could negotiate with the Allies.

It was a fiction that, for both our sakes, we had to maintain.

Knut saw me before Eduard did, barking and bounding over to me. I ruffled his fur and sat on the bench beside my husband.

'You got your wish – I'm flying home tonight.'

He nodded and looked away.

'That's best,' he said, and quickly shook his head. 'You must understand – I do not want to leave you. It is for *me* to be with you, to protect you.' He took a ragged breath. 'But to protect you, I must send you away.'

I didn't share my theory on Buck's motivations with Eduard; I didn't want this conversation marred by an argument.

His hand fell to the space between us. Moved close, closer than it should have, its warmth closing around mine. Something sharp and hard slipped into my palm.

'I don't have anything else I can give you,' he said.

'I don't need . . . I don't *want* your bloody Knight's Cross to remember you by, Eduard.'

'Then I shall collect it from you at the first opportunity.'

The edges of his mouth twitched, as if he wanted to smile, but could not, and yet his warm tone belied the stilted words.

I wanted to believe him. Hung on to that thought with every fibre of my being. And yet, the fear pervaded.

'I don't know how to do this,' I admitted.

'What? To say goodbye?' His smile was sadder this time. 'The last time, at the pier near Lourenço Marques, where your Allied ships docked, I thought it would be a week, maybe two, before I was back in Lisbon, and I would find you waiting for me. This time, it is you leaving. But I know that this time you will be waiting for me, not in Portugal, but in London.'

Maybe. Maybe not. But even if I felt inclined to tell him anything, the opportunity passed. Luard's guard began moving towards us.

My throat closed and, unable to speak, I nodded.

'I will still find you, Lisbet. Wherever you go, wherever they send you, I will find you.' His voice lowered, and he schooled his expression into one of casual disinterest. 'If you believe nothing else, believe that. We will get through this, and we will be together.' One corner of his mouth quirked. 'Maybe even, one day, in Estoril.'

I brushed the side of my hand against his, desperately wishing I could do more. My wedding ring, the fake one Barbara

378

Bertram had made me wear, caught a stray moonbeam. I stared at it, unable to breathe. Even knowing that as I changed the subject, I diverted it into more dangerous ground, I asked, 'You heard about Léonie?'

He looked at me, confused. 'Léonie?'

'Lene Deines. The German woman who helped me rescue you. She's dead.'

Emotion after emotion crossed his face, so fast I couldn't name them. Finally, he composed himself.

'I am sorry. What happened?'

I relayed the news as Dominique had told it and repeated my question: 'Did you know her?'

'I'd never met her before, Angel.'

There it was in his voice: a tone that told me he wasn't lying, but hadn't told me the full truth, either. I didn't think he would, but I understood: it wasn't his story to tell.

To hell with Luard's men. I placed my hand over Eduard's and leant forward.

'And Andreas . . . I'm so sorry, Eduard. He was a good man.'

His shoulders dropped and he looked away.

'He was more than that,' he said, his voice subdued. 'He was a good friend. The best.'

The guard moved forward; we were running out of time.

'Eduard . . .'

'It is all right.' He straightened his back and stood up. Faced me so that the guard wouldn't hear his last words. 'Keep the *Ritterkreuz* safe. Not for me, but for the man who pinned it on my chest. If our efforts do not succeed, I will need something to remember *him* by.'

He was trying to allay my fears, making it sound as if his own life wasn't at stake should his mission fail. I nodded. The guard placed a hand on Eduard's arm, and led him away, while I struggled to maintain my composure. Allowed my hand to edge out, towards the spot where my husband had sat, and blinked away my tears.

My fingers closed around the Knight's Cross, feeling its familiar edges, the Oak Leaves. 'We *will* be together again.' I stood and directed my next words at the sky. 'You can count on it.'

The Lysander came from the south; Buck had probably used the opportunity to drop another agent elsewhere. As with the planes we'd seen the other night, this also had three stripes on the wings and fuselage. Marks, I now understood, that were painted on all aircraft involved in the invasion.

Knowing Eduard watched from the château, I held my back straight and walked out to meet the plane. As relieved as I was to go home, I was terrified to leave him here, when he could just as easily be shot by the Allies as by the Nazis.

I was ordered to return, but I felt like I was running away. There was unfinished business and unanswered questions. The Allies had taken the beaches, but their toehold in Normandy wasn't yet secure. There were still things I could do to help.

With my suitcase in one hand, I gripped the fixed ladder on the side of the Lysander. Halfway up, I paused. At the line of trees, I imagined I could see Léonie, impeccable in a blue suit, one hand raised in farewell.

You have done your job, the wind whispered in my ear. *Safe travels, my friend.*

'Be at peace,' I whispered back. 'My friend.'

I settled the suitcase at my feet in the rear cockpit. The pilot slid back the canopy and accelerated into the take-off. I looked down, watching the countryside recede. It was pockmarked by bombs, blemished by the war machine.

This time the plane wasn't bombarded as we passed the coastal defences, but I could see signs of battle further west, towards Caen.

The night was clear, and with only the clear canopy separating me from space, it felt like I was flying among the stars. My gloved hand pressed against the window, as if I could touch the moon. The fake wedding ring pressed into my finger, and I looked forward to exchanging it for the one Eduard had actually put on my finger. That same hand went to my thigh, closing around the *Ritterkreuz*, hidden in my pocket.

'It is only *au revoir*.'

The Lysander slowed at the end of the runway and turned towards a Nissen hut. When it stopped, when the pilot threw back the canopy, a woman stepped onto the tarmac.

'Welcome back, Cécile.'

Vera Atkins strode forward, emanating her usual air of calm efficiency.

We shared a hot meal with the pilot on the base, before a FANY led us to the sand-and-spinach painted staff car and drove us back to London. I closed my eyes and only realised how long I'd slept when the turn off the road jerked me awake. I blinked at the landmarks.

'Barnes?' I asked. 'We're not going to Baker Street?'

'No, we'll debrief you first.'

The FANY followed the River Thames to the bend where the reception centre was located. The river was at low tide, showing a wide muddy swath on either side.

Feeling like I'd regressed back to my own schooldays, I went to my allocated room, and collected a change of clothing and a few toiletries. I'd worn the same clothes for almost thirty-six hours and by now, they weren't fit to be rags. A piece of paper peeked from between two dresses. Curious, I pulled it out. The paper was good quality, not the onion paper we'd been writing on for years. I sat down and unfolded it.

It was a simple pencil sketch – ripped from Dom's sketch pad. Three women sat on the rubble in front of the Abbaye aux Hommes, facing Saint-Étienne's abbey rather than the viewer. The woman on the right had dark curly hair and leant on an exposed beam that could have been a rifle. The one in the centre was taller than the other two, and rested a foot on a box. The one on the left had the profile of a Dresden doll. Her right one rested in her lap, delicate fingers holding a pistol. In her left hand, a quickly sketched poppy. Dom had clearly made that change after learning of Léonie's death.

In the corner, in her elegant handwriting, she'd written, 'Redeemable for an oil version by the artist once France is free. Be safe, my sister.'

I smiled, and wiped away a tear. Put down the drab wool skirt and put on a peach dress Dominique's friends had sewn for me. Held Eduard's cross for a few moments. Fearing that my belongings would be searched, I pinned it to the dress's lining, so that I could feel it against my skin, but know that it was hidden from sight. Safe, as Eduard had asked.

I took a deep breath, and walked down the hall to begin the tedious process of my debrief.

It took longer than it should have, the key questions of how far Sablonnières' treachery had spread, and why the *réseau* had not been able – or willing – to root it out themselves, not being adequately answered in the eyes of SOE. I didn't disagree, but I couldn't tell them what I didn't know, and conjecture didn't appear to cut the mustard.

Once cleared, I returned to London and resumed volunteering at Norgeby House. I learnt about the Allies' progress from the coded transmissions, the BBC and the newsreels. The Yanks had trapped the Boche at Cherbourg, and the Brits were working to liberate Caen. An RAF raid succeeded in knocking out the Panzer Group West's headquarters.

Every day, I listened for news of Dom and Jérôme, of my brothers, of Eduard Graf.

I built relationships with the operators across Europe. I heard the devastation in one man's transmission when he relayed news of the 2nd Panzers wreaking havoc as they passed through Oradour and Argenton. I'd never met 'Clive', but I imagined his tears in the unsteady dots and dashes when he told of the courier who had gone missing, presumed dead. I didn't know 'Phoebe' either, but hoped that her end had come swift and clean.

Part of me yearned to be back there with them, where I could make a difference. Every time I asked, Buck put me off, told me I was making a difference here.

The Allies entered Caen on 9 July and liberated it on the 18th, after fighting street by street, building by building. Word filtered through that Dom and Jérôme, while battered, had survived.

But there was still no news about Eduard.

A few days later, I was sitting in an officers' club near St James's, the sort of club that wouldn't allow a woman in before the war, and might just bar us again afterwards. The men beside me were half hidden by their leather chairs. They glanced at me and the younger leaned closer to his friend, whispering something.

More out of curiosity, I feigned disinterest and blocked out the background noise and concentrated. I could barely make out the younger man's words, but could have sworn he whispered about an assassination attempt made on Hitler.

Eduard. Was this what he'd been working on?

My heart skipped a beat. I had to know. I jumped out of my seat fast enough that it fell to the ground.

'What happened?' I demanded, grabbing the young officer by his tunic.

'I don't know, ma'am. Just what I heard.'

I shook him. 'And what was it you heard?'

'Someone tried to kill Hitler.'

'Wouldn't be the first attempt,' the older officer said, trying to edge me away. 'None have succeeded yet.'

'But this was different,' the young man insisted. 'Something's definitely happening.'

'Hush, fool,' the older man said, looking at me from the corner of his eye. It was clear that he wouldn't say anything, and while he was there, the younger man wouldn't either.

There was another option. Someone who would likely know what was going on, although whether they would tell me was another question.

Well, they'd just have to.

I loosened my grip on the younger man's tunic. 'For heaven's sake,' I muttered and stormed off.

I sprinted to Baker Street, and paused at the sandbagged door. Leaned against a bag and caught my breath. 'Is he in, Mr Parks?' I asked the doorman, knowing I didn't have to clarify who the 'he' was.

Parks made a step or two forward to block my entrance, but then stepped back.

'Yes, of course, ma'am.'

I pushed open the door to Buckmaster's office.

'What the bloody hell's happened?'

Buck blinked. 'Good evening, Cécile.'

'Blast the pleasantries. What's happening in Germany, and where the devil is Eduard Graf?'

'Sit down, Cécile,' Vera said from behind me.

She closed the door and went to stand beside Buck.

I slammed both hands on the desk. 'Are you telling me he's dead? Eduard is dead?'

'Calm down, Cécile.' Vera's voice was cool, but sharp. 'As far as we know, he's not dead. And as to what's happening in

Germany, you probably know as much as we do. Remember, we handle France, not Germany.'

'Fine. What's happening in *France* as a result of this?'

'It's still developing, of course. There are reports that von Stülpnagel, as military governor of France, managed to disarm the SD and SS. Captured most of their leaders, but Hitler isn't dead, and in the past, retribution has been swift and uncompromising.'

'I want to go back.'

They exchanged a glance.

'No.'

'I did what you sent me to do. Twice. The troops have landed and are making headway. Let me go back. Let me help. You don't need to send me to him. In fact, it's probably best that you don't. But you brought me here for a reason. *Let me do my job.*'

Both of them remained quiet, starting at me as if I were a deranged Valkyrie.

'Fine,' I said. 'You won't let me do my job? Then I quit. I'm sure the Yanks wouldn't leave me to cool my heels here when there's work to do.'

It was an empty threat and they knew it. Buck expelled a long sigh.

'You can't quit, and what you're threatening to do now borders on insubordination. Yes, yes, I know that's your nature. Makes you a good field agent, and all that. But right now, there is a delicate balance as we wait to see what happens in Germany. I cannot allow you to risk becoming a distraction no one can afford. Go home.'

'A distraction?' I had been called a lot of things, but not that. 'You know full well I'm more than capable!'

'Go home, Cécile. That's an order.' He held up a hand to stop my protest. 'There are more things that are going on than you are aware of. You're tired and it's late. Go home, Cécile. Cool off and come back next week and we'll discuss this in depth.'

He stood up, signalling that my interview was at an end.

I squared my shoulders; was halfway to the door when Vera called out to me.

'One more thing before you go, Cécile,' she said, rising out of her chair.

I shrugged and followed her down the hall to her office. She produced a box from a cabinet and laid it on the desk between us. It looked familiar, not unlike the one Barbara Bertram had folded my clothes into before I left for France.

'This is for you.'

I stood still, sensing that what lay within wasn't mine.

'I don't need it.'

She opened a gold cigarette case and selected two cigarettes, lighting both. 'She thought you might.'

Not *she*. Léonie. My voice was choked when I was finally able to speak.

'Why me? Why now?'

Vera shrugged in a way that was almost French, and handed me a cigarette.

'She had no one else. And she liked you. Trusted you.'

I inhaled deeply, feeling the nicotine rush through my veins. Vera sank into her seat, waiting patiently until I did the same. I placed the cigarette in a crystal ashtray and opened the box.

Inside it was a neatly folded skirt and blouse, stockings, and a battered but well-tended pair of high-heeled shoes. Underneath was a mangled stuffed rabbit, and a notebook, the sort schoolchildren used.

I opened the cover. A piece of paper fluttered to the floor. On it was written, in her precise handwriting, '*If anyone deserves to know my story, it will be you.*'

'Her journal? She kept a journal?'

'Not quite. She wasn't able to do so in Germany, but she found it cathartic, once she was here.' Another eloquent shrug.

I took another drag on the cigarette and flipped to the first page.

'*My name is Vreni Ritter, although that is not the one I was born with . . .*'

She knew she wasn't coming back, and yet, I believed that was by her own choice, and maybe this book would explain the reasons why. I closed it, unwilling to read Léonie's words in front of Vera. I placed my hand on the cover and asked, 'Did you read it?'

'I did,' Vera said, unapologetically. 'When you mentioned her reaction to the man with the triangular scar. I needed to know who he was, and if he would impact her ability to carry out the mission.'

'He didn't.'

'No. She was too much of a professional. But once the mission was complete . . .' Vera shrugged.

More than once, I'd wondered what Andreas Neumann had been like, before the scars had disfigured him, but I'd never questioned what had made Léonie as ruthless as she was, and I now regretted that.

'I hope she got him.'

'As do I, Cécile.' Vera sighed. 'As do we all.'

I walked home in the moonlight. A taxi could have taken me there faster, but the sky was clear, and I felt Léonie's ghost keeping pace with me.

I crossed Oxford Street and turned down Bond Street. Some familiar shops were nothing more than a hole in the ground, others boarded up, either for the night or for ever. The moon was rising, almost full. Would another agent drop tonight into another part of France, or Belgium, or somewhere else? A pang of envy raced down my spine. I wasn't good with inactivity. Not when I could use my skills – skills SOE taught me – to bring about a swifter end to the war. Because whether the assassination attempt was a success or not, Hitler's henchmen would put up a fight.

I turned onto Conduit Street, nodding to a pair of bobbies smoking on the corner.

'Bit late to be out, miss,' one said.

He couldn't have been much more than sixteen; the other might have been nearing sixty, and looked familiar.

I set down Léonie's box and accepted the older man's offer of a cigarette.

'It's good to be home.'

The officer nodded as if he understood.

'At least there haven't been any attacks tonight, ma'am.'

The nicotine had reached my lungs, bringing with it a sense of well-being and enough calm to realise that Buck probably did have a plan for me, and I could certainly wait until next week to find out what it was.

'Let's hope it stays that way.' I held up the cigarette. 'Thank you.'

'Evening, ma'am.'

'Evening, gentlemen.'

The neat wrought-iron fence that had been outside my town house was long gone, the metal melted down and used for arms or ammunition, but the house was still standing. I reached for my keys, eager to be home, I turned the corner and spotted a pair of unfamiliar men, further down the street, watching my front door.

Gestapo!

No, my rational brain insisted. *This is England, and the Gestapo hold no sway here.*

Still, I put the box down, transferred the keys to my left hand and reached through the slit in my pocket for the sgian dubh that I still wore. A pale tendril of light escaped the blackout curtains.

Someone was in my house.

I pulled out the knife and braced myself for attack. Eased up the first step, and then the second.

And stopped. There was music coming from within. A soprano, accompanied by a pair of guitars. Realising the haunting music was Portuguese *fado*, the music of Portugal, my keys fell from numb fingers. Inside, a dog began to bark.

Fado. Eduard had wooed me to *fado* a year ago.

My hand touched my chest, where Eduard's cross was still pinned to the lining of my dress. Buck knew. This was why he wanted me to go home. Keys forgotten, I banged on the door.

'Eduard? Eduard!'

However long we had before Eduard was moved or I was recalled for my next mission, Buck had bought us precious time together. Tears ran down my cheeks as the locks on the far side of the door were thrust aside. The heavy door opened and I allowed the momentum of life to carry me forward.

Historical Note

First and foremost, this novel is a work of fiction. The Resistance network (*réseau*) that I mention in this book is completely made up, although I've referenced real people and events where I think they would add to the story. There's a lot to cover from the historical perspective, so in this section I've mentioned some of the more remote bits of history as the broader topics (e.g., the Normandy landings) are well covered elsewhere.

Special Operations Executive (SOE)

Special Operations Executive was officially formed on 22 July 1940, at the instigation of Prime Minister Winston Churchill, as a single organisation to conduct espionage, subversion, sabotage and reconnaissance. He directed Hugh Dalton, the Minister of Economic Warfare and newly appointed with the political responsibility for SOE, to 'Go and set Europe ablaze'.

SOE recruited agents from all classes, backgrounds and occupations, and provided rigorous training that included map reading, demolitions, weapons, Morse code, fieldcraft, and close combat. It inserted agents into all countries occupied or attacked by the Axis, except where agreement was reached with other Allied countries.

In 1942, SOE began recruiting women as field agents. These women trained alongside the men (often being used as an example to spur the men on), and were commissioned either in the Women's Auxiliary Air Force (WAAF) or the First Aid Nursing Yeomanry (FANY), before being deployed. SOE sent 39 women into France, and all but 13 of these amazing women came back.

Double Cross and double agents

The **Double Cross System** (XX System) was a counter-espionage/deception operation of the British Security Service (MI5), who took Nazi agents who were captured, or who turned themselves in, and used them to send disinformation back to their controllers. While some of these agents were false from the start, having been unsuccessful in their efforts to be recruited as British agents, they then applied to be German ones. Some were used quite successfully in Operation Fortitude, which spread disinformation to the Germans, allowing them to believe that the Allies would land in Calais, and paved the way for the Normandy landings. For more information on this, I'd recommend *Double Cross* by Ben MacIntyre (Bloomsbury).

Double Cross was effective. After the war, it was discovered that all the agents Germany sent to Britain had given themselves up or had been captured (with the possible exception of an agent who committed suicide).

Germany fared far better with their double agents working on the continent. One of the most infamous ones (albeit unproven) being Henri Déricourt, but there were far too many others.

The Solf Circle, Erich Vermehren and the disintegration of the Abwehr

The **Solf Circle** was a group of anti-Nazi German intellectuals that included people from Foreign Office officials to aristo-crats, priests and businessmen. This circle was presided over by Johanna Solf, and in September 1943 one of the mem-bers, Elisabeth von Thadden, brought a Swiss doctor, Paul Reckzeh, to her birthday party. While Reckzeh expressed the same beliefs as the others in the circle, he was in fact working for/with the Gestapo and reported on the gathering. Alerted to the trap, members of the circle tried to flee, but too late. Himmler already possessed the evidence, and waited four months to act on it, hoping to catch more resisters in his net. As a result, in January 1944, about seventy-four people (including everyone who attended the party) were arrested. This event, along with the defection of the Abwehr officer **Erich Vermehren** to England, shone a light on the **Abwehr**, long suspected of harbouring anti-Nazi activity. The Abwehr was dissolved on 18 February 1944, and its head, Admiral Canaris, fired. Its functions were taken over by the *Reichs-sicherheitshauptamt* (RSHA) – the main security office, and part of the SS – with Walter Schellenberg taking over Canaris' role within the RSHA. Many of the former Abwehr officers resigned and took positions elsewhere rather than serve in the SS, while Canaris was given an empty title and marginalised. He was arrested following the failed July 20 Plot against Hitler (Operation Valhalla). While there was no actual evidence of his involvement, he had links to many of the plotters. The investigation dragged on until April 1945, when an SS court found him guilty of treason. He was executed on 9 April 1945.

The Jedboroughs ('Jeds')

Operation Jedborough saw about 300 personnel from Special Operations Executive (SOE), the US Office of Strategic Services (OSS), the Free French Bureau Central de Renseignements et d'Action, and the Dutch and Belgian Armies, train together in paramilitary, unarmed combat and sabotage before parachuting into occupied France, the Netherlands and Belgium. Their remit was to conduct sabotage and guerrilla warfare, liaise with and lead the local resistance forces in actions against the Germans, and arrange airdrops of arms and ammunition to support the Allied invasion. The men were configured into teams of three, with a commander, executive officer, and a non-commissioned radio operator. One of the officers would be British or American, and the other would originate from the country the team would operate in. The radio operator could be from anywhere.

When I first learned about the Jeds, I asked myself, 'What if there was an all-female Jed team?' It was the seed idea for this book, and then I veered from history. For starters, none of the real Jeds were women. My team are also all commissioned officers, with the wireless operator (Cécile) being the executive officer (which wouldn't have been likely), and the third officer functioning as a courier. I also inserted them into France almost a month before the first actual Jed team ('Hugh'), which only dropped into France the night before the Normandy landings. (Apologies for playing with history here.)

Operations Fortitude and Overlord

Operation Fortitude was a military deception ahead of the Normandy landings, with the aim of misleading the Germans into thinking the invasion, when it came, would be aimed at Calais in France, and Norway, thus diverting their forces from Normandy. Following the Allied invasion of Normandy (**Operation Overlord**) on D-Day, Operation Fortitude continued by working to convince the Germans that invasion was only a diversion.

There are a lot of good books on the subject. I can recommend *D-Day: The Battle for Normandy* by Antony Beevor (Penguin) and *Normandy '44: D-Day and the Battle for France* by James Holland (Bantam Press) are great places to start.

Organisation Todt and the Soviet POWs

In early 1942, German leaders decided to use prisoners of war (POWs) for forced labour. Most of the 'volunteer' Soviet POWs were employed by **Organisation Todt,** a military and civil engineering company founded in 1933, with the remit to look after the German roadways and construct the autobahn network.

In 1941, Organisation Todt was tasked with the construction of the Atlantic Wall, from Occupied France through to the Netherlands and Belgium, including the British Channel Islands.

Between 1942 and 1945, approximately 1.4 million labourers were 'employed' by Todt, with the non-Germans (often POWs) treated as slaves (the German labourers were considered Wehrmacht auxiliaries). Many of them did not survive.

Interestingly, Fritz Todt, the head of Organisation Todt, died in a plane crash on 8 February 1942. This was following a meeting with Hitler where, apparently, he felt confident enough to share his views that the war on the Eastern Front couldn't be won. While some people believe that the crash wasn't a coincidence, this theory has never been substantiated.

Pegasus Bridge and the liberation of Ranville

Early on the morning of 6 June 1944 (D-Day), in Operation Deadstick, six Horsa gliders, carrying men of the British 6th Airborne Division under the command of Major John Howard, landed with the mission to attack and capture the Bénouville bridge (later renamed Pegasus Bridge) over the Caen Canal, between Caen and Ouistreham, and the Ranville bridge (later renamed Horsa Bridge) over the river Orne. The successful capture of the bridges played an important role in limiting the effectiveness of a German counter-attack in the aftermath of the Normandy invasion.

Ranville was the first French village to be liberated on D-Day. It was liberated by the British 13th Parachute Battalion, commanded by Lieutenant-Colonel Peter Luard. The château du Heaume in the village was subsequently used as the headquarters of the British 6th Airborne Division.

If you're interested in Pegasus Bridge, I can highly recommend *Pegasus Bridge* by Stephen Ambrose (Simon & Schuster).

Lycée Malherbe and the refugees from the battle for Caen

Five 'reception centres' were set up around Caen by the civil defence to provide shelter for victims of the air raids, and days before D-Day, close to 10,000 beds had been organised in these centres or in private homes. Canteens were also prepared, and numerous dry runs were carried out in the few weeks prior to D-Day, culminating in a full-scale rehearsal on 29 May 1944, involving the crews of all areas to prove that the civil defence was prepared and ready to fulfil their mission in case of air bombing. Lycée Malherbe, a school housed in the former convent section of the Abbaye aux Hommes, was one of the five centres, and had been spared by the bombs. It became the main gathering point for families who had lost everything, and when the town hall was destroyed, the civil defence HQ was moved to the school to continue the management of the city and to help refugees.

'The Devil's Own'

The Inns of Court Regiment really did exist. Members of the Inns had been called to fight for their country in earlier wars – the first organised body was formed in 1584, and consisted of judges and barristers sent to assist with the defence of the country from the Spanish Armada. Down the centuries, it evolved into a regiment of lawyers, part of the Reserves. Several name changes later, it became the Inns of Court Regiment in 1932. Its nickname dates back to a Royal Review in Hyde Park, where King George III, when told the regiment was made up of lawyers, quipped 'ah, the Devil's own.' The name stuck. To this day, the Devil's image appears on regimental insignia and badges, an image believed to be unique in the British Army.

When war broke out, the Inns of Court Regiment was called up and became a front-line cavalry unit, equipped with armoured cars and scout vehicles. In June 1944, C squadron of the ICR was part of the D-Day landings on Juno Beach, just behind the first wave. Working with a detachment from the Royal Engineers, their (incredibly ballsy) mission was to move quickly behind enemy lines, split into small groups, and, as fast as possible, seize and destroy the thirteen bridges over the Orne and Odon rivers around Caen, to prevent German reinforcements from reaching the beaches and cutting off their escape route.

Outnumbered and outgunned, with tragedy and opposition increasing, by 8 June, despite their bravery and determination, their hopes of success had diminished. On 9 June, the remnants of C squadron were withdrawn and reassigned as reconnaissance units to the infantry coming off the beaches.

There's a really good YouTube video from Mark Felton Productions on the Devil's Own – well worth watching.

The châteaux

And finally, the reception for Erwin Rommel described in this novel was fictitious, but inspiration for the château came from the Château de Carrouges, just south of Caen. The château was relatively unharmed during the war (the only casualty was the *châtelet*, which was blown up but has since been rebuilt to the original design). Ironically, it hadn't been occupied by the

Germans; instead, it had been used to store some of France's treasures.

Ranville was the first French village liberated on D-Day. The Château de Heaume in Ranville was subsequently used by the British 6th Airborne Division.

The Château de Caen is a castle built around 1060 by William the Conqueror.

Keep turning to read

The Silke Route

a short story about Felícienne/Silke,
as featured in

RESISTANCE

The Silke Route

For the eagle-eyed reader, a version of this story was published in My Weekly magazine on 23 June 2020 (albeit under a different title). I wanted to know more about Felícienne/Silke and explored her past and future in this short story.

There was a commotion outside the front door of the Portuguese ambassador's home. Instinct saw me move towards the open window at the back. We knew the Gestapo would raid, sooner or later; the German occupation of Hungary had been quick and remarkably bloodless last month. And now they targeted anyone with anti-Nazi sympathies: Jews, journalists, priests. Anyone who might resist. Their job was ironically made easier by the pressure the Allies put on Portugal to downgrade their activities in Hungary. Foolish. Didn't they know what we were doing? How Carlos Sampaio Garrido, Portugal's ambassador in Budapest, was working to prevent refugees from deportation, or worse?

With transfixed guests providing a barrier from sight, I swivelled my legs over the windowsill and dropped onto the damp, warm earth below. Freed my hem from the brambles and stalked to the back gate.

A single plain-clothed man stood guard. There was no choice, and taking a deep breath, I stepped forward, surprising him.

Tucked my evening bag under an arm and held out my hands to show that I was unarmed.

He raised his weapon.

I moved closer, my smile tentative.

Nothing to see here; I'm just a girl in a gown. No threat to you.

A flash of indecision in his eyes, and I moved. Stiffened my hand, and brought it down on the side of his neck in a chopping motion. The Gestapo man's face went blank and he sank to the ground.

I didn't stop to check for a pulse; I pulled up the hem of my skirt and sprinted, hoping no one would see me, or wonder why a woman in evening dress was racing through the streets in the middle of the night.

After a few blocks, I was more careful. I ripped the gown at the knees to make it easier to move in. I crossed the river to my safe house, rented in the name of my alias. Maybe it would buy me enough time to leave Budapest before the Germans reconciled Sampaio Garrido's guest list to the names of the people they'd arrested, and found one name missing.

I moved quickly, changing into sturdier attire, hiding money and valuables in the seams of my skirt, as the refugees did, tucking my real papers (including the Portuguese visa that Sampaio Garrido had insisted upon) into my knickers.

The usual escape routes were south and west, through Yugoslavia to the coast, but these were now compromised. Each week brought news of friends, rounded up and sent east on a cattle train. I couldn't use that route, but there was another.

I packed a small case and forced myself to sleep for a few hours. Rose the next morning and, under my alias, purchased a ticket to Vienna. They'd look to the south – without realising that I'd fled into the heart of the Fatherland.

The train wasn't crowded, and I kept my face turned to the window, watching my beloved Hungary fly past. As we neared the border, German agents passed through the carriages, demanding papers, and answers. I willed my hand not to shake as I handed over the forged documents. Met the agent's eyes calmly, gushing about a wonderful opportunity to visit Germany. He grunted at my reference to post-Anschluss Austria as Germany, handed back my papers, and waved the next traveller over.

The train terminated in Vienna with an exhausted sigh that I understood only too well. I stayed in the crowd of departing travellers as long as I could before moving into an area that had seen heavy bombing, looking for a house that had seen better days, even before the war.

A man answered my knock, his canny eyes narrowing.

'Let me in, Sándor. It's me.'

He pulled me inside, closed the door and leant his back against it. Still-muscular arms crossed over his chest.

'Magda Király. What the devil are you doing here?'

I put down the case and crossed my own arms, meeting his gaze. He wasn't the most reliable, certainly not the most upstanding, person I knew, but I didn't need upstanding right now. I needed someone to forge me a set of German documents. And if Sándor Bauer wasn't the shiniest apple on the family tree, he was still family. And the best forger I knew.

'I needed to get out of Budapest.'

He blinked and lifted one bushy eyebrow. 'And you thought to have a pleasant summer in safe Vienna?'

407

'There's no need for sarcasm. If you can't help me, I'll find someone else to.'

Black eyes assessed me for a few moments. Finally, his mouth pursed, signalling a decision made.

'Yes, I'll help you, but I'll need you to help me, too.'

There was always a *quid pro quo* with Sándor.

'What do you want?'

His head tilted from side to side and, wordlessly, he led me through to a filthy kitchen and poured a shot of liquid into two glasses. He handed one to me and sat on a wobbly chair.

'Don't worry. It's not that bad.'

Whenever Sándor told me not to worry, I worried.

'I have a friend,' he continued. 'This friend can't travel by himself, and you ... you shouldn't be. Seems sensible for you two to travel together, doesn't it?'

The herbal liquor was poor substitute for Unicum. I ignored the burning in my throat and gestured for him to hurry up.

'I'll provide the papers – that is what you are after, isn't it? You travel together as far as Caen, in France. As soon as you part, destroy your papers. For your safety as well as his. Understand?'

It seemed straightforward, but I knew it wasn't. Travelling was only for essential purposes. We could be stopped, searched and arrested. Hell, we could be bombed by the Allies. There was something he wasn't telling me.

'What else?'

'Nothing else. A couple travelling together gathers less interest, even if it's a wife accompanying her husband to his French posting. You'll be going west – isn't that what you want?'

It was, and despite concerns about the still-missing part of the story, I agreed and Sándor left to prepare my new documents.

Tomas Kellen arrived the next day. It wasn't his real name, of course, but he answered to it the way I would answer to Silke Kellen. His dark Bavarian colouring would have made him handsome, but for a scar that ran from temple to jaw. And the dangerous intensity that emanated from him was tempered by a quiet competence. It was an intriguing combination.

Sándor walked us through the route, the safe houses. He pointed his finger at Caen on the map, his black eyes locked on mine.

'You separate here. Silke, you will go to the first café you find walking west from the cathedral. Ask for Thierry, he will take you the next leg of the journey.'

'And Tomas?'

Sándor and Tomas exchanged a glance.

'Tomas knows what he needs to do.'

Their tone was clear: *it isn't your affair and best you don't know details.*

At first Tomas was polite, if taciturn. Professional, yet driven. Handsome, but remote. On the second day, I pointed out that couples travelling together didn't treat each other like strangers, and things changed. He didn't quite open up, but he allowed me glimpses into his life: beloved family killed in a raid; friends sent east 'to work'; the dog he had rescued, shot because he'd growled at an SS officer.

He hadn't allowed his tragedies to define him and a dry sense of humour emerged, making me laugh, making me want to be the one to make him laugh. Every day brought a new challenge, which we faced together. Covering for each other, and protecting each other. Acceptance became respect. Respect became affection, and the fiction of our romance soon became reality.

Despite this, my terror grew. Not about the bombings, or the ever-present threat of the SS – but of losing him in Caen. He changed as we approached Frankfurt, became in turns more remote and more affectionate. It maddened me, and despite feeling a rising doom, I was compelled to force a brighter, happier version of myself.

On that last night in Frankfurt, he sat by a lamp, cleaning his pistol, more silent than usual. Slowly he folded the rag and put it on the table, the gun on top of it.

'Silke.'

I knew what was coming.

'Don't say it.'

'Silke.'

'It's not Caen. We still have time!'

He sighed. 'Silke, we don't.'

One warm hand cupped my face, and then his lips touched mine.

'No,' I whimpered, knowing my protest was in vain. We wouldn't separate in Caen; we would separate here. In Frankfurt.

'You knew I had a job to do.' Eyes soft, he brushed away the tear that traced down my cheek. 'You know the way to Caen. You'll get there, and you'll get to Portugal.'

I couldn't speak through the knot in my throat. Felt his arms surround me.

'When this is over, Silke, I'll come to Lisbon,' he whispered. 'I'll find you there.'

There was a desperate tinge to his lovemaking that night, and when I woke in the morning, he was gone. I followed Sándor's instructions, destroying evidence of Silke Kellen, and refused to look back.

News of the senior Nazi shot by a German officer rippled through the streets as I boarded a train for France. I almost turned around, but there was no way of connecting that officer to Tomas, and even if it was him, he would be in hiding. We had a plan, and I had to trust him to stick to his side of it. That he would evade capture and find me after the war.

I disembarked the train in Caen, but the nearest café to the cathedral was rubble. As was the one after that. In front of the third, I was surrounded by a pack of SS thugs, firing questions from every angle.

Despair lent me a sense of calm.

'There's no need for this.' I handed them my papers, hoping they wouldn't recognise the name. 'I have a safe conduct and a visa for Portugal.'

The circle tightened – a wall of black uniforms pressing close. I stared at each face. Blue eyes, brown eyes, a spot, a wart.

Was this how it ended? After everything, I would die here, in France, beaten to death?

No. I had to get to Portugal, which meant that I would have to get through this.

Help unexpectedly arrived from a pair of pampered German women.

411

'We are not animals,' one said. 'We do not treat women . . . We do not treat *anyone* like this.'

She pushed her way through the circle, as the taller one pulled me out of it. I wanted to thank her, but they weren't the words that came out.

'Why have you done this for me?'

She paused for a moment, and gave me a sad smile.

'Because you remind me of someone.' I sensed she wouldn't tell me who, so I didn't ask. 'Did I hear you tell the . . . them that you had a visa for Portugal?' she asked.

I nodded. 'Good. Well, if you make it there, you must go to the Pastelaria Suíça on Rossio Square in Lisbon. And if you find the ugliest man there, scarred, burnt and battered, give him my regards.'

She took me to a dressmakers' shop, and ordered them to make me a new skirt and blouse – on her account. I didn't know how a pampered German wife would have known about this shop, much less that the dressmakers were connected to the Resistance, but within days, garbed in clean clothing, I was again en route to Lisbon – passed from person to person, through France and Spain to Portugal.

I emerged from Rossio railway station in Lisbon into the hot summer sun, and followed a sea of refugees a short distance to a large rectangular piazza that bore the same name. Black-and-white tiles were arranged in a wave pattern around a statue, making me feel light-headed. I stumbled to a bench and sat down, bent over and held my head in my hands until the dizziness passed. I was safe. Finally safe, but I still had a job to do.

412

I looked around, half surprised when the letters above a shop in front of me arranged themselves into the words Pastelaria Suíça.

Rubbing my hands over the gooseflesh on my arms, thanking God for my German rescuer, I did my best to compose myself and stepped into the café, ordered a cup of coffee, and looked around for the ugliest man in the bar. She hadn't given me a name, but there was only one man in there fitting her description. Noticing my stare, he weaved through the tables towards me.

Sitting down in an empty chair, he crossed his hands and leant forward.

'Looking for someone?'

I matched his tone. 'A tall German woman told me to find the ugliest man at the Pastelaria Suíça.'

For a moment, his jaw sagged. Then he laughed, a rough, raw sound.

'A *very* tall woman?'

'She is. You're not offended?' I asked. 'By what she called you?'

He guffawed. 'She's called me worse. I'm just glad she's still alive. But you can call me Bert. What d'you need?'

'An audience. I have information that would be useful to the Allies.' When he didn't react, my temper erupted. 'I've spent the last two months – actually the last *four years* – fighting the Nazis. I've lost my home. My family. Someone I loved. If you can't help me, I'll find someone else who will.'

It was a bluff, as with Sándor, I had no one else to turn to. Pride had me stand to leave, but he pulled me back. Asked a few questions, then left me with instructions.

413

And hope.

When he returned a few days later, it was with an English diplomat. I told them about my work with the Resistance, how we'd tried to help the refugees. How we'd discovered what had happened to those we couldn't save.

The Englishman nodded and left me, but Bert held back.

'Do you want me to find out what's happened to "Tomas"?'

I stared at him, shocked by this gesture of kindness, but shook my head. In my heart, he was still alive, and one day, when this war was over, he would come and find me. For now, it was enough.

'Right,' he sighed. 'When you're done feeling sorry for yourself, let's talk. I could do with someone resourceful enough to get herself from Budapest to the Baixa.' Bert shrugged, then elaborated. 'Means I've got a job for you. If you're interested?'

Acknowledgements

I didn't need 2020 to make me realise how lucky I am to have a fantastic tribe around me.

I am eternally grateful to my agent James Wills for believing in me and finding the best home for my stories at Bonnier Zaffre. Katherine Armstrong has been the sort of editor every author hopes for – appreciating the story and understanding how to bring it to the next level. She's been a friend and mentor along the way, and *City of Spies* and *Resistance* wouldn't be what they are without her. While she moved on from Zaffre just after finishing the edit, she left Elisabeth and me in Kelly Smith's very capable hands. My Bonnier Zaffre Dream Team is rounded out by Nick Stearn, Ciara Corrigan, Stephen Dumughn, Eleanor Stammeijer, Ruth Logan, and Steve O'Gorman – thank you!

The publishing community has been amazing. Massive thanks to Justine Solomons (the beating heart of the Byte the Book community), to A. K. Turner and Kate Bradley, who have shared their experiences, their friendship, and often provided much-needed sanity checks along the way, and to the book bloggers, who have been absolutely amazing!

The Quad Writers have long since disbanded, but were incredibly insightful when I first started playing with the idea of my three female agents – thank you Martin Cummings, Kevin Kelly, Barry Walsh, Serena Huddle, Vesna Main and Rob Ganley.

While this is a work of fiction, I've tried to stick to history as much as I could. Many thanks to Tom McLennan for describing how it feels to take off in a WWII bomber, and to Roel op den Camp for commenting/fact-checking the draft. Regardless, all mistakes are my own.

While my parents didn't live to see my books published, they both always believed that it would happen. My brother Steve, sister-in-law Emily, and their awesome kids Matthew and Alexandra have provided incredible amounts of love, support, advice and laughs along the way. I could not ask for a better family.

Writing while you have a demanding full-time day job is always a tricky prospect, but my MoD squad have been super-supportive. Adrian Garrett was my most vocal cheerleader, talking it up in every meeting week on week. Gerry Cavanagh and Sam Bucknall – in addition to always being encouraging – were also incredibly accommodating, allowing me to take time off at short notice (during a busy period) to finish the draft.

The Girls have had no small feat keeping me sane, providing (virtual) hugs, laughs and wine along the way: Michelle Perrett-Atkins, Alison Hughes, Luma Rushdi, Sharon Galer, Monique Mandalia-Sharma, Antonella Pearce, Karen Pettersen and Martina Tromsdorf. And while they have not been in my life as long as The Girls, Zara, Brian, Harry and Nadya Ransley, and Peter and Rita Keenan were there for me during some pretty grim times.

Last but certainly not least, many thanks to my readers for coming along on Elisabeth's journey with me. I hope you enjoy reading *Resistance* as much as I enjoyed writing it.

CITY OF SPIES
Shortlisted for the Specsavers Debut Crime Novel Award

LISBON, 1943.

When her cover is blown, SOE agent Elisabeth de Mornay flees Paris. Pursued by the Gestapo, she makes her way to neutral Lisbon, where Europe's elite rub shoulders with diplomats, businessmen, smugglers, and spies. There she receives new orders – and a new identity.

Posing as wealthy French widow Solange Verin, Elisabeth must infiltrate a German espionage ring targeting Allied ships, before more British servicemen are killed.

The closer Elisabeth comes to discovering the truth, the greater the risk grows. With a German officer watching her every step, it will take all of Elisabeth's resourcefulness and determination to complete her mission.

But in a city where no one is who they claim to be, who can she trust?

AVAILABLE NOW